Mari up on a farm in the Irish Midlands. From an early age she wrote poetry, sketches and short stories for the entertainment of her family and friends.

Educated in Ireland and America, Marie holds a Higher Diploma in Education and a Masters Degree in English Literature. Having pursued a successful career in education in America, Marie returned to Ireland in the late 70's. She was a member of the English Faculty at St Paul's College, Raheny, Dublin, for sixteen years.

In 2000 she moved to the island of Crete, Greece with her husband Brian. Living in the shadow of the White Mountains she found the time and inspiration to complete this long awaited novel, *A Place in the Choir*.

Author photograph by fotolebrocq

To my dear friend Eileen, with love and best wishes,
Marie

Crete, July 2011

A Place in the Choir

by

Marie Quirke-Smith

DCG
Publications

First Published in Greece 2011

© Marie Quirk 2008

The author's moral rights have been asserted.

All characters in this book are fictitious, and any resemblance to actual persons, living or dead, is purely coincidental.

All rights reserved.
No part of this book may be reproduced stored in a retrieval system or transmitted in any form by any means with out the prior written permission of the publisher, except by a reviewer who may quote brief passages in a review to be printed in a newspaper, magazine or journal.

DCG Publications
www.dcgmediagroup.com

ISBN 978-960-99470-5-3

Typeset by
DCG Publications

for Brian with love

Chapter One
Belonging

Belonging means everything and I belonged with the farm. It was where my life began. During all those years which followed our leaving of it, my distinct memories of the land and its surroundings helped to give meaning to my existence. I was born into a soft midland cradle of green fields, woodlands, apple orchards and meadow. Whenever I think of childhood I picture again those three giant horse chestnut trees at the bottom of the long field. Here our blood red cattle sheltered in the heat haze of summer. Sometimes, lying on my back in the soft grass at the edge of the scented meadow, I watched thinning clouds tango across the sky. I was four years old then but already I knew where the sweet briars grew and where the field mice hid in the autumn leaves. My mother was a lover of nature too, taking my brother, Tom and me through the woods where we picked the first violets in early spring. In the late summer we gathered those bitter sweet and often partly green, wild strawberries sucking and crunching them until our eyes watered. Wandering slowly together along the headland we looked for hazel nuts disturbing birds and rabbits as we laughed and talked. Sometimes, in the late evenings before dusk had settled, we hid as closely as possible to the badger's set waiting until these great animals, with their black and white heads, came rooting for grubs with their young.

People said that my parents were comfortable. My father, Owen Dardis, a tall, handsome man, already in his forties, had made money in America. Eleanor Regan, my mother, was a true city girl. Although she had grown up in a small town she went to work in Dublin as a young woman. An accomplished singer and pianist, she soon gathered friends around her and her sense of fashion became renowned. She met my father at a country wake. He was at home on holiday from the States. Their first date, they said, was to the cemetery at Killmachroi. Following their marriage she and my father moved to an idyllic farm in the heart of the country. Here the local women watched her and were unable to compete with her style and talent. But they wondered how long it would all last. Farm life was harsh in the late thirties and these women were living the reality of it. There was a world crisis too, a war happening in the distance which would eventually touch us all.

When Tom was six and I was five, quite unexpectedly, at least for us, there was a new arrival in our family. Dr. Briscoe brought this child to our house in the middle of the night. I remember hearing piercing cries and thinking that a new calf had been born outside in the field. But this was a real boy baby and he had not come with golden wings like Tom. Again and again, I'd ask my mother to tell me the story about how Tom came from heaven. We listened with delight while she explained that she and my father were awakened one night by urgent tapping on their bedroom window. My father opened the window and he saw Tom floating out there beneath the stars.

'This boy is for us!' They cried. When my father leaned out and called to him, Tom flew into their arms.

Of course, I always knew that Tom was no angel. Sometimes, I would ask my mother what they did with his wings.

'They dissolved,' she'd answer, 'into holy water which we gave to the priest.'

I'd persist.

'Was it like sugar melting in hot water or was it like when we make jelly and the jelly bits disappear?'

Mother would laugh at me but say nothing. Someday, I resolved, I would ask Father Lynam all about this. But I had not flown in through the window. My beginnings were not such a spectacle of great beauty.

'You were found,' my mother told me, 'at the bottom of the garden, in that place where all the brambles and nettles grow.'

It was a terrifying story. My father had gone out with a scythe. He was about to cut away some undergrowth where the hens sometimes hid to lay their eggs. He thought he heard a baby wailing. Looking carefully, he found me, an infant girl, cut and grazed and stung. He carried me home and from that time onwards he called me, 'his little chicken.' The story of my finding always fascinated me and even though I sometimes had terrible nightmares about it with imaginings of being cut to pieces, I always thought that such a horror would have been worse for my father than it would have been for me. I suppose I loved my father dearly and never wanted him to feel sadness in the way in which even as a child I sometimes felt it.

Children, who lived on the farms around Lough Louchre and in the tiny village of Monabeag, attended the local two teacher school. It was a wonderful place and I loved it. The school itself was a stone building and the large sash windows through which we could see mighty oak trees, reached almost to the ground outside. From our places in the classroom we could watch red squirrel run up and down the branches of these trees. On the south side of the building, where the older children sat, the windows faced towards Lake Ailing. On very windy days the tall reeds which grew along its banks could be seen tossing and weaving. I longed to be an older child so that I could go with the class when the master took them to the lake before school closed for the summer holidays. They watched the water fowl and wrote their thoughts in their yellow jotters when they got back, fresh faced with delight. In the hallway of the school there were huge iron hooks on the wall where the children who had coats or jackets for wintertime hung these to dry. There was a stone basin in the hallway too. Mrs. Curtin, the mistress put warm water into this so that the children who had walked barefoot along the bog road could wash their feet. She would help to dry their feet with an old towel which she had warmed by the fire. If the master had not yet arrived, she would sit the children around the turf fire saying, 'get yourselves heated up now.'

Tom was a very reluctant schoolboy, he hated lessons and he lived mainly for his lunch and for the games of hurling which followed. I loved school, especially the stories we learned to read and the poems we knew by heart and which I recited to myself whenever I was alone. My mother knew how much I loved poetry and following one of her shopping trips to Dublin where she also met her friends for afternoon tea, she brought me a present. It was, *A Child's Garden of Verse,*' by Robert Louis Stevenson. How I treasured that book.

The school playground was part of a large field. In the middle there was an embankment which, over many, many years had been flattened on top to form a plateau. A game had evolved which was played mainly by the boys and a few robust girls. The master would hop a ball between two team captains who stood, face to face and toe to toe on the top of this hill. Below, on each side of the mound, team members waited. Whichever team got the ball had to keep it in play and prevent it from being taken by the opposition. The team with the ball could be pursued and there was much charging, shoving and sliding up and down the embankment as the game progressed. I loved hurling, I loved being in the fray. Being in amongst the bigger children didn't frighten me at all. I loved the jostling and the fierceness of battle. I loved going back to the classroom, my face red and raw, my hands sweaty and the shouts of, 'go on, Ellie, go on! Go on, Ellie! Here, Ellie, Ellie, Ellie!' Roaring in my ears.

But if I was happy at school, I did notice that at home things had begun to change. Sometimes when Tom and I returned from school we found Maggie Monaghan, known to us as, Mithy Mon, in the house and our mother in bed. We were always warned to be quiet and not to disturb her. I wanted to know what was wrong with my mother but nobody would tell me. I don't think they really knew. My father said that she needed rest and that she would soon be better. But he looked tired and worried. I wanted to help, I wanted to talk to her but she wouldn't speak to me.

Often we dallied on the way home, picking bog cotton and doing more dangerous things. We dared one another to leap over bog holes and to tease Henry Craven's fierce Alsatian dog that lunged about behind a rust coloured iron gate. I had a terrible fear of the bog holes, the dark brown water could look so inviting when the sun shone and the branches of wild fern and dog daisies were reflected on its surface. But I knew it was a dangerous place, deep and slimy and with soft edges which could crumble and from which it would be impossible to escape. Mithy Mon didn't seem to notice when we came home late from school. She was very kind in her own way but we missed the tasty dinner mother used to make and the treats which always followed. Mithy Mon never gave us a long slim bar of Cadbury's Milk Chocolate and how we loved these bars and our own special place where we ate them. We'd lie on the old sofa beside the range in the kitchen licking the creamy texture, trying to make the taste last forever. Maggie gave us each a cup of fresh milk saying, 'it's straight from the cow.'

A slice of brown bread with bitter tasting damson jam was her special treat. Tom hated this jam and when he screwed up his face in disgust, Maggie would stand over him, screwing up her own face and saying, 'you wanted jam on it Tom Dardis and you've got jam on it.'

Often the baby, who had been christened, Colin, was placed on my lap. I had to give him his bottle of warmed milk. Mithy Mon wrapped a damp cloth around the bottle and I used this cloth to wipe away the baby's dribbles. Colin was a heavy baby, with huge brown eyes and he looked at me all the time. I often wondered what he was thinking because he seemed so wise and so far away. His hot body was comforting against me. Yet I wanted him to grow up quickly, to walk and run and shout and laugh and most of all, to be able to feed himself.

One evening something happened which was to change my vision of life and the people I loved. Mother was up when we got home from school and there was no sign of Mithy Mon. We heard singing as we came up the path to the back door and we were so happy. It seemed ages since we'd heard,

> 'Mares eat oats and doe's eat oats,
> And little lambs eat ivy,
> Kids will eat ivy too. Wouldn't you?'

While mother was setting the table Tom kept chattering on, telling her about Jamesie Drew. Father Lynam had come to school on his horse and Jamesie had tried to feed his lunch to the animal. He didn't know that the priest and the master were watching from the window. Afterwards, the master gave Jamesie the cane and Jamesie cried all the way home.

'I've never got the cane,' Tom declared. 'You wouldn't let the master cane me would you, Mammy? Ellie said that the master will cane me if Mrs. Curtin tells him that I don't know my times tables.'

Suddenly, mother began to cry. Then she began to shout.

'I've had enough, I can't help my children. I'm useless I'm no good anymore.'

We'd never seen this happen before. I grabbed Tom and we hid beneath the spare wooden table which stood against the wall. I prayed to my guardian angel for help. I saw the checked red and white oilcloth hanging a few inches below the table on each side. I tried to curl my long skinny legs beneath me. I pulled my red knitted cardigan close.

Although Tom was a year older than me, he was chunky and smaller and he managed to wriggle in behind my back. He grasped a table leg tightly and I became conscious of his dark eyes boring into me below his head of copper curls. From our refuge, I looked at my mother's laced up brown shoes as though they belonged to someone else. Her lisle stockings covering her slim shapely legs met the hem of a tweed skirt. The skirt patterns suddenly seemed very vivid, all russet red and black and shimmering green. It looks like hen feathers I thought as my head began to ache, I felt sick. My mother was wearing a wrap around apron, it was patterned in red and pink flowers with tiny pale green leaves. The strings came loose and the apron slid open slowly, ever so slowly.

'Mammy,' I whispered. 'Don't cry. We'll get Daddy.'

She spoke slowly now.

'I've had enough,' she moaned. 'How can I be expected to do any more?'

From an awful silence the baby yelled. My mother flung something and a loud dong followed which filtered through the air. We waited. Suddenly, mother whipped the tablecloth from the tea table under the window, shattering the settings onto the floor. Perplexed, the young tabby cat stayed still on the ledge outside. Mashed potatoes and sausages, our favourite tea, lay scattered about. Dollops of mashed potatoes nestled in a milky stream. Mother banged and banged a saucepan against the table edge. She ran to the corner where her own chair with the embroidered cushion was. Flinging the cushion away and grabbing the chair she banged and banged and smashed and smashed until splinters flew. Tom yelped when a piece of wood hit his shin. Turning, I looked into his frightened eyes and I saw the tears coming. Swiftly, I covered his mouth with my thin fingers feeling hot tears trickle through. Tom clutched my ankles as I saw our mother slump to the floor. She rocked back and forth, her rich chestnut hair falling like the branches of the young copper beech in the woods. I couldn't take my eyes away and she saw me.

'It's you,' she screamed. 'It's your fault.'

She slithered across the floor.

'Come out of there,' she ordered. 'Come out, at once.'

I grabbed the table leg with both hands. I heard Tom whimpering. I felt my mother's hands on my legs, so strong, so forceful like steel. I was spun around on the wet lino, the debris shifting as the table lurched forward. I glimpsed Tom as he raced towards the back door, skidding on a pile of mashed potatoes. My father heard Tom's cry through the evening air. He'd finished milking and as he ran towards the house he saw Tom skid and bounce from the top step which led from the kitchen into the cement yard. Although he broke Tom's fall, Tom had already hit his head on an upturned saucepan and blood flowed. Carrying his son indoors he laid him on the couch. Tom looked very pale. I felt rigid as if I'd been turned to stone. I couldn't move, I couldn't speak, I couldn't cry.

My mother stared. From where I stood, broken wood, crockery and spoiled food lay at my feet.

I still see my father, his face tired and chilled from the dairy placing his strong brown hands on my shoulders. He drew me close the smell of fresh cow's milk lingering on his hands and the scent of sweet hay and tobacco on his clothes. Taking a strand of my honey blond hair and moving it from my face, he said ever so gently.

'Will daddy's little chicken do something very brave for mammy and daddy?'

He whispered again, hopefully, teasingly.

'Will daddy's little chicken carry the flashlight and walk along the high path to Mike Dooly's house? Just keep walking and shine the light. Don't be afraid. Mike will see the light and Mike will come.'

He fastened my fingers around the flashlight and tying my pink pixie under my chin whispered, 'you're a great little girl, now go get Mike and tell him Daddy wants him.'

I left the house. The light shone haphazardly. Mike Dooly saw it wavering in the distance. Running along the high path, he took me up and putting me on his shoulders, he asked, 'what's up?'

I couldn't answer because I believed it was my fault. I had told Tom that he might get the cane. Yet, I couldn't understand why this tormented my mother so much. When we got to the house my father was bathing Tom's head with clear spring water.

'I'll saddle the horse,' Mike said. 'I'll fetch Doctor Briscoe, there's more than one has need of him here. And I'll ask Mai to come now you're going to need to have her around for a few days.'

'Daddy's little chicken,' my mother smiled as she rocked back and forth.

Through all the days which followed this extraordinary event in our lives I was afraid. Why had this happened? Why did my mother say that it was my fault? A strange silence enveloped the house except when Colin became demanding and Mithy Mon rushed to quieten him. My father didn't turn on the radio anymore. He always turned it on for the weather forecast before mother became ill. The doctor came each day. Tom and I became afraid of him. He must know what was wrong with our mother, why couldn't he make her better? We felt excluded. Nobody told us anything. We were left free to roam about. We didn't have a routine because it was school holidays. Mithy Mon wasn't strict about mealtime and as long as we appeared whenever the food was ready, she didn't care. She was fussy about cleanliness though.

'Wash your hands,' she'd order, looking at our clay encrusted finger nails.

'No scrub, no grub,' was her cry.

It was a cry which we often yelled as we raced around the garden. After many weeks, our mother began to lie on the couch in the sitting room in the afternoon. She would call us to come in to talk to her. We'd tell who had gone down to the shop at the crossroads. We'd tell her about the animals especially Shep the collie and Sutty who was our snow white cat. Sometimes I'd pick the flowers she loved and give them to her often mixed with a few weeds. My mother would point out the weeds telling me that they were really flowers which were growing in the wrong place.

'Like I am,' she once added but I didn't understand what she meant then. Usually Colin slept in the kitchen under Mithy Mon's watchful eye. He was learning to sit up. Sometimes a neighbour came in to look at him and often a silver coin was left under the baby's pillow. Tom was always on the look out when anyone called to the house and it was he who usually found these coins.

'You'll leave that there,' Mithy Mon would order. 'That's the baby's money for a rainy day.'

Tom never understood why a baby needed money or what a rainy day had to do with it either. Tom became a professional mischief maker and I allowed him to lead me, willingly, into all kinds of trouble. I adored my brother and I would die for him. Indeed, one day, I almost did.

It was a beautiful fine sunny day when the Reverend Robert O'Hara and his wife left the rectory next door to our farmhouse for a drive into town. The rectory was a lovely old, ivy clad house to which we had been invited many times. Mrs O'Hara showed me the huge cups which she had in a china cabinet. One cup was baby blue and it had two handles. Mrs O'Hara told me that this was a French coffee cup and she gave me lemonade in it. I held this cup very carefully with both hands and longed for the day when I would go to France like Mrs O'Hara had done. I was allowed to hold pieces from her collection of china ornaments while she dusted the shelves with a soft cloth. I admired these dainty dogs and cats, frogs and rabbits. On a frosty day, a visit to the rectory kitchen was bliss. The heat from the Aga cooker was so comforting. I'd sit there in the kitchen while the housekeeper whose name was Georgie made toast which she buttered and cut into fingers for me. Georgie always gave me tea in a mug which had a picture of Little Bow Peep on one side and her flock of sheep on the other. Her real name was Georgina and she had a scrap book with cuttings from the newspaper in it. All these cuttings were about the King and Queen of England and their daughters the princesses Elizabeth and Margaret Rose. While I enjoyed looking at all this memorabilia, my mother and the Rector sat in the drawing room discussing books. Once I heard my father saying to her that he didn't think she should spend so much time in the rectory.

'I'm open-minded,' he'd said, 'but I don't want people talking.'

'People talking Owen,' my mother would laugh.

'And we, living out here in the back of nowhere. Besides, it's good for me to read. Dr. Briscoe says that I must keep my mind active and occupied.'

She reminded my father that it was very difficult to get hold of decent books with all that censorship nonsense. Rev. O'Hara could get some proper literary works from England.

'I thought I saw you going out with *The Life of the Little Flower* the other day,' my father smiled. 'Is he interested in Catholic saints?'

'It's nothing to laugh about, he's a man who has many interests,' she explained while tossing her head to one side dismissively.

I often wondered what my father would say had he seen how the Rev. O'Hara had given my mother a tour of The Church of Ireland before the Harvest Festival. While we played outside, skipping up and down the steps seeing how many we could jump at one time, I overheard Rev. O'Hara saying that he wished my mother could sing in their church and that he thought she was a very gifted and beautiful woman. When we looked inside we saw the rector and my mother walking up the nave of the church together. He had his hand against the small of her back and she walked with a sort of elegant movement, looking at him from time to time. Tom pointed to them and we began to giggle holding our hands over our mouths so that the adults would not hear us. The pews of polished wood were decorated with sheaves of corn which were tied with twine. There was a wonderful smell of apples, nuts and vegetables. Bouquets of flowers interwoven with fern and wild grasses stood in great tubs. What would it be like, I mused, if my mother had married the Rev. O'Hara? We'd be Church of Ireland then and I could marry Richard Meyer. Richard came to church with his family in a pony and trap. Richard didn't have to go into the church because his parents said he was too young. We played together every Sunday, crawling beneath the wire fence into the woods where we looked for rabbits. Our dearest wish was to see the white rabbit from *Alice in Wonderland*. I was convinced that this rabbit lived in there and Mike Dooly agreed. His wife Mai thought she'd seen it one night when there was a full moon. I'd run up and down the paths between the shining silver birch and swaying ash trees calling out.

'I'm late I'm late, for a very important date.
No time to say, "hello, goodbye,"
I'm late, I'm late I'm late.'

But I knew that I would never swap my own daddy for the Rev. O'Hara even if this meant that I could never marry Richard Meyer. Anyway, I could always marry Tom if I needed a husband.

But on the day when I almost died because of my brother our father was working in the far field. Tom took mother's bicycle, a typical upright bone shaker, to the top of the rectory driveway. This avenue curved downwards in a slope which was bordered by tall pine trees. There was a hill in the middle of the drive and from this hill it wound steeply towards the main gate.

'You lie down here, Ellie,' Tom ordered as he pointed to a spot on the ground towards the bottom of the hill.

'I will cycle down and ride over you, like the clown we saw in the circus, you remember?'

I remembered. It was such fun seeing that clown on a penny

farthing bicycle cycle over another clown who lay face down in the ring. Tom had trouble reaching the handlebars but he was inventive and managed to fix an old horse saddle above the pedals in the angle of the bicycle frame. Astride this and ringing the bell furiously, he came hurtling down the avenue to where I lay with my nose in the dust and my feet in my brown summer sandals splayed out so that my toes wouldn't hurt. When Tom rounded towards the brow of the hill, simultaneously, the rector, having not gone to town as we thought, manoeuvred his car through the gateway. Suddenly, seeing me sprawled on the ground and thinking that I had fallen and been hurt, he managed to stop the car and to leap out. Meanwhile, Tom's invention was gathering momentum and he continued to career downwards unable to stop. It was too late. Tom smashed into the wing of the car and hit off the open door. Just avoiding Reverend O'Hara, he sailed over the door, the bicycle crumpled partly on top of me and the battered horse saddle hung from the car roof.

'You cannot upset Eleanor by telling her about this,' Mrs. O'Hara warned her husband. 'She is in a far too delicate condition since the new baby arrived. Remember Owen told us that she must not get over excited her spirits have been very low. She may appear much better but we mustn't give her anything to worry about now. Tell Owen privately and let him decide.'

I was sitting beside Tom on the grass verge beneath the pines listening to them. I watched a fat worm slide past my leg and I saw pine needles sticking to the cuts on Tom's hands and face. My dress was filthy and his clothes were torn. We began to cry very loudly as we were driven to the rectory where Georgie washed Tom's cuts and put iodine on them. Tom screamed the house down.

'It's delayed shock,' said Mrs. O'Hara as she stroked his dust laden curls.

'How do you think I feel?' Her husband whined. 'I almost ran over a child, almost got killed myself, have the car badly dented and now you are telling me what to do. How can we take these children home, all cuts and bruises, covered in dirt and iodine, crying their hearts out and not explain anything? Honesty is the best policy dear,'

'Of course,' his wife agreed. 'But it's the way one imparts one's honesty which is important now. The children were just playing, there was an accident and we're all alright. Approach Owen calmly, Robert, remember calmly and let him share the information with Eleanor in his own way. I will help if he wishes me to do so.'

I became very anxious. If my mother got sick again would it be my fault or would she blame Tom too? I trusted Mrs. O'Hara though and I knew that she would be able to keep my mother calm. My mother would never shout or cry or throw things if Mrs. O'Hara was with her.

Shortly after this incident, Auntie Pat arrived from Dublin. She was not my mother's sister but her very best and steadfast friend from their city days together. We loved her, not only because she brought us wonderful presents but because she truly loved us too and she was very funny. Auntie Pat was able to lift our mother's spirit. She became animated and happier when they were together.

'What a beauty your mother was and still is, just look at her, a raving beauty.' Aunty Pat would declare.

'And children, when she was in Dublin everyone wanted her at their parties. Oh God. What a voice. I told you, Eleanor, you should have had it trained. I bet you've knocked spots off them in the choir in that freezing little church at Monabeag. God, I thought that your baby would get frostbite there on the day of his christening. You know Tom and Ellie, I had a great time too and it was all because of your mother. We went everywhere together and you should have seen the clothes. Your mother could wear anything and look like a princess.'

'Like Princess Elizabeth?' I asked.

The women looked at me.

'Georgie has a scrapbook with the king and queen and the princesses in it,' I explained.

'Up at the rectory?' My mother raised her eyebrows.

'Oh, those English Princesses, not at all!' Aunty Pat exclaimed. 'Your mother was more beautiful even more beautiful than Margaret Rose. All the men adored her. Are you listening to me, Owen Dardis? Do you realise that you stole a treasure from right under the noses of those city slickers?'

'What's a city slicker?' Tom asked.

'Oh. Wow. A city slicker is a lad who has money and a car which he drives very fast. He goes dancing.'

She demonstrated this by twirling around the coffee table, rustling her skirts above her knees and waving in the air her wrists which were adorned with many shining bracelets. Mother joined in the singing.

'After the ball is over,' they chorused.

'After the dancers leave,
Many the heart that is broken,
If we could read them all
Many the heart that is broken
After the ball.'

Pat grabbed Tom and my mother caught me by the hands and all four of us danced out into the hall and around the kitchen where daddy who had sought refuge there sat laughing and clapping.

'A city slicker,' Aunty Pat continued breathlessly when we got back to the sitting room, 'goes to the cinema and he usually has black looking hair because it's all slicked back with brylcream.'

'Can a lad with my colour hair be a city slicker?' Tom asked eagerly.

'You just get out there when you're a big lad and get yourself a fast car and the girls will come running after you looking for a drive through the streets of Dublin.'

'But I don't want the girls.' Tom scowled, 'and I think I'd rather have a tractor and I'll only let Ellie sit up on it when I go out to plough.'

'Then you'll be a country slicker, Tom,' I announced.

Aunty Pat went off to make tea. She was a very large woman whose thick black hair was usually worn in a coil around her head. Her eyes were dark and always appeared to be shining and her clothes which seemed voluminous suited her. Her shoes were what my mother called swanky and she wore high heels even when she was in the country. We knew that when she arrived back with all the tea things there would be dainty iced cakes and chocolate biscuits all the way from Dublin on the tray. We were not disappointed.

But this visit from Aunty Pat was different. She stayed in the evenings in the sitting room with my mother, the two of them in cosy armchairs before a warm turf fire. They were always talking. One night I slipped out of bed and crept towards the door. At first I couldn't hear very well so I crept closer and when I sat on the floor outside the door I discovered that they were talking about me.

'It is not a good idea,' Aunty Pat was saying. 'I know Ellie is a bit wild but she's only a child, six years old, for God's sake. I have my two girls and I wouldn't let them be away from home even for a night. I want to have them with me. I want to watch over them, to know what they are doing, to be there to help them. I'm here with you now, Eleanor but I think about them all the time. I know they're all right and they are older than Ellie. But I will be their mammy forever.'

'But,' and my mother spoke firmly, 'I think she needs to be with the nuns for a while. Ellie will be making her First Holy Communion next year and I want her to be prepared for this by the nuns just like I was.'

'Nuns, my arse,' Pat scoffed. 'Tell me what good this did for you? Why are they any better than the teachers here in her local school? I would have thought that it's much more important for her to be with her own friends for such a big day in her little life. I think that Sister Teresa, the nun you're always talking about has turned your head. I remember you mentioning the little presents which you two exchanged, the special lessons just for you, the leading roles in the concerts and all the extra tutoring for college. Did anyone else from your town get such special attention, I doubt it?'

'This is just what I mean,' my mother responded. 'I am thinking about all the opportunities which I had in that school. I want these for Ellie too.'

'That's not the point at all,' Auntie Pat sounded cross. 'Ellie is not you. She is a different personality altogether. How can you even think about sending her off to live with your mother? You will deprive her of her companionship with Tom and those two adore one another. She won't have the chance to see Colin develop or get to know about him in the way that she should. In my opinion all these things are much more important than being in the shadow of the nuns.'

'Well, why are you sending Veronica and Moira off to a convent school each day, Pat, answer me that?' Mother demanded. 'You seem to have quite an in with the nuns too and you're not behind the door when it comes to telling me about all the donations William gives to the school.'

'Look. That's different,' Aunty Pat said quietly. 'It's business, very good for the trade. Nuns need glasses so it's like an advertisement for us. When the parishioners see the nuns getting glasses from William, well, they want the same.' And she continued. 'I have not sent my girls off to live with my mother.'

There was silence for a while. I felt very cold. I had a cramp in my leg from kneeling and trying to lean forward at the same time. I sat on the cold lino, there was a draught coming in from under the hall door. I wanted to open the sitting room door. I wanted to run to Auntie Pat to beg her to tell my mother that I didn't want to leave the farm. To tell her that if I had to go to granny's then Tom should come too. Or she could send Colin. He was only a baby and he wouldn't know that he was in a different place. But I was afraid. Outside, the wood pigeons were cooing in the woods. Great shadows moved down the hall when the wind moved the branches of the trees outside, these shadows danced in the hall mirror and along the glass in the large door. Daddy who had the radio on again in the evenings was listening to a programme of Irish music in the kitchen. I wanted to run in there. I wanted to climb onto my father's lap. I wanted to smell the tobacco smoke from his pipe. I wanted to see it curl into the air until it disappeared above the tall kitchen cupboard. I wanted to ask him to stop my mother's plans. But I couldn't move. My mother's mind was made up and young as I was then, I knew that when my mother made a decision, nobody not even God himself could make her change it. I knew this too from the tone of her voice when she began to speak again.

'Look Pat, I know you mean well but Ellie is my child. I can't manage her and the baby and everything else.'

My mother raised her voice a little and I knew she was getting upset. She began to speak quickly. She explained to Auntie Pat that our daddy was not getting any younger. She couldn't expect him to come in at night time just to listen to what mischief Tom and I had been up to. She told her about us hiding behind the wall at the gates last Tuesday when we set the dog after the sergeant who had cycled passed. I didn't think she knew anything about this, I was shocked. She couldn't understand, she continued, why we disliked that man so much.

'I wouldn't mind but both Owen and I are very friendly with John and Norah. We want to keep it that way. The sergeant has to come to check on the stock and the tillage. We are finding things very difficult, Pat. There's no labourers left because so many have gone to join the British Army. There are new rules about planting crops since the war began. We can't do what we want here now. The farm has to be productive according to the rules. It's not a retirement plan for Owen anymore and it's certainly not the dream place he had in mind when we came here. Owen can't just have milking cows and beef cattle these days. It's all very hard work especially for one man and I'm no help.'

She went on and on saying how every single day she heard about the trouble we were causing. Maggie couldn't be expected to watch us all the time it wasn't fair to her because she had plenty to do in the house as well as helping outdoors. And she wasn't finished yet. She went on to tell Aunty Pat about the night Tom got it into his head that he would like to sleep with the turkeys.

'He didn't mean the ones we close in at night he meant the wilder ones who insist on roosting up in the trees beside the hen run. Of course, Ellie had to be in on this as well.' She was getting really cross now.

'They went up into the trees as far as they could climb and then they panicked. They couldn't get down and it was dark. The fowl became aggressive. If we hadn't heard the commotion and Shep barking underneath the trees we could have been looking for them all night. Owen got the ladder and I held the flashlight. He had a terrible time trying to coax Ellie onto the ladder because she was terrified. They had to have baths afterwards, they were covered in turkey droppings and their hands were shitty from trying to hold onto the branches. And, Pat, that's one smell you wouldn't like.'

It got worse and even I was amazed as I listened to our exploits.

'They disappear,' she told Auntie Pat, 'into the woods where anything could happen to them. Last week, Ellie was stung by a bee right on her eyelid. She ran crying to Mike and Mai Dooly's rather than home to her own mammy. Mrs. Butterfield came here the other day to tell us that our children were seen by the old tower at the river which is a dangerous place. Bertie Rigney hangs out down there and he's not right in the head. Last week Maggie went shopping in the village. She took Ellie on the carrier just to get her away from Tom's influence for a while. There were shoppers coming out of the Co-op and other people getting ready for the removal of Mary Larkin who died. When Maggie was cycling through the street, Ellie began to shout, "clutch me clutch me, me no brakes!" This clutch me, clutch me, is what Dan Conroy sings when he's drunk. I don't know where she heard this but the master told Owen all about the episode and would you credit it, Owen thought it was terribly funny.'

'I understand,' Aunty Pat said calmly. 'But I don't see how sending Ellie off to live with your mother and to the nun's school will sort all this out. If your mind is made up I'll say no more about it. I just hope she gets on better with your mother than you did yourself. Perhaps she will,' she added, hopefully, 'after all, Ellie is a child who does not make demands, she likes to please. I know these qualities will stand to her.' I crept back to bed and I hoped that it was all a bad dream although, in my heart, I knew it wasn't.

Chapter Two
Town Life

I lay in the iron bed which grandad had painted pink for me. The long, white, wooden shutters were partly closed and through them I glimpsed the stars shining above the rooftops of the houses opposite. Judy, my long legged, rag doll lay beside me. Her yellow hair was plaited and she wore a flowered bonnet on her large head. I didn't have Sutty now and Judy heard all the secrets which, if I was still living at home, I would have told him. This house was different from our farm house but it was interesting for a child. There was a long, curved, wooden banister leading up the stairs to a landing and to the five bedrooms. My grandmother kept lodgers and there was a smell in the mornings of soap and perfume as they got ready for work. When I went to live with granny, she had three people staying. Mr. Tobin the manager of the largest shop in the town and Mr. Green who worked in the Bank. Miss O'Grady was a teacher in the secondary school and I was listening when granny told Mrs. McGovern that while she would prefer to have all men lodgers she accepted Miss O'Grady because she came with good references. There was a status attached to the type of lodger one catered for.

I was lonely at first when I went to live in Eskeriada. I missed Tom and all the animals. I longed for the fields and the freedom of the countryside. In the town, people could see me whenever I went out to play ball on the footpath. There didn't seem to be anywhere a girl could escape to. Granny was strict. She was a person who really believed that children should be seen and not heard when there were visitors in the house or when we were shopping together and she met her neighbours. Across the road from her house there was a high stone wall. Here and there cracks and holes had appeared in it. Sometimes, from the upstairs window, if I got at the proper angle, I could look through these gaps. There was a huge field out there with hillocks and ridges. It was a wild looking place and I pictured rabbits, squirrels, dogs and cats all playing happily in there during the warm summer nights. I asked grandad about this field and he told me that it was, 'the place they wrote a song about called, *The Garden where the Praties Grow.*' Granny agreed with him. He took out his melodeon or squeeze box as he usually called it and began to play. Granny sang,

'Have ye ever been in love me boys or have ye felt the pain?
Sure I'd rather be in jail me boys, than be in love again.
The girl I loved was beautiful I'll have yees all to know,
And I met her in the garden where the praties grow.'

I tried to join in the singing but I didn't know all the words. Granny was a great Irish dancer too. Frequently, when she was in good humour and the lodgers were away, she would dance a reel around the kitchen. I would hum what she called gob music if grandad was not there or I'd beat the sounds on a saucepan bottom with the wooden spoon. I wasn't a great dancer myself, I had little notion of what to do and sometimes I hit the back of my own legs in a fierce effort to achieve.

Mr. Tobin dined alone in the lavender-scented dining room. In the evenings I would listen for the sound of the wrought iron gate being opened and for his footfall on the granite steps which led to the tall, black, front door. The house was almost on the street, there was an iron railing outside which provided a little distance from the footpath but this was not a garden. Each morning my granny swept this area and complained about the dust and papers which blew in there or got trapped between the rails. When it was time for the evening news on the radio, I had to go to the dining room door, knock and tell Mr. Tobin that he was invited in to listen to the news. He would sidle into the kitchen to his special chair under the wall clock. Sitting there he'd clasp his hands in his lap and rotate his thumbs back and forward, back and forward. I had my chair too which grandad had made. I sat opposite Mr. Tobin and clasped my hands and rolled my thumbs too. If a comment was made about the latest news, he would say, 'yes, yes, indeed yes.' And I would nod wisely.

Mr. Green, his name was Andy, and Miss O'Grady whose name was Agnes, dined later. I was not allowed to go alone into any room which belonged to a lodger. I could go in with granny when she was cleaning so that I could help her. All the rooms were large with polished lino on the floors. Each room had its own washstand with a marble top. Here a huge china basin and jug were placed. These had beautiful floral patterns all over them and there was a matching mug and a jar for a toothbrush. On a shelf beneath the washstand there was a chamber pot. My grandparents had a bathroom in the house with a toilet, a washbasin, a bath and hot and cold water. I asked granny why if she had a bathroom there were all these wash things and a chamber pot in each room. She said that there might be an emergency some day or night or supposing someone was taken short and the bathroom was occupied. I knew that my grandad loved the bathroom, it was warm and comfortable. When granny scolded him about his long visits to the toilet he'd wink at me. I knew that he smoked Gold Flake cigarettes and read his cowboy books in there. He worked away from home painting and decorating other people's houses. He did special work from time to time. This, he explained, was the work he liked best. It was called gilding or putting gold paint on altars in churches and on the decorative work around the ceilings. Granny called him Michelangelo. He was a painter who worked for the Pope, she told me. He had done a picture of the Garden of Eden. She had seen it in a book and it was magnificent. But grandad was getting older and beginning to find this special work tiring. Besides, it always meant a long absence from home when he was working in a church and granny didn't like this.

'Not at your age,' she would warn him, adding, 'and your eyes aren't what they used to be either, someday you'll have a fall or you'll go blind just like Michelangelo.' This worried me and I was much happier knowing he was in the bathroom in his own house.

One night, when I had only been in my new home for a week or so, I got up to got to the toilet. It was a cold night and very windy. I could hear my grandad snoring loudly and Mr. Tobin too. I felt frightened and lonely, everywhere looked so dark and I was afraid to reach up to the light switch on the landing. I didn't want to wake anyone or have granny appear to ask me what I was doing. When I returned to my room there was a heady smell of perfume and I walked in my bare feet on something soft. Putting my right knee on the side of the mattress I began to wriggle onto the bed. I felt Judy's hair but it wasn't her plaits. The hair I held belonged to Agnes O'Grady. It was soft silky hair which reached just below her ears. She spoke.

'Andy, stop that. I should be going back to my room anyway.'

I wriggled further down the bed trying to slide off.

'Hey, Andy, for God's sake, did you hear me, get off. You'll waken everyone and then what?'

As I tried to roll over off the bed, Andy Green's great muscled arm reached out catching me. I felt his hand on my back. He stopped moving.

'Holy Christ, what's going on? Agnes, is that your arm or your leg or what?'

'Don't switch on the light,' she gasped. 'I think we've got a visitor. Here light the candle and keep quiet.'

I sat on the bed in the candlelight. I felt like crying but I didn't. I told them that I got lost coming back from the bathroom. 'Did you get lost too?' I asked Agnes. Looking at Andy Green she whispered, 'Maybe I did.' I vaguely remember Agnes getting out of the bed, taking her soft dressing gown from the floor and holding my hand.

'Come here, Ellie,' Andy whispered.

'You are a very good little girl and we won't tell granny that you got lost if you will promise not to tell her about Agnes getting lost. Have we a penny for Ellie?' He looked at Agnes.

'Do you think I brought money with me, where would I have money?'

She was getting anxious, I could tell by her voice and I was feeling cold now and beginning to shiver. Andy told her to look in his coat pocket and to give me whatever she could find quickly. Agnes took me back to my bedroom where she reminded me not to say anything to anyone about our adventure.

'I promise,' I said. But when she'd gone, I told Judy all about it and in the morning when I looked at the money it was a half crown. I didn't feel happy though. I knew something was not quite right. Why would Mr. Green give me so much money not to tell granny that Agnes O'Grady and I got lost during the night? I was unhappy and I couldn't tell why. But it was secret and I had to keep it to myself.

☙❧

The day eventually dawned for my grandmother to take me to be educated and prepared for my First Holy Communion by the nuns. She put on her best hat and fastened it with a hat pin which had a pearl teardrop on one end. She wore her Sunday coat with the fur collar opened slightly to reveal a cream lace collared blouse fastened almost at her chin. We walked together silently to the school. There were so many children and parents gathered, much more than I had ever seen in Lough Louchre or around Monabeag. I had seen nuns before because I had met Sister Teresa, my mother's good friend and former teacher when we'd visited Eskeriada. I didn't like the nun who was to be my teacher. From the very beginning, I didn't like her. It was a child's reaction, I know but it had something to do with the way she looked me up and down while making it quite clear that in her opinion, I should have stayed in the country school where I belonged. My grandmother had a quick temper and she made it clear, that in her opinion it was Sister Mary Isobel's job to teach and to be less, pass remarkable. Sister Teresa appeared from an upstairs classroom. She was the headmistress now and she greeted us warmly.

'Mrs. Regan, how lovely to see you and here is our little Ellie coming to school with us. My you have grown since we last saw you, Ellie. I know you will be a very good pupil your mother was such a delight to teach. You do remember Eleanor, don't you Sister Mary Isobel?'

'Of course, Sister Teresa,' she answered sweetly. 'Everyone in the town remembers Eleanor Regan, she was such a star.'

Well, we never got on Sister Mary Isobel and I. I did not have my mother's gifts and if I did perhaps she would have liked me even less but in my own way I was bright and I knew it. Mrs. Curtin had always praised and encouraged me. Although I was only six years old, I was very keen to learn and to show what I knew. The little poems which the class were learning with Sister Mary Isobel, I already knew. I could read and spell as well as Tim O'Malley. Sister Mary Isobel was always praising him. One day she enthused, 'Tim O'Malley, you are a little genius.' I laughed out loudly because he'd only spelled the word "home."

'Sister,' I asked, 'what is a genius?'

'It's what Tim O'Malley is and what you are not.' She answered.

I don't know when a child begins to realise that the world is not a soft and gentle place to be. And I don't know when a child begins to learn that adults, even holy ones are often a huge disappointment. The school where the nuns taught was well organised. When a bell rang for a change of subject the subject changed even for the Senior Infants. A bell never rang in my school at home. There, Mrs. Curtin frequently asked if we wanted to continue what we were doing or would, 'you little people like a change?' She'd smile when she saw us becoming engrossed and ease us out of things if we were tiring.

Sister Mary Isobel didn't allow us to play hurling in the playground either. Indeed, I never saw a hurly in that school. All the girls had to play together and the games were real sissy games like "Ring a Ring a Rosie" or hopscotch or skipping. The boys played ball but they only threw a rubber ball to each other. Sometimes they raced one another or played tag. I tried to imagine all these children being transported to my school near Lough Ailing. They would be terrified, I was sure of that. They would be crying for their mammies and daddies.

Each child in my class took a bottle of milk to school each day so that it could be boiled up for cocoa at eleven. Sister Theresa decided that a warm drink at that hour was necessary for the younger children. At half past ten, a young nun would come very silently in to the room with a large white jug and we each poured our milk into it as she passed along. Auntie Pat had given me a present when I had to leave the farm. It was a squat fountain pen and she gave me the ink for it too. I was showing off one morning, filling the pen and when Sister Mary Isobel's back was turned I held it up so that Tim O'Mally could see it. I loved tormenting him like this. Suddenly, the young silent nun was beside me. I got such a fright that I let the fountain pen from which I had removed the cap fall into the jug as I poured the milk. The young nun became very flushed. 'What was that?' She asked when she heard a thud. She looked into the jug just as I stood up and tried to put my hand in. I wanted my pen. I could see the outline of it squatting in the jug like a great fat slug. The milk had begun to turn a pale shade of blue and Sister Mary Isobel was summoned to inspect it.

'Why am I not surprised, it's you, Ellie Dardis. Who told you to bring a fountain pen into Senior Infants? Look what's happened to the children's milk.'

'Sister, I started at the back today,' the young nun explained, 'so there are only three bottles emptied. Maybe I could ask Rev. Mother about getting some more milk?'

Her words were not even listened to. Sister Mary Isobel was already ordering me to go home to my grandmother. I was to tell her what I'd done and I was to ask her for milk, enough for three cups of cocoa. I was to hurry and be back in ten minutes. I left the classroom but when I got outside I was amazed. It was Fair Day and the streets were filled with huge animals, calves, heifers and bullocks. I could hardly find my way around them. Farmers were wielding big sticks, moving the beasts around and the streets were covered in all kinds of manure. It lay in great steaming, smelly piles gathering flies. As I passed one cow, she lifted her tail and I just escaped a drenching. When I reached my grandmother's house, I was in tears. Sobbing, gasping and spluttering, I told her what had happened. But I wasn't crying just because of my pen being in the milk jug. I was crying because the noise and the smells reminded me of home. If I was on the farm now, I wouldn't be troubled by anything. I wouldn't be troubled at all. Being surrounded by great animals wouldn't worry me. I wouldn't be worried because I loved the heat from them and their smell and the warmth of the breath which oozed from their wide nostrils.

I've already said how my grandmother was quick tempered and this temper ignited faster now than I'd ever experienced. Taking me by the hand, we went briskly back to the school. Sister Mary Isobel came to the door of the classroom.

'Well,' she said, 'so you've come back and where is the milk may

I ask?'

'Sister,' my grandmother spoke strongly. 'How could you send a six year old child out into the street in the middle of the Cattle Fair? Supposing she had been crushed by those hefty animals or had fallen and been trampled upon. Would you like to explain what right you have to send a small child home alone? I am responsible for Ellie and when she's in this school you are. And all this fuss for three cups of milk. Look at the state she's in. I am taking her home, Sister. And you must have known, Sister, that it's Fair Day or perhaps it's only incense you smell?'

The next day and for some time following my life was peaceful enough. I made friends and my special friend was Judith McEvoy. We played together after school and grandad allowed us into the back garden on condition that we did not disturb his vegetables. The back garden in Eskeriada was walled in. We would climb this wall to sit on top of it under the branches of a large elm tree. Judith had copper coloured hair which reminded me of Tom. He would like this garden I felt sure and he would love climbing the wall too. After our night with the turkeys on the farm, I imagined he would only climb the tree in daytime. There was an outside lavatory at one end of the garden beside the tool shed but it was only used in an emergency. Grandad's job was to pour Jeyes Fluid into the lavatory bowl each Saturday. It had a terrible smell like a dead bird Judith surmised. I wasn't sure what a dead bird smelled like but I believed her. Some afternoons I went to Judith's house. Her mother played the piano for us and we often had lemonade and biscuits in the garden if the weather was good. Mrs. McEvoy was a nurse, a special nurse, Judith told me. She brought babies to their mammies. How wonderful, I thought, just imagine going around bringing babies home.

'Can I see them?' I asked.

'Oh, no.' Judith replied. 'I never see them,' she continued. 'My mammy takes them out at night because they are always a surprise.'

I told Judith about Tom coming from heaven and the way I was found in the wild part of our garden.

'The doctor brought Colin.' I told her. 'It was at night too and he was a big surprise.'

I told her about my mammy getting sick and how we had to keep real quiet in the house. Her mother was sick once she told me. She couldn't speak, Judith explained and she went to the hospital for a week.

'I hate hospitals,' she added. 'They smell and people are all lying there in beds all the women in one huge room and all the men in another. And,' she added knowingly, 'there's a place for children too. The sick people look white or yellow and most of them are coughing all the time. Some people are cut open so that the doctor can see their insides, I was glad that they didn't have to cut mammy open.'

'Did you have to go to live with your granny then?' I asked her.

'My first granny is dead, that's my mammy's mammy. My other granny lives a long way away in County Roscommon,' she explained. 'My first granny was in the hospital and they looked at her insides. I heard my mammy saying that if she hadn't, "gone under the knife" she might not have died. She's in heaven now and she sends babies down from there. It's a miracle and a secret too so don't tell anyone.'

'A real miracle,' I agreed. And another secret.

❧

The months passed and the First Communion Day was drawing near. My mother sent all my clothes by the 'Harold's Cross Laundry' van. In those days the driver was very obliging and he delivered and collected messages as well as laundry all around the countryside. My communion dress was divine. I recall every detail of it. The chiffon sleeves, the pin tucked bodice and the wide satin sash which was tied in a large bow at the back. A delicate veil completed the outfit and a coronet of white wax flowers to hold it in place. This was a present from Auntie Pat.

My family came for the day. I was so happy to see my father. He called me his little chicken again and told me that I had grown a lot and that I looked lovely. My mother was fussing around, checking my clothes and trying to keep Tom from twisting the tie which he had to wear and which he hated. Colin was a toddler now and getting into everything. My grandfather had a box with all sorts of things in it, balls and ribbons and little cubes of wood which he'd painted. Granny left Colin on the floor with this box and she said that she would take care of him for the day. Other relatives came from 'round about too and Auntie Pat and Uncle William came from Dublin with their two girls.

'Doesn't Ellie look gorgeous girls? What a beautiful frock and let me see those shoes. Oh my, oh my, you are a dream. Do you feel different?' She asked. 'Are you all holy, holy now?'

'No, I'm not.' I answered. The adults laughed.

All this attention delighted me and I wished the day would never end. We were told by Sister Mary Isobel that we must keep our First Communion clothes very carefully. We would need them again for the feast of Corpus Christi. I was thrilled. We practised walking in a procession around the convent gardens. I was one of six girls chosen to walk backwards in front of the 'Blessed Sacrament' strewing flower petals on the ground as we moved. I knew that I was one of the chosen ones only because I was the right height. Sister wanted two small girls, two medium height girls and two tall girls. I was one of only two tall girls in the class.

The day dawned but when I looked out I saw dark clouds overhead and soon raindrops began to fall. Later on I saw some of the children running up the street sheltered by their parents who were holding umbrellas.

Granny exclaimed. 'You cannot wear your First Communion dress.

It will be ruined and I'll have your mother to answer to!'

Grandad intervened. He reminded her that I was one of the girls who had to strew the flowers. 'It's not going to be very heavy rain,' he added hopefully. His efforts were unsuccessful and I was marched into the church wearing a white skirt and a blue blouse. Slinking in amongst the group I thanked God that Sister Mary Isobel had her back turned. She didn't see me. The other girls gasped as I pulled the delicate veil around my shoulders trying to hide the blue blouse. When it was time to move, I slid out with the other chosen ones, taking my place with my basket of flowers in front of the priest who was walking under a canopy. All went well until suddenly I felt a tight grip on my right arm and a nun's voice hissing.

'What do you mean, Miss? How dare you.' I was hauled back, past the priest and the men carrying the canopy until having passed all the other children, I was plonked in front of the Children of Mary. I was petrified, rooted to the spot. I didn't belong to the communion class anymore because I was wearing a blue blouse and a white skirt. I was lost and confused and humiliated. The Children of Mary were behind me dressed in blue cloaks. They were all grown up ladies and I didn't belong with them either. I didn't know what to do. I didn't belong anywhere. I wanted to run away, to run to my granny's house or to try to find her amongst those who walked at the back of the procession. Mrs. Egan led the Children of Mary, she was an enormous woman and some of the children were afraid of her. Tommy Martin said that when the circus came to town, she was really the fat lady. As I stumbled forward dazed and fearful and still clinging to my basket of petals she leaned over me and said, 'Ellie, stay with us, I think you are a real Child of Mary today.'

Were you to walk out the front gate of my grandparent's house, go down the street and turn left at the Big Boy's School, you would come to a row of four houses joined together. My father's first cousin, Mary Kate, lived in the house with the white door and the brass knocker. She was married to a corpulent man whose name was Leonard Forde. He was very respectable having held a big job in the local Creamery. Mary Kate looked mournful even when she was happy enough. Her ancient mother lived in the house too. She was known to all the family as Aunty Alice. Mary Kate's brother Gerald who lived in the house as well had suffered from TB when he was a younger man. He had been a reporter with the county newspaper and he got soaked and chilled while he was covering a Horse Fair. It was said that this caused his illness. He was retired but sometimes he did write an article for the paper if he noticed anything worth writing about on his daily walks. I suppose Mary Kate had reason to be mournful, looking after all these people was no joke.

'Everyone should have a Mithy Mon,' I told her one evening and she agreed adding that she felt it would not be easy to find such a person in Eskeriada. My granny let me visit Mary Kate on a Sunday evening after our walk with her friend, Mrs. Ryan, along the road to where the waterfall gushed into the river.

I remember being outside Mary Kate's white door standing up on my toes trying to reach the brass knocker.

'Mary Kate, I've come to see you if it's convenient,' I'd announce, as granny had taught me.

'And who is this lovely little girl who has come to see us?' Mary Kate would ask.

It was a game we played until she invited me in telling everybody that there was an important visitor. Mary Kate had relatives in her house each Sunday afternoon. Two were cousins, Angela and Eilish who came from the area close by. Mary Kate's sister, Vera, came all the way from Galway with her husband Jim and their daughter Maureen.

Maureen usually had her friend, Sylvia with her. I loved to see them dressed in their Sunday clothes and with their hair done in the latest fashion. Leonard Forde was a good host and soon each lady would be holding her dainty glass of the best sherry. I loved the sitting room too. I had to go down three steps into it and the door had a thick red velvet curtain behind it to keep out the draught. On the mantelpiece above the blazing fire there were very old brown looking family photographs. These were guarded by a surly looking white china dog, one at each end of the mantle.

My position in this gathering was special. I was in charge of the gramophone. This machine stood on a round table beside the window. Gerald usually sat near me humming along with the songs. The window was actually below street level and sometimes when I looked through it I saw the feet of those walking past. There were the ends of tweed trousers and brown leather brogues belonging to the men, high heeled shoes, usually black but sometimes brown or grey worn by the ladies and the white or pink ankle socks of little girls. Boots polished for Sunday and knobbly knees were the hallmark of the boys. I think putting me in charge of music was a clever way of amusing me. It prevented me from hearing what the adults were talking about. Eventually I knew the words and the tunes for every song which the late Count John McCormack had recorded. But I had long ears and sometimes I heard more than the singing.

'What did you think of poor little Ellie in her blue blouse and white skirt?' Vera asked. 'Did you see that awful nun take her out of the procession and actually leave the poor child at the back with the Children of Mary? If I ever meet that nun I will tell her just what I think.'

'That nun,' Leonard said, 'is a Conroy from Cordubh. Her father worked in the creamery. He was a religious man always muttering prayers. He had a rosary beads hanging over his desk in the office. All he wanted was to have a priest or a nun in the family. She was pushed in, if you ask me.'

'She has a chip on her shoulder, I think,' Eilish added. 'She thought she would become headmistress and she didn't. She really has no manners she doesn't know how to speak to people. We were in her class, weren't we Angela and we know?'

'I know,' Mary Kate sighed. 'She certainly was not kind to Ellie but appearances and uniformity are everything with the nuns. And you know how odd Ellie's granny is. Ethel has strange ideas and I'd say she was afraid the dress would get spoiled if the rain continued. She's afraid of Eleanor, always was.'

'Good gracious, are you serious?' Vera asked. 'Sure there were only a few drops of rain after all. But you're right Eleanor was always a handful, very talented and far too headstrong and fiery.'

'She was such a late baby,' Mary Kate added. 'Sure you know how they waited years for her and couldn't believe their good fortune when she arrived. But she certainly was a handful right from the start. She ruled the roost in that house. And being an only child didn't help either, she was so precious.'

In my anxiety to listen I raised the needle and lifted up the lovely silver horn from the turntable. Not realising this, Vera continued for a moment.

'I pity Owen, he's so soft and by the looks of things Eleanor gets whatever she wants especially, I'd imagine, since she was so poorly with her nerves after the last baby. Did you see the style at the First Communion? There's a good many years between them too, remember that. And she can get quite hysterical you know and that temper, who would want to be at the receiving end of it? I remem …' Sensing silence, she stopped.

'How about helping Aunty Alice?' Mary Kate was addressing me sharply. This helping was a ritual. I had to take the dustpan and a small brush, wriggle underneath Aunty Alice's bed and collect all the debris from underneath it. I wouldn't really have minded too much if Mary Kate hadn't announced to everybody how her mother, 'God bless us and save us all, had been coughing up blood.' I knew that it was essential for me to make a fast entrance and exit from beneath her bed. I didn't want a great vomit of blood all over me. Usually my under the bed findings were much the same, her hair comb, crusts of bread which she had hidden down there, a penny sometimes, maybe a sticky boiled sweet, wisps of hair which clung together in little heaps and always her rosary beads. Sometimes this was caught in some broken lino and I'd have trouble releasing it. There was a spot in the middle of the springs too where the mattress bulged downwards. All these things made my job very difficult.

On the particular Corpus Christi Sunday, I found a penny and a sixpence under the bed. There were two halfpennies also which had been caught in the lino with the rosary beads.

'Oh! Look at all that money,' Mr Forde exclaimed. 'If you can count all that money, Ellie, I know that Aunty Alice will reward you.'

'Eight pence,' I beamed.

'Give her all of it,' Aunty Alice croaked. 'She's a good girl and she'll be getting married next week. I don't care for that chap she's marrying either. He's far too lanky looking. Lanky looking fellows are sly, I know all about them. But nobody listens to me. I'll need my new hat, Mary Kate, don't forget.'

Sometimes, Aunty Alice rambled but I understood how she was really very, very old. I went downstairs for tea and when Mr Forde told them that I was now very rich I, without thinking, informed them that I was already rich.

'I have a half a crown, it's at home. I've got in under my bed in the lino like Aunty Alice does. When I go home Tom and me, we'll go to the shop at the cross roads and buy tons and tons of sweets.'

There was a gasp. They thought this money had been given to me on the day of my First Communion.

'It's not.' I said. 'It's not First Communion money at all.'

'Tell us where you got this money,' the girls teased.

'Mr. Tony Green gave it to me, I got lost one night in my granny's house and I went into his room. Miss O'Grady got lost as well. She got there first, she got lost before I did she even got into his bed by mistake it was so dark you see.'

There were six gasps followed by a long silence. I looked around at the puzzled and then rather stunned expressions. I told them that I'd been given the money because I'd promised not to tell granny that Agnes got lost that night and so did I.

Mary Kate's doleful expression vanished for a few moments.

'Who would have believed it?' She giggled. 'A house of ill repute. And you know, she was actually bragging to me about having Miss O'Grady lodging with her. "Quality," she said. "That's the type of lodger I like and it's good for Ellie too having the good influence of a lady teacher around."'

I suddenly remembered my promise. What had I done, telling them this and they were discussing it now, wondering if they would say something to my granny? It would be a great come down for Ethel. She would be so indignant. She, who according to them, was, such a snob in her own way.

'You must think about this, Mary Kate,' Vera admonished her. 'In Galway they could lose their jobs if such a scandal was reported and I'm sure it's the same here. And knowing Ethel, she would be off straight away to the Secondary School and to the Bank. Their behaviour is such an affront to her belief in her lodgers. Please desist Mary Kate, don't cause trouble.'

I started to cry. What did these words mean, scandal, report, desist, affront and losing their jobs – why? I pleaded with them not to speak about what had happened to Miss O'Grady and to me. I felt all choked up as I cried even harder. I was shaking and I couldn't stop. I was hysterical. I remembered my mother and that awful day when she cried and cried. Would I get sick too and throw things and break the furniture? Then I'd have to lie in my room in granny's house for weeks and weeks? I was wheezing now and I was frightened.

Vera reached out and pulled me to her. She took me onto her lap.

'Hush hush, Ellie, dear child,' she coaxed. 'It's all a mistake, isn't it, Mary Kate?'

'Of course,' Mary Kate answered. 'It's a mistake don't cry, Ellie, please.'

I was sobbing and sobbing as if my heart would burst.

'This is terrible,' Eilish whispered. 'The poor child has had an awful day. She was forced to wear that outfit in the procession and then Sister Mary Isobel made a show of her. Is it any wonder she's distraught?'

'And living with all those adults can't be good either,' Angela added.

'Now Ellie, nobody will say anything to granny about you getting lost, it was all a dream, that's what we all think, isn't it?' Gerald asked the others.

They all agreed, yes indeed, it was all a dream. I was encouraged to run upstairs to wash my face and Maureen came with me to help. There was a glass of lemonade and my favourite biscuits waiting for me when I came back to the sitting room. Vera took a comb from her handbag and she combed my hair and braided it again. Mary Kate gave me a large wedge of her homemade chocolate cake to take home to granny and grandad. She waved to me from her hall door and called out, 'God bless you, Ellie.'

I was so unhappy. I had reached the use of reason. I knew what guilt was and I felt very guilty. They could all pretend forever and ever that it had been a dream. But I was the girl who had broken my promise.

Chapter Three
Capall Ban - White Horse

The letter arrived on a Tuesday morning and my granny looked very cross as she read it. Inside her envelope there was a small envelope for me with a little letter from my mother. She had written in large letters to tell me that I would be going home soon. I counted the days, I was so excited. Granny's lips were set in a thin line and there was a whistling sound coming from between her teeth. I didn't want to let on that I was so happy about my letter. Grandad was buttering his bread and granny stood over him.

'Typical Eleanor, she can't make up her own mind for five minutes. Would you credit this, she wants to come on Sunday to take Ellie back to the country? I thought she was leaving Ellie here for longer – and after all I've done for her.'

I thought she was going to cry.

'Now, now,' grandad said calmly. 'You must have known that Ellie wouldn't be here for ever. I know you'll miss her. I'll miss her too. It won't be the same without having Ellie in the house but she belongs with Eleanor and Owen and the boys. I always thought that she should have stayed up there anyway. If Eleanor hadn't got one of her bright ideas we wouldn't have this trouble now.'

Granny sat down.

'Can you believe this?' She asked him. 'Tom, according to his mother, is refusing to go back to school without Ellie?' And Eleanor thinks that Ellie will be able to help her to look after Colin. Sure that little boy is so clever he'd buy and sell us all.'

Eventually, things settled down. Grandad said that he had plans to go to Lough Louchre to do some house painting for my mother. At first granny was annoyed accusing him of making plans behind her back.

'I'm the last to know as usual,' she fumed.

'Come with me,' he coaxed. 'It's a Bank Holiday weekend, all the lodgers, even Mr. Tobin will be away. You can come home on the bus you haven't been in the country since Colin was born.'

'Please, please say you'll come, granny,' I pleaded.

She gave in and I ran upstairs to tell Judy the wonderful news. We were going home. And I whispered something else, something which was very important to me,

'Mammy said that I have been a very good girl.'

And there was more good news. We would go to see granny Julia on the way home. She was my father's mother and she lived in the house where my father and his two brothers and three sisters had been born. I loved that farm almost as much as I loved our own. It was called Capall Ban because in the olden days white horses roamed there and came to drink at the spring which was now the well belonging to the house.

Five days later they came for me and having enjoyed a wonderful Sunday dinner with granny and grandad we said goodbye to them. It was a lovely drive to granny Julia's. The river was on one side of the road and I pointed out the waterfall to Colin and farther down river the magnificent white swans.

'I hope your mother doesn't give me the usual tumbler of brandy.'

My mother was speaking to my father in a rather uppity voice, her visiting voice.

'You should get her a present of proper brandy balloons, Owen,' she continued.

'It's her way of making you welcome,' he answered. 'It's not the glass which counts with her, it's the welcome. And if you sip it slowly you'll be all right. She won't mind if you leave half of it anyway, leave the glass down somewhere when the tea is ready.' He advised.

'It's easier said than done,' she snapped. 'They watch me like hawks.'

Granny was waiting at the door with her sister Gracie. We were hugged and kissed and admired by granny Julia. She was so happy to see us and to see my parents especially my father who I think was her favourite child. We ran around the place checking everything. Colin, who toddled after us had to be helped. I couldn't believe how big he'd grown. Tom and I lifted him up so that he could look in at the newly born calves. We showed him the ducks paddling in a shallow pond in the haggard. We pushed him on the swing which had been made for us years before. We brought him to the gate into the pasture so that he could look at the pony and the old grey horse which were always together. Then we saw Uncle Eugene coming towards us across the field.

I always felt anxious when I met Uncle Eugene. He was younger than my father and he was really good looking. But he and my mother didn't get on, I don't know why they didn't but there was always a row whenever they met. I didn't expect anything different now. Uncle Eugene loved Colin, I could tell. My father said that Colin was very clever just like Eugene was when he was a small lad. They had the same characteristics too. I asked daddy what characteristics meant.

'Well, with these two buckos, it's their independence, they want to do things themselves, they're smart too and learn very fast.' He replied.

Uncle Eugene did not go into the house straight away. Instead he offered to put Colin on the pony so that Tom could lead him around the pasture. Eugene held Colin and they set off. I got my new skipping rope and went to skip on the cement apron which surrounded the well. This well looked like a wishing well and it had a stone wall encircling it. Down below there was a lid which was kept padlocked. As I skipped and counted I saw my father walk with granny Julia towards the paddock. She looked so small beside him but she also looked solid in her black dress and her small black boots. Granny Julia always wore a hat, even in the house. She had old hair and she didn't have very much of it. When they reached the gate my father leaned his elbows on the top rung. I stopped skipping to look at them. My grandmother was gazing up into my father's face which he had inclined towards her. They were talking earnestly and as they spoke she rubbed her hand up and down, up and down my father's arm. I wanted to cry. I couldn't explain why I felt like this. I sensed that they didn't know anyone was watching. My father looked so strong beside her and she was very caring towards him, I could tell. After a little while, they turned and without seeing me they walked towards the house, passing the old cherry tree as they rounded the gable.

My father's childhood home still had a thatched roof even though it had been raised so that a bedroom and bathroom could be put upstairs for Uncle Eugene. In the old days there was a ladder and my father and his brothers slept in the loft. It was a very warm place, he told us because the chimney breast went up through there. As boys, they had a secret piece of floor board which they could remove if they wanted to listen to what the neighbours who came to ramble at night were talking about. Downstairs there were four rooms. The main room, which was very large, had a huge fireplace. Once, when we were in granny Julia's in the summertime, she let us stand in the fireplace. There wasn't a fire alight then and when we looked up we could see the sky and the clouds. I couldn't believe it, I even saw crows flying overhead.

But on this particular day, there was a huge fire and my mother was sitting beside it on the best chair. She was wearing a deep pink dress with navy blue velvet trim and her suede navy blue court shoes. She looked so elegant. Aunty Gracie, whose own house was down the lane was helping to prepare the tea, she was bustling about arranging and rearranging the plates of food. There was a glow from the fire which caught the rose patterns on a collection of china jugs on the old dresser. There was a glow on my mother's face too and it wasn't just from the brandy. There was big news. Uncle Eugene was buying the farm next door and he had an intended.

'Mike Dooly had an intended,' Tom piped up. 'And he had to go to the hospital to have it removed.'

Everybody, even my mother laughed.

'I think you mean an appendix,' Daddy smiled. 'An intended is a lady, a lady uncle Eugene will marry one day.'

'Well, look whose here,' my mother announced. 'Congratulations are in order, I believe, Eugene,' she continued as he walked into the house. 'And when are you giving us all a day out and indeed who exactly is this girl you are planning to marry, do we know her?'

Granny Julia told my mother what I suspect she was telling my father out at the gate, that this girl was a fine lassie. Her parents had some land and her father was also a Potatoes Inspector. I could see that my mother was impressed. But before she could ask any more questions we were all called to the table which was heaving with food. I noticed that my mother had almost finished her brandy. She took huge gulps as the news about Uncle Eugene was being digested. My father was watching her closely and encouraging her to eat up.

'Eleanor,' he advised, 'have some tea now.' But her mind was on Uncle Eugene.

'Tell me,' she asked sweetly. 'Tell me, does your wife to be have a job?'

'Yes, she has a job.'

'Well, what exactly does she do then?'

I expected him to tell my mother to mind her own business but he didn't.

'Marguerita works in the chemist shop in the town, if you must know.' He snapped.

'*La Bella Marguerite*
 How beautiful to see.
La Bella Marguerite,
 Marguerites picking grapes with me.' Mother trilled.

'You have a beautiful voice,' Gracie enthused, as she tried gallantly to smooth things over. She offered some fruit cake. Everyone wanted some, even Tom who wouldn't eat fruit cake at home. But my mother hadn't finished.

'I don't suppose she's a real chemist?' She smirked. 'I imagine she is a counter clerk who sells Johnson's Baby Powder and Ponds Face Cream. Am I right?'

'I know her, I know her.' I cried. 'I know her, everybody knows Marguerita. She is so pretty. Granny says that she is the nicest girl who ever worked in Murray's Chemist Shop. She's blonde.' I added. 'And she's young, younger than Angela and Eilish.' I was breathless with excitement. 'Will she be our new Aunty, will she Uncle Eugene, please say yes, please, please?'

'Of course she will be your new Aunty, now eat up,' granny Julia encouraged us, 'let us all see what good children you are.'

'Well,' my mother hadn't finished yet. 'Are we going to have the pleasure of meeting this young girl this evening?' She inquired. 'She seems like a real baby doll from what I've heard so far.'

'There's no need for name calling, Eleanor but you can't resist the smart remark can you?' Uncle Eugene was angry. 'At least,' he continued, 'I will have a good healthy wife not a woman who likes to call herself delicate and who is too fond of the bed. And she knows a fair bit about farming too. She won't be play acting at being a farmer's wife.'

I wanted to hide. I knew that this was serious. What was going to happen next? Even Colin who had been bleating like a sheep and trying to quack like a duck went silent. My father glared at Eugene.

'We wish you well, Eugene, you know this. Now I think we had better talk about something else before things are said which can't be unsaid.'

My mother was crying and accusing my father of not standing up for her. Tom was picking the raisins and currants out of the fruit cake. Colin who had been sticking his fingers into granny Julia's cream bun had cream smeared all over his face. Because I guessed that we'd be leaving soon I tried to sample everything as quickly as possible. Our goodbyes were tearful and tense.

'Come back soon, we love to see you all,' granny Julia smiled regretfully as she kissed us goodbye. 'Owen,' she whispered, 'don't worry about Eleanor and Eugene, these things happen. They'll be good friends yet.'

<hr />

My father drove home slowly his hands firm on the steering wheel. Tom was very excited because he was sitting in the front. He kept chattering about the farm and the new farm which Uncle Eugene was buying. In the back, I sat exhausted after such a long day. Colin had his head in my lap and his clay encrusted shoes resting on my mother's knees.

'It's goodbye to our children inheriting anything from Capall Ban now.' My mother muttered sleepily. 'Eugene has such an opinion of himself he's so smart and so insulting.'

'Well, you weren't behind the door yourself, Eleanor. I don't know what gets into you two. Eugene's not all bad and he's worked hard to get the money together for the new place.'

'Thanks for taking my part, Owen,' she whinged. 'You Dardis men are all the same, always right about everything and full of yourselves. I really believe that if Eugene was made of chocolate, he'd eat himself!'

It was warm in the back of the car. I was falling asleep. I dreamed that Uncle Eugene was made of chocolate. He was sitting by the fire and he was melting. I tried to warn him but he couldn't move because he had stuck to the chair.

I didn't remember getting home or going to bed. But I woke up to the sound of bird song and Shep barking at the back door. My baby brother was standing beside my bed. He stared at me with his large dark eyes. Globules of porridge were stuck to his chin.

'Hello,' I said. He ran from the room. Jumping from beneath the cosy eiderdown I chased him up and down, up and down the hall. He was shrieking and when I caught him I tickled him. We both lay in a heap in a corner exhausted.

'Oh, it's easy to know who is home again,' my mother laughed. 'Get dressed, Ellie, don't run around in your bare feet.'

I was so happy. For a year I had longed for the safety and the warmth of my birthplace. I couldn't put all this into words, of course. But I knew that I was unafraid here. I belonged. Mike Dooly welcomed me back telling me that he thought the farm would be in a bad state had I stayed away much longer. Mai baked a special apple tart when I went to see her. 'It was very quiet without you,' she said.

'Poor Tom, he was lost,' she added. I felt so sad when I heard this. I was lost too but I had so many distractions that I didn't feel bad all of the time. I couldn't wait to visit the rectory either. Mrs. O'Hara kissed me on the cheek and called to the Rev. O'Hara to come quickly because, 'our Ellie has come back.' Georgie got her scrap book out immediately. She had some new cuttings of the Royal Family and there was now a royal baby, named, Prince Charles.

'What a fine child, don't you think, Ellie?'

'He's all right.' I replied. 'But I like Colin better.'

Granny and grandad had come and gone. They arrived a week

after my return. Tom and Colin and I waited for them at the front gate. There was no sign of them arriving and no sound of grandad's old van. We were getting anxious. Suddenly grandad appeared, laughing at us from behind the trees by the gate. He had parked the van out of sight and leaving granny with it he had walked the short distance so that he could surprise us.

'It's Michelangelo,' he called, 'come to do your ceilings.'

'Will you really paint a picture on my bedroom ceiling?' I asked later.

'What do you think, Eleanor?' Grandad wanted to be sure, you never knew with my mother. Sometimes she disagreed with what she called his quaint notions. I remember them having a huge row once because grandad hadn't asked her if he should paint the hall door black. It had always been black and he assumed he'd do it black again.

'You didn't ask me,' she scolded. 'It's my house and you don't just come here to do whatever you want. I want it done like grained wood.'

She went on and on telling her father that he was stubborn and always wanted to do whatever he decided without a thought for anyone else. I couldn't make sense of this. He was only trying to help. But he had obviously learned to keep quiet during her outbursts. He said nothing, just began to burn the black paint away with a blow lamp. Now when he asked her she laughed saying, 'do whatever you want but only in her room and don't overdo it.'

An image of this bedroom stays with me. The ceiling was pale blue. A wide white border was painted around the top of the four blue walls. In each corner of the white panel, grandad had painted an angel and all along the border there were stars and clouds. The angels had names, Matthew, Mark, Luke and John. They were to remind me to say the prayer which granny had taught me.

> *There are four corners on my bed.*
> *There are four angels at my head.*
> *Matthew, Mark, Luke and John,*

God bless the bed that I lie on.
And if I die before I wake,
I pray the Lord my soul to take.

Colin loved these angels and I taught him the prayer. He amazed everybody by learning it very quickly and amazed us all even more by saying that he didn't understand it.

'If you die before you wake, you can't wake up, can you?' He stated.

'That child is a caution.' Grandad declared

During the summer days which followed, I was joined to the life of my family once more. Tom and I were older now and we were able to do some chores around the place. I helped my mother to feed the hens and I collected the eggs each day. I had a wicker basket for this job and I loved putting my hand in under the warm bodies of the fowl. They clucked at me and I spoke to them telling each one what a good girl she was for giving us such beautiful eggs. Maybe they were impressed, I don't know. I had one special hen that I named Aunty Alice. She squawked when I came near her and often tried to push her egg out over the edge of the nesting box. She never seemed to settle as she scattered the contents of her untidy nest all over the place. Being our only White Leghorn I believe she considered herself far superior to the Rhode Island Reds. She didn't look superior though because her head was almost bald and she had a wicked eye according to Mithy Mon. She came to help my mother on two days of the week now. The days chosen by Mithy Mon, depended on the weather which had to be suitable for doing the washing. The next day she came to help my mother with the ironing.

Tom loved his job. He would stride along at daddy's side when the calves had to be fed. He had a small bucket and he wore his rubber boots. My father showed Tom how to put his fingers which he had dipped into the milk, into the calves' mouth. He must then put his hand back into the bucket until the calf realised that the milk was in there and began to drink. Sometimes I could hear Tom squealing with delight and telling daddy that the calf was tickling his hand.

During the afternoons my mother and Colin went to bed for a few hours leaving Tom and me free to enjoy ourselves. One afternoon as the long summer days rolled on and began to shorten we sat on the stile into the orchard and Tom began to talk about school. We would be returning there soon and I was looking forward to getting back to my lessons. Tom was trying to warn me that it might be different now. After all, I had been away for a year and he'd heard Iris Taylor telling some of the girls that I was too stuck up to go to a country school. I had to go to a nun's school, she told them to learn nice manners. They were all laughing, Tom said. And the boys were teasing him, saying that I was not his real sister at all and that I would not be coming back. Paddy Delaney even suggested that my parents had given me away to the Tinkers. 'She's not living with her granny at all,' he said. I knew Tom so well and I knew how awful this must have been for him. I also knew that he wasn't telling me the whole story. But I didn't worry. We would go back to school together. That bond of sympathy and understanding which linked us would be our safeguard. In my heart I knew this although once again I couldn't express how I felt.

We returned to school in September when the apples were ripening and some windfalls lay on the ground. I watched the tall sedge grass and the bog cotton wave in a gentle breeze as we passed the marshy edge of the bog. Passing Craven's gate I noticed that the big dog was not there anymore. The granite steps which led into the school felt firm under my feet. I climbed them with Tom beside me and some of the other children trying to push ahead. They turned to look at me as if they expected me to have become a different girl completely. The master held onto one of my plaits as I passed him twirling the end of it, round and round between his thumb and index finger until the tartan bow at the end of the plait became a brightly coloured spinning top.

'You've come back Ellie.' He smiled. 'Are you glad?'

'Oh yes, Master.' I answered with feeling.

'It is better here than in the town, isn't it?'

'Oh yes, Master.'

'Off you go then,' he instructed and say 'Good Morning to Mrs. Deegan.'

My place beside my hero, the black eyed, black haired, Michael Duignan, had been taken over by Iris Taylor. Daringly she looked at me from under her hooded eyes. I just stared at her but I didn't care, I could wait. The girls, in particular were acting aloof but I knew that very soon they would want to hear all about life in the town and what it was like to go to school to the nuns. It wouldn't take long until I became really important. But for the moment, I had no choice. I had to go to the back of the master's room to sit beside the twin Rowleys in a long school bench. Nobody wanted to sit beside the twins. As I moved towards them, they gyrated in unison to make a space for me. They were very fat boys who kept so close to one another that they seemed to merge together. I was reminded of a picture of Buddha grandfather had shown me. It was in a book he had borrowed from the library and was called *Travels in India*. The twins had their hands on the desk top. I looked at twenty fat fingers splayed out. The fingernails were loaded with black clay all twenty of them. If Mithy Mon saw these she would say that one, 'could plant spuds underneath all that dirt.' I couldn't understand my sudden feeling of delight. Why did I love these boys who had dirty fingernails? Was this because Sister Isobel had checked our hands each day? She wouldn't let us use our good copies if our hands, including our fingernails were not spotlessly clean.

Smiling at the boys I took out my wooden pencil case for them to see. There were birds painted on this box and it was like magic. I could swing the lid over to reveal a second compartment. Hidden in here was a selection of coloured pencils. Grandad had given me this pencil case when he returned from a job. He gave me extra coloured pencils also which I kept in a small cloth bag. Impulsively, I took two red pencils and two green ones from the bag. I handed one of each to the twins. After all, I was fortunate, I was given lots of presents and I did actually believe Sister Isobel when she told us how good it was to share with one another. But I did have my doubts when she said, 'Throw your bread on the water and it will come back sandwiches.' I had tried this and it didn't work. But the twins were a double reward. They smiled simultaneously, their eyes disappearing, their upper and lower lips merging, their teeth vanishing, their fringes dropping to the tip of their nose. I had never seen anything like this before. I tried to smile like them twisting my face this way and that, sucking my teeth down over my lips, clenching my eyes tightly shut… until I suddenly heard the master's voice.

'Children in the back seat,' he called. 'Pay attention.'

Tom found me at playtime to tell me that he had a hurley for me. But I didn't want to hurl now. I was afraid, afraid that I might not be chosen anymore. Supposing I was left to be the last man out, not wanted by either team? I wasn't taking any chances after all it was my first day back. Besides, when I realised how big some of the boys were I began to wonder how, as a five year old I had battled amongst them. Perhaps the nuns had made me soft, perhaps I was now a Ring a Ring a Rosie girl? I hoped not. Sitting on the school steps, I watched the melee until I became conscious of some girls sitting beside me. Others joined them to hear all about my year with granny, just as I had expected. I told them about my fountain pen falling into the milk jug. They laughed and laughed. I heard an adult laugh too and looking up I saw the Master and Mrs. Deegan. Exchanging glances they turned away but I could see their shoulders shaking.

Around this time of the year the Tinkers came to camp on the side of the road. They choose the same place each time. It was near the gate which opened into the largest field on our farm. We could see the tops of their green barrel roofed caravans through the trees and the smoke rising from the turf fire. Mary Riley was always the first tinker woman to call to our house. It was so exciting. Her basket was filled with the kind of things a housewife would want, little things which might be forgotten during a trip to the shops in town. There were needles, threads, elastic, buttons, ribbons, hair slides, fasteners, trimmings and paper flowers. My parents had great respect for the Tinkers and they taught us to value their way of life. A visit from the boss man of the Tinker family followed. My father would take him to the garden to show him what vegetables they could pick and where they might walk across the fields for turnips and potatoes. He gave them hay for the horses and straw as well. 'These people,' he told us, 'are a part of our tradition, we must do all we can to help them to survive in Ireland.' Each evening and morning two children came with small milk cans for milk for the childer. In return if my mother needed pots mended, knives sharpened or indeed if there were farm tools to be repaired, the men did this refusing adamantly to take payment.

When I was eight years old and the Tinkers were camped in their usual place, we travelled to Dublin for the day with my mother. Daddy did not come because he had too much to do and he had a bad cold. Mithy Mon arrived early to look after Colin and to keep house. Daddy drove us to the town of Ballinfir where we got the train. I loved the journey, the train sliding through the countryside as I viewed green fields stretching for miles. Cattle, horses and sheep grazed contentedly or looked up in curiosity at the great machine which was chugging by. The stations along the railway line looked so pretty with great tubs of flowers outside and all the railings and buildings painted green. Aunty Pat met us at the station in Dublin and we spent a day going from shop to shop choosing new winter coats for us, a red one for me with a black velvet collar. And a brown one for Tom which Aunty Pat said looked like tweed and was, 'oh so smart.' There was a coat for Colin too, his first real new winter coat. Aunty Pat insisted on buying this. 'He can't always have Tom's old coats,' she said, 'even a three year old likes new clothes.' My mother bought a beautiful coat too. It was black with a fur collar which looked like curly lamb's wool. The collar was a blackish grey.

'Eleanor, you wear that coat so well.' Aunty Pat exclaimed. 'I know Owen will approve.'

'I wish he had been able to come,' my mother sighed. 'He could do with a coat himself. Maybe he will come up with Eugene soon. Eugene is getting married you know and he will have to get things in Dublin, I suppose.'

She did buy shirts for daddy and two beautiful jumpers.

'I hope he likes these, I usually knit all the jumpers myself but I don't seem to have the time these days, Pat'

'Of course, he'll be thrilled,' Aunty Pat gushed. 'You never make a mistake when it comes to buying clothes, Eleanor.'

We had emptied our money boxes the night before our trip. I had my half crown in there. 'Mr. Green gave it to me,' I explained to my mother when I came home to the farm. I didn't tell why.

'Easy to know where he works,' laughed my mother. 'These bank fellows earn plenty of money.'

Tom and I shared our money and Aunty Pat gave us some when mammy wasn't looking. I'm quite sure that mammy knew this because she smiled and said, 'Pat,' in her, Oh you are terrible voice. We bought socks for daddy and a big red handkerchief. There were sweets and a story book for Colin and for Mithy Mon, a bottle of perfume. I bought one for Mrs. O'Hara for Georgie and for Mai as well. The bottles were glass. There was a pink bird, a yellow teddy bear, a green cat and a purple dog. Aunty Pat helped us to buy a surprise for mammy. This was a beautiful scarf. It was pink with grey swirls in it, perfect to wear with her new coat. I think Aunty Pat paid most of the money for it and for everything else we bought too. We came home with more money than we had at the beginning.

'The Reverend O'Hara met us at the station instead of Daddy, 'Mrs. Monaghan asked me if I would mind,' he told mammy. 'She didn't think Owen should drive. It's such a wet evening and his cold is worse.'

'Well thank you so much, I'm sorry you had to come all this way. I'm afraid Margaret can be a bit of a worrier.' My mother apologised.

'It's no trouble at all and there's no point in dragging Owen out when I am free, is there?' Reverend O'Hara smiled at her.

Arriving home we all rushed in with our packages. The bigger items were left behind at Aunty Pat's. We were disappointed because except for Colin's coat we would all have to wait for a fortnight to wear ours. Uncle William would be free then to drive Aunty Pat to the country.

'It's the most sensible thing to do,' she told my mother. 'There's heavy rain forecast and you won't be able to manage all your shopping and these big bags as well. If they get wet you'll be upset. And it gives me an excuse to visit,' she laughed.

There was no sign of daddy when we got into the kitchen but Mithy Mon was sitting by the fire warming his pyjamas. My mother guessed at once that there was something wrong.

'Where's Owen?' She asked and without waiting for an answer she ran into the bedroom. We followed. Daddy was propped up on the pillows. His face was flushed, perspiration gleamed on his forehead, his eyes were closed and he didn't even seem to realise we were there. The Reverend O'Hara who had followed us into the room suggested calling the doctor. My mother agreed.

'You must go at once,' she cried. 'And please,' she added, 'go to the Post Office and ask Peter Egan to let you phone Dan. Tell him it's an emergency. When you speak to Dan tell him we will need some help here for a few days and explain the situation to his wife, Bridie as well. They told me to call on them if we were ever in trouble. I know Dan will come. Here, take my address book, the number is in there. Dan is Owen's brother, look under Dardis.'

Uncle Dan was the oldest boy in my father's family. And according to my father he was the best farmer of us all. He preferred machines though and he had a big business outside Mullingar. Here he sold tractors, haymakers, binders and other implements. He stocked fertilisers too and seed potatoes, grass seeds and binder twine, everything a farmer might need. We didn't see him very often and he did have two grown up sons who helped him with the business. The Reverend O'Hara returned with the good news that Uncle Dan would be with us the following evening. Meanwhile, Mike Dooly, was alerted about the crisis and he took charge with James Rigney another good neighbour.

When Mary Riley's grandchildren came for milk Tom told them that daddy was very sick, maybe he would die, adding that the Reverend O'Hara was with him and praying like the priest did but not in Latin. Mithy Mon insisted on staying for the night so that my mother could get some rest. Between them, they kept cool cloths on my father's forehead, tried to get him to drink plenty of fluids and gave him his medicine. We were packed off to bed and told not to worry at all.

'Daddy will be better soon,' mammy said.

I looked at Matthew, Mark, Luke and John.

'Make sure my daddy wakes up,' I ordered. 'If you don't, I'll never pray to you again.' During the night Colin crept into my bed.

Doctor Briscoe arrived early the following morning. There wasn't any change. 'He's got pleurisy,' he told mammy and I saw tears in her eyes.

'Don't be upset Eleanor. It is early days and he's a strong man. He will be fine but it's going to be a long haul.' The doctor said gently. Hospital was mentioned but my mother was adamant, she would nurse daddy at home. I have often been reminded that when I heard about the possibility of my father going to hospital, I stood in front of the doctor, hands on my hips as I glared at him.

'My daddy will not go under the knife, Judith McEvoy's granny did and she died.' I told him.

'Don't worry, Ellie, your daddy will get better at home,' he spoke kindly and apparently added that someday he would tell me all about hospitals and what good places they can be. Afterwards while doctor Briscoe was having a cup of tea at our kitchen table he saw four big Tinker lads coming up the road. 'Are you expecting company? There's a gang on the way, I think. Would you believe it, they're Tinker lads, what do they want I wonder.' My mother went out to the yard.

'Morning Ma'am, we heard all about the boss,' the biggest fellow told her. 'Our father has sent us up to do whatever you want doing on the farm. If someone can show us we'll get started. We'll come every day,' he added, 'until the boss is on his own two feet again.'

'Well, I'll be darned. Is this all right with you, Eleanor?' Doctor Briscoe seemed doubtful. My mother was really tearful now. She was so grateful, she said, so very grateful. 'Mike will show you,' she sobbed, 'and tomorrow the boss's brother Dan will be here with you.' Dan arrived as he said he would. He was long and lean not at all like daddy or Uncle Eugene. But he was so funny and he managed to lighten the atmosphere and to encourage my mother to look forward.

'Owen will make a full recovery,' he announced. 'Why wouldn't he, he's a Dardis?'

Mithy Mon had made up a bed for Uncle Dan in Tom's room. She put a hot water jar in the bed to make it really comfortable. Later that night everybody heard the roar.

'Jesus Christ almighty, she's trying to do away with me, she's burned the bloody backside off me,' he yelled. Leaping into bed Dan hadn't noticed the hot jar. He sat on it. My mother and Mithy Mon rushed into the room. Tom was sitting up in amazement watching Uncle Dan doing a jig around the floor while trying to hold the seat of his pyjamas away from his backside.

'Look, I'll get something to put on it,' my mother offered. 'What do you think, Margaret? Should I use cold water or Vaseline? I can't remember and I've done a First Aid Course.'

'It's Zambuck, mammy, use Zambuck, that's what it says in the advertisement.' It was Colin who had crept from my bed to peep round the door.

'That child knows more than the lot of you put together.' Uncle Dan said between gritted teeth. 'And I'll put the stuff on myself, thank you very much ladies.' He growled. Doctor Briscoe was very surprised next morning because he now had two patients instead of one.

Chapter Four
Changes

My father was wearing one of his new jumpers which my mother had bought in Dublin. It looked very loose on his thin frame.

'I may look a bit on the fragile side but I'm getting stronger, I'm improving day by day.'

He was speaking to Aunty Pat and Uncle William. We'd had dinner and I had helped my mother to clear the table. Aunty Pat wanted to help with the washing up but we wouldn't let her. Afterwards, my mother suggested that we three children should put on our new coats and go to see Mike and Mai. I knew that the adults wanted to talk. Uncle Dan was still with us but he would be going home in a few days. There were plans to make because daddy could not work the farm alone any more. The Tinker's camp was gone. They had moved all silently one evening, without us knowing. Uncle Dan had been told that they were ready to leave and like my father he accepted their need to move on. Two men had been hired by Uncle Dan, men we didn't know. We were told not to bother them because they had plenty of work to do. I realised later that Uncle Dan was helping to pay their wages. When he left a few days later, my father was thanking him for the money.

'Look here, when you were in America you kept us all going,' Dan reminded my father. 'Now it's my turn and I'm glad to have the chance to help.'

They put their arms around each other, slapped one another on the back and said we'd all meet at Eugene's wedding. Uncle Dan called out to my mother as he set off, 'Eleanor, if you need me here again, anytime, just "Say the Word" – but no hot jars next time. I'm branded for life.'

☙❧

The months passed until winter became spring. Little buds were appearing on the bushes and the birds were busily building nests. My mother was watching for the first swallows which always came to nest in the eaves of the house and in the barns. They wouldn't come for many weeks but she didn't want to miss them. Tom became an altar boy when he was nine. I thought all the altar boys were gorgeous especially Tony Butterfield. He had blonde hair and deep blue eyes, he was tall and he was the head altar boy. Tom looked very handsome too, a real little miniature priest in his black soutane and white surplice. My mother helped him with the Latin responses in the evenings after tea.

'What does, mea culpa, mea culpa, mea maxima culpa mean?'

'It means, my fault, my fault, my terrible fault,' she explained.

'Is that what you say when you are kneeling down and bending over with your bottom up in the air and thumping your chest?' I wanted to know.

'I don't have my bottom up in the air and I don't say mea culpa, mea culpa, mea maxima culpa at all.' Tom was cross now.

'Well, Tom, what do you say?' Mammy was puzzled.

'I say me a cowboy, me a cowboy, me a Mexican cowboy. Other

boys say this too.' He was letting us know that there was a posse of them at the altar.

When my mother told daddy about this, he said this story made him feel so much better already. I couldn't understand my parents sometimes.

It was early March and because it was cold we were amusing ourselves indoors. My parents were not in the house, mother had gone up to the rectory and daddy was in the haggard.

'It's time for Colin to be prepared for his First Confession and you can do it.' Tom told me. He would be the priest.

Colin was a willing student and he knew the rudiments of confession very quickly. To teach him, I had put a white pillow case on my head. A black skirt of my mother's was pinned to my shoulders by its waistband with clothes pegs. I became Sister Isobel. We decided that the spare wardrobe in our parent's room was the ideal confession box. My mother's fur coat hung in it and my father's heavy winter coat which had come with him from New York. There was an assortment of hats and shoes on the top shelf. The fur coat, rolled up, became a kneeler for the penitent. Tom practised swishing daddy's coat back and forth on its hanger to give the effect of a shutter opening and closing. All was prepared. The priest came into the room in his altar boy outfit, a purple tie belonging to my father draped around his neck. We sat on the bed waiting until we heard a swish inside.

'Now, Colin,' I said, 'remember what you have been taught.'

Beaming he entered the confessional. I really shouldn't have listened.

'Bless me father, for I have sinned.'

A good beginning, I smiled with satisfaction.

'This is my first confession.' He went on.

'And have you any sins you want to tell me about?'

'No. No. I don't.'

'Yes, you have.' I shouted from outside. 'You wrote on mammy's mirror with a crayon.'

'No, I did not. I only drew a picture of mammy.' Colin protested.

'Look, my child, don't be afraid, Jesus will forgive you no matter what you've done.' The priest encouraged him. 'Have you ever told a lie?'

'No, I haven't but you have.'

'I think you did tell a lie once. Do you remember when you told Ellie that you hadn't been looking in her school bag? Do you remember, my son?'

'I don't remember and I'm not your son.'

'I remember,' I called out helpfully.

'Somebody is listening. You're not supposed to listen.' Colin yelled.

'It's all right, she's Sister Isobel so she can listen,' Tom decided. 'Now begin at the beginning again, Colin. Say, bless me father again.'

'I won't, I won't.' He shouted and there began a great commotion inside the confessional.

'You've hit me,' Tom yelled. 'You've hit a priest, that's a mortal sin.'

'And I don't care,' shouted the penitent hitting him again. A great scuffle followed. I noticed the confession box beginning to sway.

'Stop it, stop it, you'll bring the whole thing down.' I warned.

It was too late, the wardrobe leaned towards me. Leaping off the bed, I watched in horror as the confessional fell forward. Luckily it did not fall flat onto the floor. It was caught at the top against the bed but the door was closed. Priest and penitent were imprisoned.

'Don't move, don't move.' I told them. 'I'll get daddy.'

I ran in my mother's black skirt across the yard and into the haggard. My father saw me and at first he thought we were playing some game. But seeing my white face he came towards me.

'The priest and Colin are locked in the wardrobe,' I yelled. 'It's fallen down and they can't get out.'

In the bedroom he told the boys that everything would be all right. He would tell them what he was doing. When he tried to lift up the wardrobe he didn't have the strength. I had to run again, this time to the Red Shed where Padge and Liam were getting some fencing posts ready. With my father they lifted the confessional and when it was upright daddy opened the door slowly.

Colin crawled out from under the fur coat like some dazed animal. The priest trying to be as dignified as possible stumbled out with a red velvet hat which had fallen down perched on his head.

'It's a Cardinal, we have,' my father laughed but it was a laugh which was filled with relief.

We were in the village later in the week, my father and I when Tommy Rigney called out, 'hello there, Owen. I believe there's confession being heard down at your place now. Do you think I'd get off easy with that new priest?'

'Not a hope, not a hope.' Daddy laughed.

There was very bad weather for the last two weeks of March in 1949. The Harold's Cross Laundry van didn't come because the roads were so bad. Farmers were worried about their crops and the potatoes. The cows were indoors and we all longed for the evenings and the warmth from the sitting room fire. My mother hung our night clothes on a pulley above the range so that they would be warmed up for us at bedtime. The talk was of Uncle Eugene's wedding which was to take place in early May. His house was finished. It was an old farmhouse which went with the land. Marguerita was busy decorating and furnishing it granny Julia wrote earlier in a letter.

'We must get them a decent present.' My mother was looking through a magazine which Aunty Pat had given her. 'See all these beautiful bedspreads, something like this would be good, I think. There can never be enough bedclothes, she mused. 'I think I'll ask Pat to get one like this, what do you think, Owen?'

'I rely on your choice, Eleanor you are the one with an eye for a beautiful thing. I'll go along with whatever you think is best.'

'That's it then,' she said. 'I'll write to Pat and send her the money.

Knowing her, she will make William drive down with it and we will see them all again. This thought made her very happy.'

A couple of weeks later we were getting ready for school and it was a Tuesday morning. Spring dithered and so did we because we saw Dessie O'Brien from the post office cycling up the road. He stopped at our gate. 'Good Heavens!' My mother exclaimed, 'what does he want at this hour of the morning.' It was a telegram. My father sat down when he read it.

'Eleanor, there's been an accident.'

'Oh my God. Who? What?'

'It's Marguerita,' he said in disbelief. 'You read it Eleanor.'

We didn't go to school that day. My parents thought that we were too upset and we would be worried and anxious.

'Stay with us,' they said sadly, 'and we will pray for Marguerita and for Uncle Eugene who must be very sad.' Daddy went to the rectory where they now had a telephone. He got the details from Uncle Dan. The roads were very icy and Marguerita was cycling out before work that morning anxious to leave some things in the new house. Crossing the little stone bridge she was hit by a van which skidded on an icy patch. She didn't stand a chance, he told daddy. She was pinned against the wall of the bridge and she died there.

My mother was fraught with worry. She said she didn't want to go to Marguerita's funeral. I heard her asking daddy how she could face Eugene and the family after the way she behaved during our last visit? He would never forgive her she was saying, it was too terrible to think about – singing that song and everything. Daddy told her that, 'this is all water under the bridge now.'

'Don't mention the bridge,' she wailed. 'Marguerita died on that old stone bridge. How will we ever cross it again?'

Mammy was becoming hysterical. Everything to do with Capall Ban was unlucky, she declared. It always brought out the worst in her. Whenever we went there she became so infuriated and it was all

Eugene's fault. He knew everything and he had always disliked her and he didn't mind letting everyone know this.

'Don't you remember, Owen, how he didn't think I was good enough for you?'

'We all know where the Dardis family have come from but who knows where you lot have crawled out of. Do you remember that, Owen? I haven't brought it up before but I was so hurt then and you didn't stand up for me either. "You've no land" – he said that too. But I told him I had education, well, that put a halt to his gallop.'

'Eleanor,' my father looked exasperated as he spoke firmly, 'This is not the time to go over this. Stop thinking about yourself all the time. Stop it now. The children are listening and they're upset enough as it is and so am I. Eugene is the one we had to think of now,' he added, 'and Marguerita's family.'

'You will come with me, Eleanor, I'm quite sure Eugene is not proud of what he said either but I know that it will be the last thing on his mind. He will be glad to see us and to know that we are there for him when trouble strikes. After all, blood is thicker than water.'

'And,' my mother sobbed, 'Dardis blood is thicker and better than anyone else's. But, yes, you are right, Owen, I'll have to go.' And she ran sobbing loudly into the bedroom.

I could tell that my mother was feeling very bad. She had said things and now she was worried and ashamed. I understood because I had felt like that when I broke my promise to Miss O'Grady and Mr. Green. I had revealed their secret in Mary Kate's house when I'd been upset. But they didn't know what I had done. Perhaps this was worse for me? I knew that I had let them down and I couldn't make things better.

Mithy Mon took us for a walk on the day Marguerita was buried. I told Tom and Colin that people said she was like an angel.

'Everybody loved her,' I said. 'She would have been a beautiful Aunty.'

Reverend O'Hara was at his gate, when we were returning. Mithy Mon was uncomfortable, I could tell.

'Good Day, Your Reverence, it's a chilly afternoon, isn't it?' She murmured.

Tom laughed nervously. We'd never heard him called, 'Your Reverence,' before. Looking at us, he suggested that we might like to go up the rectory to get warm. Mithy Mon was not agreeable at all. We had a lovely fire in our own house she explained, she had fixed it herself.

Impetuously I asked, 'Will you come to our house, Reverend O'Hara? Mithy Mon has made a beautiful sponge cake and you can have some.'

'How lovely, I would love to accompany you but only if this is convenient for Mrs. Monaghan, I know that she is very busy.'

'Not at all,' Mithy Mon smiled, 'you must come, Reverend. Now it'll be a bit rough and ready, we're all a little out of kilter, you understand.'

When we sat down in the sitting room Mrs. Monaghan placed a coffee table near the fire and poured out milky tea for us. Speaking rather poshly she enquired, 'Is it milk and sugar for Your Reverence? Do you like to have milk in your cup before I pour the tea? Some people have this preference?'

'Marguerita must be in heaven by now, mustn't she?' Colin brought us all back to reality.

'Yes, yes, the dear girl, gone to the Lord and to Paradise where she will always be happy.'

I wanted to know what it is like to die. What happens exactly? Is it like a clap of thunder - would I look around afterwards to discover that the people, the places and the animals I knew were gone forever? The Reverend O'Hara didn't think so. He said that everything would stay on the earth but I would leave it for a place so marvellous it couldn't be described. Colin was puzzled.

'If it's so good why doesn't everybody die now?'

'That is a difficult question. I think myself that we have to live here for many years. We see all sorts of good things and sometimes bad things. We meet good people and sometimes bad people. We see beautiful places and sometimes ugly places. If we didn't know the difference, we wouldn't appreciate heaven. It would be like having Christmas everyday. We'd have nothing to look forward to.' Reverend O'Hara looked at us hoping we understood.

'Yes indeed.' I nodded. 'Indeed yes.'

'Do people know they are dying? I mean how do they know that they are not still alive?' This was Tom. The questions were getting more complicated for his reverence.

'A long time ago, I asked my grandfather that very question. He was an old man then,' Reverend O'Hara told us, 'and he had been a minister too. "You know, he said to me, it's like being on your father's lap, you are very young and you are very tired. You are in a warm and a safe place. You fall asleep and when you wake up you're in your own cosy bed. Well, he said, that's what I think dying is like."'

'What a lovely way to explain it.' Mithy Mon was overcome. 'You have a great way with words. None of our clergy has a way with words like that. 'May god bless you,' she smiled.

My parents returned home during the night as quietly as the snow which fell. They were fortunate to have made the journey at all. Nobody had expected the snow. It fell in great fat flakes which built up into mounds in the flower beds and on the window ledges. I couldn't believe all the whiteness when I looked through the frosted bedroom window. Tall pines were enfolded in white mantles and the red cattle looked speckled where the hide was showing in spots through the snow. Everyplace was silent and enclosed. I thought of Marguerita. Was she wrapped in snow like someone wearing a silver and white spangled dress?

Mike Dooly had come on his tractor to see if we were all right. He was sitting at the breakfast table with mammy and daddy. Mithy

Mon was getting the porridge ready.

'I hope I never have to witness anything like it in my life again, it was terrible,' my mother was saying. 'Her poor parents and her brothers and sisters were inconsolable. But it was a lovely mass and the neighbours were so good. There was such a crowd.'

'A terrible tragedy,' Mike agreed. 'But God is good and they will come through it.'

'Eugene is like an old man, isn't he Eleanor?' She didn't look up or say anything.

'He was in total shock,' my father went on, 'but he was brave. I had to admire him. He thanked all the people on behalf of her family because her poor father was unable to speak he was so grief stricken.'

Mike spoke.

'Death it's a funny thing God between us and all harm. It's hard to understand, you're here one minute and you're gone the next. God bless us and save us all.'

'The Reverend O'Hara explained death to the children,' said Mithy Mon. When the adults heard the story they were moved.

'I'm so glad,' my father said. 'I Hope they will remember it always. I know I will, isn't it a very helpful way to think about death?'

Mithy Mon was very happy. She had, reluctantly at first, entertained Reverend O'Hara. Now she was rewarded, she could tell how consoling his words were for my parents. Liam and Padge appeared for breakfast. They couldn't do much more until evening and they were wondering if we'd like to make a snowman, if it was all right with the boss.

I have the photographs. One shows our snowman, wearing daddy's old hat and a striped scarf. His impressive nose is a carrot specially chosen by Mithy Mon. He is smoking a clay pipe, one Mike Dooly fetched from his tractor. Down his front are gleaming buttons. I remember washing the pebbles in soapy water to make them shine. Wide eyed, he looks at the camera while his mouth, a creation which

Liam worked on using bent twigs, smiles at me. We are all in the photographs which were taken with my mother's Box Brownie camera. Shep is photographed too beside Colin and they are both grinning. Being together and creating something took the edge off our sadness.

A few days later, the snowman began to melt. His nose sat on his shoulder and then his shinning buttons fell at his feet. We rescued the scarf and hat for another time and watched until our creation became a little hard lump of icy snow lying in the slush. He was gone. He was gone but we didn't forget him because he was linked forever to that snowy time and to our memories of Marguerita.

A month later my parents were going back to Capall Ban. There was a special mass for Marguerita and we wanted to go. It's going to be a long day mammy explained and you would be too tired. There won't be anybody to mind you down there and no other children to play with. It's too cold for rambling around the place and all the talk will be for grown ups this time. Listening to her, we agreed that we could have more fun at home.

'And don't forget, you have homework to do.' She reminded us.

When April came it brightened the land with cowslips and primroses. I wandered around the woods and brought small bunches of these flowers into the house. They adorned the mantelpiece in a glass vase and there was an arrangement on the hall table where the flowers sat in a bowl embedded in damp green moss. Outside, the buds were coming on the whitethorn and all the hedgerows greening up almost while we watched. Frequent showers caught us off guard and we sheltered under the huge trees until the raindrops fell through the branches in a sudden wind. My father wanted to take the two huge shire horses for a grooming. These animals were special because they had won awards at the county show. My father asked me if I would like to go with him to see Sam Murphy clip Sally and Nancy. Sam was a perfectionist and he knew exactly how a shire horse should be presented.

'Would you like to get up on Sally's back?' My father asked.

'I don't think so.' I answered. 'She is so wide. I'd have to lie down or go side saddle.'

'I suppose you're right.' He laughed. 'But you'd have a great view.'

Walking along, the horse's halters and blinkers creaked and their mighty feet pounded the road. Sometimes one of them snorted as she shook her great head. Their breath gushed over me like a spray of warm steam. We greeted neighbours along the road or in the fields. Some asked daddy if he was feeling better. Others offered their sympathy on the death of Marguerita. They had read all about the accident in the local paper and were very sorry.

I had never been to Sam Murphy's place before and it was a long walk. I felt tired but I didn't want to let on. Having climbed a steep hill, we rounded a bend. I couldn't believe my eyes. In front of us were the mountains. Such a scene as I'd never witnessed in my life - all purples and blues leaning upwards into the darker blue sky. Shades of pinks and mauve hovered and drifted in and out between the white clouds. Lower down were the greens of the forest and nestling below, a tapestry of fields. Smoke rose from chimneys and roofs of yellowed straw, red corrugated iron and grey slate were sprinkled in the distance. I stood watching as the shadows moved amongst the peaks and the sun appeared or disappeared at random. My father and the horses stood too. My father was aware of my excitement.

'It's a wonderful sight, isn't it Ellie?'

I was speechless. I couldn't imagine anything grander. These mountains which had been here forever, held a perfect stillness about them. I felt as if they knew me and that they had held all the secrets of the earth from the beginning of time. For thousands of years they had stood guard. In my imagination I recognised them as guardians, as a great unmoving protector which would shelter our farms forever. My father was watching me.

'You sit here, Ellie, enjoy the scenery. You won't know Sally and

Nancy when we're finished with them. I'll call you when Sam's doing their manes, you'd be interested in that.'

But when he did call me the horses were ready for home. I wandered into the horse parlour as Sam called it. Sally and Nancy gleamed from withers to tail. The white tuffs of hair at their feet and fetlock glistened like white ice. Their thick manes were spread out in an elegant cut. When they moved, their tails swung in wide free movements as in a great waltz. Knowing they were beautiful they nuzzled Sam.

Our shire horses won the championship class again just as we had expected. 'When you take them to Sam's place again, can I go too?' I asked daddy. I wanted to see those mountains once again. It was a scene I thought about often, it was a place I wanted to re-visit.

'I hope so, Ellie.' He sounded uncertain.

Had I known what was on my father's mind that day, I'd have realised that I would never return to that place as a child. Within three months our farm had been sold.

We heard about this one evening when Tom and I were playing snakes and ladders. Colin was busy drawing and colouring and my parents, who sat by the fire were gazing thoughtfully into the flames. I shook the dice in an old egg cup but before I could see the numbers on it, my mother leaned forward as daddy began to speak.

'We have something to tell you. Maybe you will be upset but you have to know it sooner or later.' He spoke reluctantly. 'We are going to live in Eskeriada, to be near to granny Julia and Uncle Eugene. And we'll be almost beside granny Ethel and grandad as well. Now, before you get worried, we will still have a farm to work, I'll take care of the home place and help Eugene with his.'

I was stunned. Tom cried out in an anguished voice.

'No, I won't go down there. Ellie hated Eskeriada, she told me she did. What will we do with our animals? Daddy, you said that this farm will be mine one day. I'll stay here. I know what to do, Mike will help me.'

'Oh Tom, you will have a farm one day if you want one but you're only ten now and even though you are the best little farmer this place would be too much for you. Besides, Mike has his own farm. He can't be here all the time.'

'What about our animals?' I wailed. 'I won't go either. I won't go back to that Sister Isobel. You can't send Colin to her, mammy, she's awful.'

My mother tried to reassure us. They'd all had a long talk after Marguerita's Memorial Mass. Granny Julia was not getting any younger and Eugene felt that he should stay in the house with her. He wanted to sell the new farm, mammy explained. 'We told him not do anything in a hurry. He needs someone to help him and your daddy is finding all the work here too much.'

'What about Padge and Liam?' Tom asked. 'They can work here forever.'

We didn't realise that it was not that simple. It cost money to employ men to work on the land. Daddy couldn't expect Uncle Dan to keep helping out financially.

My mother wanted us to have a good education.

'It's about your future too.' She tried to encourage us. 'If you stay here you'll have to go away to boarding school to get an education and we won't have that kind of money. You must all get an education it is most important. In Eskeriada there's a secondary school in the town. Going to live there will make things so much easier for us. In a year all this change won't seem so bad you will realise that it's a good thing.' She promised.

We were not listening. I cried for the cows and our hens and for Shep and Sutty.

'Now now, Ellie, you don't think we'd leave Shep and Sutty behind? They will come with us,' daddy was adamant. 'And the red cattle will come to granny Julia's farm and we'll take the chickens and the hens too. It's not the end of the world, not at all.'

'But what will happen to the cows?' Tom was getting desperate. 'What will happen to the cows, daddy?'

'I have good news about the cows. All the cows, Daisy, Buttercup, Rose, Daffodil, Holly, Cowslip and the others will all go to live on Mike's farm. He knows them and he loves them as much as we do.'

Our parents promised that we would come back from time to time to visit Mike and Mai and The Reverend O'Hara and Mrs. O'Hara.

'Mithy Mon, Mithy Mon.' Suddenly Colin spoke. She had minded him since he was a baby. During all those months when my mother was sick, it was Mithy Mon who had been there for him. 'Will Mithy Mon come to Eskeriada, she has to come? If she doesn't come I'm staying here with her.'

'I had a little chat with Mithy Mon.' Mammy spoke soothingly to him. 'She is very sad but she did tell me that the time has almost come when she has to stop working for us anyway. She is a granny now and she wants to take care of the new babies. She will come to Eskeriada for a holiday sometimes though. I think you will see her very often, Colin and you will be able to show her everything.'

Our protests had been anticipated. There was nothing we could say which would change anything. Once again a sense of loss overwhelmed me. I could not envisage the future and I didn't want to think about it. I tried to pretend that I had imagined everything but when I looked at Tom and Colin I knew that I hadn't. I didn't think about my parents feelings at all not even when I came upon my mother sitting beside the range. She was lying back in the old sofa waiting for the kettle to boil. She looked tired and anxious but I didn't care.

'I hate you and I hate daddy,' I blurted this out with all the feeling I could muster. 'None of my friends in Monabeag School have to leave their farms. Their daddy's and mammy's wouldn't do that,' I continued. 'And what about Colin, Sister Isobel will murder him?'

Drawing me towards her onto the sofa and putting her arms around me.

'My poor little girl,' mother murmured. 'I know how you feel. I feel sad too and daddy is heartbroken.'

'Well, if you are, why can't we stay here?' I reasoned.

'It would be foolish of us to try to continue here, Ellie. We cannot manage,' she explained. 'When I came here with daddy so many years ago, I was young and I was filled with enthusiasm. We bought this beautiful place and I had it furnished and decorated. I planted the sweet scented roses which grow by the hall door and I knitted your jumpers here during the winter evenings. We had so many plans which included you and Tom and Colin. I wasn't really a farmer's wife though and your daddy had not farmed for a long time. Things changed and the government made rules for farmers. Money is becoming short now, Ellie. But we have been offered a wonderful chance to improve our life. Please, don't be too upset, Ellie. Let daddy see what a brave girl you are.'

'I don't want to be brave,' I protested. 'You only think of yourself,' I screamed. 'Daddy told you that when Marguerite died and he was right. None of us want to live in Eskeriada except you – I hate you.'

I felt the cold slap of her hand across my face.

'How dare you speak to me like that, Ellie Dardis. Who do you think you are? You are the boldest girl – how could I rear such an ungrateful child. You need an education with the nuns and that's what you'll get. They'll put manners on you sooner or later.'

As I cowered on the sofa waiting for another blow my mother just put her head in her hands and cried. During the night while I lay there sobbing and planning how I would run away in the morning, my mother came into the room. She had something special to tell me. It was a great surprise and it would make everything better. This was a surprise which I could tell Tom and Colin about all by myself. We were going to buy a big house in the town. It was three stories high and the sitting room was upstairs. From the windows, we would be able to see the river and the waterfall too on a clear day. Downstairs had been a shop when my mother was a young girl. It would be a shop again – our shop.

'What sort of shop?' I wanted to know.

'A drapery shop, this is a shop which sells clothes and hats and maybe shoes. There will be materials for curtains and blankets and babies things. Aunty Pat has great ideas,' my mother enthused. 'She knows the wholesalers in Dublin. When the place has been decorated by grandad and the new counters made, you and I will go to Dublin, Ellie. We'll stay with Aunty Pat for a few days and we'll choose all the stock for our shop. I think we will have a section for men and boys too. What do you think, Ellie?'

'Maybe it's a good idea,' I replied. 'But can we have a sweets and cake shop too?'

I was excited but I didn't want to let on. I knew the house and I liked the look of it. I told Tom about the shop. Colin was more interested. He was always drawing houses and a house which was three stories high appealed to him.

I'd forgotten to ask about a garden. 'I'll find out Tom,' I promised. I can't imagine daddy buying a house without a garden.

'Don't bother, I'll be farming for granny Julia anyway and I'll be too busy for a garden.'

His eyes were shining with unshed tears. I watched him pulling on his rubber boots.

'I've got to help daddy to check up on the calves,' he told me.

In the dim morning light I watched him march towards the haggard, his shoulders squarely set, his hands dug deep into his pockets. My father coming out from the shadows put his arm around Tom and they walked on together out of sight.

Chapter Five
Dardis Drapery

Five years passed and with them all the changing seasons which mirrored the growth, departures, and love within the collective life of our family. I did go to Dublin with my mother to choose stock for Dardis' Drapery. She was getting carried away until Aunty Pat reminded her that she would be catering to the needs of farmer's wives and other women whose daily lives did not demand high fashion. Such women needed sensible clothes which didn't cost the earth. 'A few select items were fine,' she said, for special occasions.

'I really want to stock some clothing which will give my customers a lift,' mammy told her. 'We're all fed up with make do and mend. It's the new look now and I'm sure I will have some customers who will want to look fashionable.'

Coats with fur collars and skirts which reached to mid calf and sedate blouses were ordered. My mother longed to choose beautiful lingerie but she had to admit that a selection of interlock bloomers, warm vests and substantial brassieres would be better sellers.

'Listen to her,' Aunty Pat, beamed. 'She's got all the shop talk down to a T already.'

It was agreed that she would sell children's clothes too but not many woollen jumpers because the mothers knit these themselves. Aunty Pat suggested stocking the wool, the patterns and knitting needles.

'I'll put a little skirt in the window and a boy's pants. Beside these I'll put matching wools and a suggested pattern. What do you think Ellie?'

I thought it was a good plan and I asked if I could help her to decorate the window.

'It's dress the window, Ellie, that's what we will be doing.' She replied smiling at me. She was delighted that I was finally, after weeks of sulking, becoming interested in the shop.

The house we'd moved to was beautifully decorated by grandad. My parents had bought all the furniture which had been in the place originally. It was heavy mahogany which shone in the sunlight from the large windows. We were intrigued because we had an upstairs parlour. It was a huge room and the windows did give a view of the river. We could see the Guinness barges chugging downstream and Tom often watched until they came near the bridge. Then he'd race down the street to be alongside when they tied up. During our first year in Eskeriada, I worried about Tom. He told me that he didn't like the Boy's School.

'Why not?' I asked him. 'Tell me what's wrong with it, Tom?'

'The boys call me a "culchie."' He said. I had to laugh. 'Most of them live out in the country themselves,' I told him. 'Don't take any notice and they'll soon get tired of teasing you.'

I knew that he found the lessons hard too. I tried to help him but he had a real problem. He didn't seem to see the same words I saw and when he wrote something it looked as though he had written the words backwards or sometimes upside down.

'If I wanted to do this, Tom, I wouldn't be able to,' I told him. 'What are you trying to do?'

'I can't do it at all,' he said, 'I can't read or write and I'm nearly eleven.'

There was a lady teacher named Mrs. Moore who really liked Tom. Seeing his struggle she was determined to do something about this. It was agreed that she would take Tom for lessons after school three days a week. He protested. There were his farm chores out in Capall Ban. But my parents insisted that he go to Mrs. Moore's house on the evenings which suited her. I knew that he was embarrassed and he was afraid that some of the other boys would see him going into her home.

'Pretend you are bringing her shopping.' I suggested.

For a few days we saved cornflake packets and we wrapped a sod of turf in brown paper to look like a loaf of bread. We put apples in a bag and an empty sauce bottle filled with tea. For weeks he carried this shopping with him, leaving it inside Mrs. Moore's gate going in and collecting it on his way out. Gradually he began to forget about it and eventually he didn't mind who noticed his visits.

He didn't mind because at last he was making progress. It was a miracle really. If Mrs. Moore was alive today she would be a famous teacher and a much sought after consultant. Between her and Tom they worked out his problem. She'd discovered how he saw things and they worked out a code. It may have taken longer for Tom to write or read because he had to use the code to translate the words and then use it again to write or read but it worked. He became faster and faster doing whatever it was he did. I couldn't work out his system and neither could mammy or daddy.

'Tom speaks a different language.' They said.

'Moore's Melodies,' my father called it.

Each Christmas my mother gave Mrs. Moore a beautiful cardigan because she would not take anything for helping Tom. Without her, he might have known the song but he'd never have been able to sing it.

Daddy was very relaxed during the years which followed our move.

He had beef cattle on granny Julia's farm and he helped Eugene run his new place. Sometimes my mother scolded him for spending so much time in Capall Ban.

'There can't be that much to do,' she stated.

She was annoyed because the three girls had come home from America to see their mother.

'Such a fuss when they should be ashamed of themselves. Imagine away from their mother for more than twenty years then they come back full of hope and glory.'

I knew what was wrong with mammy. The aunties were very American, all make up and with different nail polish each day. Their clothes were not at all like the clothes in our shop, they were very frilly and colourful. They had really flashy jewellery too. I'd never seen so many rings on one hand.

'Do people really buy those mighty dull looking things which you sell, Eleanor?' Aunty Helen asked her. My mother was livid.

'Easily known you ladies haven't suffered through a war.' She snapped. 'I suppose you'll expect dancing at the cross roads next?'

'Oh Gee, honey, wouldn't that be something, can you fix it for us, Owen?'

'God give me patience.' He muttered under his breath.

Of course, deep down, he was delighted to see his sisters. Sitting in granny Julia's house by the big fire they talked about America. We heard all the stories of their younger days and about their husbands and their children in Long Island. Daddy got the latest news about his friends who were still in New York. I began to realise how successful he had become over there. Aunty Anna was very forthright. She told my mother that we would all have had a better life in America. Why hadn't she agreed with daddy and gone over after their marriage?

'Because,' my mother snapped. 'Because I'm an only child and because I've got a mother and a father and I care about them which is more than I can say for some people.'

'Oh boy!' Anna exclaimed. 'Pardon me, I guess I've misunderstood.'

'Don't take any notice of Anna,' Aunty Eileen tried to be conciliatory. 'She doesn't talk a lot of sense sometimes. She's up in the clouds always, that's our Anna.'

'Well, the sooner she's up in the clouds again the better I'll like it,' was my mother's furious response.

And she, who loved a party, refused to have one in their honour. Daddy was upset.

'They have never heard you sing Eleanor,' he cajoled. 'I've been telling them about your singing,' Mammy wouldn't budge, not an inch.

Granny Julia never saw her girls again. She died a few weeks following their return to America. My mother employed Nellie Grant to work in the shop so that she could be with granny Julia. The priest came and this annoyed granny. 'What's he fussing about?' She wanted to know. We were told about her death. I wasn't upset, well not in the same way as I was when Marguerita died.

'This is highly irregular,' the priest had said to Eugene when he heard that granny Julia wanted to be outside in the fresh air. She heard him.

'Who says, it's highly irregular? Who says I have to meet the Lord in my bed. If I want to die outside under the cherry tree I will die outside under the cherry tree.'

Daddy, Uncle Eugene and Uncle Dan took a mattress outside. Wrapping their mother in her well worn patchwork quilt they carried her and settled her down on a bed of soft blankets. Her sons sat on the ground beside her and she told them again how she and their father, John had come to Capall Ban. 'He wanted this farm,' she said. 'We sat here under this very tree and it was in blossom then. We decided to get married - and he got the farm too.' She laughed. Neighbours called and busied themselves doing odd jobs around the haggard. Aunty Gracie made tea. Granny said she didn't want any.

'Is Eleanor around?' She enquired.

My mother knelt beside her, granny Julia whispered into her ear.

'How about a little drop of brandy for the two of us, you know where it is?' Holding granny Julia's head my mother gave her a little sip. 'That was nice,' she smiled, 'Very nice indeed.'

At her funeral mass, I pictured granny Julia wrapped tightly in her patchwork quilt sailing over Capall Ban, over the rooftop and the great chimney. Sailing away into the blue sky, away above the trees and beyond the clouds where she would wake up amongst the stars.

Aunty Gracie moved into Capall Ban following her sister's death. Someone had to look after Eugene and the hens, she decided. My mother was very satisfied because it seemed that Eugene was resigned to being a bachelor. There was a chance that we might inherit something after all. Eventually, he rented the other house to a vet. It was a good arrangement especially when there was a sick animal on the farm.

Colin did meet Sister Isobel when he started in the convent school. He terrified her. She had finally come face to face with a real genius. When children were asked to write a few words about their favourite animal, she expected them to have ideas about cats and dogs. Colin wrote six pages about the badgers, their habitats and their strength. As his schooling continued and he moved to the Boys School, his intelligence became a problem. He could not get enough books to read or find people who understood his need to learn more and more and more. Again, Mrs. Moore came to the rescue. There was a young male teacher in the Christian Brother's School in Ardcais about three miles away. He was very bright and could do with some extra money, she said. He could give Colin some challenging work to do. Should she speak to him?

'It's very difficult,' she explained to my parents. 'Colin is only eight emotionally and physically but intellectually he is thirty. 'I always think,' she added, 'that a gifted child carries a heavy burden.' It took many years for me to appreciate what she meant.

If you came in through our hall door from the main street in Eskeriada you could enter Dardis Drapery through a door to the left. Wide stairs led to the upper floors and to the right of the hall door a small room had a window looking onto the street. My mother made this room into a cosy corner where she could sit and have a cup of tea, sometimes with a customer when she was not too busy. This room was now set aside each evening for Colin and Michael. When I saw Michael for the first time I fell in love with him immediately. I told my friends in school about him. I almost swooned as I described his jet black hair and his piercing blue eyes.

'Is he tall, dark and handsome or is he not?' I gasped. The girls wanted to see him. It became a ritual. Each evening a group of us walked past the window. Conveniently someone had to stop to tie a shoelace or fix a stray lock of hair. If Michael looked up there were giggles, smiles and blushes.

'Oh, he's a knock out,' they screeched.

Colin told mammy. I was furious especially when he said that we all looked silly and stupid. 'You should have seen their red faces and the way they were trying to make googly eyes at us,' he told her.

'Don't get carried away,' I retorted. 'We weren't looking at you. You're just a little boy with a big head.'

We were growing up, Tom and I. He had some pals who were girl mad. Joe Scully was one of them. One Sunday evening when my parents had gone to the pictures with Mr. and Mrs. Kenny I went into the shop to look at the new stock. There was a big glass door into the shop which was the entrance for customers. Dardis Drapery was scrolled on this. Grandad had painted the words in gold. When the shop was closed another wooden door behind the glass one was closed and locked. Opening this inner door I switched on the light in the store room. This area was divided and the middle part of it was visible from inside the shop. Here my mother had a display of hats and shoes. The stock was hidden away on shelves and in presses to the left. On the other side there was a private changing area with a big cheval mirror. I was happily admiring the new skirts and wondering if I could ask for one for Easter. Cuddle skirts were in fashion then. These were made in soft tweed and in pastel shades with a wide waistband and a flared skirt. Hearing a knock on the outside glass door I saw Tom and Joe. I let them in through the hall door.

'What are you doing, Ellie?' Tom wanted to know.

'Oh, just looking at the new things, that's all.'

'Ellie, show us a brassiere.' Joe coaxed.

'What size, madam?' I was playing their game now.

He didn't know that there were different sizes. I explained that he could have anything up to a double D cup. I showed him the largest we stocked.

'God, that's mighty.' He gasped. 'And this hold them up bit is called a cup?'

'Yes indeed, Madam.'

'Look at this, Tom, what do you think, this would hold some bosoms wouldn't it?' They were tittering. Tom asked to see some corsets.

'I'm not certain if we have what would suit your requirements,' I laughed as I got out an oblong box of these pink undergarments. 'You might like to try one on, madam, to see if it's comfortable.'

Soon the boys were outfitted. Their socks were rolled up over the legs of their pants and each boy was harnessed into a strong laced up corset.

'God these are awful yokes,' said Tom. 'If you crashed into a fellow while you're wearing one of these you'd send him flying.'

'Madam,' I advised, 'you really need to wear a brassiere to get the best outline to go with your corset.'

'I'll take two double D cups then and the bigger the better,' Tom laughed.

I stuffed the brassieres with tissue paper. I could be in trouble if my mother discovered this because she kept this paper for special purchases only.

Hearing all the laughter, Colin came downstairs. His eyes came out on stalks.

'Are you off to a fancy dress dance?' He asked.

Tom and Joe began to prance around the shop. My recorder was lying on the counter. Colin took it up and began to play a dance tune. The boys became more rowdy. Tom and Joe swung each other around and around and whooped. I joined them. The metal suspenders on the corsets jangled and sparked in the light. The tissue bosoms heaved and bounced beside me. We kept dancing. Colin increased the tempo. We sang:

Come into the parlour boys and make yourselves at home.
Come into the parlour sure you won't be on your own
There's Mick McGee, there's Rafferty, there's Murphy and Muldoon,
Thy say McGilligan's daughter, doesn't know the taste of water
So if you're Irish come ...

The music stopped, my dancing boys raced into the stock room, my parents and Mr. and Mrs. Kenny were staring through the glass door. I'd forgotten to close the inner one. They had seen the performance. Colin had vanished.

The adults stood watching while the blushing boys struggled to undo their fasteners and laces. My mother and Mrs. Kenny helped them. 'I don't want these garments destroyed my mother was trying not to laugh. If there's a mark on anything you boys will have to pay up. Ellie, I'm surprised at you...'

She couldn't continue she had to sit down she was laughing so much. Later, I could hear the four of them still laughing upstairs where they had gone to have a nightcap.

I had been learning the recorder. I wanted to belong to the marching band in Ardcais. During my Intermediate Certificate year when I was fourteen and going on fifteen, I took the bus for a ten o'clock band class each Saturday. Since I had to wait for a bus home at three o'clock, my mother arranged for me to have lunch with the wife of my father's cousin. Majella was married to Dermot Daly who owned a butcher's shop. He had a farm too and reared his own cattle. When my father was selling animals he always sold to Dermot Daly.

Majella had six small children but she had a part time housekeeper, a nurse for the younger children and a cook to help her. I admired her style. She always looked so perfect rather like the American aunties - without the gloss. Her brother was a priest who had come home from the missions in South America. Everyone thought the world of him. 'It was Father Cyril this and Father Cyril that.' I met him for the first time at lunch one Saturday. I didn't like him. I thought I must be the only person in the whole world who didn't.

After lunch I sometimes played with Majella's children for a while. It's a nice thing to do, my mother told me. I played the recorder for them and at other times I'd read a story. Afterwards, in the parlour, which was upstairs like our own, I'd try to do some homework.

Father Cyril came into the parlour one afternoon. I couldn't understand why people thought he looked like an angel. He did have very blonde curly hair but I thought his mouth was too wide. It reminded me of a crocodile because when he smiled he opened his mouth really wide and his teeth were visible from ear to ear. He was short and squat and his skin was very brown. He had a record player, a present he told me, from an admirer. I was on guard, don't ask me why. What had I to fear from a priest? I didn't know but I was uneasy. Noticing his suitcase lying on the floor, I asked him hopefully if he was going away.

'Oh indeed, I'm not. I suppose you think I am because of the suitcase. Wait a minute and I'll show you something,' he smiled.

Taking an item from the suitcase, he disappeared behind the heavy brocade curtains. I was thinking of making a run for it as he reappeared. He was wearing baby blue silk pyjamas. He turned the music up.

'Come and dance with me, Ellie, please.'

I was mesmerised. I sat still and perplexed in the chair. Suddenly he grabbed me. My schoolbook fell to the floor. 'Dance with me, come on Ellie.'

He was very rough, he hurt my arms. Trying to kiss me he began to rub himself against me. I pulled away. I hit him, very hard, beneath the chin just the way Tom had shown me. It was a real uppercut. My own strength amazed me. Catching his foot in the suitcase he fell back against the table his jaws wide open. He was furious.

He warned me, 'You won't get away from me that easily, Ellie.'

Majella wondered why I asked her to fetch my recorder and my school books from the parlour. Smiling at me as she came downstairs, she said, 'I understand, Father Cyril came in. He didn't expect you to be there. He was going to have a sleep on the couch near the fire. He likes to do that you know. You've probably never seen a priest in pyjamas before, have you? I think he looks even more like an angel in that blue set.'

'A very bad one,' I wanted to say but I didn't know how to. My hand ached as I sat on the bus for home. My knuckles were beginning to swell. I stopped taking lessons with the band. I had too much study to do I told my parents.

I didn't tell anyone about Father Cyril. It was a very upsetting experience which made me fearful of adult men. A customer who caused trouble in the shop added to my anxiety. He was a rough diamond, a farmer who held the purse strings tightly. My mother was serving him at the far counter which was the men's outfitting area. He wanted to see some combinations - the all in one vest and long johns preferred by the older men. When one garment was spread on the counter for his inspection, he whispered, 'Do you think my little mannin would have enough room in here, Ma'am? I think I'll need to check for size, let me show you, tell me what you think, I'm sure you're a good advisor on these matters.'

I was studying behind the other counter, sitting on a low stool but I could see him in the mirror. He began to undo his trousers right there in the shop with only my mother watching, as he thought. I stood up and running to the bottom of the stairs, I shrieked, 'Daddy come quickly, there's a terrible man down here tormenting mammy.'

My father took the man by the collar, 'Get out of here,' he ordered, 'Take your filthy custom elsewhere.'

My mother was shaken.

'I didn't know you were there, Ellie,' she said, 'I'd forgotten all about you. I'm sorry you had to see that terrible behaviour. If she hadn't been there,' she looked at daddy, 'I don't know what I'd have done.'

My mother became very protective of me after this. She didn't want me to be alone in the shop especially on a Friday evening. Many men came into the town then and sometimes one or two drank too much. Daddy had a few talks with Tom. I knew this because Tom was going around looking all smug and behaving very grown up.

'Tell me,' I implored. 'Tell me what daddy told you. I'll tell you, if you'll tell me,' he replied. He knew that mammy and I had had a heart to heart too. I remember her telling me that she hoped our lives would always be free from danger and disappointment. This came between her gentle explanation about babies and how they were conceived. Being a farm child I was not unduly amazed. But I did think about the strange acrobatics required to make a baby. Who would I like to make a baby with I wondered? For a woman of her day, my mother was far seeing and sensible. Some boys will try to take advantage of you, Ellie.

'Always trust Tom,' she advised. 'He is a good brother and he will know the good boys from the bad ones. He won't let anything happen to you.'

Tom was the only person I eventually told about Father Cyril. He wanted to confront him. 'If that Father Knickers ever sets foot in our house, I'll kill him,' he told me. Unfortunately, my mother admired this priest. She invited him to a party at Easter. My parents had many friends. The house was crowded. My mother played the piano, guests sang or told stories. Father Knickers had brought his record player along, 'a present from an admirer,' he told everybody. Where had I heard this before? There were gasps of delight when he played a record. It was a South American melody, he told us. They dance to this music he continued while removing his clerical collar and opening some buttons on his shirt to reveal a tanned, hairy chest and a gold cross on a chain. He wriggled around with his arms in the air, twirling his hands this way and that. I wanted to tell him that he was sweating under his arms. Tom's face was like thunder. The next morning my mother enthused about Father Cyril. 'He is so down to earth, so unaffected,' she beamed. 'Could you imagine Father Lynam in Monabeag dancing like that?' She asked.

'Father Lynam has respect for his calling.' Daddy's voice held a warning. 'I'm surprised at you Eleanor. I don't see anything to admire in his antics. I've seen fellows like him in the States, Eleanor. They're no good and quite frankly, I'd prefer if you didn't invite him again he's no example for the children. And don't think, for one minute that anyone other than you admired him last night.'

Mammy was flabbergasted. 'We'll see,' was all she could say.

During the night of the party granny had a mild stroke. Grandad didn't realise something had happened to her until he woke up the next morning. She didn't answer him when he spoke to her and she didn't seem to know who he was. There was consternation in our house. Mammy became hysterical. Mrs. Kenny was called and she calmed her. I had to look after the shop. A pattern developed during the summer which followed - a pattern which didn't suit me at all.

While my friends were playing tennis or sitting by the river I had to stay at home. Sometimes Mammy would come in and tell me to go and enjoy myself. But grandad would soon appear in a panic asking her to come back to granny. He imagined all sorts of things were happening to her. My parents wanted granny and grandad to come to live with us. We had plenty of room for them but they didn't want to move. We were all unhappy. Daddy had to serve in the shop on Friday and Saturday evenings. He took charge of the men's outfitting and he hated it. He knew I hated being in the shop too. Often when he came back from the farm, he'd find me standing at the shop door or sitting forlornly on the window ledge. Often when I sat there or on the low stool inside the shop I thought about granny. In an instant during that night of the party, unknown to anyone, her life was changed forever. She was so fragile and vulnerable now. I wondered what she was thinking. Did granny long once more to be outside sweeping up the papers and dirt which came in through the front railings and which annoyed her so much? Did these everyday things matter to her now? Sometimes she had a look of desperation on her face and at other times a look of gratitude for the kindness of everyone. I was feeling sad and lonely. I think daddy noticed my vacant look. I think he spoke to mammy because she decided to employ Nellie Grant as a shop assistant.

During this time Colin took over my visits to Mary Kate. He did her shopping and stayed to play chess with Gerald. Leonard had died two years after our move to Eskeriada. Aunty Alice outliving him by one week, she was over a hundred years old when she died. Mary Kate now devoted herself to Gerald. Whenever I did go to her house we now sat in the kitchen. We couldn't disturb the chess masters. Sunday afternoon gatherings no longer happened for Mary Kate

'I used to love having everyone here,' she told me. 'If they hadn't come during those years, I would have gone stone mad.'

A new metal bridge was being constructed over the river. Tom spent all his time down there watching everything. Daddy got cross with him sometimes because he was neglecting his jobs at Capall Ban. They had words more than once until Tom shocked daddy by telling him that he didn't want to be a farmer after all. He wanted to be an engineer, he wanted to build bridges.

I think I was more shocked that my father by his outburst. I didn't know everything about my brother. I would love to be a farmer if I could. There was a presence within the land which could not be replaced. It was something I felt, something I always wanted to be near.

❦

When granny died, grandad did come to live with us. He was lost for a while until he met James Lamb. James and grandad became interested in railways when a new line was opened into Eskeriada. Railways became their hobby. They actually built a model railway in the attic of our house. Colin read details and information about engines for them because their eyesight wasn't the best. Daddy found pieces of wood, metal and wire for the enterprise.

'I'd say they're like children playing,' my mother laughed, 'if it didn't take them so long to get up off the floor.'

The railway took shape over a year. Eventually, daddy made a long, wide bench for it. Grandad and James could now stand or sit while awaiting the train's arrival. They chatted at the station, smoked and drank cups of tea in their own new world. When word reached the town that there was a model railway in the loft of Dardis Drapery we had so many children and adults tramping up our stairs to see it. We didn't mind. Where would one find another such railway with the carriages and the scenery painted by Michelangelo?

Uncle William had shown my mother the proper book keeping system for the shop. She liked doing the accounts and she was good at it. When granny was ill she let things slide for a while. When she went back to the shop herself, she made a terrible discovery. Nellie Grant had been helping herself to money and to clothes, especially underwear and stockings. Nellie had been extra generous with her relatives too. She gave them discounts and she gave credit to people who would probably never pay. My mother had offered Nellie part time work when she herself came back to the shop. She was surprised when Nellie turned down the offer. Now she knew the reason for her refusal. My parents had a serious discussion, they asked Nellie to come in to see them. She wouldn't. There was talk of solicitor's letters and court appearances. Aunty Pat and Uncle William came to see us. They came all the way from Dublin on the new train, its first journey into Eskeriada. It was marvellous, Uncle William told us.

The situation was a very difficult one, they agreed. Nellie Grant should make some sort of restitution. She obviously had a problem and she could not be trusted. Mammy could never give her a reference, they said. Perhaps her husband should be approached. Solicitors and court cases were all very well but we were in a small town and so many people were interrelated – such a move might do the business more harm than good. Besides, Aunty Pat pointed out. 'I don't think it would be good for you, Eleanor, to have all this trouble. It could hang over you for a long time before even coming to court. Think of the headlines in the local paper. I don't think your nerves could take it, Eleanor. And remember, you've gone through such a bad time, up and down to your mother and of course her death is still so recent.'

I listened to their conversation while I was helping to get the dinner ready. I silently agreed with my father when he said that they were right. He should have thought about the repercussions especially on mammy's health and on the children too. 'No money would be worth having her ill again,' he said. Grandad, who was supposed to be deaf and who appeared to be reading the Sunday paper, reminded mammy that there was a house to sell.

'Remember that,' he said. 'It's yours Eleanor to do whatever you want with. What you've lost in the shop is nothing compared with the value of that house. Use it and forget about the likes of Nellie Grant.'

'And so say all of us.' Aunty Pat exclaimed. My mother was laughing and crying as she hugged her elderly father. I felt ashamed. Had I thought anything at all about my generous grandad and his awful loss? He had lived with granny for more than fifty years. Everything had changed for him. How his heart must have been broken. I never pictured granny Ethel sailing beyond the stars. I was finished with that sort of dream. If I thought about her in that way, she would probably be, in my mind, brushing feathers off the floor of heaven. But I didn't believe in angel's wings anymore either. I had seen her interred in the good earth, her grave covered with flowers. My drifting thoughts were interrupted by Colin who was looking for his dinner. Passing grandad's chair he instinctively put his hand on his head, 'Grandad,' he said, 'you are an extraordinary man.'

Chapter Six
Someone to Love Me

Tom and I began two years of study for our Leaving Certificate together in 1957. He changed to the Christian Brother's School in Ardcais so that he could repeat a year and have the subjects which he would need for engineering. My parents were worried they didn't want Tom to be disappointed and they knew how difficult school subjects, especially those which required a lot of reading, were for him. Mrs. Moore reassured them. She said that the Brothers would be very aware of Tom's needs, indeed she had already spoken about Tom to the Head Brother. 'Besides,' she added, 'he will have Ellie to help him.'

But we had more on our minds than school work. As the summer holidays were drawing to a close, I realised that Tom's interests were not entirely centred on the new bridge. A group of young people met down by the river, girls and boys whose thoughts were turned in a new direction altogether. While I was minding the shop they were chasing one another around the callow land. When I joined them, I was on the fringes. I was an observer rather that a participant. I felt left out when I very much wanted to belong. Sometimes, I left the twittering girls to walk alone in the rough hay trying not to upset the shy corncrake that nested alone hidden away in the warm ground. I disturbed game birds during my wandering because they were so tuned in to every danger. Flying suddenly from the ground they'd warn a mate with a wild cry. When the river was in full spate, the callow lands became water logged and dangerous. Through the windows at the back of our house we could see the flood waters creeping forward. Eventually we would be looking at a lake. During the dry months cattle could graze on some parts of these meadows after it had been cut for hay. From our garden in Eskeriada, it was possible to climb a wall at the back and walk along a well worn path through the callows to the old forts which had been built by Cromwell. We were warned not to take this path except when the weather was really dry. One could easily fall or trip over a clump of rough grass and no one would see you there or be able to find you for a long time.

My father had cultivated the long garden at the back of our house. It was a reminder for him of his garden at Lough Louchre. When we left our farm Reverend O'Hara had given daddy dozens of dahlia bulbs which were his own speciality. Our garden was ablaze with many wonderful blooms in reds, purples, yellows, orange and some exotic varieties. The nuns who looked after the church, were given great bunches of these flowers for special Holy Days. My mother was always so proud to see them on the high altar. Daddy grew all our own vegetables. He had a fruit garden of strawberries, blackcurrants and raspberries also. The birds were his biggest problem and Sutty, who was my own age of sixteen years, had gone well past caring about their intrusions. Daddy made a bird scaring device. It was a coloured pole with short coils of coloured rope attached to it. These were supposed to spin in the wind. He was setting this invention on top of the garden wall, the one leading into the callows when he heard giggling. It was Tom and Mary Mahon. They were cavorting in the long grass and they didn't notice daddy until he called out: 'Tom, tell me, is it true that a bird in the hand is worth two in the bush?'

My brother was mortified. Mary Mahon, who was a brazen girl and twenty if she was a day, stood her ground.

'We're only having a little court,' she said, 'I'm giving Tom a few lessons – as if he needed them,' she smirked. 'He's really hot stuff.'

'Miss Mahon, I think you should give your lessons to those of your own age,' daddy advised. 'I don't ever want to see you hanging around with Tom again, is that clear?'

'Suit yourself,' she snapped. 'You're only an old stick in the mud anyway.' That did it. I don't think daddy would have been so severe with Tom if she had been a more innocent type of girl. He was forbidden to go outside the house on any school evenings until further notice and he had to return to Capall Ban and resume his chores there, chores which he had conveniently forgotten about and which Daddy had attended to while Tom studied bridge building!

'Tom,' I said in my most serious voice. 'Mammy told me that you would look after me but you're not able to look after yourself.'

He gazed at me with a far away look in his eyes.

'Ellie,' he said. 'You'll understand better when you find someone to love you.'

Before the Easter of our final year in secondary school, a Retreat was carefully planned for the girls. This very special event was supposed to be a help, a final summing up of our obligations as catholic young ladies. We, who would be the wives and mothers of the future, had many obligations to consider. If one or more were favoured by Almighty God to become a religious sister then the time of Retreat was essential to nurture such a vocation. The nuns and lay teachers would have been severely disillusioned had they known that the young ladies were looking forward to the retreat for all the wrong reasons. We were indeed weak and we were influenced by a girl named Yvonne Bailey, a doctor's daughter. She brought medical text books into school. We huddled in a group at the end of the playing field during break and studied these. We studied them during hockey practice too, getting into huddles as far away from the games mistress as possible. We'd hear Miss McCarthy, in her short green skirt and green stockings shouting. Her cries of, 'stop playing about with the ball, stop playing about with the ball,' sent us into peals of laughter. The medical books were full of information and diagrams showing men and women's bodies, even the most secret parts. Yvonne spoke with great authority, using the correct names always.

'This is important,' she told us. 'Never say Willy, saying Willy is silly,' she warned us. We were her eager students and we passed all her anatomy tests with flying colours. I believe we had sufficient insight into human reproduction, diseases and remedies, to become specialists.

A sincere priest who had more insight than we realised came to conduct the retreat. He looked like Alan Ladd and in no time at we were all in love with him. Yvonne had an idea for the day when the priest would tell us, as they always did, to write down questions which he would do his best to answer. These questions were placed in a box which was left in the chapel. We all wrote the exact same question which was dictated by Yvonne and waited. Father Colm read the first question. He left it aside. We looked at one another surreptitiously. He took the second question and the third, we giggled nervously. Taking the forth and the fifth slip of paper, he left them aside very delicately. We stirred uncomfortably. Sister Agnes was sitting in the back row. She walked up to the priest. 'I'm sorry to intrude father,' she whispered, 'but is there a difficulty?'

He answered so quietly the we couldn't hear him. Some girls blushed furiously. Yvonne stared straight ahead her face was impassive. Sister Agnes returned silently to her place. Father Colm spoke.

'There are some things, ladies, which are best answered by a girl's mother, I think. Since you all seem to have the same question I'm wondering if I should invite each girl's mother to come in this evening.

They could have a little talk amongst themselves and then each mother would probably feel comfortable enough to answer her own daughter's question. It would help me greatly to know how this question should be dealt with. One never knows, it may be asked again in some other school for young ladies. If you want me to ask Sister Agnes to contact your mothers, please raise your hand.' Not a hand was raised.

'Very well, ladies, I want each of you to go home after the talk which I am about to give. You are, on your word of honour, to ask your own mother the question which you have written here.'

We were stunned. I heard little of the talk which followed. There were some words which suggested that a decent young lady should have the courage to reject the bad example of others. We should be strong enough to do the right thing. My mother was puzzled when I dragged her into the pantry. 'Father Colm said I have to ask you a question,' I told her.

'Oh yes, Ellie, what's the question?'

'It's what do I do if a boy tries to put his hand up my knickers?'

'My God.' She gasped, 'the priest told you to ask me that question?'

I had to tell her the whole truth.

'We all wrote the same question, to put in the question box,' I said.

'And whose bright idea was it?' She wanted to know.

'We all agreed,' I told her.

'I want to know who thought up such a disgraceful question for the priest?' She insisted.

'It was Yvonne,' I answered reluctantly, 'but we all agreed. Please don't tell Rev. Mother that it was Yvonne,' I pleaded.

'That girl knows more than is good for her. She is a right sneaky little madam. Just what does she think she's up to?' My mother was fuming.

'Where's my hat and coat?' Rushing to the hall stand she grabbed them and her gloves as well.

'What are you going to do?' I cried. My mother went to the cosy room and looked out through the window.

'I'm waiting to see all the mothers marching to the convent. I intend to go with them.'

I was terrified. I ran upstairs to my bedroom and falling onto the bed, I grabbed Judy and sobbed with shame and frustration. Eventually I fell asleep. I was awakened by mammy coming into the room.

'Ellie,' she spoke softly, 'tea is ready, come downstairs now.'

'Did you go to the convent?' I asked fearfully.

'No, I didn't, not this time but Ellie I am ashamed of what you have done and I hope you are too.'

'Oh I am,' I cried, 'I am and I'm very sorry. I won't ever do anything like that ever again, I promise.' She touched my face.

'Ellie, you are far too innocent,' she said, 'to let yourself be led into such nasty and underhand ways.'

'You didn't tell daddy, did you?'

'No I didn't tell daddy, we'll keep this between you and me, Ellie. At the weekend I think we should have another little talk though, what do you think?' I agreed and we smiled at each other. During tea, Tom kept looking at me and raising his eyebrow. He was able to raise just one eyebrow which usually made me laugh. I didn't laugh now as I helped myself to a large piece of mammy's apple tart. He collared me later.

'Hey, Ellie, what's going on? Jimmy told me that Roisin was crying in her room all evening and when I was in the Post Office I heard Mrs. Keane yelling at Lily out in the back. She was calling her a "dirty minded little imp." What's it all about, Ellie?'

'Search me,' I sniffed.

'And guess what, Ellie? Doctor Bailey nearly ran over Miss Feighry. He came up the street at such speed just as she was crossing over to the bakery with that blind dog of hers. You should have heard the screech of brakes and he didn't even look back. His car swerved through the convent gates on two wheels. Mrs. Bailey was in the front seat and Yvonne was in the back, they were looking serious. What do you think has happened, Ellie?'

'I heard,' I whispered in his ear, 'that Reverend Mother has had a fit.'

❦

Irene Wilson, who was born in Ardcais returned from England that April. She wanted to work closer to home. She was a trained nurse who had worked in a large hospital in London for many years. My mother liked her because Irene bought good clothes in the shop and she wore them very well. Her hair was cut in an Audrey Hepburn style and she did look a little like the movie star. Soon, many young girls and older ones too began to wear a similar hairstyle. I pleaded with my mother to let me have my hair cut. I'd had long hair all my life. 'I look like a little girl,' I moaned. She agreed but she said she didn't think it would suit me at all.

'You don't have Audrey Hepburn's face you know.' But I thought I looked beautiful until Tom's pals said they didn't like it because they didn't recognise me anymore. Colin remarked that I looked like an overgrown tadpole which he added, 'is essentially an immature frog.' I did have an oval face and my eyes were round and a grey blue colour. But for him to say that I looked like a frog.

'You are the most insulting snotty nosed little boy, I've ever come across. Why don't you go read *The Dandy,* where you get all your smart remarks,' I sulked. I knew this would annoy Colin, he thought he was far too clever for the comics every boy of his age loved.

The older boys who hung around with Tom were coming in to our house very often. I really thought they were all keen on me. I was mistaken, they were thinking of ways to bribe my mother. They wanted her to teach them to dance. She couldn't understand their unexpected offers of help. 'Would you like any grocery shopping done,

Mrs. Dardis?' 'Can we clean the windows for you, Mrs. Dardis?' 'If you have a sweeping brush handy, Mrs. Dardis, I'll sweep up outside.'

'All right,' she laughed, 'what do you boys want?'

Her classes were a great success. They were held in the kitchen after tea. Only boys came because we girls learned ballroom dancing in school. We had a record player now and Colin was in charge of it. My mother marched around straightening elbows, giving directions, counting, beating time and sometimes taking the floor with a boy in order to demonstrate a step. I had to dance with each boy in turn so that they would get used to holding a girl. Sometimes my shins were black and blue. We waltzed, did the tango and the samba and the quick step. I accused Tom of practically dislocating my shoulder and I yelled when Jerry Breen almost crushed my fingers. Jerry Breen was my favourite dancing partner. He kissed me once, ever so quickly, when mammy had her back turned. I smiled at him blissfully. A couple of the boys who were dancing nearby made sick noises.

Irene Wilson had relatives who lived near Capall Ban. Tom told me that he had seen her out there and that she had been talking and strolling around the land with Uncle Eugene.

'So. She's allowed to speak to him isn't she?'

I wasn't interested. Well, not until Tom added that he thought it was serious. This would be alarming news for my mother. We decided to keep quiet. Suppose she went out to Capall Ban to ask Eugene about this? Our mother was quite capable of interfering in his affairs. We knew that she didn't expect any changes out there. In her mind we would inherit something. But there was a difficulty which Uncle Dan had pointed out when the girls were home. Granny Julia had refused to make a will. Whenever she died the farm would belong to all her children. The girls had opted out saying they wouldn't take anything out of Ireland and the home place. Dan said he was financially secure and he would not be claiming either. Eugene and daddy worked the farm together, daddy grazing cattle on two large fields and Eugene tilling the rest. My mother was not entirely happy with this gentleman's agreement. She annoyed my father when she nagged at him to get the matter sorted. This came to a head when Eugene told daddy that he and Irene were to marry. What a shock for mammy. She had no idea. Tom and I felt quite guilty

'Eugene again, I always said he was a sly one. Owen, did you know anything about this friendship?' She asked.

'Well…'

'You did, you did.' She shouted.

'Don't get carried away, Eleanor, the man has a right to have a friendship if he wants to. I don't know everything about Eugene. I'm glad for him though. She's one steady woman and she's very friendly too.'

'Very friendly, steady, how do you know she's very friendly? You did know about them. You wouldn't be bothered telling me. Here I am working my fingers to the bone in this shop and I don't know what's going on. I was supposed to wait for a customer to tell me, I suppose. Yes, that's it I could hear it from a customer. I should have been told, Owen, I do belong to the family after all.'

She was furious.

'I'm quite sure Eugene talked to you about her, Owen,' she went on. 'Now where do we stand? What have I been telling you about sorting out your share in the land? Eugene will want it all now. Will nobody listen to me? Now there won't be anything for our children.'

'We'll sort it,' he said. 'I'll go out there straight away, will that satisfy you?'

Before mammy could answer, daddy had gone. My father became the owner of three fields. This was approximately forty acres of grazing for his cattle. It was a good arrangement. Eugene had forty acres as well and he had his other farm. But my mother was not satisfied. 'What about the house?' She asked. 'That house is worth some money and Eugene has taken it over.'

'Oh. For God's sake Eleanor! I don't know what's come over you. We've got a fine house here and you have grandad's house rented. What more do you want? If I hear anymore about land and houses, I declare to God, I'll give Eugene my forty acres.'

My mother was surprised again when Irene came into the shop during the afternoon. Putting on her special voice mammy congratulated her on her forthcoming wedding to Uncle Eugene.

'We're all thrilled, aren't we Ellie?' She beamed. 'A real surprise for everyone, I must say. It will be a new lease of life for Eugene, the poor man, he was becoming really odd but I'm sure you've noticed this yourself? He, if anyone, deserves to be happy. He went through hell when Marguerita was killed.'

I cringed, and she hadn't finished.

'Don't get me wrong, Irene, I wish you all the personal happiness in the world, of course but you'll have your work cut out for you. Eugene has been on his own for a long time now.'

Will she ever stop, I fretted? Irene smiled and thanked mammy for her good wishes.

'But I've come in to ask your advice,' she gave my mother a we're in this together sort of look. I think mammy hoped for a split second that Irene was going to say she was calling the whole thing off.

'Would you help me to choose my wedding outfit?' She asked. 'And do you think I could ask Ellie to be my bridesmaid?'

There's one clever woman, I thought and I beamed with pleasure. Mammy was totally wrong footed but she recovered quickly. Naturally she would be delighted to assist. She became animated.

'You know what we could do Irene, you and I and Ellie? We could go to Dublin for a day. I have an in with the best clothing people. You will have a great choice. Come upstairs, Irene, let's have a cup of tea.'

This was the unexpected beginning to a friendship which endured.

Aunty Irene would not hear of Gracie leaving the house in Capall Ban. Gracie's own little house which had been idle now for a couple of years had fallen into disrepair.

'I'm insisting,' Irene told mammy. 'After all, Gracie kept Eugene safe and well when things were hard for him. Now it's our turn to help her.'

Aunty Irene told me about her plans for the Capall Ban house. She loved decorating and I believed she could make a chicken coop comfortable. But her plans had to take second place when she and Eugene became parents. Their twin boys arrived early their tiny lives hanging by a thread for days. My mother saw the doctor driving out the Capall Ban road but she didn't think anything of it. Soon afterwards an ambulance drove at speed down the street, its siren blaring. We had no idea that Irene and Eugene were in the ambulance with their babies. Eugene telephoned from the hospital in Galway to explain what was happening. He was terribly upset and anxious, daddy said. We were praying desperately. To lose these boys would be unbearable for everyone. But one month later we were able to rejoice because Peter and Paul had come home to Capall Ban.

❦

Tom and I had finished the Leaving Certificate and a long summer stretched before us. It became a time for discovery and for decisions about our future. I had no idea what I wanted to do. I don't think my mother wanted me to be a shop keeper.

'If you want to work here in the shop, Ellie, you can,' she told me. 'But I think you would get bored very quickly. There's not enough business for me to pay you very much and you'd have to learn that you can't have clothes for free either. I would be the boss, Ellie and we might not get on when we're together all the time.' Her thoughts were turned towards a profession.

'If you have a profession you will always have a job and a good position in society,' she declared.

'I did not want to be a teacher under any circumstances and I had refused to take the exams at Easter which could open the way into a Primary School Teacher Training College. There was talk of the Civil Service - I didn't even know what that was. University was not an option. It would be expensive enough to keep Tom there if he got in and besides what would I do at university? Colin would win a university scholarship that was certain but me, I was a problem. 'I'll find myself a rich farmer,' I announced, 'that's what I really want to be, a farmer's wife who works on the land.'

'There's no such thing as a rich farmer,' daddy laughed, 'and you'd have to have a big dowry, Ellie. Now what about someone like Mikey Lyons? I think he has lots of money.'

'Mikey Lyons,' I screeched, 'he's filthy dirty, he never washes and he's old.'

'But he's rich,' daddy was still laughing. 'He's rich because he works day and night. There's money in muck, Ellie, remember that.' I was disgusted.

Whenever I wasn't needed in the shop I cycled to Capall Ban to see the twins. They were delightful babies. Aunty Irene said that she was blessed, they didn't keep her awake all night and they were great feeders too. Uncle Eugene had all kinds of excuses to come into the house so that he could look at his little miracles. Often I sat outside with Irene and Gracie. We'd take turns holding the babies, talking baby talk to them and chatting to each other. Nobody could tell the boys apart, they were identical. Each baby had the blackest hair I'd ever seen on an infant. Their eyes were the bluest of blue.

'Usually, the eye colour is not so pronounced at the beginning Aunty Irene explained but these boys are so beautiful. I can hardly believe they're mine. I'll let you into a secret,' she whispered. 'You will be the only person apart from their father and me to know them apart. Peter has a crooked little finger on his right hand, look, you'd hardly notice it.'

'It's not uncommon,' she continued, 'for this to happen and it won't get any more obvious as he grows.'

I was privileged and I promised Aunty Irene that I would not reveal Peter's secret to anyone. I told her that I was worried because I couldn't decide what to do with my life.

'I should be thinking about something,' I sighed, 'but I don't want to.' Most of my friends know what they want. Judith is going to train for teaching, Iris has had an interview for the Hibernian Bank and I know Mary and Roisin have done the civil service exams. A couple of the girls are going to Dublin to do a secretarial course. That's what Lily is going to do. I'd hate it. I'd hate to be stuck in an office all day. Mammy keeps going on about a profession,' I said.

'Ellie, would you like to become a nurse, what do you think? I can tell you all about that profession. And,' she added, 'you could train here in Ireland. I'm sure your exam results will be very good. I had to go to England because the Nursing Schools were very selective then and all the places had been filled by girls who did better in school than I'd done or who had the right connections.'

I was astounded, why hadn't I thought of this myself? It was an ideal profession. I remembered loving all those medical books which Yvonne Bailey had shown us. The diagrams of the skeleton and the individual bones fascinated me. I remembered the structure of the heart and the diagram of the eye which was unbelievable there was so much detail there. I imagined wonderful scenes of me, dressed in a nurse's uniform, standing beside a sick bed, walking along beside a handsome doctor, dressing wounds and even assisting at an operation. Irene brought me back to reality.

'Of course, it's not an easy profession,' she explained. 'It's like a calling really and you have to have an aptitude, I mean a real liking for the work. It's not easy caring for the sick, Ellie. Sometimes patients are very frightened and sometimes one or two can be difficult and ungrateful. The study is hard as well but I will be able to help you, Ellie. I've still got all my text books and even the copies I used in

Nursing School.'

Irene said I must think carefully before I made any decision and I must talk to my parents, they would have to be agreeable.

'I know, I know,' I told her, 'but it's what I want. I never thought of nursing but its ideal for me. I know I'll love it. I'm so excited! Oh I do hope I will be accepted in a good hospital. My mother won't agree unless I get into the best, I'm sure of that.'

My news was welcomed at home.

'It's splendid, Irene is a God's send,' mammy enthused. 'I thought of nursing for you myself,' she said, 'but I didn't think you'd like it, Ellie. You are always going on about not wanting to work indoors and saying that you want to be a farmer. It will be great to have another nurse in the family. Now I won't have to worry if I'm sick or sore when I'm an old woman.'

I was accepted for the College of Nursing in Galway, conditionally until my leaving certificate results were known. I was confident these would be satisfactory. I would begin Nurse training at the beginning of October. Three long months stretched ahead and I was determined to make the most of them. We, Judith, Iris, Roisin and Lily danced our way with Tom and Joe and their friends through the weeks which followed. The tennis Club became our meeting place. Here we planned each frenzied foray to the local dance halls. Not a carnival, a gymkhana dance, a tennis hop, a rugby club social escaped our presence. Some towns had their own dance hall and often a marquee was erected after a County Show when large crowds were expected. Any young man who owned a car was desirable. Nobody could leave town for a dance without having his car tightly packed with highly perfumed and gaily dressed girls. Each girl sat on the lap of a proud and possessive boy. There was no end to our happiness, no obstacle to our desires and no satisfying our need to belong with the crowd. Just to have a lad, to be wanted for one self was like a terrible pain, a pain which wouldn't go away. And I was in pain for a long, long time. Or so it seemed.

The hall was crowded. Jerry Breen had assumed that he was my partner. I sat on his knee all the way to Ardcais. I had my arm around his neck, my head resting on his shoulder. Holding my hand Jerry told me that I smelled like a bed of roses. We all smelled the same – we shared the same scent bottle before we got into the car. Arriving at St. Mary's dance hall, he paid for himself and walked in. I had to buy my own ticket. The embarrassment of it. Would you believe he had the nerve to ask me for the first dance?

'You're a mealy mouthed, chicken livered, miser. Jerry Breen,' I spat. 'I can't believe I liked you once upon a time.'

'Ellie, Ellie, what's wrong, what have I done?'

He didn't even know. I was fed up being treated like one of the lads.

'What can I do to make it up to you, Ellie?'

'Go blacken your arse and jump in the river.' I flounced away.

Tom came along. He always wanted to dance with me, 'to get warmed up,' he said. I was fed up with him too. Tom was still being influenced by Mary Mahon. When they danced they gazed into each other's eyes smiling their syrupy smiles. They didn't care who was watching. She was far too old for him, I thought. Tom was so handsome all the girls loved him. He could choose any girl he wanted. We danced a change partner dance I was about to scold Tom when there was a tap on my shoulder. I turned to face my new partner. I nearly fainted. I was looking into the eyes of Richard Meyer from Monabeag.

'Ellie, Ellie, I thought it must be you, I recognised Tom but you have changed so much. You look great Ellie, really wonderful.'

Richard had changed too. His face was longer and he was so tall now. I just kept looking at him. It was really Richard, the blonde hair and the blue eyes were still the same. There was an air about him. How far we'd come from those Sundays when we looked for the white rabbit.

'I can't believe this I've never seen you at any of the dances. We go to most of them, you know. Where have you been Richard?'

He said he had come to Ardcais because another lad wanted him to drive. So he had a car.

'I don't usually come over in this direction, Ellie,' he explained, 'but I am glad I've come here tonight.'

We went to the balcony to have a glass of orange each. I was so happy and so glad that I'd worn my new dress. It was pale blue with white spots. The style was A Line with a dropped waist. There was a petticoat attached which had a stiff edging at the bottom so that when I danced a layer of beautiful lace was revealed. It was a sleeveless dress and on each shoulder strap there was a soft white bow. My parents had given me this dress because my Leaving Certificate results had been so good. My mother did not stock any other dress like it. I saw Roisin and Iris looking up towards the balcony. Seeing me with this young man stunned them and they stood still gazing in amazement. They didn't know Richard. I could see the questions on each face. Who is he, where did you find him, he's gorgeous? I looked away when Jerry Breen approached me. He seemed dejected and I wasn't a bit sorry for him.

Richard became my constant companion. We talked about our days in Lough Louchre and Monabeag. He had attended a Church of Ireland Secondary School and in a few weeks he would be going to an Agricultural College. I wanted to change from nursing. I would go to the same college as he.

'Sorry, Ellie,' he said. 'They don't take girls.' I was disappointed. 'But,' he smiled, 'we can write to each other and we'll meet at weekends if we're home at the same time. I might be able to drive to Galway sometimes to see you, Ellie.'

I would just have to let him know whenever I had time off. I lived for Richard for the feel of his arms around me, for the softness of his kisses, for the security of being his girl exclusively. Our life was an adventure. We were the same yet filled with differences. We could relate to each other. When we were together we were not confused or frightened. We both loved the land. Sometimes before a dance, we would drive through the countryside, to think, to remember, to hope and to love. Richard had a dream. He wanted to go to New Zealand where he would become a sheep farmer. We could get married and go there together. His father mightn't like the idea but Richard knew a lad who had gone over there and by all accounts it was a wonderful country. We might not stay there for a long time. We could learn all about the farming methods in New Zealand and come back eventually to take over his father's farm.

'It's an exciting idea,' I agreed. 'I could work out there as a nurse. I think I would like that. I'd want to work with the sheep too. I wouldn't like to stay there for too long, Richard,' I added. 'My father lived in America. He told me that it was great for a while until he got lonely for home. I think I would get lonely too.'

Tom was not very happy about my friendship with Richard. I told him about our plans. He couldn't believe it.

'Are you going crazy or something? He's the wrong colour,' he said. 'He will not want you later on, Ellie. They always marry one of their own.'

'You're just jealous,' I was annoyed with Tom.

'You shouldn't talk,' I told him. 'You're the very one who's running around with your mother.'

'Ellie, don't. Mary and me, we are not fooling each other. She knows that I am going to university. I expect I'll meet loads of girls there. She is a good friend and I like her more than any other girl I know around here. We are not going to get married Ellie and we're not planning to raise sheep or kangaroo or whatever it is in New Zealand either. And where will you get the money to go there? He would have to work for a sheep farmer he wouldn't own his own place for years and years.'

'We can get an assisted passage,' I answered knowingly. 'It will only cost us ten pounds each.'

'I know all about assisted passages,' Tom surprised me. 'You will have to give an undertaking to stay in New Zealand for a certain number of years. It won't be all plain sailing there either. You'll have to live where you're told to live and you'll be an outsider. They'll probably watch you all the time. What will you do, Ellie if Richard decides he doesn't love you anymore? You'll end up out there all alone and...'

'Why are you going on like this, Tom? I thought you'd be happy about me and Richard. You always liked him when we lived in the country. Why are you so envious of our plans?'

Tom said that Richard Meyer had a girlfriend already.

'Everybody knows it,' he told me. 'She is in Dublin. Her name is Ester Dillon. Why do you think he hasn't been around here at the dances before?'

Tom tried to explain how the Church of Ireland held special socials in Dublin where the young people meet.

'That's why you haven't seen him around here in the catholic parish halls, Ellie. It's all planned, they're very well organised. Richard Meyer will not become a catholic just to marry you, Ellie. If he does he won't get a penny from his father. Besides, I don't think mammy or daddy would want you to marry him, Ellie. You wouldn't fit in no matter what you think, they're different.'

'You're right!' I yelled. 'They are different, they're honest and upright and they don't have mean, nasty minds like you have, Tom.' I burst into tears. 'Where is this Ester girl?' I cried. 'Where is she? If there is such a girl, Richard would have had her with him at the dances, he wouldn't be pretending that I'm his girlfriend, would he?'

'I did ask his friend Keith the same question.' Tom looked so sorry for me now. 'She's in England on a holiday. Her mother is English and they go over there to see her family. They go every summer I'm sorry, Ellie. It's a rotten thing for him to do to you. He'll answer to me some day,' he added.

My mother was collecting the post in the hall.

'Everything all right?' She wanted to know.

'Fine,' I spoke as the tears flowed.

'Tom, what's happened to Ellie?' She was looking at him knowing that he had something to do with my distress.

'It's Richard Meyer, I was talking to Ellie about him. She won't believe me when I try to tell her that he is spoken for. I know he is because Keith Summers told me all about the girl in Dublin.'

Keith Summers was Church of Ireland too but he didn't practise his religion. His sister had married a catholic boy. I remembered how people were scandalised at the time. Everyone wondered if she would let him bring up the children as catholic. He had to sign a form in front of the bishop before the wedding promising this. I heard my mother and Mrs. Kenny talking about it.

'But they're not that different,' I sobbed. My mother was very friendly with the Reverend O'Hara. I reminded her of this and of our visits to the rectory when we were children.

'That was exceptional,' my mother said. I really didn't understand her sometimes.

Mammy told me that there was no use fretting about any boy.

'You are too young, Ellie to be thinking of marrying anyone yet. There are lots of boys out there for you to meet. Wait until you get to Galway, think about all the young doctors you will be meeting and working with. Maybe you will marry a doctor, Ellie.' She was the one who was getting carried away now.

A parcel arrived from Aunty Pat. She sent presents to us because we'd got our leaving certificates. There was something for Colin too because he was starting secondary school. I loved the make up set. The box was yellow with a see through lid. Inside on a bed of white velvet lay a jar of pancake makeup, lipstick, perfume, eye shadow and even a little comb and a mirror. I got dressed for what would be the last dance of that summertime. Richard said he would collect me but he didn't come. I had to go with Tom. 'He'll probably be there later, don't worry, Ellie,' Tom was trying to be helpful. I was very doubtful. After all that had been said, I knew that I couldn't relax anymore if I was with Richard. I would have to ask him if what Tom said was true. Did he have a girl named Ester and would he never marry a catholic? But I knew I'd never ask him because I was afraid of what the answer might be.

Richard didn't come that night. All Tom's pals asked me to dance. I was on the floor constantly. The pancake make up which I had used felt sticky. My face was getting very hot. Jerry Breen and I were quick stepping.

'Hey Ellie,' he said, stopping and standing back, 'your face is melting.' Moving his finger across my cheek and drawing it away, we both saw it covered with a creamy caramel coloured liquid.

'It's dripping down your nose, Ellie and there's a bubble on your chin. Here take my hankie.'

I ran to the ladies room. There was only cold water in the tap. Furiously I dipped Jerry's hankie in water and tried to wipe the liquid off my face. My skin had become red and blotchy, my eyes were getting puffy my fringe was stuck to my forehead. There were brown specks on the Peter Pan collar of my white blouse. I was a mess. I had to get fresh air. Jerry was outside the door of the ladies.

'I've got the car,' he said, 'come with me, Ellie. I've told Tom we're leaving now.'

'I feel sick Jerry.' He stopped the car along the roadside and held my head while I vomited.

'God I think you need a doctor, Ellie. Was that some sort of poison you had on your face?'

'No, it was a present from Aunty Pat,' I told him.

'I feel awful, Jerry.' I blushed. 'I was not very nice to you was I?' It was a few days after the dance and we were sitting in the cosy room talking.

'Look Ellie,' he laughed. 'I feel awful too I totally forgot about paying for you that night. We're all so used to you being with us. I completely forgot I was so anxious to get in there and to dance with you. I can't explain how it happened, really. I felt terrible, I know people noticed. You weren't the only one to call me mean. I've been miserable for weeks since and when I saw you with that Monabeag fellow, God, it nearly killed me.'

'You have been the best friend ever, Jerry.' I spoke lovingly now, 'You didn't let me down the way I let you down. You probably saved my life the other night too Doctor Bailey said it was an allergic reaction to the make up.'

'I know all about allergic reactions,' said Jerry looking very serious. 'Can you imagine what happened to me when I blackened my arse?'

Chapter Seven
Student Nurse

'What do you think, Katie?'

I was standing in front of the full length mirror in the room which we shared.

'It's a bit of all right, Ellie,' she answered as she fixed my apron at the back. I was wearing my student nurse uniform for the first time. The white collar on the knee length navy blue dress sat perfectly. I looked neat and professional. A new watch, a special one for nursing was pinned to the bib of my snowy white apron. In a special side pocket, my stainless steel, surgical scissors awaited its first assignment.

'You look perfect, Katie, I wish I could get this head dress to fit properly.'

'I'll do it for you,' Katie offered. She removed my starched white veil.

'Anyone would think you had a bird's nest in here,' she giggled.

My ponytail was long and thick. I'd tried to fix it into a bun but Katie was right, it did look rather like a colossal bird's nest. Strands and wisps of hair were sticking out over my ears and forehead. I didn't want to have my hair cut or thinned even though my mother thought I'd have difficulty trying to keep it tidy.

'Sister Tutor is very particular from what I've heard. She inspects the students each morning and afternoon for tidiness, so be warned, Ellie.'

At that time dancing had very quickly turned from the waltz and quickstep to jiving to rock and roll and I loved the way my ponytail swung back and forth as I danced. It added momentum to every movement on the dance floor. It gave the right look.

'It's a dangerous projectile,' said Tom. He was showing off again using new words and mentioning university at every opportunity. But I was glad to see him so happy. He had worked very hard. To know that he was not finding the lectures too difficult was a relief. He still sang Moore's melodies with variations. His natural aptitude for engineering stood to him according to his tutor. Tom would always get plenty of help. He was that kind of fellow. He looked so beguiling when he wanted to. His facial expression could be filled with pleading. 'I'm a good lad, willing and appreciative, please help me.' And help fell into his lap. And I don't mean in the shapely form of Mary Mahon. They had gone their separate ways. Tom, like me, had left home to plough a different furrow.

Our first six weeks in the nursing school were spent in the classroom and I loved every minute of it. Anatomy and physiology were taught by the senior tutor, Sister Alphonse. I delighted in drawing diagrams with labels and explanations. Every procedure had to be known exactly. Keeping bed sores at bay was so important. Any nurse whose patient developed bedsores would be disgraced. And it would be the fault of the student. We would begin ward duties doing simple procedures. I was quite happy to disinfect beds when a patient was discharged. Having a bedside locker spotless and the flower vases looking fresh, the water glass and carafe for the patient gleaming, preoccupied us. Later, we were shown by the clinical tutor who was a nun, the correct method to use when turning a patient, how to administer an enema, how to collect and measure urine samples, how to make a patient comfortable when using a bed pan. The patient's privacy is paramount, we were warned. Tom wanted to know all about my training. 'I was washing doors this morning,' I told him, 'we have to see that the jambs are free from dust and we wash the bed frames too.'

'Hey, are you sure you're not unpaid cleaners?' He asked.

I reassured him that this was a sort of initiation and that very soon I would be giving injections. Tom was very proud of me and he suggested that his new friends should speak to his sister if they were ever sick.

'They needn't wait until they're sick,' I laughed.

The hospital was called Saint Mary of the Wayside and it was administered and staffed by a religious order. There were lay nurses too, many of them had been students in the school. It was a university hospital and we girls were on the look out constantly for young doctors. It was very important to get assigned to a ward where one might come upon such a specimen. My mother came to Galway to visit a neighbour who was a patient. Later, she met Sister Tutor who told her that I was their star student. I was, 'a natural,' she said. I had the right temperament for nursing. I could go places. Mammy was thrilled.

'I can't believe it Ellie, you took so long to decide what you wanted to do, you were so unsure of yourself. I'm delighted and daddy will be too. Aren't the nuns exceptional?' She continued. 'At Benediction, which I went to with Mrs. Byrne, I saw them in the chapel wearing those cream veils and I must say I was carried away. It was like being in heaven. The sun shining through those amber windows seemed to make a halo over each sister. They are so happy too, there's such a lovely atmosphere here. It's a wonderful hospital,' she enthused.

When we had a day off, Katie and I cycled to the seaside or into the city where we drank lemonade and watched the talent passing by.

'I think Doctor Flood has his eye on you, Ellie. He's a lovely fellow.

Not the best looking mind you, and a bit mature but God, he's nice.'

'He must have broken his nose once upon a time,' I laughed. 'He's all right I suppose but I don't think he's bothered about me. Did you not notice how Mary McCarthy follows him around? When you see him lo and behold you see her.'

'Come on now, girl, I've seen the signs.' Katie was laughing.

We cycled out of the city along a country road one afternoon. It was quiet. There was some traffic but not enough to make our trip unpleasant. I watched the mighty Atlantic crashing against the shore in the distance. Over our heads the seagulls screeched and the wind blew sea spray all the way up through the dunes. Lough Louchre was in my mind, the fields there and the woods. What was happening now to all the places I had loved? It seemed such a long time ago since I had sat in the kitchen with Mike and Mai. They would be amazed to know that I was training to become a nurse. Some day, I dreamed, when I have a car of my own, I will drive to Monabeag and surprise them. Stopping for a rest in a small village we leaned our bikes against a low stone wall. Sitting there in silence I thought about Doctor Aidan Flood. I did like him but for reasons I daren't tell anybody.

After three months in the classroom I was ready for my assignment of two months nursing duty on a ward. Male medical was my first assignment. A stint on the female medical followed. I realised, to my horror, that I didn't like ward duties at all. And what I had to do was nothing compared with Katie's work in the surgical wing. What would I do when I had to go over there? When this happened, I realised that I couldn't bear to see people in pain. I hated looking at huge incisions and at all those stitches which would have to be removed. How awful that a young girl to have a tube put down her throat. She cried and lashed out trying to make us go away. I wanted to cry too. A woman with a swollen stomach had to have a huge needle inserted right into her abdomen in order to remove fluid. It was all so terrible. I felt sick myself when I had to hold an old gentleman while he vomited a vile green substance. It was even worse I thought when I was called upon to hold a bottle while an embarrassed post operative man tried to urinate. The urine had to be measured and a chart kept of intake and output. What a carry on? I was in a panic. Settling a lady on a bed pan wasn't too bad. Women seemed to be managers of their toilet affairs better than the men. Sometimes, standing in the male ward and hearing through the drawn bedside curtain all kinds of farting and belching, I'd feel like shouting but what to shout I didn't know. Once a patient in another bed asked me if there was a volcano erupting beside him or was that the sound of an earthquake? I wished it was, I wished the ground would open and swallow me and all the sick people in the country. Wouldn't this be better for everyone? I became ashamed of my terrible thoughts.

'A penny for them,' Katie was looking at me. 'Let's go, we don't want to be late for supper.'

I agreed. We tried to talk as we cycled along. We were against the wind and very soon our words were lost in the air. It's surprising how the weather changes so suddenly in the west of Ireland. It was like my life and the uncertainties facing me. Aidan Flood had noticed my phobia. He had taken blood from a patient handing me each vial as he did so. Suddenly I felt myself getting hot and dizzy, I knew I must look very pale. My hands began to shake. The doctor turned to pass another vial.

'Nurse,' he asked, 'are you all right?'

'No doctor, I'm feeling a little faint I don't know why.'

Taking the blood samples from me he told me to walk slowly to the Dressings Room. 'I'll be over in a few minutes,' he added. And he was. Very gently he asked me some questions about my health and my feelings about nursing.

'I wanted to be a nurse,' I explained, 'and I still do. It's just that I'm finding it more difficult than I expected. I'm quite sure things will improve. It's all so different on the wards I mean. I don't like to see people suffering. I don't like broken things,' I said. 'I couldn't bear it when any of our animals were sick. We lived on a farm,' I told him. 'I looked after sick birds and rabbits and field mice and even a baby badger. Now I want to run away from sick people. I can't understand why.' I was trying not to cry.

Aidan Flood told me that when he went to medical school he didn't like it at the beginning. He thought he had made a terrible mistake. But it was the reverse for him. He actually enjoyed his calling more when he started doing the practical training. I should give myself time.

'Would you speak to Sister Alphonse, she's a good sort?' He suggested.

'Oh no, I can't.' I told him what Sister Alphonse had said to my mother. 'If I talk to anyone, it will be to daddy. I'll just see how I get on for the next while.'

'And I'll help you all I can,' Doctor Aidan Flood promised. 'You are a fine girl Ellie. Don't be too hard on yourself. I promise I won't mention this to anyone, it was all nothing really.'

After supper that evening Sister Alphonse sent for me. Oh no. He couldn't have, he promised not to say anything. I was embarrassed and angry.

'Nurse,' Sister Alphonse smiled, 'there is a visitor to see you. I knew you had a free day but I did tell him that I was quite sure you'd be back for supper. I know my girls, I told him that they all eat well.' She laughed. 'Anyway, Father had supper in the convent and he's in the garden now waiting to see you, so run along dear.'

'Father,' I gasped, 'Father who?'

'Father Hayes, Father Cyril Hayes, nurse. How remiss of me thinking you would know immediately. He was in South America, such an interesting and humble man. Do run along dear, don't keep Father waiting.'

I couldn't believe it, the nerve of him. I wondered if I should phone Tom. If I said Father Knickers he would rescue me but Tom was probably on a sports field somewhere. I'd have to sort this out myself. I was raging. There he was. He didn't see me at first. He was gazing up at the nurse's residence hall. There was a garden bench and while his two hands rested on the back of it his right knee was on the seat.

'See anything interesting?' I was as sarcastic as possible.

'Oh Ellie, this is such a surprise. But where is your uniform? I expected to see you dressed as a nurse. You look beautiful though, just as I remember you.'

'Really,' I snapped. 'And what brings you here. Do you know someone who is a patient in the hospital or what?'

'You forget, Ellie, or perhaps you don't know that I am actually from Galway? I was born and bred in this ancient city. I know its every nook and cranny.'

Born, I thought but without breeding. Of course, I should remember because when Majella Hayes married Dermot Daly, my parents had to travel to Galway city for the ceremony. He told me that he'd had a beautiful supper in the convent parlour.

'Sister Tutor speaks so highly of you, Ellie, I believe you are a star student. You came first in the Preliminary Exams, congratulations. Now I have a little outing in mind to celebrate your success. I did want to take you out for a meal but I'll do that next time instead since we've both eaten already. Would you like a drive down to the beach, Ellie? I know a really secluded place where we will not be disturbed. We can relax first and then try out the water.' Beaming, he gazed lecherously at me. I was glaring at him. What was he talking about?

'And I brought something for you to wear. We'll have a lovely swim together. He went to the boot of the car. This is all you'll need.' He was holding up a pair of men's underpants, briefs, not boxers, I think they had some coloured pattern on them but I can't remember I was so stunned.

'How dare you,' I yelled. 'Who do you think you are? Get into your little puddle jumper and make yourself scarce. If you ever come near me again, I'll call the Guards. Don't you dare come near me ever again, I'm telling Tom and I'm telling my father about you. You're crazy!' I was screaming. A window opened in the Nurse's Residence, a staff nurse in a blue uniform looked out. He leaped into his car and sped away. I heard him shouting. 'I'll get you yet.'

~~~

March came in cold and wet. Sometimes sleet belted off the windows of the hospital. I often watched visitors battling against the wind with bouquets of flowers dead headed before they ever reached the ward. We were back in the nursing school again and I relaxed. Our focus was on the eye and the ear. I was fascinated by such wonderful mechanisms at work within the scull. Soon we would sit our first state exam but before that we had a week at home for Easter. It was 1960 and possibly the last Easter when I would be free. Katie told me that she was not looking forward to going home. Gradually I had learned that her mother had died when she was born. There were seven children in the family and her older sister took over the role of mother.

'She is not a nice person my sister but I do know what's wrong with her. She's had to miss out on so much. She didn't have time to enjoy herself because of us. She never loved me. I know it. I was the cause of my mother's death and of all the upset in the family which followed it. That's why I came up here to do nursing,' she added. 'I wanted to get as far away from home as I possibly could.'

'That's terrible, Katie,' I was really upset for my friend. 'You could come home with me. We'd have a great time and I know you like Tom.' I grinned at her.

'That would be gorgeous. It really would but I have to see my father. He is paying all the fees here and we don't have much money. You know what farming is like nowadays, Ellie.'

I told Katie that I did know all about farming but we were lucky because my mother had a shop in the town.

'Daddy doesn't do any tillage anymore and he doesn't have dairy cows to worry about. He only deals in beef cattle.' I explained. 'But I do know what you mean, Katie.'

Then I reminded her about the nurse's dance. We had it to look forward to.

'Think about it while you're at home. I could lend you one of my dresses if you like, I've got loads.' I thought the blue would suit her best. 'Or would you like red? Yes, maybe the red with your dark hair. Tell you what, I'll ask mammy to have it turned up a bit. There's a lady in the town, who does alterations for the shop.'

Katie was delighted. She would wear her black patent shoes and a black velvet band on her hair. I didn't know what I would wear I told her although I was hoping that mammy would have a surprise for me. She did. It was a present because I had done so well in the first hospital exam. But I needn't expect a gift every time I did well. Next year when I'd be getting some payment each month I would have to buy my own clothes.

'I might give you a little discount,' she laughed.

My mother was becoming quite annoying, I thought. At every opportunity she told people how successful her children were.

'My son, in university, is doing engineering,' she'd manage to say while wrapping a customer's purchase or, 'When my daughter, who is training to be a nurse, qualifies,' or 'have you read Colin's article in the *Shannon Valley Times*?' It was all quite painful.

Colin had indeed become a local phenomenon.

Already he was writing a column for the local paper. He was a humorist. People were queuing each Friday to get the paper as it arrived in the newsagents. Hugh Lyons, the town barber told daddy that he nearly cut off Paddy Glynn's ear. Paddy had insisted on reading aloud the article which Colin had written about local barbers while

Hugh tried to give him a short back and sides. It could have been a terrible accident. But not everyone was so pleased with Colin. The staff of the *The Shannon Valley Times* did not appreciate having a young lad receiving such accolades. A strike was threatened. Daddy went to see the editor, who told him not to worry. He had offered the staff a substantial rise. My mother was furious saying that she knew who was behind the idea of a strike.

'It's Paddy Hensey, who else? Well, the next time that overbearing wife of his comes into the shop I won't be giving her a discount. And knowing her, she's too haughty to ask for one. And if you only knew where she came from originally, talk about "putting a beggar on horseback."'

I had put my problems and anxieties about ward duty to the back of my mind. But when I went to see Aunty Irene, I had plans to talk to her about this.

Perhaps she'd had a similar experience. I might even tell her about Father Knickers too. The twins were thrilled to see me they smiled their toddler smiles and tried to say something like, 'Lelei.' I hugged them in delight and gave them each a little, woolly, white lamb, a cuddly toy all the way from Galway. Irene told me that her boys had become quite a handful. They were into everything and eating her out of house and home. I could see what she meant. She didn't have a minute and any chance to have a private conversation with her began to look more and more unlikely. Besides having the children to look after, neighbours were always dropping in to see Irene. Gracie was older now and although she helped as much as she could it took her a long time to do very little. When the boys were asleep that afternoon and Gracie had gone to town with Eugene, we sat down together to have a cup of tea.

'At last,' Irene sighed with relief. 'At last I've got a breather. Now, I want to know everything about the nursing school. I've been waiting for this chance to get all the details, Ellie. Are there any nice young doctors around? Come on, you can tell me, Ellie. Are you glad that you choose nursing? I wonder if it's changed since my day?'

I was so relieved but as I was about to open my heart to her a shadow crossed the door.

'God bless all here,' an old man saluted us as he came in, crossed in front of the fire and settled himself in an arm chair. Taking out his pipe, he began to smoke and he talked non-stop until it was time for me to leave for home. My wonderful opportunity was lost.

The dress which my mother gave me for the annual nurse's dance was a glamorous grey taffeta shot with a pinkish hue. I was so excited returning to Galway with such an event to look forward to. I had the red dress for Katie and Tom said that I must ask her to be his partner.

'She mightn't want to,' I said dismissively.

'Oh she will, I know she will, so stop trying to fool me,' he laughed. 'And Ellie, just get me six tickets because there's two other lads who want to come and they have a couple of nurses lined up as well.'

'Who are these nurses?' Tom said that he hadn't a clue but the more the merrier. I was so disappointed when Jerry Breen told me that he couldn't get off duty. He was training to be a Garda. He phoned me during Easter.

'The sergeant in charge of the depot is a holy terror,' he was saying this between gritted teeth I suspected. 'I can't get off, Ellie and I'm as mad as can be. I was looking forward to seeing you again. God, I could do with a good night out.'

Jerry was so disheartened. I didn't want to make things any worse for him. There would be other dances, I reassured him. Maybe we'd both be free during the summer. I tried to console him by suggesting that we could then go to the carnivals and the marquees together. He might even be assigned to Galway in the future.

'It's all right, Jerry, I know there's nothing you can do about it.' I reasoned. 'I'll go with Tom and Katie but I'll be thinking of you all the time.'

I didn't think of Jerry at all. Well, I did think of him at the beginning as I danced with Tom and with his friends. But it was Doctor Aidan Flood who stole my heart that night. At the first opportunity he asked me to dance and I didn't leave his side after that. I knew that I was the envy of many nurses. After all, I was just a student and a first year at that. He was so dashing, so tall and such a dancer. My head rested on his chest when we danced a slow waltz. I felt his arms safe and comforting around me. Suddenly, I was pushed slightly.

'Sorry,' I whispered to Aidan.

'It's not you,' he teased. Looking around I saw Mary McCarthy with her sickly smile. 'Cosy aren't we?' She smirked then looking back at us she danced away.

'Some bitter pill,' was Aidan's comment.

'She thinks she's somebody just because she's a theatre sister. I don't care for her at all,' I confided.

'Oh, there's not that much mystery to being a theatre sister, Ellie,' he laughed. 'Once you know the ropes, concentrate, and keep calm its plain sailing. Being a good ward sister is far more demanding, I think. After all, an anaesthetized patient can't talk back or make that many demands.'

We giggled, Aidan was holding me tightly and kissing me just as Mary McCarthy waltzed passed us again. She looked haughty and displeased. I smiled serenely. Dancers began leaving the floor because it was time for dinner. We looked at our tickets, mine said first sitting, Aidan's second.

'I'll get someone to change with me if you like,' I offered.

'No, no, Ellie. I have a better idea. Let's get out of here. Have you a wrap?' I fetched it and we left the dance hall as surreptitiously as possible. My feelings were in turmoil. I hated sneaking off without telling Tom or Katie where we were going. Doctor Aidan Flood had a Hillman car, which was very comfortable. 'A drive into the city would be lovely. Would you like that?' He asked.

'We could go to "The Great Western Hotel" for a proper meal Ellie. That food which I saw them dishing up at the dance is all right but I think you deserve something more special. After all, you look so lovely in that dress you're my very own princess.'

I was overcome, hardly able to speak. The lights of Galway shone in the distance. I was never so happy. The moon beamed over the waters of the Atlantic and across the bay. Bright stars, the brightest I had ever seen hung overhead. This was a dream coming true. In Eyre Square, Aidan rushed to open the car door for me. I would have to tell Tom about this. When we crowded into his Morris Minor, we were lucky to get out of it without falling into the road. My elbow was held ever so gently as Aidan guided me towards the dining room of the hotel. I really wanted to go to the Powder Room but I'd wait. This was all so new for me but it was not new for the doctor. I realised at once that he was well known in the hotel. The manager came to speak to him and Aidan introduced me very formally.

'Delighted, I'm sure,' the manager held my hand briefly. 'And what would you like to drink, madam? Complimentary,' he advised Aidan.

I was rightly stuck. It was hardly the place to ask for an orange juice or a cidona. What did my mother ask for when she went to a hotel? My mind went blank for a minute. Then I remembered, Leonard Forde and the Sunday afternoon gatherings at Mary Kate's.

'I think, a sherry,' I smiled. 'A nice cream sherry would do very well, thank you.' This was like something from the movies. We studied the menu.

'Darling, would you like an appetiser?' Darling unsettled me enough without having to think about an appetiser. Some of the dishes were in French – oh what did they do in the movies?

'Darling,' I replied, 'I really don't think I would like anything fishy, have you a suggestion?' I hoped he wouldn't suggest soup. I would definitely spill soup all over myself, I knew I would. But Aidan was looking so pleased with himself, so in control, very happy that I was with him. The order was given. This included a bottle of wine which was presented in a silver ice bucket. Asking Aidan to sample it, the waiter said that he hoped it would be to his liking, it was. If I'd been asked to taste it I would have died. I'd never had wine in my life except in Lourdes when we were on a school pilgrimage. I didn't know that I was about to drink wine at the time, I thought it was lemonade. What a shock – it was local French wine which tasted awful.

I had to excuse myself, I couldn't wait any longer. In the Powder Room, I touched up my lipstick and admired myself in the full length mirror. I was walking on air, my eyes were shining and I couldn't stop smiling. I imagined what was yet to come, his kisses his desire for me alone. Spinning around, I gloried in my appearance, I was truly irresistible. Aidan looked up admiringly as I returned to our table not taking his eyes off me for a minute. But we were interrupted a few times which annoyed me. I was annoyed because I began to realise how many sophisticated, mature women he knew. I did look almost like a little girl in their company. They commented about me as if I was some sort of treasure he'd dug up.

'What a pretty little thing, where did you find her, Aidan? Are you kidnapping from the training school, ha, ha?'

'This is Ellie Dardis. We were at the nurse's dance,' he told them. 'There was a big crowd and we escaped to have a proper meal. There's a chance of having a bit of peace and quiet here too, the music was horrendous, you know what these local bands can be like,' he grimaced.

'Oh but you do so like your food, Aidan,' one lady smiled. 'We know all about his taste, don't we girls?' She drooled.

'We're having coffee in the lounge later perhaps you'll join us there darling?' A lady with huge white teeth coaxed.

'Lovely idea,' Aidan smiled. 'Perhaps, I will see you then?'

Aidan was looking at me. I held his gaze. He cleared his throat.

'I wanted to get away from that noisy dance hall, Ellie,' he said. 'It's not my kind of place at all but I had to put in an appearance. It's true what my lady friend has been saying - I did want a decent meal. I'm so glad you agreed to come along. When we have finished here …' We were interrupted when the waiter arrived flourishing our very decorative baked Alaska. It was my favourite dessert and it was the in sweet of the day which I couldn't wait to devour.

'Mm,' I managed as I tasted a mouthful. 'Mm, this is gorgeous. You were saying, Aidan?'

'Oh yes, I was about to say that I will take you back to the dance and to your own pals when we are finished here. As you can see, I have several friends in the lounge and I'd like to return to have a chat with them. We've all been friends for many years.'

I was stunned. I felt as if he'd poured icy cold water on top of my head. But he didn't seem to notice my shock. He continued to speak.

'I'm going to Toronto soon, you know. I have a place in the hospital there. I will work under Mr. Archibald Clarke. He is the leading paediatrician in the world today. I don't expect you've heard of him, Ellie?'

I stared at him. I felt dizzy.

'Archibald Clarke I know him very well,' I laughed. 'Archibald Clark who sings like the lark.'

The wine had gone to my head I'd never had so much to drink in my life. I was quaffing it back like lemonade.

'Toronto,' I asked Aidan if he'd ever seen the movie *Rosemarie*,

'When I'm calling you oooooooooou oooooooou,' I sang.

I knew that I was behaving disgracefully but I couldn't help myself. I could see what I was doing, hear what I was saying as if I was watching and listening to myself from above. I was powerless, completely out of control, it was frightening. Aidan tried to calm me. Calling the waiter, he ordered coffee. He asked me if I was all right? Did I like nursing at last, would I continue with my training?

'I'm happy, it's great,' I giggled. 'Who cares anyway? People are sick, we make them better. Give them a good dinner, is what I say. "No dancing," the priest said that dancing is dangerous. Did you know that? But of course you did, you're a doctor and you like a good dinner better than - you ou ou, ou like me ee, ee ee,' I tried to yodel.

I started to cry. I remembered what Judith had told me. I continued talking.

'Cut them open and look at their insides. Everything all right in there and we stitch 'em up again. Is Mary McCarthy a good stitcher?' I asked. 'You know what? Judith McEvoy's granny went under the knife? She died of course. Oh yes, she died stone dead.'

Aidan poured the coffee from a silver pot. It looked hot and steaming. My father loved coffee. I wanted him now. I wanted my father to tell Aidan Flood to stop treating me like a child. I felt unusually mutinous as I eyed a third bottle of wine which had been delivered to our table. Aidan reached for it he was trying to keep me away from any more drink. I beat him to it.

'You need to be quicker on the draw, doctor or the Mounties will get you.' I warned as I grabbed the bottle. Filling my glass I drank it back. I knew I was in an alcoholic haze and I couldn't do a thing about it. It was a most awful feeling as everything around me seemed to be swaying. I could still hear my own voice as if it was hitting off the corniced ceiling. It sounded so loud. Other diners looked at us. Sniggering I held my wine glass aloft.

'Dwaling,' I stuttered, 'dwaling, you are a big dlis-al ploint-ment to me. Take me home, I'm such a pwetty little twing. You are a kidnapper, you know. I hope you enjoyed your big, big dinner. What about coffee, dwaling or shall we dwance?'

I vaguely recall what followed. The woman with the big teeth returned to tell Aidan that they were waiting for him.

'I'll be with you Daphne,' he said, 'just as soon as I can get this silly girl back to her residence.'

She had to help him otherwise I would have fallen. I think the manager hovered behind us as we made our exit. There were steps down from the hotel entrance and I do recall continuing to step down when there weren't any steps left. I kept lifting my foot and stepping out like a horse pawing the ground. When the night air rushed into my face I sang. *'I'll be with you. I'll be with you in apple blossom time.'* I was assisted firmly towards the car and all the while, I sang.

Katie told me that she and Tom were frantic when I disappeared. She knew Doctor Flood's car. They looked in the car park and it was gone. Tom was furious she told me because he didn't get a hot dinner. He was chasing around trying to find me instead.

'That's all men think about,' I snapped, 'Big Hot Dinners.'

Aidan Flood had driven me back to the Nurse's Residence where Katie and Tom were waiting in Tom's car. It was three o'clock in the morning and I was out of my mind. When I sobered up my heart was cold and dead. I'd ruined everything. I'd been stupid to think that he cared for me at all.

'Why did he take you away from your own crowd, Ellie?' Katie wanted to know. 'We were having a great time. I thought the band was super and Tom did too. He's too old for you, Ellie. He just wanted someone for a dinner date on the spur of the moment.'

'It wasn't a spur of the moment,' I answered crossly. 'We were dancing together all the time.'

'Look, I'm not saying that he's not a nice fellow, Ellie. He's just older and he obviously mixes with a different crowd. You'd soon get tired of it all and anyway, you say that he's going to Toronto.'

I felt embarrassed and ashamed. It had all begun so beautifully now I would be the laughing stock of the hospital. Mary McCarthy could rightly smirk but she didn't. Katie was right nobody seemed to know that anything had happened. Some of the trainee nurses told me how jealous they were, 'he's such a dream,' Elsie Galbraith sighed.

'He's going away,' I told them. 'He's going to Canada.'

They couldn't believe that I was taking it so well. But I wasn't taking it well at all. I was very confused, life was getting far too complicated. I felt very sad and disappointed with myself. Where did I really belong? When Katie told me that the nuns were going to show us a film about their Order and its work on the missions and around the world I wasn't interested. She was going to see it she said, why wouldn't I come? There would be tea and sandwiches afterwards.

'No drink?' I queried. 'If there's no drink I can't possibly go.'

We laughed for the first time since the dance. I was only joking and I did go with her.

The film didn't interest me at all. It opened telling a little about the history of the Order and about its missions throughout the world while liturgical music played softly in the background. But when it recounted the adventures of a young girl who entered the convent and explained everything about her training to become a missionary, I was mesmerised. Seeing myself in that role, I too travelled in my own mind to far away places doing God's work. It was a spellbinding account of such a wonderful existence. This girl shone with an inner peace. Her contentment reached out to me from beyond the screen. I read a message within the story as if it had come to me straight from God himself. Had Ellie Dardis discovered where she truly belonged?

Chapter Eight
Longing

I had crossed a threshold and I had finally told my parents what I wanted to do. It was the first Sunday in June, 1961. We sat together on a wooden bench overlooking Silver Strand. In the bay a couple of fishing vessels lay at anchor. Farther out a great ship appeared over the horizon. I was watching Tom and Colin who were walking along the beach. Over their heads seagulls wheeled and screamed.

'Really Ellie, I just don't understand you at all,' my mother sounded exasperated. 'You decide to become a nurse, you're happy and you're getting top marks. Why this sudden rush to become a nun? You really are the giddy limit. Do you think about anyone's feelings except your own? We have spent a lot of money on you, Ellie and you now expect us to fork out again for all the things you will need going into the convent. I know that when Molly Daly entered her mother told me that she might as well have had a trousseau. Say something, Owen,' she ordered. 'What do you think?'

My father was silent for a few moments.

'I'm at a loss, Eleanor. Ellie, where did this sudden notion come from? You have never been one for the nuns as far as I know. It all seems to have come out of the blue. Tell us, why do you really want to go into the convent?'

I could hardly tell them because I couldn't explain it to myself. Something had crept into my mind so slowly, like a rhythm which wouldn't leave. Since I'd viewed the film about the life of a nun I had begun to think seriously about my own life. I had to admit that I didn't like nursing. I had been let down by Richard Meyer, I had been demeaned by Aidan Flood and pursued by a priest with sex on his mind. Did I love Jerry Breen? I wasn't sure because I hadn't seen him for ages. Maybe he had another girl now and if he had I didn't really care. I didn't really know why I wanted to devote my life to the service of God. I just knew that I had to do it that was all.

'Ellie,' it was my father speaking again. 'Give your mother and me some idea about this vocation, how has it come about? Who has been influencing you? Have you told Tom? Does your friend Katie know your plans?'

Katie knew all right, she was joining the convent too. I knew what my parents would say. I was following Katie's example, and they did.

'No, I'm not. I want to do this. I would want to do it myself even if Katie wasn't,' I told them. 'These nuns are modern, they are different. Do you know that their Mother Foundress is still living? They have convents all over the world. I may travel to places I've never heard of before. They drive cars too and the nuns are trained in all sorts of professions.' I continued enthusiastically. 'When I saw their film last week I was convinced that I must become a nun.'

'A year ago, Ellie,' my mother spoke fiercely, 'you told us that being a nurse was all you ever wanted to be. What is wrong with you that you now want to change? I suppose by next week you'll have changed your mind again. It's very difficult to have patience with you. I want to speak to Reverend Mother Elizabeth about this. What do you think, Owen?'

My father agreed. I wasn't there when they met because we were on night duty. Besides, I didn't want to hear what my parents had to say to her. My mother would speak her mind, she would make conditions. Reverend Mother had agreed to one of them – when I was professed, I would come back to Galway to complete my training. Then my parents could visit me frequently. Daddy told her that he would object very strongly if there was ever any talk of me being sent off to one of those African places. I imagined Reverend Mother Elizabeth smiling and telling him not to worry. I wasn't happy about the idea of continuing my nursing training but I said nothing. There were so many other possibilities. In the film the nuns were shown attending college to become librarians, horticulturists, dieticians and even stained glass artists. I was sure that there was something other than nursing which I could study in Galway.

Entering the convent would be a strange transition for me, I knew. But many girls entered convents in the 1950s and 1960s. It was a huge honour for a family to have provided a priest or nun for the Church. My family were not overly religious although we did have relatives in religious life. Their serene photographs were hung strategically throughout the house. They were a status symbol whose names were dropped in conversation whenever my mother wanted to impress. But this was different altogether. I was her daughter, her only girl and I was still "daddy's little chicken."

Tom was upset. He said that he thought I was crazy.

'Supposing you don't like it what will you do then? You know what it's like for a girl who leaves the convent, she almost has to disappear. Look at Hugh O'Meara, he was almost ordained a priest when he left. His mother hasn't gone outside the door since, she's so ashamed.'

My parents were listening.

'Well, you must promise us that if you want to come home again, you will tell us. Let's say that you're just giving it a try.' My father advised.

'I still can't understand you,' my mother sighed. 'I wish you'd just make up your mind and stick with it. You're never happy with anything, Ellie.' She scolded. 'When I think of all I've done for you and now you won't even be around when I'm old and in need of you. I looked after my mother but you have no thought for your mother at all.' Crying, she ran from the room.

'Don't mind her,' daddy advised. 'Your mother is upset but secretly we know she'll get over it. Just tell her that she'll have a whole convent of nuns to look after her and she'll be all right. And Ellie, if you ever want to leave the convent, we won't be ashamed. We will never be embarrassed. I think that people who are embarrassed about these things are very foolish. Now, off you go and have a word with herself.'

<hr />

When I had watched the film about the Sisters of St. Mary of the Wayside with Katie and other girls from our nursing year, I admired, subconsciously, a group of women each of whom was leading an extraordinary life. To belong with them became so important to me. I believe that at that period in my life, I longed for harmony, I longed to be loved, to be respected and to dedicate myself to something beyond the ordinary. I knew, within the core of my being that such a life would be more rewarding than I could possibly understand. Within the convent, I would find peace and tranquillity. I would wear garments which would set me apart. I knew that I could be happy there, just like the sisters I worked alongside in the hospital. Within the convent, I would truly understand what having a vocation meant. I was prepared to trust those who had seen the possibility of a vocation within me before I became aware of it myself. When I was on night duty with Sister Callist she smiled so much that I had to ask her why?

'Because I'm very happy,' she replied. 'I'm serving the Lord, that's why, Ellie.'

'Oh,' I sighed, 'How I wish that I could be happy like you.'

A signal seems to have reverberated around the convent after this. I became the centre of attention. Convent literature was left where I would find it. Katie began to talk to me about her own vocation. She had seen the film once before when two nuns had come to her secondary school to speak about vocations to the religious life.

'It was so wonderful, I wanted to enter immediately,' she explained.

But her sister Mairead had objected. She had not looked after Katie for seventeen years for her to up and enter the convent.

'Daddy,' Mairead had pleaded. 'You tell Katie that she will have to get out and work at something first. She will have to bring some money back into this house, won't she?'

But Katie's father was a God fearing man. He would not he said, 'fly in the face of the Lord.' He told Katie to begin with the nursing school and if after a time she still wanted to become a nun, he'd allow it. Before we went to sleep each morning after our nights on duty, we talked and talked about our future. We expected to be together always.

'Tom, what about Tom, will you miss him Katie?'

'Oh yes, I will but that's the sacrifice I have to make. Tom will always find someone to love him. I'm sure of that.'

'I think, Katie, that our families will be making more sacrifices than us.' I muttered, because I knew how much Tom thought about Katie. My mother's outbursts were upsetting too but I took my father's advice and waited for her to get over her grievances.

When I went to Capall Ban to tell Aunty Irene about my decision, she threw her arms around me and cried. She didn't want me to go away at all and certainly not into a convent. She had worked in hospitals, she said and the nuns in charge were not always very nice. They were very strict and so particular and they expected the nurses to do all sorts of extra duties. They were powerful women. Nobody could stand up to them – not even the doctors.

'Well, the Sisters of St. Mary of the Wayside are not like that.' I told her soothingly. 'They are so modern, they drive cars. When I come back to Galway, I will be able to drive out here to see you and Uncle Eugene and the twins.'

But Irene was not convinced.

'Why don't you join an Irish Order? At least you would be here in your own country and we would be able to visit you more easily. I'm afraid you'll find the English composure very different. I'll worry about you, Ellie.'

'Well, there's no need to worry. Anyway, daddy and mammy said that I must come home if I'm not happy. They won't be ashamed if I change my mind. It's just a trial, you see, to find out if it's right for me. There's girls from many countries in the Order,' I added, 'that's what makes it so exciting.'

'The convent – exciting? I hardly think so, Ellie,' she laughed.

Aunty Pat arrived at the hospital in Galway in a great flurry of indignation following a phone call from my mother.

'I've come to make you see sense. Where's that Reverend Mother? I know all about nuns, I've had dealings with them all my life. You have been influenced, Ellie, you've absolutely no idea what you're letting yourself in for. Just think about what you are giving up. What about your boy friend? What about marriage and a family of your own? This will never happen for you now. You're too young to be making such a drastic decision. And your mother, she's really upset even though she's not letting on. Oh, Ellie, do think again and don't let these religious women turn your head.'

Somebody must have been watching us because Aunty Pat and I were invited to have afternoon tea in the convent parlour. Reverend Mother Elizabeth listened to Aunty Pat's concerns.

'I do know what you mean, dear,' she said, 'but when the Lord calls we must answer.'

'Well, I've known Ellie since she was a baby, Mother. She is very sensitive and I am really worried about her. She will be crushed in the convent, made to become someone she is not. Ellie is not a person to stand up for herself. I know nuns very well and I know they have a great desire to increase vocations at any cost. I wouldn't let a daughter of mine become a nun for anything in the world.'

Aunty Pat was tarring all nuns with the same brush and I was mortified. But Reverend Mother remained composed.

'It's a great blessing for Ellie to have an Aunt like you to voice such concerns. But we have great hopes for Ellie, and she is not as easily influenced as you might think. If she were, we wouldn't be advising her to join our congregation would we?'

Aunty Pat was not convinced but she did agree that having a Foundress still living was exceptional. Perhaps, these nuns were more reasonable, more in tune with the real world. She would agree to wait, as I had to, for the Mother General to tell me if she thought I truly had a vocation.

Mother Angelus, the woman who had instituted the order in the mid 1930s arrived in Galway. Nuns and nurses who were off duty lined up on the driveway to welcome her. There had been so much cleaning and polishing beforehand. I had never seen anything like it. Huge floral arrangements were everywhere. The nuns were alert, there was not a stray leaf on the drive not a smudge on a window pane and even the convent dog was moved from his place in the sun. Meeting Mother Angelus was a highlight for everyone but she was not the tall elegant lady I'd expected to see. In the film she looked taller but she was in reality small and dumpy. Unlike my saintly looking imaginings, she wore horn rimmed glasses and held her head to one side as she walked.

'Ellie Dardis,' Reverend Mother Elizabeth introduced me. 'She may be joining us,' she whispered.

'I will see you later, dear.' Mother Foundress smiled. And her smile was beatific; she had presence. I thought she could read my very soul. Her bright dark eyes lit up when she spoke. I couldn't help smiling broadly.

Later, I did have a special audience with Mother Angelus. Those who passed the door where I had to wait to be called inside smiled their encouragement. One sister murmured, 'we are all praying for you, Ellie.'

Taking my hand in hers and looking at me very closely, Mother told me that I did indeed have a genuine vocation. Then she asked me a few questions about my schooling and my family.

'I look forward to meeting your dear parents and your brothers sometime in the future – but this visit is just for us,' she smiled. 'Your vocation is very precious, it is the most precious thing in the world and you must not let it slip away. You must not let anyone deflect you from serving the Lord. Some people, well meaning people, of course, dear, will advise you against becoming a religious sister. Be kind to them, Ellie. They don't understand what the Lord has in mind for you. To become a member of our religious family is your calling. Your destiny is to work in whatever part of the world He ordains. Do you understand? Are you willing to give your all?'

'I am, Mother,' I replied with great confidence. How could I have any doubts?

Colin cornered me one evening when I was at home getting packed for my departure.

'Don't forget,' he said seriously, 'I will look after Pixie and Dot until you come back. I know you will come back because all that convent stuff is a big mistake. You'll only need about a month or less to find this out.'

'Thanks,' I stuttered. I hadn't thought about my cats at all. I would miss them terribly.

'The nuns have a farm,' I told him there's probably a cat or two there but thanks anyway.

When Jerry Breen telephoned, I was truly shaken. It was the morning when I was to leave home forever. Tom had told Jerry everything and they had worked out a plan to stop me. Jerry told me that he wanted to marry me, not straight away but he'd never imagine marrying any other girl. To him I was the most precious person in the world, did I not realise this? He couldn't understand how I could come up with such a daft idea, the convent was the last place I should be, he said. Would I not wait a while until he could get to Eskeriada to have a talk? Had something happened? What was I running away from?

'I'm not running away, Jerry. I have to follow my vocation. If I'm wrong I will come home. I've promised daddy and mammy. Jerry, you have been my best pal. Don't wait for me,' I sighed. 'You will meet somebody else and when you do, make a good life for yourself, you deserve this.'

'I'll wait.' He insisted. 'Ellie, I'll wait.'

༄༅

Five of us were leaving from Galway to take the night boat to Holyhead. Sister Pauline was to accompany us. Parents and relatives came to the convent to say, 'goodbye.' We had changed into our postulant's dress.

'We'll see you as soon as we can,' my mother whispered. 'Write and let us know everything.'

Trying to smile my father told me to be good. He reminded me that I had a home if things did not work out.

'Remember, I didn't like America all that much and I came home. You do the same, Ellie, if you're not happy.'

'Tom, I hope all goes well for you next year,' I heard Katie saying. 'And don't worry about Ellie and me. We'll look after each other.'

Looking at my brothers, I didn't know what to say to them. The enormity of what I was doing suddenly struck me. I had hardly ever been away from Tom except for that year with granny. I had seen Colin grow up and I had been amazed by his brilliance. Now he spoke up for both of them.

'If you're in trouble, Ellie, tell us and we'll come and get you.' Tom nodded.

'You're the first I'll call on,' I replied earnestly.

Close to tears I got into the car. Slowly we were driven away. I looked back as we left the Galway convent behind. They were half way down the drive, all my family and they were still waving.

After a night of travelling we were in the order's house in central London. Sitting with the other postulants around the Formica topped table I wondered about home. Were they still asleep or were they awake, thinking about me, worrying about me?

I pictured my mother in the big bedroom with its dark furniture. Did she wake up crying? Had she buried her head beneath the deep plumb coloured eiderdown trying to pretend that I hadn't left at all? My father was probably silent. Was he remembering that day I wondered, that day about which my mother knew nothing – when he had cycled all the way from Eskeriada to Galway? He hadn't taken the car because if he had, my mother would want to know where he was going and she would want to be with him. But he didn't need her, he needed to come alone. I pictured him cycling along the country roads, by the river and over the new bridge, past blackberry hedges dripping still with the previous night's rain. He would have greeted the farmers as they herded anxious cows home for the morning milking. He cycled wearing his good overcoat and his felt hat.

I recalled that morning when I had come off night duty. I could feel the tiredness again, that deep sleep which attached itself to me as soon as I got into bed. I could almost feel the fullness of the breakfast, a taste of gritty toast and tangy marmalade in my mouth. I imagined again the comforting hot bottle at my feet and the weight of my faded pink dressing gown on my legs. I remembered my surprise – waking up suddenly to see my father standing at the foot of my bed.

'There's nothing wrong, Ellie,' he whispered. 'I've just come to see you.'

We sat in the kitchen sipping tea. His hat was on the chair beside him, his overcoat across the back of mine. I sensed the morning chill on it, I noticed the mud spatters around the hem – mammy would ask questions.

'Don't go, Ellie,' he urged. 'Look, I think I'm right when I say that you don't like nursing. I wouldn't like it myself.' We laughed.

He tried to persuade me that he would find something else for me to do. I was a bright girl, I could go anywhere. He could write to Aunty Anna in New York. He knew we would get on very well even though mammy thought Anna was in the clouds. I could go to college over there. I would be able to come home for holidays it would be a great new life. America had changed since his time over there. If I remembered the photographs which the girls had of my cousins, it was clear that they were all doing well because they had so many opportunities. Wouldn't it be great to meet the American branch of the Dardis family?

But I had let him go, let him cycle all those miles home again. I had told my father that I was sure about what I was doing. But how confident had I been really? Why had I suddenly run after him, through the back door of the bungalow where we slept when we were on nights? Why had I run to the small iron gateway which fronted the street, calling for him to come back, wanting him to help me to sort out my confused thoughts? But he was already out of reach and he didn't hear me. He didn't look back. I went inside consoling myself – I did have a vocation. After all, Mother Angelus had said so.

It had been a horrible journey from Dunlaoire to Holyhead. We did not have cabins which surprised me. Up on deck it was very chilly. I had been sick and leaning over the railings I had spewed yellow green bile into a sea which was as dark and frothy as a barrel of Guinness. Sister Pauline was very annoyed. I had been indiscreet. I should not be sick, I should exercise control and refrain from vomiting in such a public place. This was not the first time I had travelled by boat. When I had gone to Lourdes on the school pilgrimage I was seasick and the nuns were concerned. Sister Joseph Mary had held my head. She had taken me to a bunk where she had given me brandy to sip while telling me not to let anyone know about it. But last night I had been scolded instead. I had been warned that I must keep my clothes clean, I was told to stay on deck so that the sour smell would not linger.

Now the shunting, hissing and groaning of the train from Holyhead to London still jolted my bones. Sitting at the table I felt as if my body was rolling with an unrelenting motion, inhaling the smoke and the smuts, my eyes blinking against the glaring lights from factories which crouched near the railway stations of industrialised British towns. A white enamel basin was placed on the breakfast table for us to wash up our breakfast crockery. The sparsely clotted soap suds made me feel nauseous again. I had often helped my mother to wash up at the kitchen table in Lough Louchre. I was a child then kneeling on a chair, delightedly flicking a wooden spoon up and down beating more and more suds into the warm water. I remembered my mother taking a huge sud onto her index finger and setting it deftly on the tip of my nose. I tried to blow it away or to reach towards it with my tongue. We giggled together until mammy flicked it off with the edge of her apron. My revulsion now at this harmless basin of water perplexed me. Here we were silently scraping, washing, drying and surreptitiously fishing bacon rinds from the grimy depths as though our whole future in the convent depended on our efficiency.

When we were told to gather our things and follow Sister Pauline it was misty outside. The dimpled cement steps which we climbed from the basement kitchen had metal railings which were cold and damp to the touch and covered in verdigris. Strange greeny shapes reflected onto the ground in the light which came through the open door. I expected two cars at least but we were directed by Sister Pauline into the back of a large black van which was parked by the kerb. This was, as we later learned, the market van.

Inside, squatting on bags of turnips, crates of cabbages and sacks of potatoes, we tried to balance. We mustn't fall over. It would be disaster if our white cuffs got dirty. The van lurched forward and onward until we became part of London's early morning traffic.

Visibility was limited, two small windows, one in each back door had misted over. Between the great hulking forms of the driver and Sister Pauline fierce bright lights from oncoming traffic stabbed at us through the gloom. I wondered what had happened to the box of Cadbury Milk Tray chocolates which had been given to me for our journey by Aunty Pat.

'Enjoy these,' she said. 'I know they're your favourites.'

There was no sign of them and I couldn't ask anyone if they'd seen the box anywhere because we had been forbidden to speak without permission. How I longed for a sweet chocolate covered toffee to eliminate the taste of the streaky bacon. As morning light began to filter through the skyline, I craned my neck and I realised that we had left the wide roads behind. Now we were turning into a smaller country road, the traffic had eased and we were sheltered by tall trees and hedges of hazel and blackthorn. Great black crows circled above the stubble of cornfields and farm houses were dotted here and there between the rolling hills. Across a headland I saw a group of race horses being led out for a gallop and my heart lifted.

A tangerine sky hung over the Motherhouse of the Sisters of St. Mary of the Wayside which was named Mary's Way. Tired and crumpled I alighted from the van and saw the beauty of the buildings before me. There was a low red brick main house with several wings. The roof turrets, the wide arches, the blue grey roof tiles, the great oak doors, the gleaming leaded glass in the windows and the tall chapel spire with it's mighty bell tower proclaimed order and tranquillity. I looked at Katie her face was pale but she was smiling with happiness. Beyond the tree lined drive I pictured the road to the farm. I knew that the kitchen gardens were enclosed by a high old stone wall which was visible to my left. The apple orchards were not too far away and beyond these I would discover the woodlands and a fine lake. It was just as I had seen it in the film and for the next two and a half years Mary's Way would be my home.

※

We were called Sisters, never again would we address each other by our baptismal names. Katie became Sister Clarissa and I was named Sister Stella. Later, when I received the habit of the order I would be given the name which I would carry for the remainder of my religious life. I didn't mind Stella but I did hope that my enduring religious name would be very pretty and very meaningful. We were taken upstairs by the head postulant, Sister Cecily. She was English and like the other postulants who were already in residence she had come to Mary's Way some weeks before us. The others were senior. I learned very quickly that in religious life even one or two days before or after could make a huge difference to one's status. We were taken to the dormitory where each bed was separated by a wooden partition. I was disappointed because I had expected a proper room of my own. There was a washbasin with running water in each cubicle, a small black iron bed and above it a large crucifix. The windows were latticed, sparkling clean and reflecting light onto the polished floor boards. There was an atmosphere of simplicity and cleanliness here. I liked it.

'Please, place all the contents of our suitcases onto our bed,' directed the Postulant Mistress. She was Belgian and her accent was difficult to understand. I wondered why she kept saying 'our' all the time. It was our bed, our shoes, our hearts and souls. Eventually, we realised that we would not have possessions of our own any more. All our worldly goods had been given up and belonged in common in accordance with holy poverty. I tried to lift my suitcase onto my

– I mean our bed. Mother Beatrix came over to me.

'No, no, no,' she said very sternly. 'We do not put anything on our bed, only our mortal bodies and our blessed soul.'

Why did I want to laugh? Sister Pauline who had come upstairs with us shot me a warning glance. I knelt down and began to unpack all the clothing and bedding which had been so carefully chosen by my mother. Mother Beatrix, Sister Pauline and Sister Cecily stood watching. I was embarrassed. I wanted to ask them what they were looking at but I didn't dare. When I held up a beautifully embroidered nightdress, Mother Beatrix gasped and it was not in admiration. This was a gift from Aunty Irene.

'It's not on the list,' my mother agreed but, 'take it Ellie, let them see we have class.'

Flannelette nightdresses were on the list, full length and with long sleeves. Luckily I had these too. But my knickers, what a scene these created. There was no doubting their unsuitability,

'These are quite immodest, Sister Pauline,' the Postulant Mistress announced. 'Surely Sister Stella must have known that knickers with elastic in the legs are what she should have.'

I was mortified but I didn't think they were immodest at all. Most student nurses wore Airtex brand like mine all the time. They were not immodest girls.

'Well, I don't think having elastic in the legs is a good idea,' I spouted. 'It causes varicose veins you know.'

Unceremoniously, I was handed three pair of off white bloomers from the stock cupboard. We were allowed a few hours sleep after our journey. When I awoke the weak afternoon sunshine drifted through the window. I glanced out to see postulants and sisters returning to the convent from their various occupations. I was not happy when the expensive pure wool blankets which my parents had supplied were not left on my bed. They had been taken away along with my apple blossom soap and talcum powder. The blankets on my bed looked worn and I saw a bar of carbolic soap propped uninvitingly on the wash basin. My two suitcases had been removed – our blankets were in them. I would have to ask mother Angelus about this.

I didn't know at that time just how much the rest of my life would hinge upon waiting for mother. I now stood with my four companions outside the office of Mother Angelus. This would be our first meeting with her since our arrival. I was so excited. I had done everything I had been told to do. I had said goodbye to my family and to my friends. I was ready to put my shoulder to the plough. I waited and watched so many nuns glide past us. They moved so silently along the polished corridor, heads bowed, hands hidden beneath their robes. The air was filled with a scent of lilies. From the kitchen downstairs there were sounds of pots and pans being moved about. I could smell freshly baked bread. Soon it was my turn to knock and enter Mother Angelus' study. I knelt down and kissed the floor at her feet just as Sister Pauline had demonstrated for us. Mother smiled as she reached out from a softly upholstered leather chair. She made the sign of the cross on my forehead. This reminded me of my time with granny who always did this after my prayer to Matthew, Mark, Luke and John. Now Mother Angelus called me Sister Stella. She spoke to me about dying to earthly things and of being prepared to do God's will always.

'You belong to this congregation and great things will be expected from you,' mother was staring into my eyes. I was puzzled. I was blushing. Had she heard about my immodest knickers? Why hadn't she asked about the journey over to England or if my parents were well? There was no inquiry about how I felt, if I was tired or hungry or if I needed anything. Mother didn't ask me if I had any worries at all or even if I liked Mary's Way. I supposed she knew that I hadn't been given a tour of the Motherhouse yet. I was dismissed when mother straightened my collar and told me to, 'go in peace.' I forgot to ask her about the blankets.

Because we had been last in we were assigned to the lowest places at table. We occupied the front stalls in the chapel. We were new. I sensed all eyes upon us. I nearly fell over when I genuflected. Sister Clarissa, who was beside me laughed nervously. Mother Beatrix announced that the Irish sisters were giddy. She would have to do something about us.

I was not dreaming. It was October and the morning air was raw with a lingering touch of dawn. I stood within the walls of the kitchen garden inhaling the sweet smell of the earth. Around me there was richness in the branches of the ripened fruit trees. The long twisted arms of the walnut espaliered against the old brick walls seemed resigned, just as I was to its calling. Almost two months had passed and already I was losing touch with the outside world. I was shocked to realise how little I thought about my parents or my brothers now. Each day was filled to overflowing with new things to learn and experiences which delighted and sometimes astounded me. I couldn't understand why we were not allowed to speak freely to one another until it became apparent that silence was necessary for spiritual growth. Our communion was with the Lord, who was the beginning and the end of all things. The Constitution of the Order of Saint Mary of the Wayside, directed that the sisters must never turn anyone away from the convent door. Any pilgrim along life's way must be greeted with a kindly word. Nobody in need, spiritual or material, who was known to any Sister of St. Mary of the Wayside should be left without help. But we must not linger ourselves, idleness was forbidden. Each individual journey was a road where the signs along the wayside were clearly posted. These read: lose yourself, surrender in all things and seek real freedom in obedience to the Rule. I shouldered our hoe and began to work. There was a nip in the air and a glint of frost on the bluish slates. My fingers were freezing.

I was frightened to think about the way my life had altered. Like a process of osmosis my very self was being absorbed into religious life. My friends would hardly recognise me now dressed for work in a black apron which hid everything except my rubber boots and my scarf wrapped head. If they saw me in a long black dress, gliding along the chapel cloister, my head slightly bowed and inclined whenever I passed a senior nun, would they know me? My once proud ponytail lay subdued in a coil at the nape of my neck, its place in the history of rock and roll forgotten. Had I looked for the last time on youth and youthful things? Soon I would be twenty but for my birthday there wouldn't be any party. The day would go unnoticed except for the cards from home. Would I be given these, I wondered? Seeing Mother Beatrix reading the letters which arrived from my mother shocked me. I considered these to be private between my mother and me. As an individual, I owned nothing – not even letters from my parents. And my mother was outspoken.

'Do you get enough to eat?' She wanted to know. 'And I just wonder what that Postulant Mistress is like? Mother Elizabeth told me that she is Belgian. We're not happy about you being out in the fields picking potatoes. You father is very displeased about this. He said you would never be asked to do this sort of thing at home. It's not work for a young girl and certainly not for a nun. You are to tell the nun in charge that there is to be no more of it.'

The nun in charge forbade me to mention any manual work in my letters ever again.

'They don't understand,' she said. 'Manual work is good for the soul. It has always been part of monastic life.'

I wanted to say that I didn't know I had joined a monastery but I had already learned not to challenge those in authority. I was puzzled when we had morning classes because we couldn't ask any questions. Mother Beatrix whose English was often difficult to understand, spoke about the order being an active contemplative one. We were unique, she explained, because of this. We had managed, under the guidance of Mother Angelus, to combine a monastic rule with a life of apostolic activity. I couldn't follow this reasoning in my head. There was an order of nuns in Dublin who were contemplatives. Aunty Pat knew one of them very well because they had gone to school together. These nuns were dedicated to prayer even in the middle of the night. They were, she told me, enclosed and they were never seen by the public except through a grill. I had always understood that we were active nuns because the order was portrayed as being for modern women who were trained to work amongst the people. But following the monastic tradition as well, wasn't this a contradiction? I remained silent.

However, the rituals which we studied did fascinate me. True, these were monastic in origin. We sang the Divine Office in Latin three times a day. I liked Gregorian chant which was solemn and rich in meaning. I had studied Latin in school which helped me to understand what I was reading and singing. We had learned at the beginning of our postulancy, how to enter the chapel in two's and how to genuflect then turning around gracefully, how to bow to Mother Angelus whose pre-dieux directly faced the altar. Indeed, should we meet Mother Angelus anywhere else, we had to stand aside, bow our heads and observe custody of the eyes. The chapel was magnificent with stalls of polished wood. There were green leather kneelers in front of these from which we could face each other across the aisle or face forward to the wonderfully carved wooden altar. Later on this chapel became my refuge, not always for the right reasons – sometimes, I was so tired I slept there when I should have been reading a spiritual book and I wasn't the only postulant overcome with fatigue. One afternoon there was a loud crash. Sister Maud had toppled over, her fall sending her holy book skidding across the floor. She stumbled forward and sat on the floor in a daze with her glasses perched awry on her nose. She was mortified and scolded in public for her disobedience and for breaking the silence. Maud's penance was to do the cross prayers for three days. These penitential prayers were said before the main meal of the day. So while we sat down to eat, Sister Maud had first to kneel on the refectory floor with her arms outstretched in the form of a cross. Holding aloft the offending book in one hand and her glasses, which had been damaged in the other, she prayed earnestly and silently for forgiveness. I thought that these penances were comical especially when I saw a sister holding a well worn saucepan aloft from which the handle was missing. Obviously it had broken off but how, I wondered could she be responsible for this? I realised eventually that I would have to cultivate a better spirit of humility within myself.

Maud was Irish, she had come over with us on that awful journey but I knew nothing about her. We never discussed our private lives, our family, or where we came from; such talk was not permitted. Soon after this episode in the chapel, Sister Maud was missing from table, her place was empty. Nothing was said but we all knew that she had left. She didn't exist anymore.

The postulants didn't rise at 5 o'clock with the other nuns. We were called when a bell rang at 6 o'clock. Often when I'd hear soft footstep on the stairs I'd know that the bell ringer was on her way. I'd try to snuggle down in my little iron bed savouring the heat which curled around me in that hollow which had been moulded by others who had gone ahead of me. But such small comforts were short lived and soon another day would have begun. I loved the days when we went on long walks through the English countryside. Walking in two's we didn't speak until Mother Beatrix gave permission. Sometimes she would give this permission at the very beginning of the walk and at other times she would decide to withhold permission altogether. I didn't know which was worse. What had we to talk about anyway except a bird in the sky or a calf in a field? We had to walk with a different partner each time because particular friendships were discouraged. I wasn't sure what a particular friendship was except perhaps being somebody's best friend. But there were sinister overtones when Mother Beatrix used the phrase – maybe it's her accent, I reasoned.

I longed to walk with Sister Clarissa. I longed to ask her what news she had from home. Had Tom written to her like he said he would, was she all right? But Ellie and Katie had become anonymous even to each other.

There was a house which we passed on one very scenic walk which reminded me of our farm house at Lough Louchre. It was more beautifully kept though and it was clear that the owners had money. Once I glimpsed a tennis court at the back. I imagined each room within that house as if it was the place where I grew up. There were woodlands at the back of it and cows in the fields. Sometimes I glimpsed the face of a young boy at the window and for an instant I'd think of Colin. I should have confessed my day dreams to Mother Beatrix and done penance for hankering after that which I had given up. But I didn't confess because if I did, the walk would change direction. I couldn't bear never to pass that house again.

Chapter Nine
The Habit

We went into retreat six months after entering. This was our final preparation before taking the habit of the Order of St. Mary of the Wayside.

The retreat priest was solemn, a man who had studied the Rule Book of the Order and who laid very clearly before us our obligation and rewards. Remembering the question which the class had left for the priest when I was in Secondary School, I blushed. There were no naughty questions for this priest, indeed there were no questions at all. Once again I waited outside Mother Angelus' door. It was a tremendous privilege we were told to have her speak to us individually at this time. Mother was extremely busy but she knew each of us intimately, we were in her prayers always and we could speak freely to her. When it was my turn, I had many questions prepared about my future in the Order. Where would I go? What would I study? How could I still be sure that what I was doing was the right thing for me? But mother didn't want any questions. She knew that this was the life mapped out for me by the Lord. She reinforced the message that there must be no turning back, no giving in to self doubts which in essence is self pity. Did I want someone to tell me how wonderful I was because I had given up everything to serve God? No, I was not wonderful at all. I was a lowly creature chosen by God and He alone knew why. God was the Wonder in our lives. I belonged here as part of this great Religious Family.

Even though I left Mother's office feeling elated this euphoria was short lived. Mother was charismatic. She was so convincing, so in tune with God's will that I didn't dare question her. But I felt a huge uncertainty within myself. I couldn't honestly say, had I been asked, why I had entered the convent. I wanted something new and different, a life which would be meaningful and from which something good would emerge. When I was an adolescent in the late 1950s there wasn't much choice in life. I might have hoped as indeed I did, that a man would come along to sweep me off my feet and marry me. If this man was a farmer I might eventually become worn down by the daily grind of feeding calves and chickens and working on the land during the busy times. I had seen women like this who raised large families too. Many of these children had to go to England or to America to find work and never came home again. I didn't want these unrelenting duties, this heartache and seeming deprivation. I had loved our farm in Lough Louchre and I thought about it often but the reality was different and I knew this. Working on the farm at Mary's Way was religiously romantic and an escape. Was I basically selfish? I didn't think so. I was looking for a commitment from Mother Angelus. I wanted my own identity within the order and it took a long time for me to realise that what one did within the religious family was of significance only in relation to the whole. If I was a talented nurse that was good but it was not for my own personal satisfaction. It was rather a small facet of that perfection which the entire congregation must represent to the world.

That night I had a terrible dream. I was in the centre of a circle of sisters who were dressed in white. I was holding a candle which flickered in front of my eyes and made me dizzy. My family were trying to break through the circle. They were calling out to me. I shouted to them but I had no voice and they heard nothing. When I looked again, I was within the circle of white clothed nuns. My family was gone, I woke up and my pillow was wet with tears.

Had I been getting married in the outside world, would my marriage have taken place in February? Maybe, but I'd never know. The spring day of my religious clothing dawned with a scent of jasmine. A clear blue light from the sky drifted through the stained glass windows at Mary's Way. I could hear the strains of *The Magnificat* being sung softly and then more strongly as we processed down the cloister towards the chapel. The atmosphere was one of expectation and longing, an end to the old life and a new beginning. From their places in the side chapel and quite near to the high altar my mother and Aunty Pat watched.

'Receive this habit of the Congregation of the Order of the Sister's of Saint Mary of the Wayside,' the bishop chanted. 'Wear it to the glory of God. Let it be your inspiration to do good works. May God and his Blessed Mother guide you along the way until you will take the three vows of Poverty, Chastity and Obedience.'

I waited to hear the name by which I would be called during my life within the Order.

'No longer,' the bishop pronounced, 'will you be known as Eleanor Veronica Dardis. You are, in the service of the Lord, given the name, Sister Mary Jacob.' For an instant I thought I heard Aunty Pat giggle.

There was a celebratory lunch for us that day. Afterwards, Mother Mary Claude, the Novice Mistress, gave permission for us to visit our parents in the parlours. My mother and Aunty Pat were in St, Joseph's parlour. I could hear my mother just as I reached the door.

'What were you thinking of?' She was challenging the novice mistress.

'Where,' she demanded, 'did you resurrect that wedding dress which my daughter was wearing? It looked like something from the rag bag, something pre-flood.'

My mother's anger did not surprise me. I had been upset when I had been handed the dress which I had to wear. It was very old fashioned a faded cream with the remnant of what had at one time been a long train. What remained after this had been shortened looked like a long slinky tail. As I walked this appendage kept winding and unwinding behind me.

'I'm so glad my husband, Owen, is not here today,' my mother continued. 'What would he think, seeing his daughter in that get up? And you know, I do have a high class drapery shop myself.'

'That's right,' Aunty Pat chimed in. 'Very high class, indeed.'

'We would have provided Ellie with a beautiful gown worthy of the occasion,' my mother continued. 'Marrying the Lord, I ask you. A modern order,' she laughed derisively. And she didn't stop there. She suggested, quite rightly and I had realised this too – all the pure white stylish dresses had been worn by the English girls. 'You didn't think we'd come, did you think...?' Seeing me standing there she burst into tears and Mother Mary Claude made her escape.

We had so much to talk about. Daddy was all right. He had been helping Uncle Eugene to fix the roof on the hay shed and he had fallen. His ankle was broken. He couldn't travel but he would come for my profession which would be even better. The boys were fine and they would come next time too. Indeed, my mother had a surprise for me – Tom might be able to visit sooner because he had to do some study in London. I could sense how proud my mother was of him and Colin. Irene sent her love and a coloured picture from Peter showing what was supposed to be a cow and one from Paul of his parents. I was overcome with emotion but I tried not to show it.

Grandad was not getting any younger, mammy said. He and Jamesie still watched the trains coming and going. It was a wonderful pastime for them.

'Daddy was thinking of bringing the entire model railway down to the cosy room,' she added because grandad's knees were so bad.

'The cosy room suits your father too now that he has his ankle in plaster. Anyway, we'll see. I just think we'd have no end of callers if that train was downstairs, it would be seen through the window, you know.'

'Wait 'till they hear your new name,' Aunty Pat laughed. 'Where on earth did they get it from?'

I told her about Jacob in the bible.

'He had a dream,' I said, 'where he saw angels ascending and descending on a ladder which reached all the way to heaven.'

Aunty Pat was not impressed. She thought my name was comical.

'When I heard it I could only think of Jacob's biscuits, did you hear me giggle?'

'You do look like a Kimberley biscuit, Ellie,' she laughed. 'All that brown habit like ginger and your little white veil just like marshmallow. You take the biscuit all right.'

I wanted to cry. I was upset myself, the name did not appeal to me at all. It was a man's name. I didn't know anybody called Jacob and I'd have this name for the rest of my life. But I didn't cry, instead I laughed and I don't know why. Maybe I had to have some relief from the tensions and drama of the day. I laughed loudly and my mother laughed too. Aunty Pat joined in and other visitors who had no idea what we were laughing at laughed as well. Suddenly, Aunty Pat left us and racing down the cloister she called out urgently, 'toilet, toilet please, toilet,' to the great alarm of two very discreet sisters who took her away in a great hurry. Very soon, St. Joseph's parlour was converted into a scene of unseemly merriment. I became aware of Mother Mary Claude. She was standing just inside the parlour door and she was not laughing.

Katie was happy because her father had come from Cork and her two brothers who worked in England were also with her for the day.

My mother talked to them and I managed to tell Katie that I thought her name, Sister Mary Davinia was lovely. She said that she liked my name too although I really knew deep down that she probably thought it was quite odd. I smiled, 'It's all right,' I said. 'And I don't mind if you laugh, it could be worse, I suppose.'

That night I felt drained and exhausted. Seeing my mother again and Aunty Pat brought a terrible longing for home. I should be detached but I wasn't. Why couldn't I say goodbye to them without feeling that I was betraying a promise to God, a promise to belong to Him alone? On my way to bed I was passing by the work room where our outdoor clothes were kept, when a hand clasped mine and pulled me into the small windowed room. Vaguely, in the moonlight, I saw Sister Dympna's face. She was crying. I didn't know what to do because it was absolutely forbidden to speak. After night prayers there was 'The Great Silence' until after mass the following morning. Nobody uttered a word except in an emergency. But Sister Dympna spoke.

'I've got to talk to someone,' she said. 'I don't want to get you into any trouble I don't want you to say anything at all but I'm so upset, I can't believe what's happened. If I go to bed in this state and if Mother Mary Claude comes along I know I'll probably hit her because I'm so disgusted.'

I was speechless - well, I was supposed to be wasn't I? But Sister Dympna, ready to clout Mother Claude? I couldn't believe it. Sister Dympna was a tiny, very pretty girl from Dublin. I knew this because her accent and her use of words reminded me of Aunty Pat. I stared at her willing her to tell me and yet at the same time, not tell me, what was wrong.

'The way my family were treated today was terrible,' she sobbed.

I knew her family because they were in the parlour with my own visitors. Her parents and two brothers and one sister were so proud of her and so excited. I overheard them admiring her religious habit.

'God bless us, what a little charmer you look, Anne, a real little saint if ever there was one.' Her mother declared.

They had joined in heartily when we were all laughing in the parlour. Maybe Mother Mary Claude blamed them? I felt guilty because I had begun the hilarity.

'Tell me what it's all about.' I implored with my eyes. I was actually very frightened because if we were discovered together and talking too, there would be serious trouble ahead.

'When I went out of the parlour to get some more tea,' Sister Dympna explained as she began to sob again. 'I met Mother Mary Claude coming along by the parlour kitchen. You won't believe what she said to me.' Fresh tears welled up in her eyes.

'"Have you not managed to get rid of them yet, Sister?" That's what she said.'

'No.' I gasped.

'Oh yes. That's exactly what she said and she meant every word of it too. In the morning I'm going to leave this place. If that's what she thinks of my family what does she think of me – are we not good enough or what? Think about it, Sister Mary Jacob would she say something like that to one of the English girls? You bet your sweet life she wouldn't dare because they'd have their parents up here in a jiffy. I'm going back to Dublin to join an Irish Order where I'll be happy and where my family will be respected.'

I didn't know what to think. I was in a difficult situation. Was this a temptation from the devil – already? Had I fallen into a trap which He had prepared for me? Sister Dympna was in the refectory for breakfast. I avoided any meeting of eyes and sadly, I never saw her again. This was something I couldn't understand. Postulants left and novices too but they were never spoken about. For a while there would be a vacant space until we moved up one place in the chapel and elsewhere as it dawned on us all that a companion had gone. I'd wonder what had happened, why had the girl left, where was she now?

Why couldn't we have said, goodbye? After all, we had shared the same home and the same religious dream if only for a while. And Mother Mary Claude was always going on about the great family spirit of the order. I didn't see much family spirit in all this secrecy. Were we to think that the girl who left had done something very bad or that she was not fit to become a nun? I didn't know. However, I admired Sister Dympna's courage although I was secretly and guiltily glad that she had gone. It was terrible to think the way I did and I knew that I was simply protecting myself. Had Sister Dympna stayed, would she have felt obliged to confess to Mother Mary Claude that she had broken The Great Silence? If she did this, I would be implicated too. But had I been really honest and a truly repentant and scrupulous novice I would have gone that very night to Mother Mary Claude's room, kissed her feet and confessed my transgression on bended knees. Well, I was not that scrupulous, not yet anyway.

We were not told that there would be a Novice's Concert. This was a tradition which we heard about surreptitiously. A surprise supper Mother Mary Claude called it – a surprise all right. We were seated at the top tables but not in the place reserved for Mother Angelus and her advisors. The professed sisters waited on table. We could speak to anyone but since we were all together this meant to any other novice only. I noticed that the postulants were not present. There was real party food, sandwiches, cakes, ice cream and chocolates. Mother Mary Claude stood up, there was silence.

She welcomed Mother Angelus, the council, the senior nuns and she welcomed the junior professed too.

'In our religious family, we have forty two novices, twenty senior novices and twenty two who received the religious habit on Sunday last.' Everyone clapped. 'Our new novices are ready to entertain us,' she beamed. This was news.

'However, since twenty two items would take a long time,' Mother Mary Claude continued. 'And we must finish by 9.00 pm. Mother

Foundress who has the name of each novice in a box will honour us by picking a name at random. What is different for this concert, is, that Mother will decide if the piece to be performed should be a dance, a song or a recitation.'

We gasped. What a horrible idea, I thought. It spoils everything. There was confusion on every face. Mother Foundress smiled – she was in control.

I was watching the clock, it was now 8.30 pm. The novices who had already been called upon could relax while I was becoming a bundle of nerves. I was not a great singer, not like my mother and not even as good as those who had already been required to sing. If I was asked to recite a poem I would use the very beautiful poem by the Irish poet Joseph Mary Plunkett:

'I see his blood upon the rose,
And in the stars the glory of His eyes.'

'Sister Mary Rosa, please.' Mother Angelus smiled and beckoned her forward. 'Dance, sister,' she commanded.

How could she do this to Sister Mary Rosa who was a huge girl, very much overweight and whose flushed cheeks now registered complete amazement. I watched her fists clench while at the same time a bright smile spread across her countenance. I liked Sister Rosa. I felt that we could have been friends in another life. In a very loud voice she asked for some ballet music.

'*Swan Lake* or *The Nutcracker*, whatever you have handy.' She beamed.

Everybody laughed. Sister Rosa stood in the middle of the refectory and launched herself into a fleet footed routine of pirouettes, great leaps and tiny steps. She looked like an aeroplane in an aeronautics display, a mighty force weaving and bending as if on air. Suddenly, she flung her head back and with her arms outstretched took a flying leap into the air. All this time her face was a vision of angelic delight but beneath this I sensed a sly grin in hiding. As cups and saucers shuddered on the tables Sister Rosa spun around and around until halting in front of Mother Angelus' chair she effortlessly performed the splits. The place erupted as pent up tensions and emotions were finally released. I was hurting inside because I thought that this had been a mean and cruel trick to play on Sister Rosa. What did it accomplish except to make everyone uneasy and embarrassed? Sister Rosa had been equal to the challenge but I wondered if her efforts were a lesson in abandonment and humility or an act of defiance? Would I have had courage equal to hers? I didn't think so. Suddenly, the clapping stopped, Mother Angelus was standing and we waited heads bowed and silent within our own thoughts as she passed.

※

I understand now that when I began my novitiate, I was spiritually, physiologically and emotionally immature. After all, my life until this time had been a sheltered one. I was a perfect candidate for religious moulding within the walls of a convent. I was once again living within a circle of interdependence where there were people to guide and direct and watch over me. And so believing in what I had been told – that there would be room for me to grow here, I submitted gladly. Within the daily hours of silence, work and prayer, I did not feel vulnerable anymore. I belonged where I was training to become religious in its truest form. Over many months I became unselfish with my time, generous in my thoughts and dedicated to a disposal of my old selfish self. I would become new by choosing freely to fight the good fight.

While such thoughts drifted within my head I looked out over the fields which formed part of the farm at Mary's Way I was so happy. I couldn't believe that I had been assigned to work here for a while. The farm was replacing the home of my childhood. But I did not write to my parents with this news. I didn't say that I cleaned out the cow parlour or that I fed pigs. I didn't let on that I carried bales of hay on my back or that I helped to spread manure over ploughed fields. I was wise enough not to jeopardise the harmony which had suddenly entered my soul. This contact with nature was a gift from God. How I loved each cow, each animal had a name just as our cows had in Lough Louchre. How I loved the smell of the milking parlour in the early mornings. I helped Sister Mary Joanne carry the huge milk cans to the gate for collection by the milk lorry. She and I had an unwritten attachment to this farm. We were two of a kind – land girls and Irish. Sister Mary Joanne protected the girls who worked for her. She made sure that we got finished in time to get back to the convent and properly cleaned up before lunch. She warned us to get our outdoor jobs done first whenever it seemed like rain. And it was she who saw my tears when the news came that grandad had died.

One afternoon, during recreation, I had been handed the sad letter without any comment. How could Sister Mary Claude be so unfeeling? She had read the letter from my mother thoroughly and I had recognised the handwriting immediately. Yet she passed the letter to me and said nothing at all, no warning about what news it contained, no words of comfort or sadness on my behalf. I was so upset when I read the news. Mother Mary Claude was watching me, I knew that.

She was an impressive looking woman. I thought that she would have made a lovely Foundress because she had a special radiance about her which inspired others. Her quiet dignity belied her strength of character. Mother Mary Claude was self possessed and charismatic, an authentic witness to the spirituality of the Order. I knew that every novice admired her, some even walked the way she did with an erect carriage, downcast eyes and a serene smile playing about the lips. Nobody wanted to disappoint the Novice Mistress, her silent approval was essential to keep us focused on our vocation. In some strange way our identity was linked to her. As she would have expected, I folded the letter and continued the mending which I was doing. It was recreation time and we could speak to one another. There was subdued chatter and an occasional laugh. I wanted to bang the table furiously. I wanted to shout: 'Listen here, everybody, my grandad has died. We called him Michelangelo because he painted churches. He and Jamesie Lamb made a model railway. It was the talk of the town. Now he's gone on his last journey and the train won't stop for him anymore.'

But I daren't say anything. Nobody knew of my heartache. No sister was able to console me or offer to pray for him. It didn't make sense. We helped people we didn't know at all yet we were forbidden to speak about our own family and the inevitable changes which were taking place within it. But on the farm Sister Mary Joanne sensed my distress and she did not behave like a stranger to my sorrow.

'Have a quiet chat with the little animals,' she said. 'I always do and they listen, you know.'

That night I prayed that God would grant grandad, 'a quiet night and a holy rest.' And I added, 'In the morning, Lord, give him a pot of golden paint and set him free to gild the stars forever.'

In the days which followed the news of my grandfather's death, I began to suffer anxiety, the beginnings perhaps of a state of mind which would plague me for years to come. I was angry of course but I had to subdue this feeling. I thought a lot about death and what it meant. Did it really happen the way Reverend O'Hara had explained so long ago after Marguerita's death? I tried to ask about this when questions were unexpectedly permitted one morning during class.

'Mother Mary Claude, please,' I said. 'What do you think death is?'

'It is going home to God, dear.' She replied sweetly. 'I will talk to you later, Sister Mary Jacob, in my office.'

Mother Mary Claude said that she knew exactly why I had asked the question. I was not accepting God's will. My grandfather had died well over a month ago – wasn't that right? And I was still looking for sympathy. I must do penance. Remaining silent, as I was supposed to do, I wondered what grandad would think about this. I began to withdraw further into myself punishing myself by trying to live a religious life of daily demands as perfectly as possible. But this routine had no relation at all to how I was feeling inside. I had loved grandad dearly and he had loved me but now I felt that nobody cared about me anymore, nobody loved me for myself as a person. I became almost immobilised emotionally.

Towards the end of May in that first year of my novitiate I continued to work on the farm. It became my salvation my escape from the smell of furniture polish and cooking within the convent. Sister Mary Joanne gave me more responsibility. I was like an overseer, checking on the animals and making sure that each novice working beside me knew what to do. Mother Angelus came to visit the farm one morning which was unexpected. She had some people with her including a bishop from Australia.

'This farm is truly wonderful,' he beamed. 'I have never been to a convent anywhere in the world and I've been to many, which has its own land and cows. Such self sufficiency, Mother Angelus, we could learn a lesson from this down under.' He laughed. 'It's admirable'.

With Mother's encouragement, he took photographs using his cine camera which was something very new to us. I was holding two tiny black piglets. Mr. Shiels came along. He was a local man who helped out by assisting the vet, ordering feed stuffs and driving the tractor. When Mother Angelus introduced him he knelt and kissed the bishop's ring.

'I've been telling Mother how impressed I am,' the bishop said. 'You must feel very privileged to work on this farm, Mr. Shiels. There is such a wonderful atmosphere. It is so calm and so beautiful, I don't see any sheep though. You probably know that Australia is crawling with these creatures. Maybe I should send a flock over to you.' He laughed.

'Aye, it's a great farm, goes like clockwork, My Lord.' Mr. Shiels answered. 'The animals can be holy terrors though, especially the pigs.' Everyone smiled. 'But you see Sister Mary Jacob there,' he continued, 'she's the best little farmer I've ever come across, has a real way with her especially with the cows. She's the only one of us who can get Lobelia to cooperate.' Mother Angelus frowned.

'Oh Aye, the red and white cow over yonder, she's a dandy, never wants to do what she's told. Isn't that right, Sister Mary Jacob?' I saw Sister Mary Joanne out of the corner of my eye willing Mr. Shiels to shut up.

'Yes, that's right,' I murmured as the party moved away.

It was evening time and a few days later when I was summoned to Mother Mary Claude's office.

'Now dear,' she smiled at me. 'Your work duties will change from tomorrow. It will be good for you and it's necessary to develop all your skills not just those associated with animals no matter how well you handle them. From now on you will be assisting in the parlours. Sister Mary Basil is in charge there and Sister Gabriel will be the senior novice who will work with you.'

I felt the colour drain from my face as I kissed her feet and standing up I obediently thanked her.

The convent parlours were beautiful rooms. There were four altogether and each one was used in accordance with the status and importance of the guest. The small cream parlour was used by the chaplain who breakfasted there each morning after mass. There was a massive oak room which overlooked spectacular gardens of green lawns and colourful flower beds. The cloister parlour opened into the library which could become an extension of it whenever there was a crowd and the chintz parlour which was my favourite had windows which overlooked the rose gardens. This particular room was intimate and comfortable and many girls who entered the order had their first convent tea there. Of course, each parlour also had a Saint's name.

My early days as a parlour trainee were testing because I kept thinking about the farm and the animals. Half hourly I wondered what was happening there and if Lobelia was behaving herself. I couldn't believe they could manage without me and for a while I kept expecting a summons to rescue a situation. But such a call for my help never came. I knew that Sister Mary Joanne was annoyed by my sudden change in occupation. She passed me a few days later just as I was emerging from the parlour kitchen in my crisp white apron, a damask serviette in hand. A wry smile was exchanged between us. I almost thought I saw her wink her encouragement. I didn't like working in the parlour, it was so boring. Just how many times can one clean the silver or wash and polish the crystal? But I did admire the beautiful cutlery and glassware and the spotless linen. How my mother would love these. I learned how to serve from the left and take away from the right. I discovered also that there was a correct way to serve wines and particular glasses for red and white and glasses called flutes for champagne. I recalled getting tipsy in Galway with Aidan Flood and how I grabbed the bottle of wine before he could reach it. I blushed all over again with embarrassment and guilt dropping a serving spoon to hide my rising colour.

'Sister, be careful, retrieve that spoon at once and be quiet.' Sister Mary Basil commanded.

Each morning Sister Gabriel and I arranged flowers in crystal vases which were then placed on the dining tables and on occasional tables in the parlours and corridors. A special bouquet was always placed in front of the statue of St. Mary of the Wayside which was in the main entrance hall. Sister Theo who was the head gardener made us suffer by taking an age to decide whether we could or could not have flowers. Terrible decisions had to be made about which blossoms she would pick for us. I hated it when it was my turn to approach Sister Theo. If her decisions were lengthy I would have to rush to finish the tables or do other work assigned to me by Sister Basil. Often, Sister Gabriel helped out on the quiet so that I wouldn't get into trouble. I liked Sister Gabriel. She was obviously older than any other novice indeed she was probably much older than Mother Mary Claude who was about forty. Once I thought that Sister Gabriel was an assistant Novice Mistress, that is, until I realised that she did not wear the medal of the Order and she did not have a cream veil. But she was a wonderful character who could let things wash over her and I supposed that, being more mature, the petty things didn't bother her very much. One afternoon she had words with Sister Mary Basil. We were on red alert because the sister of Mother Angelus was arriving for lunch in the chintz parlour. The hollandaise sauce was put into a china sauce boat instead of the silver one which matched the cutlery.

'It will get cold, Sister Mary Basil if we change it into the silver. The china sauce boat has been heated in the kitchen. The silver one is stone cold.' Sister Gabriel declared.

'We are serving the sister of our Foundress, if you would care to remember this.' Sister Mary Basil announced as she turned the sauce into the cold silver sauce boat and marched off with her tray to the parlour.

'You'd think we were entertaining Queen Victoria,' Sister Gabriel said to me.

'And you know, that same lady in the parlour is as mad as a hatter. She wouldn't notice if the hollandaise was served in a teapot.'

I couldn't believe it. And it never occurred to me that the passing on of such information to me by another novice, this breaking of the silence and this criticism of a visitor should be confessed to Mother Mary Claude. A sister should not retire if she had a violation of the rule on her conscience. I didn't confess.

I believe that Sister Gabriel recognised in me the struggle, the self doubt and that loss of an initial sparkle which had first led me through the convent doors. She watched over me like a guardian angel and often took the blame when I'd forgotten something or put things away in the wrong cupboard. I was frequently sad and I didn't know why. I think this inner turmoil became apparent to Father Philip Power too. He was the convent chaplain and it became my duty to serve him breakfast on alternate weeks. This man had status within the convent. The professed nuns sought his advice. Mother Mary Claude consulted him, and Mother Angelus walked alone with him in the convent gardens. One morning as I served his bacon and egg, he looked at me and said, 'smile, Sister.' I wanted to ask, 'what for?' But I was wiser now. I was wary and apprehensive even though Father Power was not in any way threatening towards me. He was no Father Knickers. He was thin and ascetic looking with long white fingers and dark circles beneath his eyes. I doubt that he could harbour any inclinations to swim with a near naked girl.

'Here,' he said. 'Have an orange, Sister Mary Jacob. You are looking very pale this morning and it will do you good.'

I stared at him, was he out of his tiny mind? He knew that I couldn't accept an orange from his table or eat anything anywhere without permission.

'I'm giving you permission to take an orange,' he said. 'Take it, Sister, look I will even peel it for you.' He reached for the fruit knife.

'Father, I am not permitted to eat outside of our own refectory but thank you all the same.' I smiled sweetly, lowered my eyes and walked with as much dignity as I could from the room.

Sister Gabriel called him Pip and although she admired his holiness she did feel that he was full of his own importance. She was talking to me on one of our walks and I told her how he wanted me to have an orange with him.

'Wouldn't it have been fun,' she giggled, 'if you'd sat down at the table and eaten the orange? You could have asked for a share of his toast and why not his bacon and egg? Gosh. What a scene.'

'Yes, I agreed and an even more dramatic one if Mother Mary Claude or even Mother Angelus came along to have a wee word with Father.'

One morning during that same week Mother Mary Claude arrived for morning lesson looking very serious indeed. I wondered if she'd had a conversation with Father Power about the novices who were on parlour duty because she began the liturgy class by saying that Father Power had just spoken to her. I began to shake and I could feel cold sweat breaking out at the back of my neck. But I needn't have worried because he had spoken to her about the novices who had pimples on their faces.

'It was appalling,' said Mother Mary Claude, 'to have our chaplain draw this to my attention. I should have been aware, of course, and I should have noticed that there are novices here who are obviously careless about personal hygiene. But my dear Sisters, it's not something which has ever happened before and I would not have expected the like. Sisters, you are obliged to wash carefully with the soap provided. If you do this, facial skin problems will be avoided. Obviously some novices think that using carbolic soap is beneath them.'

A special paste was being prepared by Sister Claudia. She was a chemist and we would have to follow her instructions to the letter. We didn't have mirrors which meant that we had to point out each offending pimple to a fellow novice who would then anoint the spot. We performed this caring and sharing duty during recreation. I couldn't stop laughing when Sister Mary Claire called the ointment pimple paste. Eventually, all visible spots had been coated with this substance which dried out to resemble grey cement, the result was worse and more obvious that the initial malaise. When we trooped into chapel next morning and bowed with due deference to Mother Angelus she gasped in amazement. Beckoning Mother Mary Claude we could hear in the silence of the chapel as she spoke sternly to her asking what on earth had happened to the novices. Sister Joanne laughed unashamedly and many senior nuns hid behind their breviaries to have a giggle. I thought for a moment that Father Power would refuse to give us Holy Communion. He looked so disgusted as if he thought we were playing a joke on him.

Sister Gabriel escaped because she did not need any pimple paste but Sister Matilda was nearly destroyed by it. She already had a skin problem which this paste aggravated. Her face became the colour of beetroot. It looked red and raw and was bleeding in places and she was obviously in pain. She had to go to hospital and on her return to Mary's Vale, had to remain indoors for weeks. While we were at recreation Sister Matilda had to go to her cubicle to have special facial masks applied. We were told to stop using the pimple paste. All the jars of this cream were taken away but Mother Mary Claude had the last word.

'Sisters,' she said, 'if you had been faithful to cleanliness and to the rules of the Order, Sister Matilda would not have had to suffer on your account. Each novice here is to say the cross prayers while holding a bar of carbolic soap. I will assign the days for a group of six novices at a time to perform this exercise. I can't have forty of you on the refectory floor together.'

Sister Gabriel laughed out loudly and promptly received three days of carbolic penance for her insolence.

I admired Katie – Sister Davinia so much during all the time of our novitiate. She was born to religious life. Nothing perturbed her. While I was working as a parlour maid she became assistant sacristan. She moved about the chapel looking diligent yet prayerful. And there was much work to be done there, so much polishing of the wooden floors and so much dusting, flower arranging and changing of altar linens. But she worked steadily and unhurriedly in an atmosphere of tranquil peace. Two senior sisters worked with her and taught Sister Davinia how to prepare the altar for different ceremonies. I was confident that she would only need to be shown once and she would remember – unlike me. The priest's vestments were hung in very tall wardrobes which had to be checked daily for moths. Sister Davinia was responsible for doing this and for setting out the vestments for morning mass and she never made a mistake.

One morning when Father Power was vesting, we who were at the front nearest to the sacristy heard loud crunching, scrunching and tearing. These sounds were followed by gasps and muted groans. Sister Davinia and the senior sacristan stood up and having bowed to Mother Angelus walked quietly to the sacristy. We could hear Father Power's masculine tones and the softer, soothing voices of the nuns. As we later discovered, the priest had been trapped in the alb – a long white linen garment which had been starched to the stiffness of cardboard. The front and back of the alb were stuck together and the sleeves, which were very wide, were also stuck. Father Power had been trying to beat his way into this vestment like an adventurer cutting his way through the jungle. Fifteen minutes late for mass, Father Power appeared looking indignant with a very red face and with bits of white fluff in his hair. He was not seated at the table when I took his breakfast to the parlour that morning. He was at the window, his foot resting on the window seat as he tried frantically to remove starchy remnants from his black trousers. I resisted the temptation to say, 'smile.'

The laundry novices were summoned but Mother Mary Claude could not find any reason to chastise them. Sister Mary Rosa said that she had ironed the alb but she hadn't starched it. This had been done as always, in the machine. No. She didn't notice that it was extra stiff. I wondered. Sister Davinia was questioned. She was very sorry because she should have realised that the vestment was not properly laundered. I wondered again – someone had substituted a rigidly starched alb for the normal one. Sister Mary Rosa was looking very pleased with herself. Sister Davinia had to say the cross prayers but not holding aloft a blessed vestment, instead she had to make a paper cut out of an alb and use it. This was the first time I had ever seen her having to do penance in the refectory. The entire episode intrigued me – it was pimple paste revenge and we all knew it.

The feast of Easter came upon us for the second time since we entered the convent. The time of Lent which preceded this great feast was severe and trying. We fasted daily which meant that there was no break at eleven and no special tea on Sunday. Our daily intake of food was very plain and less plentiful also. Before Holy Week everyone in the Motherhouse was on Retreat. Four priests came from a monastery nearby to conduct a separate time of reflection for postulants, novices, junior professed and final professed sisters. We were very busy in the parlours even though the priests were themselves fasting. New postulants had arrived from Ireland and elsewhere three months previously. There were four girls from the Far East. I watched them in the same way we had been watched on our arrival. One English girl in particular intrigued me because she was so tall, fair, elegant and fragile looking. She will be crushed in no time I surmised because she is certainly not the type to relish mucking out a cow shed. Neither did she appear to be a girl who would take the hard knocks easily. She had obviously been brought up in a very protective family. I served her parents in the parlour and her welfare was of great concern to them. They quizzed me about the order and our life within it. I was very embarrassed because I couldn't tell them anything.

'I'm sorry,' I hedged, 'but it would take a long time to answer all your questions. I'm sure Mother Beatrix will be very pleased to tell you about our life here. I would love to stay but I have to go to the other parlours because we have several visitors today. Ask Mother Beatrix,' I advised, 'she is the Postulant Mistress and she will be able to tell you everything.' I smiled.

Had I been free to speak I might have told them to take their beautiful daughter straight home. And this would have been better for her as I later discovered. During this time of our Lenten Retreat I accidentally came upon their daughter, now known as Sister Marianne. She was being chastised in the chintz parlour by Mother Beatrix and

Mother Mary Claude.

'How dare you speak to Father Bernard like this, sister,' Mother Mary Claude was saying. 'You have just told me that you spoke in confession about a custom which is private and which is for the edification of the Postulants only. You have been taught that our internal affairs and customs are not for discussion with anyone. Isn't that correct Mother Beatrix? And sister,' she continued, 'I really don't want to know what you said to Father Bernard and I'm not interested in his reply either. If the custom of confessing your faults to the Postulant Mistress upsets you perhaps you are in the wrong place. Do you agree Mother Beatrix?'

'Of course,' Mother Beatrix replied. 'Sister Marianne knows these rules. She is very disobedient and Mother, she is filled with an inordinate pride. Father Bernard came to question me also and just fancy, he said that he had been given Sister Marianne's permission to do so, I ask you. He thought that we were acting as mother confessors. He just didn't know the...'

They had seen me. I excused myself and closed the door as if I had only just opened it. But I was puzzled and disturbed. I decided to be very careful in the future. I would watch what I had to say to any priest in or outside the confessional.

Lent was a time of great hope and longing. We were awaiting an awakening and a new sense of life which Easter would bring. The convent was cleaned from top to bottom. Chants were learned and the wonderful Easter ceremonies rehearsed until they were perfect. New habits were made, one for each sister. Sister Mary Theo could be observed in the greenhouse inspecting freesia or walking by the huge flower beds where the Easter Lilies were ready to bloom. But the weather was grey and dismal. Huge rain clouds hung over Mary's Way threatening to blot out the sky. It was Good Friday, a day recalling great grief and loss for the Christian. We venerated the Holy Cross in a moving ritual. We mourned in prayer and in our thoughts for the death of Christ. The rain became torrential. It mirrored our tears. Through the wind I heard the sound of the front doorbell. Scurrying along the corridor I saw beyond the rain drenched windows tall trees bending, swaying and shuddering. From somewhere nearby I heard Mother Mary Claude's voice calling, 'leave it, sister.'

She was too late. I had opened the door. Sister Marianne stood outside. She was soaked her beautiful hair clinging to her cheeks in great strands of dampness. On each side of her a policeman stood. As I moved away they were handing their sobbing charge over to Mother Mary Claude. This was a terrible scene to witness. I wanted desperately to know what had happened to Sister Marianne, to know the reasons which had caused her to run away from us. I waited for a summons from Mother Mary Claude. I was quite sure that she would want to give me some explanation about what I had seen. No doubt she would tell me not to speak about the matter and to forget it altogether. But I wasn't called to her office and this made me sad. I was sad for Sister Marianne whom I never saw again and I was sad for myself because of a silence which left my mind once more in a state of fearfulness.

⸙

I couldn't believe it. It was the week after Easter and Tom was coming to see me. Sister Mary Claude met him in the front hall and made a big fuss of him. Perhaps she remembered my mother's outburst on the day of our clothing?

Tom was really handsome now and I was so proud of him. He spoke with such maturity to Mother Mary Claude telling her how impressed he was by the beautiful buildings and the gardens. When he saw me, his eyes grew wide with amazement.

'Ellie,' he laughed. 'It's really you. For a minute I thought I'd seen an apparition – one of the children of Fatima or something.'

'How delightful,' Mother Mary Claude gushed. 'I'm glad, Tom, that you associate our religious habit with those saintly children.'

I had permission to spend the entire day with my brother. His lunch was served in the cream parlour from where he could see the gardens. Sister Rosa, who had been moved from the laundry to the kitchen – not long after the starched alb incident, gave me extra helpings for Tom.

'He's a grown man and a bonny one too.' She whispered to me. 'What they dish up sometimes wouldn't feed a wee sparrow.'

I was so grateful to Sister Rosa. Tom loved his food and I knew that all the convent daintiness would not impress him half as much as a good meal. He appreciated the farm. I didn't tell him about the hard work I'd done there but he did meet Sister Joanne who let me know, indirectly, that I was missed. If she could manage it, she told Tom, she would have me back on the farm, maybe next year. I was delighted. Tom told her that we had grown up on a farm and that our father still had land and cattle. They talked about combines and tractors. She heard all about Uncle Dan and his farm machinery business. Tom was an expert on the latest farm machinery and equipment and he answered all of Sister Joanne's questions. It made me happy knowing that she now knew something about my background. I knew that when Tom's visit was over there was no one I could talk to about him and all the news he'd brought to me from home. When Sister Joanne said goodbye to Tom, she said that she looked forward very much to meeting him again. This made me very happy.

Tom didn't ask about Katie and I wondered if I should mention her at all.

'Tom,' I said. 'Do you have a girlfriend now or are you still hankering for Katie?'

'I have a girl,' he answered, 'but I'd like to know how Katie's doing.'

'She's fine,' I told him. 'She's in the right place. The convent seems to be made for Katie and Katie for the convent. Would you like to meet her?' I asked. I'm sure Mother Mary Claude would agree. She was falling over you. I've never seen her so charming.'

Tom didn't want to see Katie.

'Maybe when we all come for your profession or whatever it's called, I'll see her. I just feel a bit awkward. I wouldn't know what to say.'

'That's all right,' I reassured Tom. 'She doesn't know you are here anyway so it won't matter at all. Tell me about your girl now,' I pleaded. 'I want to know everything.'

Tom laughed and I could tell that he was very happy.

'Her name is Bridget and she's from Galway,' he said. 'She's in the university doing pharmacy. It's a long course and I will finish ahead of her but we do have plans – sort of, for the future.'

'What does she look like?' I wanted to know.

Tom handed me a photograph. A lovely smiling girl looked back at me. Her hair which was very fair and naturally curly fell below her shoulders. She was slim and quite tall. Her eyes were deep blue, trusting and honest looking.

'Oh, Tom,' I cried, 'she's beautiful.'

'She is,' he agreed, 'and she's even nicer than she looks in the photograph. I don't think I could live without Bridget,' he added.

We talked about our parents. Tom was a bit worried about daddy.

'He seems to have got older,' he warned me. 'I think grandad's death affected him very badly. They got on very well you know even though daddy was not his son just his son in law. He still works at Capall Ban, of course and he is as busy there as he ever was but the ankle is troublesome, a bit of arthritis, I expect.'

Mammy was in good form and very busy in the shop.

'She's going in for all the latest First Communion styles,' he laughed. 'She knows every child in the town and she knows which ones will need new clothes and when. She speaks to the mothers before she orders anything. This way she can guarantee that everything will sell. She's very smart and I often think, Ellie, that she's a bit lost sometimes

– there's not much going on in small towns like Eskeriada'

I reminded Tom about the night he and Joe Scully dressed up in corsets.

'We still laugh about that,' he told me. 'Do you remember how fast Colin made his escape? He's a wonder, really. He has no problems in school and he'll be in the Galway soon.'

Tom didn't know what Colin wanted to do.

'He has so many choices,' he agreed. 'It's actually harder for him to make a decision. I just hope he chooses what suits him best.'

Looking at me Tom suddenly asked, 'Do you think that you are made for the convent Ellie, and the convent for you? I'm wondering because you haven't asked me about Jerry at all.'

'Well, how is he, Tom?'

'Working in Donegal,' he replied. 'I see him sometimes when he comes down to Galway. Jerry is still the same and when I told him that I was coming here he said to tell you that he sends his love.'

'Does he have a girlfriend at all now?' I wanted to know this.

'He does,' Tom replied.

'Well?' I looked quizzically at Tom.

'He tells me that she's in a convent somewhere in England and he's waiting for her to come home.'

Chapter Ten
A New Experience

I had not been outside Mary's Way for almost a year except for those walks which we took in the immediate vicinity of the Motherhouse. Any idea I might have had about driving the convent car up the Main Street in Eskeriada with my veil blowing in the wind had gradually diminished. I would probably never do this and indeed I would never hear the words from my former imaginings.

'Oh, there goes Ellie Dardis. She's a nun with the order in the Galway Hospital. Isn't she a great young one all the same?'

Such notions of acclaim had no place to hide within my awakening life of spirituality and sacrifice. Mother Mary Thelma was driving this car, the first time I'd been in a motor vehicle since that horrible journey from London in the market van. I was now on my way to a small convent called Mary's Grove near Tunbridge Wells. This was an opportunity for me to live within a smaller community where I could see and be seen. Mary's Grove was a home for small babies who were awaiting adoption. These infants were adopted before becoming two years old. I was advised that I would not have anything to do with these children. There were four sisters who were qualified nursery nurses and two staff nurses to do this. The accommodation for all these sisters was self contained. I would be assigned to the convent proper and I would take on the duties of cook and housekeeper. As I admired the beautiful scenery through which we drove I was not worried about the jobs which lay ahead. I was quite sure that there would be good guidance and help to get me started.

It was a beautiful September afternoon. The tall trees by the roadside reminded me of the great horse chestnuts at Lough Louchre. I felt so happy being outside of the Motherhouse and its stuffy parlours. I felt so happy to see cattle and sheep, orchards and meadows. The undulating hills threw interesting shadows that danced within the valleys. Mighty oak trees gave shade and a sweet scent from the wild roses growing amongst the hedgerows drifted through the car windows.

Sister Angel sat beside Mother Mary Thelma. She had belonged to an order that for undisclosed reasons had disbanded and she made a choice at that time to join the Sisters of St. Mary of the Wayside. Sister Mary Claude had told me this before I left Mary's Way.

'Sister Angel is one of us now and you must respect her accordingly. She is our sister in Christ,' she said.

Sister Angel was elderly and quite stooped. She began the rosary which we completed just as the car veered into the convent drive. I looked around admiringly, acting like a visitor and forgetting my place. Suddenly, Mother Mary Thelma ordered me indoors to prepare the tea. I didn't even know where the kitchen was, how many were for tea and where it should be served.

'I'm sorry, Mother,' I said. 'Can you tell me where to go? I have never been in this convent before.'

'My dear, how remiss of me, of course you haven't,' she gushed, 'just go indoors, sister and take your things upstairs first. You will see the kitchen to your right. Hurry along now.'

What a beginning I thought as I rattled about in the most old fashioned kitchen I'd ever come upon. There was a horrible smell of sour milk and the old iron stove was covered in soot and grease. Who on earth had been here before me I wondered? I opened a cupboard but found nothing except an empty cornflake packet a few tins of peas, Bisto and an earthenware jar of rice. Was I dreaming? Was I a character in a Dickens' novel? How could I be expected to work in this place? I heard shuffling behind me, it was Sister Angel.

'I'm afraid this place is a disgrace, Sister Mary Jacob but you know all about the previous housekeeper, I suppose?'

I didn't know anything and I didn't dare ask. If Mother Mary Thelma caught me gossiping, I'd be sent back to Mary's Way.

'Look, I will help you,' Sister Angel offered. 'We will have to do something about this mess.'

Mother Mary Thelma made a grand entrance. She was a very large lady with a florid face and big flat feet. Her accent was ever so posh.

'Dear, dear,' she sighed. 'I'm languishing for a nice cup of tea. Do hurry along sisters.'

I couldn't believe how she didn't seem to notice the state of the kitchen. I had a feeling that my time in Mary's Grove would be a strange one. Each morning we had lesson during which Mother Mary Thelma read from a *Life of the Saints*. She liked to have a discussion amongst the five who were present although she herself did most of the talking.

'Sister Mary Jacob,' she asked, smiling her sweetest smile one morning, 'can you tell us anything about St. John of the Cross?'

I hadn't opened my mouth to question anything or offered an opinion for such a long time that I was tongue tied.

'Come, come, sister. You must have something to say,' Mother Mary Thelma urged. 'Tell us anything at all about this great saint. Perhaps you don't know anything at all, do you, dear?' She laughed.

'He was an ascetic,' I answered, 'he gave his life to spirituality alone and he wrote about meditation. I know that he wrote *The Dark Night of the Soul.'*

'My, my, did you hear that sisters? And what do you mean Sister Mary Jacob by asceticism?'

'Well, Mother, it's giving up worldly things, it means going without ordinary comforts.'

I wanted to add, such as a decent bread knife and a few tea towels which are not threadbare.

'I am very impressed, sister,' said Mother Mary Thelma. 'Fancy an Irish sister being so articulate. You have learned all this from Mother Mary Claude in the Novitiate of course. Am I correct, dear?'

'Oh no, not at all I smiled. I heard all of this from my father.'

Sister Angel looked at me in amazement and smiled. What I had said was a downright lie. I knew it was and Sister Angel did too. And of course Mother Mary Thelma could see through me and my cheeky attitude but she didn't know what to do or say. I waited. But she didn't challenge me, I think she was too shocked and wrong footed. And in my own exalted and far from humble opinion, she was not very intelligent. I was furious because she had spoken so sarcastically about the Irish sister. How dare she speak like that. We were not supposed to talk about our family or our past. Yet Mother Mary Thelma kept putting in little asides to let us know that she was from an aristocratic background.

'Sister Mary Jacob,' she'd ask. 'Are we having fresh carrots today? I can remember when the kitchen gardener used to bring vegetables for Cook each morning. We had such a wonderful kitchen garden at The Hall…, oh, dear I mustn't talk about this, forgive me my dear sisters.'

Sister Angel would look at me, her look saying it all.

I could not have managed without Sister Angel. Between us we served the meals on time. Gradually the cupboards were fully stocked with essential foodstuffs and the old cooker brought back to life. My only association with the babies was for fire drill and when the prospective parents came to visit at weekends. Fire drill could happen at any time of the day or night. I was assigned the cot called, St. Valentine which was in the Guardian Angel's room. I hurried there whenever the alarm sounded and took the baby in my arms wrapped in a blanket and got outdoors to the station as fast as possible. Here heads were counted by Mother Mary Thelma and when she rang the bell we went indoors and returned our charges to the nursery nurses. I loved having a little baby in my care even if it was just for a short time. I was reminded of Aunty Irene and the twins and I often wondered how they were getting on. I didn't think I was great with infants but of course I had nothing to do with them and my life had gone very surely in another direction. At weekends I had to stay for a few minutes beside the cot of this particular baby until the adoptive parents came along to visit. I was permitted to have a short general conversation with them before leaving them to play with and cuddle their future child. Three nursery nurses and two sisters always stayed within sight during these visits. Sister Angel told me that this had to be done because a woman who wanted someone else's child had once tried to take the baby away with her. Now a discreet watch was kept on all visitors.

I slept in the attic sharing a room with Sister Angel. This was irregular, I suspected. Novices and Senior Professed did not share the same sleeping quarters at Mary's Way or in any other convent - everything at Mary's Grove seemed to be more than a little bit out of the ordinary. Sometimes Mother Mary Thelma was in a black mood. It was frightening and it reminded me of those times when as a child I hid from my mother when she was out of control. Mother Mary Thelma would lose her temper and begin to shout at us. Sister Angel and Sister Sarah would close all doors and try to guide Mother Mary Thelma into the parlour from where her screaming could not be heard so easily. Once she shouted at me in the corridor. I got such a shock because there were never raised voices there. I'd left the door open and Boniface the dog, had come in. I couldn't understand this outburst because Mother Mary Thelma had that dog with her all the time except in the chapel. I knelt down as was customary to beg pardon for my transgression while Mother berated me for my carelessness. She was in full flow when the bakery van drove up and parked outside the window. Mother Mary Thelma actually kicked me on the leg.

'You are a stupid stupid girl,' she cried, then kicking me again she screeched, 'get up at once can't you see a man outside?'

I was shocked. I looked at her and I hated her.

I remember going to confession where I told the priest that I was guilty of the sin of hatred. I expected him to be disgusted but after some questioning he declared that he would feel exactly as I did.

'You know what I'm beginning to think, sister? I think that this is a crazy place. Why do you stay with the order? You know, there is such a thing as a temporary vocation?'

I'd never heard of this and I told him so.

'We all want to give something to God in our own special way but that doesn't mean that a particular way of life has to be pursued forever, sister.' He explained. 'You should think about getting out,' he went on, 'because this outfit reminds me of a cult. There are people in religious life who have too much power and in turn too much influence over the minds and hearts of others. Young girls and boys are very impressionable. Sister, I think you should leave, go home before it is too late. Leave now, that's my advice because I know that you have done as much now as you have been called to do as a religious. There are other ways to have a good and meaningful life.'

The words of the priest really disturbed me. I think my anxiety and my inner confusion caused the accident which followed. I was using a meat cleaver. I was distracted. Suddenly, there was blood everywhere – my blood. I had almost severed a finger. I tried to hold it underneath the cold tap but the pain was excruciating. The middle finger of my left hand was cut to the bone from nail to knuckle. I ran looking for someone to help me. Hearing voices I opened a door not registering that it led into the parlour. Mother Mary Thelma was seated there in an armchair with two other sisters. They were drinking coffee, the aroma of the freshly ground beans engulfed me, making me feel ill. They were watching horse racing on the television and for a minute I thought I was hallucinating.

'Leave at once, get out of here,' Mother Mary Thelma roared. 'What do you mean, dripping blood all over the carpet? My, but you are such a naughty, naughty sister.'

Feeling weak, I couldn't speak from the shock. Sister Angel ran for the first aid kit and fortunately there was a bandage in it. I held my hand aloft when she told me to but the blood kept pouring through down my hand and into my sleeve. During the night I was so overcome with pain that I had to awaken Sister Angel. Although she bound the finger again I couldn't sleep. I got up and went outside. As I opened the back door I saw in the shadow of the moonlight, one of the lay nurses with her boyfriend. They were in each others arms, oblivious to any outside presence. She looked so loved, so cared about. He had his arms around her in such a protective fashion. As they whispered together, I slipped indoors and I cried. I cried for my family because I needed them to ease my pain and I cried for Jerry Breen because I needed him to ease my breaking heart.

In the chapel the following morning, I avoided eye contact with the chaplain who just the day before had advised me to leave as quickly as possible. I was anxious and embarrassed. He knew who I was, of that I was certain. I fainted. It happened in front of him, almost at the altar. Earlier I could see how my hand was badly swollen. The pain was terrible. Suddenly I had become weak and dizzy. Sweat began to pour out all over me. The room went black and the walls which were covered in mosaics of the saints came forward to meet me. I tried to stay standing, I tried to walk forward. I heard the voice of Mother Mary Thelma.

'Sister,' she hissed, 'stop looking for notice, get up for goodness sake.' I didn't recall anything else.

I awoke in hospital where there was a drip beside me and a nursing sister was leaning over my bed.

'How are you?' She asked. 'Doctor Elliot will be along soon to check on you. You've given everyone a terrible fright.' And then she winked at me.

I'd had blood poisoning, it was under control but I was lucky not to have lost the finger. Had it been left without attention for much longer surgery might have been unavoidable. The sepsis had travelled to the glands under my arm and I'd had a lucky escape.

'It's been an anxious time,' the nurse told me. 'Mother Mary Thelma said that you cut your finger with a meat cleaver. How on earth did you manage that? You didn't come in to hospital straight away either, did you?' She asked suspiciously.

I couldn't remember very much. I recalled seeing a thin red line going up my arm and so much pain.

'It happened yesterday,' I whispered. 'Sister Angel knows all about it. You must ask her.'

To my surprise, the nurse, whose name was Sister Maria, told me that I'd already spent four days in the hospital. She suddenly stopped speaking because Mother Mary Claude was being ushered into the room.

'My dear sister,' she began. 'What a shock you've given us all. Mother Foundress has been so worried and she has been praying specially for your recovery as indeed we've all been doing. I believe you are over the worst now. How do you feel, dear?'

Momentarily, I became confused.

'Do I know you?' I asked.

Sister Maria said that I was not out of the woods yet.

'It's the drugs, Mother Mary Claude. Sister Mary Jacob is reacting badly to them and they are making her very confused. I'm afraid they're necessary though to clear the infection completely.'

As she held a glass of water to my lips I could tell that she was trying not to laugh.

'I want my mother, I want her to come here,' I cried. 'I want her to know what has happened to me. I was picking potatoes, you know. My father said that I was not to do farm work. A glass of sherry would do nicely.' I added.

Sister Maria was recounting this for me a few hours later.

'It was hilarious, I have never enjoyed anything so much,' she laughed. 'Mother Mary Claude didn't know what to say, especially when Doctor Elliot came along. You kept rambling on about Mother Mithy Mon whoever she is and you said that she was a fine ballet dancer in her day.'

But I didn't care anymore, I didn't care what I'd said or to whom I'd spoken such foolishness. I just wanted my parents and I couldn't understand why they hadn't come to England to take me home.

It was such a surprise to see Sister Davinia who had come over from Mary's Way a week previously. She was living with the hospital community for a while and working on the wards as an assistant nurse. Reverend Mother had asked all the novices to pray for me and they were all shocked but didn't know what had happened to me and they wouldn't dare ask. Sister Davinia had waited for a week before asking for permission to visit me. Mother Crispin, who was in charge, was a kind person and she allowed her half an hour in my sick room. I didn't know what to say, I didn't know what I could tell her. I longed to reveal all the secrets of Mary Grove but I was afraid to do this. I was afraid because I would be asking her to listen to my criticism of the order and of those who had control over us. I would be dragging Sister Davinia into something serious, invading her thoughts and looking for support which she might not feel able to give. I couldn't do this to someone who had been my dearest friend. If I told her what the priest had said to me she would think that I was breaking the seal of confession. It was such a dilemma because I didn't know how much Katie might have changed since entering the convent or if indeed she had changed at all? It was a terrible thing to realise that I was actually afraid to trust her, afraid to open my heart to the one person with whom I had once shared my deepest thoughts. We were together but we were also alone – in a limbo of silence. I was relieved when Sister Davinia told me that she had something funny to tell me, something to make me laugh, something to cheer me up and to stop me looking so serious. Mr. Standish Havers was the hospital's top surgeon. All the sisters were in awe of him and treated him with due respect because he brought very rich patients to the hospital. He was valued and he knew it. One morning when a very young novice was on room cleaning duty, Mr. Havers breezed in wearing his trade mark red carnation in his buttonhole.

'Sister,' he called out. 'I need a chaperone immediately. I'm beginning my rounds starting with Mrs. Hepburn. A chaperone, sister, at once.'

Well the ward sister was elsewhere and having been told to use her initiative if ever there was an emergency Sister Agnes rushed out and returned with a white enamel basin.

'I trust, sir,' she gasped, 'that this will meet your requirements.'

And this was not all. It appeared that Sister Agnes was making a name for herself. One evening when a priest asked her if she could direct him to Father John, she led him along to the toilet. Well, why not? In the convent euphemisms were used for terms which might be considered offensive or indiscreet. Imagine professional women having to ask permission to go to Father John. I couldn't believe this at the beginning of my religious life. People who were making life saving decisions outside the convent had to act like children within it. I found it so difficult to have to ask permission for the smallest thing. We couldn't have a drink of water without asking. Imagine longing for a cup of tea after a hard day or wishing that there was an easy chair into which one could collapse. There was none of this but I gradually learned that such sacrifices were just a small part of the overall picture. This was a self denial which after a time would become my second nature. Was I slowly being conditioned by daily routine and by an eagerness to fulfil the expectations of those who had charge over me? Or was I voluntarily undertaking this life of seeming contradictions? I was not intellectually ready yet to tackle such dilemmas. Of course, I knew very well that there were women outside the walls of the convent who were also leading lives of self denial because of poverty or circumstances or personal choice. I had a choice too but I'd lost the will to choose.

I recovered but I never returned to Mary Grove. Instead I was brought back to the Motherhouse to recuperate. For a while there was a great fuss made and I had to have extras. There was a glass of fresh orange juice each morning and bread with marmite at elevenses – I hated marmite. And I did not like being singled out. This was in itself a humiliation which I had to endure. I'm sure some of the other novices would have loved a glass of fresh orange juice which looked so delicious and inviting, a real contrast to rolls and dripping. I could not tolerate dripping and when I first realised that we would have to spread this on our bread, I was disgusted. The taste was utterly revolting, lingering and reasserting itself within my digestive system all day long. To overcome my loathing I developed a method of taking as little of it on my knife as possible in the hope that the Novice Mistress would interpret this as an act of mortification.

Mother Angelus always had a special breakfast prepared for her but that was different, she had initiated the Order. Each morning her aide carried a tray to the top table where Mother Angelus sat at the centre beneath a huge picture of St. Mary of the Wayside. There were three sisters on each side of her. These women formed the General Council of decision makers. There was always a little vase of fresh flowers beside Mother's place and her orange juice, porridge and toast were served by the sister who carried the tray. This privilege of waiting on Mother was reserved for one sister only, a sister who was filled with devotion and discretion. During all my time in the Motherhouse it was the same sister who day after day waited upon Mother anticipating her wishes and attending to all her needs. She fluttered around Mother Foundress like a little bird. The sisters who were Council members could have something extra for breakfast if they wished and generally they each had orange juice and a boiled egg. I didn't feel privileged by being in this special breakfast company. It was an embarrassment because none of my fellow novices had anything extra to eat not even those who were about to undertake heavy manual work. Mother Mary Claude kept a close eye on me. I had lost so much weight and I was very thin and probably very pale.

'We can't have you looking like this when your family come over for your First Profession. We have to build you up dear.'

'Does my family know that I have been ill?' I asked her.

Mother Mary Claude appeared disappointed.

'Sister, we do not think about ourselves and our own comfort especially when we are ill. It's a chance to offer up our sufferings without self pity. I do hope that you have not squandered the opportunity given to you to do this?' She added looking at me severely.

I didn't know if my parents had been told anything but I guessed that they hadn't. I was feeling guilty again. I had expected changes within myself which were not happening. I was still so self centred and so blind to the opportunities for self sacrifice – I was pitiful. I wanted my mother. How weak my sentiments must have appeared to Mother Mary Claude. I was being very hard on myself but I didn't realise it. I had a long way to go before this fact became clear to me.

At Mary's Way I was initially assigned to the library. How I loved being there amongst the books. The sister in charge was lost most of the time because she was so totally absorbed in her work. There were two other professed sisters in the library with me and they let me do whatever I wanted. It was like a little holiday. Sometimes I helped to attach *ex libris* labels onto new books or to replace existing labels which were on books gifted to the convent. Some of these books were beautiful. I loved leafing through those which showed pictures of other countries. There were many books about meditation and penance too and there also were books which were decidedly ancient. The saints were given a special section but I did notice that there was not one volume about St. Patrick or about The Saints of Ireland. I decided to ask permission for my parents to bring such books as a gift for my profession. They couldn't bring anything for my personal use but I was sure that some books for the library would be acceptable. During my library searches I uncovered books by theologians, philosophers and the fathers of the Church. The more modern writers such as Hans Kung interested me. Some dealt with the religious life in the then modern world. Such books did not seem to circulate at all. Maybe I could ask Mother Mary Claude to let me read some during my spiritual reading time. As I wondered about this I surmised that such a request might lead to my dismissal from the library for good. In the novitiate, we were handed books which were chosen for us by Mother Mary Claude. Some of these volumes were really battered looking having done the rounds and which had probably been bought second hand. Not one of these books would raise questions about the validity of religious life or the vow of obedience. They were either frothy lives of the saints or difficult to fathom methods of meditation and prayer. Even in the refectory where we listened to spiritual reading during dinner and supper, the books were light weight. Sister Gabriel obviously thought the same because one evening she caused a major distraction. She was reading to us from the *Lives of Women Saints*, about a particularly holy woman who was also a queen. This lady was quite unaware of the poverty of her subjects who were hungry and cold and who lived in shacks outside the walls of her palace. One day she came upon a clamourous group who were crying out for help as they tried to enter the manicured gardens. The queen's silk apron was filled with sweet smelling roses as she walked towards them.

'We're hungry,' they cried. 'Please give us bread.'

Kneeling down the mortified queen asked pardon from God and from her suffering subjects. She had neglected them and she was sorry. As she stood up the roses miraculously became loaves of freshly baked bread which she blessed and gave to the people. 'Such utter bunkum,' quipped Sister Gabriel. Heads were raised

Mother Mary Claude left her place at the table and sidled up to the podium. Her words were audible although she whispered. She was unaware that the microphone was still switched on.

'Sister Gabriel, did I hear you insert a word into the story, a word which I'm quite sure is not there?' She asked.

'What, Mother? Did I indeed? I don't really recall. What was the word, Mother?'

'Sister, stop playing games, you know very well that you said bunkum.'

'Oh dear, how terrible, Mother I am so sorry. I can't imagine myself uttering such a word as bunkum. But if you say that I said bunkum then I must surely have used that word. And pardon me Mother for asking but what does bunkum mean anyway?'

The audience tittered. And I discovered some time later that Sister Gabriel had been a speech and drama teacher. Inadvertently, Mother Mary Claude had become an actor on her stage. The next morning Sister Gabriel could be seen taking to the boards with her breakfast - on the refectory floor. I don't mean directly off the floor because we who had to do such penance placed our table mat on the floor first. Afterwards we knelt down to eat in some discomfort. While such a penance was not hygienic or indeed good for the digestion, it was warm down there because the radiator pipes were underneath the floor. If one was accustomed to doing frequent penances, as I was, then one got to know where to find a hot spot.

Soon it was early December. Advent prayers and chants filled the chapel as preparations began for the celebration of Christmas. The sisters who had joined the order from the Far East made wonderful decorations. They made gossamer angels with golden wings for the tree which would be placed in the sanctuary. The room in which they worked was beside the library and sometimes I was called upon to help them. I admired these girls who had come from so far away. How they must miss their own country and their very different culture. They moved so gracefully and had such delicate hands with which they produced the most artistic creations. But they were allowed to use their talents and this must have been wonderful for them, I supposed. Yet, I often wondered about all the other women with whom I lived. Who were the other artists amongst us? Who were the writers, the gardeners, the flautists, the confectioners, the seamstresses, the pianists? I had no idea and I was sure that there were many lights which would remain hidden for ever under the bushel of humility and mortification.

Christmas day was so special in Mary's Way. There was such a sense of great joy. The mass was sung and this was very beautiful. Father Philip wore gold vestments and he wished his sisters in Christ a blessed Christmas. The voices of the nuns rose into the heavens, the melodies were truly celestial. Sister Mary Adrienne almost levitated in her efforts to restrain, add tempo, exalt and encourage us while she conducted the singing. Music came from the great organ which lifted the spirit and filled the soul. Happiness was all around. Peace and rejoicing was everywhere. On St. Stephen's Day there were celebrations too. We got our Christmas presents then during a special afternoon tea. I had helped earlier in the busy kitchen where I iced queen cakes with one hand. Our presents were different from the usual tinsel wrapped gifts of home. We were each given a new pair of stockings and in one there were small gifts – elastic, buttons, pins for our veils, a hankie, suspenders, a holy card and a little bag of sweets. These were wonderful presents for novices who had to make do and mend constantly. Yet there was a snag even here – we had to ask Mother Mary Claude for permission to keep each item. And she could withhold permission or take back anything which she felt was not necessary. What a nervous wreck I became. Supposing she wouldn't allow me to have the suspenders when my stockings were literally hooked to a thread. And the pins for our veil were to the recipient a treasure beyond all treasures. How fortunate was the Novice who had a pin in reserve for the awful day when one got lost and the veil hung at right angles to the eye. But Mother Mary Claude was filled with the Christmas spirit too and very seldom spoiled our day. I suppose it made her life easier otherwise she'd have novices constantly seeking her out in the future to ask permission for buttons, needles and such sundries. We were allowed to speak to the professed sisters that evening and they came to serve tea wearing fancy hats over their veils. Some had huge straw hats while others wore little pill boxes in a variety of colours. The Asian sisters had made these wonderful creations for the professed nuns. Some of the hats looked like birds while others resembled exotic flowers. Mother Angelus surprised us by appearing in a boy's black school cap. Everybody clapped. As I stood there beside the hatch in the refectory waiting for the food which I was helping to distribute Mother Angelus spoke to me.

'Sister,' she asked, 'are you better now, I do hope that you are fit and well?'

I opened my mouth to reply when quick as lightening she pulled a water pistol from behind her back. Taking aim she squirted water at me – right between the eyes. The sisters who were watching dutifully laughed and cheered. I stood there wiping the water from my face. Mother Angelus was staring at me. I stared back. I was daring her to try it again. She didn't. I had a terrible urge to grab her, to shake her, to ask her why she thought her antics were so funny. If Colin had done this to me I would have retaliated. I saw her harmless prank as a threat, a challenge of some sort and I was seething inside. Was this just her idea of fun? Her personality puzzled me. There was always something about Mother Angelus which in some strange way frightened me.

Three months lay ahead and during this time we would prepare for the taking of our first solemn vows. Lessons became more intense. We studied the Rules of the Congregation which had been authorised by Rome. The Order of St. Mary of the Wayside was a Pontifical Order answerable to the Pope alone. Local bishops had no control over the Congregation. They could and often did, submit requests for sisters to come to work in their diocese. In this way the Order had spread from England to many places around the world. I was surprised to learn that the Customs of the Order and the Rules by which we lived had been drawn up by men. One priest in particular had been instrumental in assisting Mother Angelus to get the Order of St. Mary of the Wayside established and recognised by Rome. We constantly heard about the goodness of Father Samuel and whenever he came to Mary's Way there was an air of delightful expectation everywhere.

Father Samuel spent many hours talking with Mother Angelus and we were warned to be extra quiet as we walked past her private sitting room which was beside the chapel. A Cardinal in Rome had been appointed as our Protector and if there were problems to be sorted or requests to be made, the Mother General submitted these through His Eminence. It was a great honour to be a Pontifical Order at such an early stage in the life of the Order, Mother Mary Claude told us. But we didn't learn anything about the life of our Foundress at this time. Sister Gabriel did ask, in her own feigned innocent way if Mother had been a nurse or a teacher perhaps? All would be revealed following her death, Mother Mary Claude answered curtly, adding that she hoped that such a terrible event would not happen for many years to come.

Mother Angelus did not wish for praise or acclaim, she continued. Her dearest wish was for each sister to show such example to the world that other young women would follow their example by becoming members of the congregation too. The three vows were studied in depth now. Poverty was so essential. Its practice embodied poverty of spirit as well as total disinterest in worldly and material things. There was no point in living the simple life, making do with its basic necessities if the mind hankered for comforts. Chastity was embodied in our Love for Jesus alone. We must not admit any other lover but Him. Our hearts must remain unsullied and free from any human attachment. However blind obedience seemed to me to be emphasised much more than Chastity and Chastity was the vow I wanted to ask about. Surely it meant more than observing the sixth and ninth commandments in a new and dedicated way whatever that implied. Must I now forget about Jerry Breen forever? Would it be a sin if I just pictured him in my mind? I didn't know and I certainly wasn't going to ask. Obedience Mother Claude insisted was the most crucial vow because it released us giving our hearts and minds the freedom to adhere to Poverty and Chastity. Essentially, we surrendered all our personal choices and accepted the ultimate and only authentic choice of total obedience to the Rule. I was puzzled. I couldn't give up my thoughts, could I? I asked Mother Mary Claude about this when she, much to our amazement invited questions one morning.

'You can't give up your thoughts, dear, but you can channel them. You must learn how to think by listening to those whom God has put in charge of you. You alone are responsible to banish any thoughts or criticisms which may hinder your path to salvation. You must trust those who are guiding you, you must hear God's voice through them. This is the choice you have. Do you understand?'

I wasn't sure at all. I knew I wanted to sift through what she had said. There were more questions but I didn't know how to piece them together. I said, 'thank you Mother,' and kept quiet.

I was going through a bad time again. I was confused and frightened because I didn't understand what was happening to me. Where could I turn, who could I speak to? Mother Mary Claude had all the answers which sometimes seemed reasonable. But later, during the day or while in the chapel for private prayer I was in turmoil again. I needed answers, I wanted to understand. Did I not have any fighting spirit which would help to formulate my thoughts? I wanted to grow, to progress spiritually and I couldn't.

And then a miracle – I was sent back to the farm. I was happy again. Here I could worship and pray. I was reconnected. I was enriched again just as I'd been in my childhood. My anxieties and tensions eased amongst the familiar fields and stables. Indeed, the smells and sounds became instruments of healing. I discovered a balance in nature which restored my spirit. And I think I saved Sister Joanne's life. While I was sorting some feedstuff for the animals she had taken the tractor into a nearby field. I could hear repeating revving as the engine spluttered and strained. For some time this continued. Looking over the fence, I realised that Sister Joanne had tied a rope around an old tree stump which she was trying to loosen. The rope was also attached to the tractor. As she reversed quickly away from the stump the tractor suddenly tipped. I saw the front of it rise in the air. Sister Joanne tried to hold on. I ran. The tractor tilted sideways as she shot backwards and was somersaulted onto the ground where she lay unconscious. As she came round she tried to stand and couldn't. Oh my God, I thought, she has done some terrible damage to herself.

She hadn't. Mr. Shiels had seen the accident from the road. He was on his way to warn Sister Joanne about the danger of the tractor overturning but he was too late. Together we got her onto her feet and eventually back to the farm. Her big worry was not about her possible injuries but about what would happen if news of her exploit got to Mother Angelus.

'I will be removed from the farm,' she sobbed. 'They'll say that I'm not responsible, not fit to be in charge of the Novices and Junior Sisters. If this happens I may as well die. I can't think of not being outdoors, I'll go insane.'

'Now, now,' Mr. Shiels chided. 'We're not saying anything are we, Sister Mary Jacob? How do you think we'd manage if you were not here, Sister Joanne? I'll tell you what, have a mug of tea now out of my flask, the wife makes great tea, and, for the next few days you just take it easy down here, do the accounts or something in the office and we'll look after everything.'

'Thank you,' she smiled. 'Thank you for your loyalty and may God bless you both.'

I couldn't sleep that night. Maybe Sister Joanne had serious injuries which we didn't know about. What if she had broken ribs or had some internal damage? Would I be responsible if she was taken to hospital and this was discovered too late? What if she died? I was in a terrible state. By morning I was in a cold sweat and I had Sister Joanne buried in the graveyard behind the chapel. It was such a relief to see her at mass. She did look very pale and when she walked I could tell that she was bruised and sore beneath all the folds of her habit. From then on we shared a secret which I knew I would never reveal.

A few weeks later Mother Angelus came to the Novitiate to conduct morning lesson. We were all a bit edgy. The entire place had been cleaned and polished. A special chair, with a soft cushion was brought along from the Library and placed at the head of the table. Mother Mary Claude's plain chair was moved to the left hand side. We stood and bowed when Mother Angelus came in. We sat down when she instructed us to do so. We inclined our heads in her direction and listened attentively. Mother Angelus spoke about the three vows which each of us was about to take. There must be no turning back. We had put our shoulder to the plough and we had arrived at our goal which was to become part of the family of St. Mary of the Wayside. Each one of us was a precious member of that family and we must not lose our God given vocation. She then told us about a sister who in the early days of the Congregation, reneged on her vocation. She had turned her back on God and on her religious family. Eventually, this woman became very ill and she knew that God was punishing her. In terror, she sent a relative to Mary's Way to beg her former sisters to come to her.

'I did send two very mature sisters to the small house in the village where she lay dying.' Mother Angelus told us as her expression became very sad. 'This nun had lost her vocation. She had thrown it back in the face of the Almighty, thrown it back into the hands of the loving God who had called her in the beginning. She was crying out to Jesus now, begging Him to forgive her for what she had done. "I can't face death," she gasped. "I gave up my vocation, the most precious gift from God, what can I do? Please sisters don't ever, ever think of doing what I've done." She pleaded. "With my dying breath I'm telling you to banish any such temptation," Oh they prayed with her, our poor lost soul who left this earth in such inner turmoil and fear. And I'm quite sure, my dears that she had to pay a heavy price for her decision in the next world. Remember, as I've already said, you have put your shoulder to the plough and my dears, there's another part to what Christ said about this, which is, "if you look back you are not worthy of me." Don't look back, sisters, don't ever look back, never, never, never look back.'

Following this solemn warning Mother Angelus joined us for a rare treat of tea and chocolate biscuits.

Chapter Eleven
Commitment

I awoke long before the rising bell. Lying in bed I watched the sharp morning shadows flit across the white ceiling. It was 19th March, the feast of St. Joseph and the day on which I would take my first vows. I was not afraid any more. During the novitiate I had been tried and sometimes I had been found wanting. But I was human and so I was not any better or any worse than those who were to take religious vows beside me. I was idealistic too and my youthful exuberance could still overcome any lingering fears. Yes, there had been challenging thoughts and questions, which in turn had led to other challenging thoughts and questions not yet answered. But I knew that the answers would be out there along the wayside I must continue to travel. If there were no answers then I was perhaps asking the wrong questions. I marvelled at the calm and composure of my fellow sisters and I wondered if they'd had doubts too. Was all our piety a veneer or could I trust enough to believe that I had gradually, through prayer and contemplation begun to glimpse my God? Seeing a crown of roses on the bedside locker, I smiled. These roses had been left by Sister Beatrice who would be my helper on this my profession day. She had made the crown herself. It was a circle of pink and white roses on which a perfume still lingered. But, in spite of all the euphoria of this day, I couldn't help wondering about the thorns which would surely follow.

My parents were now in England. I was so excited thinking about them being in a hotel, a little distance from the Motherhouse. It was like Christmas Eve when I was a small child. The anticipation of seeing them soon was overwhelming and I tingled all over with acute happiness. I had not seen my mother since the day I had received the habit and I hadn't seen my father or Colin since the day they waved goodbye at the convent in Galway.

Tom had been to visit, but I couldn't wait to see him again and to hear more about Bridget. We were each allowed to have six guests. I invited Aunty Pat and Uncle William because they were part of our family too. It would not have been the same without them.

Eighteen girls who were to be professed stood in the cloister. Our helpers fussed about checking that we had our booklets for the ceremony, that our crowns were secure and that each one held a lighted candle in a silver holder. I remembered those who had left, especially Sister Dympna. I hoped she was happy. I thought about Sister Maud too and her fall from grace in the chapel. Katie stood beside me. We were the sole survivors from that horrible journey in the market van, a journey which now seemed so long ago. When the choir began to sing the entrance hymn for the High Mass we walked into the chapel two by two. Suddenly, I felt embarrassed when I thought of my family watching and looking out for me. It was such a strange and unexpected feeling. How did they see things now? Were they satisfied that I had chosen to become a nun? What were my brothers thinking as they watched their only sister walking past them, clad in white and brown and wearing a crown of roses on her head? We had never had the opportunity to discuss our life time aspirations and dreams as adults and now we never would. But this

I supposed was probably the case in many families.

I became aware of Sister Beatrice standing beside me telling me that it was my turn to move forward. I knelt down in front of the bishop and prepared to pronounce my vows of poverty, chastity and obedience in public.

'The foundation stones have been put in place,' the bishop had said earlier, now I was taking those vows which would set me free. I would obey the Lord's will and do good works in the name of His Mother, St. Mary of the Wayside. Sister Beatrice removed the garland of roses. Placing a cream coloured veil made from very fine fabric over the white one and replacing the roses she led me from the altar. I was now a professed nun.

For March it was a surprisingly warm, sunny day. I walked in the convent garden with my family. Daffodils, tulips, and freesias were in bloom. There were many fragrant rose blossoms too. 'It was heavenly,' my mother announced. She looked wonderful in a short fur jacket over a black skirt and a cream hand stitched blouse.

'You wouldn't believe it,' she whispered. 'This was May Kenny's fur. Her sister, Eileen, sent it to her from London. Mary thought it was too posh so I did an exchange with her – two new suits for one exceptional fur.'

'It is a beautiful jacket,' I told her, 'and you are by far the best dressed woman here today – apart from me, of course.'

I knew that my mother would be delighted with this praise because clothes had always been so important to her. My father looked very well too and I was so happy to see him again. He didn't have any limp and his ankle had knitted perfectly he told me. There was some arthritis but this was a common complaint in Ireland.

'You look the part, little chicken,' he laughed, 'or maybe you are more like a little pullet now especially in those colours.'

The boys were so good looking, I felt really proud to be seen with them. Colin had a sketch pad with him and he had already drawn his unique impressions of the Motherhouse. Suddenly, there was a flurry of excitement and Sister Beatrice, her cheeks flushed, approached our group.

'Mother Angelus has come outside and it's possible you may meet her somewhere in the garden. She would like to speak to all the visitors, and it's likely that she'll meet you out here instead of in the parlours later. Just thought I should let you know,' she whispered.

'Hey. What's the big news?' Aunty Pat wanted to know. 'Is it top secret, are we going to meet the Pope?'

I was about to enlighten her when Mother Angelus and her aide appeared beside us.

'Ah, Sister Mary Jacob's family,' she smiled. 'I'm so pleased to meet you, so glad that you could come to Mary's Way for this important event in your daughter's life.'

'We wouldn't miss it for the world,' my father replied. He then introduced everyone and I was delighted. My father, was so polished when he wanted to be. Mammy made a point of letting Mother Angelus know that her two sons were in university.

'One almost finished, an engineer, you know and the other just beginning. Colin, my youngest, has so many options,' she gushed. 'He is a genius.'

'Praise the Lord,' Mother Angelus' companion pronounced.

Colin smiled at them, he was very precocious.

'Indeed, Mother, believe it or not, it's true and what a problem I have. Sometimes I think I would like to become an architect but on the other hand I'm very interested in journalism. But speaking of architecture, I would like to give you these,' he added, handing her some sketches. For a second my heart almost stopped beating. Earlier, Colin had drawn some rather unedifying cartoons of nuns and I thought that he was giving these to the Foundress. Watching Mother study the drawings we could all see just how impressed she was.

'You know, sister,' she said turning to her companion, 'I will have to have these wonderful sketches of Mary's Way framed. You have a God given gift Mr. Colin. I wonder if you would also do a sketch to show the east cloister with the bell tower on the roof. That would complete a set of six, would it not?'

Everybody beamed because we were getting special attention. Other visitors who kept within view were making polite conversation amongst themselves and obviously restless because they were kept waiting for Mother. Colin turned to Mother Angelus.

'Tell me, Mother,' he asked seriously, 'why did you establish a Religious Order of women? I mean, it is rather intriguing.'

'The Good Lord inspired me, I know that,' she replied. 'I'm just a poor instrument doing His will.'

Colin persisted.

'But how did it all begin. Did you wake up one morning and say, what will I do today? Oh yes, I think I'll found a Religious Order.'

Out of the corner of my eye I saw my father take a step forward. Colin was being too cheeky. But he must have seen daddy too because he apologised very quickly, saying, 'I beg your pardon, Mother Angelus, I've been very impolite. Let me rephrase the question, please? What I'm trying to say is how I'm truly amazed by the growth of this institution. I mean, look at all the women who have followed you including, Ellie, here. It's a strange phenomenon, really, seeing all these girls walking the same, dressing the same even smiling the same. How has all this happened in such a few years? It is amazing.'

Mother Angelus agreed. Yes, it was probably amazing to those who belonged in the outside world but all these women, including Sister Mary Jacob had chosen freely. It was a life which had its difficulties and its own joys and sorrows. It probably didn't always make sense to those who didn't understand it.

'You only see the outward appearance, Mr. Colin,' she admonished. 'You do not, of course, see or understand the ascetic and spiritual dimensions to our life.'

Was Mother Angelus putting him in his place? I felt uncomfortable and Tom coughed loudly. But Colin had the bit between his teeth and my mother had that look in her eye which said, 'go for it my boy.'

'Of course, I do know that there is an ascetic and spiritual dimension to religious life,' Colin replied. 'It would not be religious life in the strict sense of the term if that was not so, would it, Mother? But what bothers me is the sameness, the conformity, the seeming importance of trivia. It sort of reminds me of, *Animal Farm* by George Orwell. It's a good book, Mother and I'd recommend it to you. It's interesting because all the animals think they are equal but they're not. Orwell says in the book, "all animals are equal but some are more equal than others." A telling phrase, I believe, when it is used in relation to any institution religious or secular. What do you think, Mother?'

'It's not the sort of book we read, Mr. Colin,' she answered tersely. 'I may be wrong but you strike me as a young man who likes to probe complex issues. Don't let the simplicity of life pass you by and don't get too carried away by the praise of others. Now I must leave you all for the present,' Mother announced. 'There are other people who have been waiting a long time to talk to me.' And smiling indulgently at Colin she began to move aside.

'Thank you so much, Mother, for giving us so much of your time.' My father smiled. Then we watched as she turned from us while her aide tucked Colin's sketches carefully underneath her own outdoor shawl. I was breathless. Did Colin have any idea at all to whom he was speaking? He was challenging the Foundress, how awful. Aunty Pat wasn't so concerned.

'Wow.' She gasped. 'Is she a formidable woman or what?'

Ignoring her, daddy advised Colin to be more respectful.

'It's all right to ask questions,' he said, 'but there's a time and a place, Colin, and it is Ellie's day after all and we don't want to spend it all with Mother General either, do we? Let's go and have a look at the rest of this beautiful place, Ellie how about showing us the walled garden for a start?'

We sat on a bench in the fruit garden, my father and I. My mother and Aunty Pat had gone indoors out of the chill which was beginning to descend. Uncle William and my brothers had decided to walk by the lakeside.

'Ellie, I do hope you're happy,' my father said. 'Remember, you have only taken these vows for one year. I believe you have to request to renew them each year now for three years? So if you ever want to come home there's still an opportunity to do so without any disgrace, you know.'

I didn't know what to say. We had been told from the beginning of our Novitiate that even our very first vows were forever. The renewal of vows, Mother Mary Claude explained, was a formality, a reminder of what we had sacrificed. First vows, second, third or final, it was all the same. Once pronounced today there could be no going back. 'It would be better,' she had concluded, 'to be lying dead in the gutter than to forsake one's vows.' Years later, I discovered that, according to Canon Law, this was not the case at all – for years I was misinformed and misled.

'Daddy, don't worry. I'm fine and I do know that I can come home at any time.' I lied for his peace of mind hoping that such a motive would make it all right. 'I promise I'll tell you if I ever want to do that. But I'm really happy here, really and truly happy, so stop worrying. And I'll be back in Galway soon,' I added reassuringly.

I left him sitting there waiting for the rest of the family to return for lunch. The newly professed had a special lunch in the refectory after which we were given permission to rejoin our relatives. My mother asked about Sister Dympna, where was she, her parents didn't seem to be around? I explained that she had left.

'I believe that she has joined an Irish Order but I don't know which one or where she is now.'

'Why don't you know?' My mother snapped. 'And why couldn't you do something like that? But of course, you couldn't, you have to be different, Ellie.'

My mother was getting tetchy and I wasn't sure what to say to her.

'And where's Katie?' She continued. 'My God, you girls are so timid so wishy washy that I'm finding it hard to have patience with you, Ellie. I expect Katie has to ask Mother General if she can speak to us or something silly like that.'

'She will come,' I said, looking at Tom who pretended indifference. We met Mother Angelus again when she came to the parlour to cut the Profession Day cake. She and Sister Christine, the senior newly professed, held the silver handled knife and sliced through the cake while the visitors clapped politely.

'Oh it's lovely to meet you again, Mother. We are very privileged today.'

Mammy spoke now using her special customer voice. For a minute I almost expected her to tell Mother that she could order an outfit which would suit her perfectly but Colin got in first. He would like, he said, to write the biography of Mother Angelus. Would she allow him to do this? It could take about two years because, as she knew, he was a student and would not be able to work on it full time. He would have to gather a lot of material, do research and set up many interviews. We were stunned and so was she.

'I don't know if it's appropriate, Mr. Colin. I do know that you would do an authentic life story but I also know, or at least hope, that I will have many more years ahead of me in which to continue the Lord's work. I've always said that such a biography, if it's ever to be done, should be written after my death.'

'Well then, how about a brief article about the Order, perhaps incorporating the first profession of Ellie, pardon me, Sister Mary Jacob?'

I knew that I was blushing furiously. Colin was so persistent that it was mortifying. Daddy did not looked pleased.

'Or perhaps I could show how this modern Order has developed,' he suggested. 'Or I could pursue a more theological angle like, let's say, the tenets of the Order. I mean, what theological masters do you adhere to? Are you and your sisters interested in the Christian Philosophers who are writing at the moment, the existentialist people, for instance? In what way does the Order cater for the creativity of the sisters? This is a big issue in schools today, Mother, even in Primary Schools. People must be allowed to express and develop their talents in all walks of life, I believe this firmly. You were surprised, Mother, by my art work. Why? Have you not seen any of my sister's drawings? She was showing great talent before she entered and she hand painted pots in the local pottery one summer which were so popular that they couldn't keep up with the demand. You have the one she did of a horse and foal, haven't you Tom and its very fine isn't it?'

'Yes, lovely.' Tom looked at me while raising his eyes heavenward.

'Perhaps when Sister Mary Jacob goes to America she may be able to pursue some art as part of her course,' Mother Angelus smiled.

'America! America! America!' – was the agonised collective cry from my family.

'America? What exactly do you mean, Mother?' My father looked shocked.

'America. You are making a big mistake, Mother.' Mammy was adamant. 'My daughter is coming back to Galway to complete her training. Mother Elizabeth told me so herself. In fact it was a condition. Her father and I would not agree to let Ellie enter the convent unless we had this guarantee. You can ask Mother Elizabeth yourself.'

'There's obviously been a misunderstanding,' Mother smiled graciously and there was a communal sigh of relief.

'Mother Elizabeth could not have foreseen what the requirements of the Order are at the present time,' Mother continued calmly. 'Sister

Mary Jacob has good exam results. We are sending her to America with the first members of St. Mary of the Wayside to be invited there. She will be a pilgrim. It's all arranged. She and one other sister will go to university in Upstate New York. They will train to become High School teachers.'

'Teachers!' I almost shrieked. That was worse than nursing. I didn't want to be a teacher – ever.

Tom spoke up.

'Ellie never wanted to be a teacher she wouldn't even do the exams for it. Why are you going to become a teacher now?' He asked me.

What could I say? I was in shock and as I looked at my stricken family I wanted to ask them to take me home with them. I wanted to be taken away from such insensitivity to be kept safe and respected but I didn't have the strength to act or even to speak.

'I've made an exception by telling you this news.' Mother Angelus was speaking again. 'Usually, the newly professed are given their assignments later in the evening when the visitors have left. This time I've decided to tell them before their families leave. America is a wonderful country, you know. We have been invited to staff a school there. All the arrangements have been made by the bishop and a new convent has already been built. Sister Mary Jacob will be going back for a holiday in Ireland. She may stay with you for ten days. Don't be afraid, my dears, she is doing God's work and He will bless you all. America is a new frontier.'

'It certainly is. I lived there myself for almost twenty years and all I can say is that it's probably better for our daughter than some of those African places might be.' Daddy sounded furious.

'Indeed, do you think so?' Mother Angelus retorted. 'If your daughter did go back to complete her nursing studies as you so ardently wish, she might well be sent to one of those African places Mr. Dardis. Perhaps the Lord has been kinder to you than you realise.' And so saying she turned on her heel and left us.

'Wait, Mother Angelus, wait.' Mammy shrieked. But Mother Angelus walked on, walked out of earshot seemingly oblivious to the cries which followed her.

'I have not finished talking to you, you cannot dismiss me like that, you have not been honest with us,' my mother cried out. 'And that same nun was horrible to you too, Owen, so rude. Did you not hear her caustic remark? Are you not going to do anything about this because if you're not then I am? And she's in charge of our daughter and she's sending her off to America just like that, I ask you. Owen Dardis, do something.'

She was becoming hysterical just as Katie appeared with her sister, her father and her two brothers. Sensing that something was wrong she was about to turn away. Tom strode over and spoke to her and Katie, knowing what to do as always took my mother to a garden bench and sat beside her. Aunty Pat sat on the other side. I stood as if paralysed unable to say or do anything feeling like a spare part in my own family.

'Oh Katie, how could you two girls enter such a convent as this?' My mother sobbed. 'Off to America when you were supposed to be coming back to Galway to finish your nursing course. I just don't believe it.' She gasped as she clutched Aunty Pat's hand.

'America?' Katie asked. 'Whose going to America, I'm not anyway.'

'There, you see, what did I tell you, Ellie, you're not forward enough, you don't stand up for yourself? See how, Katie is coming back to Galway and you – what are you doing – saying "yes Mother" "no Mother" "three bags full, Mother" and off to America without a thought for me.'

Daddy came over then and he told my mother to calm herself. She was making a scene and he was sure that everything would work out for the best in the end. After all, I would be able to see the aunties and all my relatives in the United States. I would be in New York State where they lived. It wasn't such a big place, just about the size of Ireland and they'd be able to keep in touch and to visit me as well.

'I should have known that you'd think of this, Owen. Your first thought has to be for those dolled up sisters of yours. Well, for your information I don't want them next or near Ellie. She's coming back to Galway or else we're taking her home. I want to know why Katie is being allowed to continue with her nursing and Ellie is not?' By now mammy was out of control.

Katie's sister, Mairead, who was listening to all of this chimed in.

'Oh yes, Katie is coming back to Galway and if she thinks that we'll be up to see her at the drop of a hat she's got another thing coming. It's a pity she isn't going to America.'

Katie blushed as my mother's face brightened.

'What a great idea,' she almost shouted. 'Katie would you like to change places with Ellie? It wouldn't make any difference to Mother Angelus. She just wants to oblige a bishop. She's not worried at all about people's feelings only about his.'

'Eleanor, stop this nonsensical talk, you cannot interfere like this and you know it. These girls have just made vows, they have to obey the rules and they want to follow the plan which has been mapped out for them. Stop now before you have everyone upset.'

'Now it's all my fault,' my mother sobbed. 'Am I the only one who finds the carry on in this Order intolerable?'

'You're bloomin' well not,' said Aunty Pat. 'It's like a secret society. But let's look on the bright side, Eleanor – you and I will get a trip to America out of this.'

Colin stood muttering to himself that, 'all animals are equal, ha, ha, ha.' And then Tom tried to say something to calm us all.

'Look, it will be great,' he smiled. 'Ellie, it will be terrific going to an American University. You'll have real news to write home at last. And think about the holidays, teachers always have good holidays and I'm sure it's the same over there. You'll be able to come home for much longer periods than you would as a nurse. We can go to see you as well, myself and Bridget will anyway.'

Everyone began to cheer up. Maybe the future wasn't so bleak after all.

'Tom is right you know,' Aunty agreed. 'You and I we'll go to America too, Eleanor, why not? Those sisters of Owen won't know what's hit them. You remember them asking you over, Eleanor? "We'll show you a good time," remember that? Well, let's go then. Let's put on the style and let them entertain us. What do you think, William?'

'Yes, of course. You ladies go and Owen, Colin and I will go another time. And Tom says he will go over with Bridget. God Ellie you'll having us crossing the Atlantic for the rest of our days.'

We laughed, the shock had diminished and we could look forward. I heard Katie's father speaking to her, telling her not to fret telling her that there would always be someone to visit her, telling her how proud they were of her, even Mairead although, 'she will never admit it,' he laughed.

How I wished that my mother could say that she was proud of me.

My family left that evening saying how much they were looking forward to my ten days at home. It was an effort for my mother to hide her disappointment, disapproval and anger. After all, she and my father had been given an assurance which had been so curtly dismissed by Mother Angelus. I knew in my heart that my mother would not forget this. But for the moment so many plans were being made for my enjoyment that this was at least a temporary distraction for her. It would never console her though for having believed that I would return to Galway. She envisioned a time when she could visit me regularly and where, Colin, could as she presumed call in for a chat from time to time. I knew the reality and I knew that had I been returning to Galway the rules about visiting would not make any sense to my mother and she would speak her mind. I felt guilty when I thanked God for preserving me from the possibility of such future conflict. Being sent to America was really a great idea.

As newly professed we lived in a different part of the Motherhouse and already we had carried our few possessions to the new quarters. I was in the original building in a room which overlooked the kitchen garden. The roof tiles slanted downwards and when it rained I could hear the water gushing along in the guttering. From time to time I glimpsed a small bird enjoying a quick wash in the cool water. Flying away it perched high on the roof opposite where I watched it spread its wings in the early morning sun. Sometimes I wished that I too could be free to fly away. I longed to loll under a blue sky, to be unfettered just for a while. How I missed having free time for myself. I longed for my own space in which I could totally relax. Within the convent every minute had to be accounted for. I wanted to spread my wings and I wanted to be able to dream again. But I knew that I couldn't let these feelings last. In my room with its tiny latticed window I was slowly learning to be solitary and spiritual.

Mother St. John the Baptist was in charge of all those who were professed but who had not yet taken final vows. There were sisters under her guidance who had returned to Mary's Way for a break from mission work. Others who were in convents in England or elsewhere in Europe spent time at Mary's Way following medical or dental treatment which was carried out at the private hospital owned by the Sisters of St. Mary of the Wayside. But most were like me, newly professed and ready to learn more by meeting sisters who had some experience of life outside the Motherhouse. Mother St. John the Baptist was easygoing. She had a calming effect on everyone and she was aware of our worries and our excitement. Many of us saw the future as a time of joy and exploration, an adventure awaiting us in a new place. Yet, the sisters with whom we now associated did not really have much opportunity to tell us about their experiences because recreation was just as controlled as it had been in the Novitiate. Questions had to be asked through Mother St. John the Baptist. It was ridiculous.

'Mother St. John the Baptist, please,' I had to say, 'I would very much like to ask Sister Mary Rita about her work on the missions. What is the name of the particular language which she had to learn in South Africa and is it a difficult language to master?'

And Mother St. John the Baptist would say. 'Sister Rita would you like to answer Sister Mary Jacob's question?'

Then all our attention would focus on Sister Rita while she attempted to deal with this query. I couldn't ask her if she expected to be going back to that particular mission. I couldn't ask if she enjoyed her work or if she found it difficult or the place frightening. Such personal or casual questions were not permitted. Consequently, we knew nothing about their personal experiences or the views of our sisters about any new ideas they discussed – that is, if such modern ideas shaping the world at that time were ever heard or spoken about. Sometimes, in the Novitiate or when Mother Angelus visited the newly professed sisters, tales of heroism were recited. However, these related to Mother Angelus herself or some of her cronies. Often the stories were ludicrous – about Mother tackling a cobra or Mother Rosario converting a witch doctor only to discover later that he was a missionary priest playing a joke on the nuns. But healthy curiosity about the real life of a missionary was subjugated. I knew that the life of the missionary was a combination of hard work and deprivation. Often the conditions were primitive and unsanitary. Nuns died on these missions at an early age because they had little protection from tropical diseases. Mother Angelus once remarked while giving a talk to the novices that she actually hoped that a sister would die while doing the Lord's work abroad. 'It would be a sign,' she declared, 'that the Lord is pleased with the sacrifices the order is making in His name.' I tried with difficulty to follow this reasoning and I felt very disturbed when Mother said that the work which we were doing, especially on the farm, was a preparation for such an event. But now I was professed and my inner thoughts became centred on America.

I wondered what life would be like for us over there. It was a strange coincidence that I was following in my father's footsteps although in a different way. There was a great deal of excitement about this American venture. We were going to prepare the way for the Order in the New World, Mother St. John the Baptist reminded us. We must begin as we intended to go on, faithful to our vows, loyal to the Order, dedicated to our studies, prayerful at all times and proclaiming the joy of Christ by our refined demeanour.

I left for my holiday in Ireland travelling with Sister Lucia who was from India. She was elegant and reserved. I knew that there wouldn't be any chance for us to have a little heart to heart on the journey. She simply wasn't the sort to deviate from the rules and she didn't have any sense of humour. I was unsure as to how I felt about going home again. I was nervous and excited, happy yet anxious. When I was a student nurse I loved having a weekend off so that I could go home and sleep in my own bed again. I'd hop on my bicycle and cycle to Capall Ban to see Aunty Irene and the twins. I'd stroll around the town with Judith if she was home too or with some of my former friends who happened to be in town. This visit would be very different I knew. Grandad was not there anymore and even though Tom and Colin would have time at home it wasn't likely that they'd want a nun hanging around with them even if this was something I could do. It would be strange being a religious sister while living in the same house as my parents. I would have to try to accommodate their wishes to the sort of restrained life which I had vowed to live. On the boat with Sister Lucia I prayed that I would not be seasick. Again there was no cabin booked for us so we sat facing one another across a red topped table. All around I could hear Irish voices and lots of laughter.

It was early May and the boat was quite crowded. I don't think Sister Lucia noticed this. She was reading prayerfully from *The Imitation of Christ* when a young couple came to our table which was for four people. 'Is there anyone sitting here?' A rather pleasant young man asked. Sister Lucia nodded that he was welcome to sit down. He beckoned to his wife who came over with a baby in her arms and a little boy in tow who was about three years old. I smiled at her as she sat beside Sister Lucia who didn't even look up. The man sat beside me with the little boy on his knee. The child was staring at Sister Lucia. He was mesmerised and looking up at his father he exclaimed, 'Daddy, Daddy, look at the chocolate nun!' I almost laughed.

His father answered softly,

'No, no Sean, she is a holy nun from a far, far away country.'

'Are all the people in the far, far away country made from chocolate?' He enquired.

Looking at me for any possible help the man tried to distract his son by reminding him that we would soon be sailing on the sea. The child was not fooled.

'Daddy, if I was a boy in that far, far away country would I look like chocolate too?' And then he giggled and putting his hand out with a finger extended, tried to touch Sister Lucia. He couldn't reach her and she continued to read while observing custody of the eyes. I shifted uncomfortably. I looked directly at the child's father because I felt that I couldn't ignore them any longer.

'You're a great little boy,' I said. 'Do you like this big ship? Listen there's the siren, what do you think of that loud noise? I think it's a bit like the noise an elephant makes.'

Fortunately, the little boy had been to Dublin Zoo and he began to tell me about all the animals and birds he'd seen there. Sitting next to Sister Lucia, the mother tried to keep her little baby happy by bouncing her up and down. I could sense that my companion was not pleased. From time to time the baby kicked out and once or twice she tried to grasp Sister Lucia's glasses. Later on the couple ask us to mind their seats while they went to have something to eat. They did not return to their places.

215

'We are not encouraged to entertain people while we travel,' Sister Lucia said as she looking at me from under her glasses. 'I know you meant well but don't let it happen again, sister.'

'Thank you, sister,' I murmured. 'I'm sorry.'

I wanted to ask her what it had all meant then – our pledge not to pass anyone on the wayside needing our help. This couple needed help. They were put on the spot by their inquisitive son and I had come to their aid, I had helped them. What was wrong with that? But, Sister Lucia had been the subject of the child's curiosity. She didn't know how to handle the situation, perhaps she had been embarrassed too. I felt guilty for not being more aware of her feelings.

The sky was grey over Dunlaoire as the boat edged into the harbour. Drops of rain were spattering the windows, there was a slight wind blowing. People stood aside to let us pass as we disembarked. Men, young and old doffed their caps. I was amazed and yet delighted, I felt important. A lady turning to her companion remarked, 'Doesn't she look so young?' I knew she was talking about me and I smiled sweetly. Her companion remarked that, 'the other lassie's not Irish and that's for sure.' I hoped that Sister Lucia had not heard this. We didn't speak at all during the taxi ride to Kingsbridge Station. I remembered that journey we'd made as children to get winter coats. That was the year daddy became very ill but I mustn't dwell on these thoughts now.

Sister Lucia didn't bother taking money from her bag, it was understood that we would not be charged for the journey to the station. Irish people at that time had such respect for nuns that they did everything to try to accommodate their needs. I gradually began to expect such service and to accept it with gratitude and humility.

'God bless you, sisters,' said the taxi driver. 'Please say a prayer for me and the missus.'

I adored the train journey to Galway. Seeing the green fields, the tall trees and the noisy crows circling overhead gladdened my heart. Two sisters met us at the station with the convent car and having greeted one another with a holy kiss we set off through the city. Galway was bustling. How I longed to look at everything, the shops, the houses, the river and the cathedral. I had to restrain myself and my senses and so I kept my eyes downcast. We were welcomed by Mother Elizabeth who told me to go to bed for a rest as soon as I'd had breakfast. Officially, I was on holiday but I must be in the refectory at six o'clock for supper.

'Your brother will be here to take you home in the morning, Sister Mary Jacob,' she informed me. 'I have asked Sister Matilda to check with you. She will make sure that you have sufficient clothing and so on to see you through your ten days in Eskeriada. I'm sure I don't have to remind you, sister, to observe religious decorum during the visit. If you need permission for anything you must telephone me – your parents have a phone isn't that right?'

'Yes, Mother.' I said.

'Now,' she continued, 'You do know that you may stay only in your own parent's home. You may not go someplace else to stay overnight or anything like that. It's possible too that you may be given gifts of money. Remember that these gifts are not for you personally but must be handed in and accounted for when you return to Mary's Way.

'Thank you, Mother, I understand.'

'And, sister, wait a minute. Here's a nice tablecloth for your mother,' she added, her face colouring a little. 'I believe she is disappointed that you are not coming back to Galway. You must explain that the needs of the Order have changed. We have sufficient nurses in training but we need teachers now. You are privileged to be chosen for America, sister.'

It was obvious that Mother Angelus had said something to her concerning her promise to my mother. Had she been told to present my mother with this gift? I rather thought that she had decided to do this herself. Mother Elizabeth was probably just as surprised as anyone else when she too realised that I would not be returning to

Galway to complete my training there. It didn't make much sense since I was already half way to becoming a fully qualified nurse. I took the tablecloth which was hand embroidered and very beautiful. I felt certain that my mother would love it. Whether this would be accepted as a peace offering from Mother Elizabeth was a different matter.

I knew that all the sisters with whom I had worked during my months as a trainee nurse were delighted to have me back. I was so proud to have come this far. I had repaid their faith in me. Sister Alphonse who had been my tutor, smiled a warm smile of welcome. I belonged with her now within the religious family which we had both vowed to serve. At early morning mass, which was always attended by lay nurses who would go on day duty later in the morning, I glimpsed many of my friends who had been student nurses with me. I tried not to feel superior, not to look self satisfied in my religious habit, I kept my eyes downcast and in some strange way I did feel separate from them. A barrier had risen between us. I was in their world but not of it anymore.

As I stood inside the convent door with my bags on the floor beside me my heart lurched and beat frantically when Tom's black Morris Minor rounded the bend in the drive. I could see through a glass panel beside the door that he drove with one hand on the steering wheel. His right elbow rested casually on the edge of the driver's window. It was so typical, he always drove like that and it made me smile. Mother Elizabeth walked with me to the car. Tom leaped out and I realised then that Bridget was with him. What a lovely girl, I thought. I almost envied her relationship with my brother, she was his best friend now. Bridget had an engaging smile and was quite at home talking to Mother Elizabeth. When Tom opened the car door Bridget pulled the passenger seat forward, she was getting into the back.

'Not at all, Bridget,' I protested. 'I can get into the back, it's no trouble.'

'You will not, Sister Mary Jacob,' she cried. 'You are on your holidays and you must have a good view.'

Tom laughed.

'We don't want you getting tangled up in all that yoke you're wearing, Ellie. What would mammy say if we brought you home in shreds?'

Bridget asked me if I'd had a good journey from England. She hoped that I was not too tired after all the travelling.

'There's so much for you to do during the next ten days,' she laughed. 'I hope you are fit for it all, Sister Mary Jacob?'

I asked her to call me Ellie.

'After all, everyone else will once we get home.' I said, 'and you are practically one of the family now.'

She and Tom exchanged coy glances in the rear view mirror. I was happy for them. Tom tried to cover as much local news as he could while we continued our journey. I was distracted. I was thinking of that day when my father had come to reassure himself that I really knew what I was doing by entering the convent. He'd cycled all these miles alone with his own thoughts. What did he think during his bicycle ride back to Eskeriada? What a perplexing journey it must have been for him. And if he had heard me calling him back on that same morning would anything have changed, would I have become a nun at all? He had suggested that I might go to Aunty Anna in New York and now I was going to America but for an entirely different reason. Destiny had led us both along a path which had ended so surprisingly.

We reached Eskeriada. We drove over the new bridge from where I could see the callow lands and the small fishing boats tied up at their moorings below us. It was a cool day with white clouds scudding across the sky. Tom's car was recognised and once or twice we had to stop so that I could be welcomed by old friends and neighbours.

'God bless you, Ellie,' one lady smiled with tears in her eyes. 'What a great day for your dear mammy and daddy to have you home with them again.'

My stomach was churning. I never expected this. I thought I would slip into the house unseen. Driving up the street Tom sounded the horn and nearby neighbours came to their front doors to wave to us. I waved back, like a queen. My parents were at the shop door. Daddy rushed forward to help me from the car. My mother held out her arms 'Ellie,' she cried, 'home at last.' I couldn't bring myself to rush into her arms. I just stood there like a statue until I started to cry, it was all too much for me. My mother was not usually emotional but I had been away for a long time and she was in high drama mode. She exuded gladness and affection and I didn't know how to respond. The house was just as I had remembered it but it seemed so small even though it was three stories high. Compared with the convents I'd lived in the house and the shop looked unremarkable. Even the doors which had been painted so lovingly by grandad looked ordinary.

'Ellie, come into the shop.' My mother was excited. I followed her. I think half the population of the town were in there and spreading out into the hallway and even up the stairs. Laughing and clapping, they hugged and congratulated me. Since my entry into the convent nobody had praised or admired me. Such love and friendship was trapping me and for a split second I knew what was wrong. I had lost my sense of spontaneity, I didn't know how to react, how to become reconnected to these people. They had seen me grow up and had been there through my teens. They had only too often been aware of my joys and my sorrows too. Now I was wearing a mask. I had become refined, rarefied and almost untouchable. I think my father sensed my discomfort.

'Let's have a cup of tea, everybody,' he invited. 'This is a wonderful homecoming for Ellie. She will be here now and you'll be able to meet her again during the coming days. I think there are some cakes and sandwiches in the cosy room. Help yourselves.'

Shaking hands with as many people as possible I escaped upstairs as soon as I could without causing offence. My mother took me to my old bedroom where she had left some pretty night clothes for me, a dressing gown and some perfumed soap, bath oil, and talc.

'Use these while you're at home with us, Ellie,' she was almost pleading. 'I want you to have a lovely holiday. I want you to have some nice things just for yourself because you'll be back in the convent soon enough.'

I didn't know what to say to her until I noticed my special doll, Judy under the bedclothes with her head on the pillow. Her yellow pigtails were spread out and her chapped red lips were smiling.

'Oh mammy,' I gasped. 'You kept Judy for me.'

My mother's face crumpled as she stumbled from the room. Sitting on my old bed I took the doll in my arms.

'Oh Judy,' I whispered, 'I have so much to tell you.'

Chapter Twelve
A Visitor

'Ellie, for God's sake will you stop creeping up on me like that.'

My mother was standing at the kitchen sink her arms in the air, her hands covered in soap suds. I had said good morning to her and she'd jumped. Like a visitor, I was padding about in my own home unsure about my place there.

'Sorry,' I sighed, 'I'm sorry, I didn't mean to frighten you, mammy.'

'And please stop saying, I'm sorry. It's sorry this and sorry that, what's wrong with you, Ellie? You're like a little mouse. You used to be so noisy. I'd prefer if you had a bit of life about you. I'm finding your behaviour quite unbearable.'

'Sorry,' I was almost in tears.

'Ellie, what did I just say? Oh, go on, put the kettle on.'

She sensed my uncertainty. And perhaps she thought that by suggesting a nice cup of tea for just the two of us and a good chat some sort of understanding might happen. Taking our cups and a slice of home made Madeira cake we went down to the cosy room. I was feeling so tired. Since arriving back in Eskeriada I'd had so many late nights. Nobody realised that I was accustomed to retiring at nine thirty. Staying up until one o'clock in the morning had become a penance for me because, holiday or not, I was obliged to attend mass in the local convent chapel at seven thirty each morning. People rambled in by chance to my parent's house and often by invitation to see me and to welcome me home. They spoke about politics and about television programmes of which I knew nothing. They discussed the neighbours and the sick and the dying. I was so out of touch with all of them, so removed from their interests and their worries that I was like an outsider looking in. Already I'd been escorted by mammy to visit an old lady who was dying. I'd had a harrowing session with a young mother who had lost her baby. A neighbour whose son had been killed on a building site in London sought consolation. I was ill equipped to help any of them. My mother was able to comfort, soothe, and console them better than I. She always knew what to say while I stood by fearful and silent. Whenever I did manage to utter a few words they were always the same.

'I'm terribly sorry, I will pray for you of course and I'll ask all the nuns to do the same.'

This seemed so inadequate. Why was I unable to throw my arms around these suffering souls? Why could I not suggest that we pray together? Why was I so embarrassed in front of my mother? Why was I so formal, such a misfit and so afraid that I might make a mistake? It was a consolation to know that the people I visited did not expect me to be other than I was. I was Ellie Dardis, I'd come to see them. I'd promised my prayers and the prayers of all the nuns. They were happy to be able to say that I'd been in their house, that I'd taken the time to visit and that I'd remembered them.

Through the window of the cosy room I could see Mrs. Dixon come out of the chemist shop across the road, the place where Marguerite used to work. A mother came by with her child in a push chair. Jimmy Devine cycled down the street with a little boy on the handlebars of his bike.

'That's son number seven,' my mother explained. 'Jimmy is so happy now because he has the seventh son of a seventh son. Let's hope that the boy has the cure for all our ills. There will be a few bob there if he has the gift.'

As I watched, a farmer in filthy rubber boots and with his coat tied in the middle with a piece of binder twine, drove a few cattle through the middle of the street.

'He looks very content,' I remarked.

'More content than his wife,' my mother laughed. 'He'd drink Lough Erin dry and he's a nasty old devil when he's drunk.'

I flinched. My sanitised convent mind found criticism of any person totally wrong. We had to think good of everyone we met along the way. I disliked all the gossip and backbiting which seemed so ingrained in town life and I felt ill at ease having to listening to this.

Two little girls stopped outside the window.

'They're Alice Kavanagh's twins. Aren't they the image of her?' My mother smiled indulgently.

I couldn't believe it. I had been in school with Alice. She'd been part of that group of school girls who'd lingered with me outside the cosy room window when we were all in love with Colin's tutor. Her girls tried to climb onto the window ledge and even though it was low they couldn't quite manage this. I was standing now to get a better look when one of them spied me. Calling to her sister they stood back on the pavement and stared at me in utter astonishment. I could see 'what's that?' written on their faces. Going to the front door, my mother asked them if they would like to meet Sister Mary Jacob.

'She was my little girl once,' she told them, 'and she was your mammy's friend in school too. Maybe one day, you Daisy or Trixie will be a nun. Come in and meet her.' Holding each other tightly by the hand they turned away and raced down the street.

'We'll stay outside for a few minutes,' mammy suggested. 'Maybe we can chat to a few locals for a while. May is looking after the shop today so I don't have to worry.'

It was true that May had volunteered to look after the shop whenever mammy wanted to be free during my holiday. May was a good sales lady although she didn't approve of the mini skirts which had become so fashionable. As we sat on the window ledge my mother and I were joined by grandad's old friend Jamesie. He perched beside us panting a little after his uphill walk. Some young girls from the secondary school came along free and happy because it was Saturday. Each girl wore a mini skirt. I wondered if I would have done so had they been in vogue when I was a young girl. I supposed I would have although with my now prim attitudes I thought that these outfits were immodest and vulgar.

'Oh look,' said Jamesie, giving my mother a dig in the ribs. 'Look at the one in the red skirt. I'd say that's dangerously close to the high water mark. What do you think, Sister Mary Jacob?'

My mother laughed so loudly I was horrified. What a disgusting thing for the old chap to say. It was terrible and then to ask me, a nun, what I thought. I was very insulted. My mother repeated this incident to several people. She even told daddy and the boys. I couldn't believe the coarseness of my family. Everybody laughed. It was hilarious, what a great description – trust Jamesie. It was appalling or was I too obsessed with correctness now and preoccupied with purity of mind and heart? I had become unrealistic and detached. To have sufficient sympathy and humility in an often harsh world seemed to be beyond me. I'd lost the value of a sense of humour.

When a black car slid to a halt outside our front door I realised with a feeling of dread why my mother wanted to be outside. She had mentioned a surprise visitor and here he was – Father Knickers. Before I had time to protest he was out of the car and hugging me and then my mother.

'Come inside, Father,' she giggled. 'Let's go upstairs before you scandalise the neighbours.'

He sat in an armchair leering at me. Mammy had given him a brandy. I was sipping a glass of orange. He would have to stay for lunch, my mother insisted. She was going this very minute to prepare everything – no excuses, Father. I didn't mind because I knew that the boys would be back from their tennis match soon and daddy would be in the house too.

'Ellie, you look a dream,' he simpered. 'You're so sexy although I know I shouldn't say such a thing about a nun. Are you well? You certainly look stunning even though you are what shall I say, "gift wrapped?" I'd love to be the one to unwrap you, Ellie but I don't expect to be able to do so for a while.' He laughed. 'But I said I'd have you one day, Ellie and I will.'

'So you are still pretending to be a friend to this family,' I managed to stutter. 'You come here like a sheep in wolf's clothing with the very worst of intentions. You should have yourself seen to. I could arrange this, you know. Someday you will destroy a young girl's life. I warned you before that if you pestered me again I would speak to my father about you and I will.'

My courage had returned and I felt suddenly free of restrictions. This blast from the past had awakened my long subdued real self. I spoke up now because I was not prepared to accept this sort of innuendo. My sense of justice was as real as it had always been. How I hated this man, this pretend priest this paragon of virtue to those who didn't see the predator behind the clerical garb. This realization was a new experience too. I was sad because he had probably been steered along the wrong path in life. He had been nurtured within a religious order which didn't or pretended not to see how carnal needs had become his obsession. These warped desires could eventually destroy him and others because he had the freedom to roam and to make his mischief out of sight. Which was better, I wondered, to be confined and controlled within a rigid set of rules and regulations or to be given personal space and responsibility? With sudden and frightening clarity I realised that within religious life one could not expect emotional or psychological comfort. If I could not progress spiritually against all the odds then I, like Father Knickers, could quite easily be led towards a path of darkness and evil.

I became aware of Tom and Colin standing together in the room staring at Father Knickers.

'So, it's you.' Colin was narky and dismissive.

'What do you want this time?' Tom demanded in a surly fashion.

'Boys where are your manners?' My mother had just popped in to see if we needed anything. Now her face was red with temper.

'Father Cyril is staying for lunch and we'll have it when your father gets home. The chicken will be fine and it's your favourite, Ellie, with the stuffing you like. There's roast potatoes too, Colin. Tom, get another brandy for Father, no mixer he likes it neat.'

'Brandy.' Tom looked amazed. 'Brandy and the day still so young, Father?'

'The day is young and you are beautiful,' the priest grinned while winking at me.

Father Knickers explained that he found brandy before a meal really good for his digestion.

'A very good aperitif,' he advised, 'if sipped slowly – not that I follow this advice all the time.' He laughed.

My brothers sat opposite Father Knickers and looked him up and down. I knew instinctively that Tom had told Colin everything. And I knew that Colin could be dangerous. Quickly, I excused myself and escaped to the kitchen to help my mother. She wouldn't agree to this because the priest had, she said, come specially to meet me. I must go back at once to the parlour and entertain him.

Luckily, Colin had already decided to do this. Strumming his guitar he sang:

There are three lovely lassies in Bannion, Bannion, Bannion.
There are three lovely lassies in Bannion

And I am the best of them all ...

He stopped playing.

'You know who I mean, I expect, Father. You know the three Coakley sisters who live a few miles out the road on the way to Ryanalto? For some reason I always think of that song *Three Lovely Lassies in Bannion* whenever I see you. I think I've seen your car outside that house quite often, Father?'

Tom laughed.

'An eye for the ladies, is that the case, Father? Who would have thought it? Could I make a suggestion?'

'I suggest that you all come in for lunch,' it was my father's voice. He was standing by the sitting room door. Had he been listening? I didn't know.

The table looked lovely with the new tablecloth which Reverend Mother Elizabeth had sent over. Mammy had gone to so much trouble. Could she not see what this priest was really like? It was obvious that she couldn't. Would Father like more chicken, potatoes or any other vegetable? He wouldn't – he couldn't – unable to eat another bite. His face glowed as he lolled back in the chair. He told stories and became confused 'I'm getting one head-a-step of myself.' He slurred.

'Interesting,' Colin smirked, 'very interesting.'

Daddy yawned and Tom suggested that coffee might be a good idea. We often drank coffee because it was part of my father's heritage from America. My mother explained, without revealing her disappointment that I was, off to the States. It was an honour to be chosen because I had such good exam results. I would be going to university over there and eventually I would teach in a Catholic High School. Father Knickers beamed. He went to America most summers, he said, to relieve Irish born priests for holidays. They needn't worry about me being over there because he'd look me up and bring back all the news. America was a great place, he loved it. The people were so generous. He always had a car and he got lots of gifts and greenbacks too – 'You know what I'm talking about,' he guffawed.

'Yes, I know what you're talking about,' my father replied. 'I've seen priests from Ireland on holiday relief work in the States. They do have a good time and the Americans are generous, over generous in my opinion. It's a pity some priests lose the run of themselves though. I've been quite embarrassed watching them. They think they're out in the wilds or something and that nobody notices. It's a very bad example.'

'Some priests lose the run of themselves here in Ireland. They don't have to go to America to do it, daddy.' Tom nodded knowingly.

'Tom.' My mother cried looking aghast. Father Knickers stood unsteadily and announced that he would have to leave. So rude to go so soon after such a wonderful meal, he apologised but he'd stayed longer than he'd planned and he was expected elsewhere. Colin hummed, three lovely lassies in the background.

'Now, before I go,' Father Knickers beamed. 'I have a lovely gift for you. I hope it will be seen as a gesture of thanks for your hospitality. I'm sure Ellie will be pleased. It will be something different to take her to see, something to remember.' He handed my mother six tickets. 'Oh!' He said, taking one back,

'I must have one too. We can all sit together then,' said he, looking at me slyly.

My mother was overcome with excitement.

'Tickets, tickets,' she cried, 'tickets for *The Desert Song* in the Weir Theatre in Galway, on Wednesday night, how lovely, how absolutely wonderful. Oh. Father Cyril, what a surprise,' and throwing her arms around him she hugged him in front of everybody. I felt sick.

'I can't believe this,' Father Knickers had gone and my mother was looking at the tickets almost in disbelief. 'This show was advertised, Owen, in *The Shannon Valley Times* but I never expected that we'd be going to it. I thought it would be so impossible for us to get tickets that I didn't even try. I know that the new doctor couldn't get any and he and his wife go to the theatre in Galway regularly. Ellie, this will be a lovely treat for you, Father Cyril is so kind, Owen, no matter what you think of him.'

'But I can't go,' I almost whispered. 'We are not permitted to go to places of public entertainment at all.'

'Listen to her,' my mother gasped. "We are not permitted to go to places of public entertainment," she mimicked. 'Really, anyone would think we were taking you to some sordid drama. Ellie, it's a musical for God's sake. Of course you can come, there's no question of you not coming with your family. Owen, talk some sense into her. Did you ever hear the like?'

'If Ellie says that she can't go to this show then she can't. Think about it, have you ever seen the nuns from the convent here at a show or at the pictures? Remember when Ellie's class went to Dublin to see the play which was on for the Leaving Certificate the nuns couldn't go to that even though they were teaching it? Do you remember, Eleanor?'

'Oh, that's right,' my mother shouted. 'Take her part, you always did. If Ellie is not going then I'm not either. You can phone Father Cyril and give him her stupid excuses. Go on phone him.'

'Mammy, I'm sure there's a way round this.' Colin spoke up. 'It's obvious that Ellie has to obey the rules. It's not fair to try to make her do something just because Father Knick – I mean Father Cyril has a bright idea.'

'You keep quiet.' My mother was really in a temper now. 'You, Colin, are the greatest little know all on God's earth. You think you have an answer for everything. Well, I'd like to know about this so called modern order which Ellie has joined. They're driving cars, travelling the world but not able to go to a decent uplifting musical in Galway. I ask you.'

Tom was looking desperate.

'Maybe you and daddy should go and take the Kenny's too.' He suggested. 'They would be so thrilled and it would be a perfect thank you to May for minding the shop. There are five tickets here so why not ask Majella as well. She is his sister after all and he shouldn't have left her out.'

'When I want your opinion, Tom, I'll ask for it. Who do you think you are? You were so rude in front of Father Cyril, you and your father talking about priests losing the run of themselves. You're the ones losing the run of yourselves. Father Cyril didn't give us these tickets so that we could take the Kennys and Majella to the theatre. You are all so ungrateful, especially you, Ellie. I have gone to so much trouble to have everything right for you here. I have tried to remember all the things you like and the places you might like to go and the people you would want to meet. And what thanks do I get – you can't do this and you can't do that? The fact that I'm your mother doesn't seem to mean anything anymore. I just wonder if it ever did?'

'I'm sorry,' I muttered.

'Sorry, sorry, sorry, stop this meaningless I'm sorry, what did I tell you?' She screamed.

'There's nothing I can do.' I was shaking now. 'I'd be seen in the theatre. Father Cyril would be introducing us to his friends. It would get back to the convent, I'm sure of that. I would be recalled and it would mean the end of my holiday.'

'You're sorry, Ellie? Well, you're not half as sorry as I am. I'm sorry you ever entered that English Order. I'm sorry we didn't get it in writing that you would be back in Galway to finish your training. I'm sorry that you have no spunk. And this is real sorrow, Ellie, not like your little maddening, "I'm sorry, mammy." I'm going to phone that Mother Elizabeth and I'm going to get this sorted out. You are coming to, *The Desert Song*, Sister Mary Jacob, whether you like it or not.'

'Eleanor,' my father stood beside the telephone table. 'You are not to make any telephone call which might make things unpleasant for Ellie. If she can't go to the theatre, that's that. I think Tom's idea is a good one. Why don't I phone Father Cyril and explain the whole situation. He's bound to be agreeable.'

'So it's all right to make things unpleasant for me. Oh yes, protect "daddy's little chicken" at all costs. Well, do whatever you like, I don't care anymore.'

My mother ran upstairs. The bedroom door slammed. I sat on the stairs. My father couldn't reach Father Knickers but he telephoned Majella who told him that Father Cyril was actually asleep in her house. He'd been drinking too much brandy again she supposed. She understood the situation perfectly and she would see to it that Father Cyril agreed to the new arrangements.

'Father Cyril seems to think he has the powers of a bishop,' she'd said. 'He gets these bright ideas and expects everyone to row in behind him. He should know better.' She was cross and she'd sort him out, daddy reported.

Daddy went upstairs and I could hear him talking to mammy. I couldn't hear her tearful responses but she seemed to calm down eventually. I heard my father say, 'Yes, an apple tart will be lovely when we get back. You have a good sleep now, you need a rest. You've been overdoing things – all that cooking. I'll take Ellie to see the new calves.'

We were going to Capall Ban.

'I think we need a change of scenery for a while,' daddy said as we drove along by the river. 'Your mother is very highly strung, Ellie and she's getting worse. It's her age of course and she'll get over it. Wait and see, when we get home she will act as though nothing has happened so don't you worry at all.'

I didn't answer. I didn't want to talk about my mother.

Being back in Capall Ban was wonderful. I had been so upset, so confused and so unable to cope with my mother's outburst. Here was the perfect escape. The twins ran to meet us. They were three years old now, filled with curiosity and very talkative. I had seen them earlier in the week when they were dressed for the occasion. Now each boy wore dungarees and little rubber boots. They were smaller editions of Uncle Eugene and my father loved them. He was their surrogate grandfather. Watching them walk away, each little hand holding his, I was overcome with sadness. My father would never hold my children by the hand or have an opportunity to be a grandfather to them. By joining the convent I had deprived him of a joy which he might, at one time, have expected. Such thoughts had crossed my mind before and I hoped that in the years ahead Tom and Colin would compensate him for this loss. I remembered being in Dublin earlier in that week and battling similar emotions. Aunty Pat's daughter Veronica came to show us her new baby girl. As I watched my mother bounce the baby on her knee, coo over her and kiss her, I realised that we would never share such intimate moments. This special bond of experience between a mother and daughter which was so evident between Aunty Pat and Veronica, would never happen for us. We would grow apart over the years because my experiences would be alien to hers, there would be little in common for us to talk about except memories of Lough Louchre and my school days in Eskeriada. My life would be lived out in silence and my desires, especially if these were physical, would remain forever unspoken. But I could try to be her listener while she continued, as I knew she would, worrying about us in her own way until the day she died. If I considered my vocation to be an awesome calling it was, I realised at that moment, no more awesome in its demands than hers.

Aunty Irene smiled as she watched her boys walk off hand in hand with my father.

'They are just gorgeous,' I laughed. 'They walk like Uncle Eugene and they're so busy.'

Irene had put on weight. Seeing how she'd changed in appearance surprised me. I knew very well that she worked hard feeding chickens, breeding turkeys and doing other chores around the farm. The boys took much of her energy as well. Gracie had died shortly before grandad and Irene had looked after her, which had not been easy because for the last few months of her life Gracie was bedridden. But Irene had insisted that Gracie would die with her family around her just like granny Julia.

Sitting at the kitchen table Irene admitted that she did feel very tired. She should have her thyroid gland checked. She knew this because she'd had a thyroid problem years before. It was simply a matter of getting the time to organise everything. I told her that she shouldn't wait any longer.

'Ring now,' I said, 'and make an appointment, the doctor is only a couple of miles away. You're a nurse Irene and you know that you need to have a check up.'

'I know what I'll do, I'll get in touch with your mother. I've been telling her to have a check up too. I've been telling her this for the past six months. She's going through the change Ellie, and it's not easy for her. I know that she had trouble with her nerves years ago and she's getting jumpy again. I'll phone her and we'll go together.'

Hearing her speak like this was such a relief. I had to talk to someone and I told Aunty Irene everything that had happened earlier. But I didn't tell her the truth about Father Knickers or give him this title in front of her. Somehow I felt ashamed guilty almost when I thought about his behaviour and the way he tried to ingratiate himself into the family. He'd shadowed me, followed my footprints and sought to ambush me down all the years which had followed my Saturday afternoons in Majella's upstairs parlour. No. I couldn't bring myself to tell Irene.

I did tell her about some of the attitudes I didn't like within the convent. I believed that the Irish girls were not treated as well as girls who came from other countries. I talked about the rules of silence, telling her that we couldn't speak outside of recreation except about our work. I was in tears when I recalled grandad's death and the letter telling me about it. She heard about the farm and how I'd loved working there. I was frightened I said about going to America because I'd never wanted to be a teacher but maybe this would be different. I didn't think I could manage a room full of small children but I'd be teaching in a High School so I'd probably be all right. I'd never been in an aeroplane before though and this would be exciting. Aunty Irene asked why I'd never written to her. She couldn't believe it when I told her that I couldn't get permission.

'I would love to be able to send the boys something nice from America,' I told her, 'but it's impossible. I'll ask Aunty Anna to send them a present, she is very kind and I know she'd love to do that. I know their age and their size and I'll tell her. I know that you and she could be very good friends,' I added.

'Ellie,' Aunty Irene held my hand. 'Don't worry about these things. I know that there are rules and I also know that in your heart you would do anything for the boys and for your family. Forget what your mother has said. I'm sure she is very sorry now. She has a fiery temper and she can be a bit hysterical but she doesn't mean any harm. She doesn't seem to know how to show her pride in you, Ellie. But believe me she is very proud of you. She loves you and she still sees you as her little girl. You will enjoy America, Ellie and your father is secretly pleased that you are going over there. And if you don't like it, come home – promise me.'

'I promise,' I whispered.

But I was afraid now; afraid that I'd said too much. I'd revealed things about my life within the convent I never imagined I'd speak about. What would I do? I'd have to tell Mother Elizabeth. Irene was watching me closely.

'Ellie,' she said, 'we all need someone to talk to. It's impossible to carry these burdens within yourself all the time. I'm so glad you've spoken to me. How could you go to America not knowing why your mother is so difficult to understand these days? I will not repeat a word you've said. You remember how I worried about you going to an English Order? The English have been through such difficult war years, Ellie. All that hardship taught them to have a stiff upper lip. We Irish have suffered too but we fight against life, we grieve and cry and when that doesn't work we can laugh at ourselves. But in England you've found a different outlook I think. I've always admired the tenacity and determination of the English nuns I've worked beside. They were very efficient and they were able to keep their emotions in check, not like us at all, Ellie,' she laughed. 'Now what were we talking about, I've forgotten already? – Did I say something about going to find your father and the boys? I expect Eugene is out there too.'

Together we walked to the well where a tin mug now hung on a chain. Irene lowered it into the cool water and taking turns we sipped from the refreshing spring, just as my ancestors had done in the past.

❧

From the hall door we could smell the apple tart. Daddy winked at me as we climbed upstairs to the kitchen. Mammy sat at the table, her hair neatly combed and her make up impeccable.

'I suppose, you've eaten lots of nice things out there in Capall Ban?'

'Hardly,' daddy answered, 'after that great dinner here, how could we? But we're ready for some apple tart, aren't we, Ellie?'

'I can't wait,' I smiled. 'I haven't eaten proper apple tart for such a long time. They don't know how to make proper apple tart in England, you know and they'd never be able to make them like you do anyway.'

'Oh Ellie, go on with you, now, you're a right little plaumass isn't she, Owen?'

'Indeed she is but we wouldn't have her any other way, would we, in spite of her crazy rules and regulations?'

Daddy was smoothing over life's creases again. He winked at me when she wasn't looking - we understood each other.

'Majella phoned,' my mother spoke casually. 'Tomorrow I'm going to the hairdresser with her. She is looking forward to the musical in Galway just as much as I am. May and Tony will come too and they're thrilled. Well, any normal person would be,' she added. 'But of course, you have your crazy rules and regulations as you father just said, Ellie, so I'll say no more about it.'

'When I come home next time the rules will have changed,' I said. 'There are supposed to be new things happening because of Vatican II.'

'Well, that will be welcome I just hope I'll be alive to see it. You nuns could do with some light entertainment from time to time. You all go on with so much nonsense – tell me one thing that's modern about the order, Ellie, just one thing because I can't see anything.'

She was becoming sarcastic now and fortunately I didn't have to answer because Tom and Colin came in noisily demanding apple tart. Tom told me that he'd just met Judith and Joe and they'd planned a drive for the next day.

'How would you like that, Ellie?' He asked. Bridget will come as well and Colin, what about you?'

'Count me in,' Colin replied.

'Take a picnic,' mammy urged. 'I have an extra large apple tart here as well as this one and you can have it.'

'Where would you like to go, Ellie?' Tom asked.

'To Lough Louchre,' I answered. 'I would love to go back to Lough Louchre.'

My parents beamed, Tom and Colin smiled and I felt happy. Was I being held once more in the bosom of my family? How I had longed to feel really at home. Would our return to the place of our childhood reinforce this bond? Were my parents happy to know that Lough Louchre, that once so familiar place, still meant so much to me?

Joe Kenny had a new camera. It was the latest model and he wanted to photograph everything. Before we left Eskeriada, we drove around the town and its environs so that he could set up his pictures of us and of me in particular. Everyone was in high spirits. Judith and Joe were doing a line. Tom was besotted with Bridget and Colin and

I were just pleased to be in such contented company. I thought about Jerry Breen - had I not been in the convent would we be together now? Jerry was stationed in Donegal but he'd been ill Tom said. His parents had been to visit him in Letterkenny Hospital where he was having tests. I had asked Tom about trying to visit him but it was such a long way and I wasn't sure if it was a good idea. Tom sensing my difficulty promised to go to Donegal as soon as he possibly could. It wouldn't be too far from Galway where he had part time work with an engineering company. Tom expected a permanent position there following his graduation.

'I'll keep an eye on Jerry, don't worry,' he laughed.

Colin, who had won a university scholarship, would begin his studies in October. He had decided about his future, he wanted to become a professional journalist and eventually a foreign correspondent.

'What about the life and times of our Mother Foundress,' I quizzed. 'You were very keen on writing this a few months ago.'

'That prissy one,' he laughed, 'A complete waste of my intelligence writing about her. She's Napoleon all right. God, Ellie. You've really landed yourself with the animals - make sure you keep in with the top dogs, all animals are equal and all that.'

I didn't know what he was talking about and I didn't want an explanation. Colin's subversive ideas were best left alone. But years later they did come back to haunt me.

In two cars we set off through the countryside. Tom's Morris Minor was gleaming and I sat in the front once again with Bridget in the back. I agreed to this on one condition, Bridget must sit beside Tom on the way home. They agreed. Colin travelled with Joe and Judith in Joe's Volkswagen Beetle. This was one of a few such cars around at that time and Joe was really proud to own it. It was grey with little split windows and the engine was in the back. It was a noisy car but that's what the boys liked. Colin took his guitar along, his notebook and his sketch pad. He and Joe were in competition – would Colin's art be superior to Joe's photographs. Nobody would accept the role of judge.

Travelling through the countryside I became aware of how close we had actually lived to granny and grandad. When I was a child the distance seemed enormous. Not many people owned cars at that time. Tom and Colin had been back to Lough Louchre several times to visit Mike and Mai and Mithy Mon. Unfortunately, I was too late to visit Mike. He had died and Mai had left to live with her sister. Mike's nephew, Joachim was running the farm where he had already built a new house. Reverend O'Hara and his wife had been moved to a Church of Ireland ministry in Sligo. The church which we had once seen decorated for the Harvest Festival was being renovated. The stables, now demolished were replaced by a small car park. The garden where Reverend O'Hara's prize dahlias grew was completely overgrown and the old, iron gate leading to the cemetery within the shadow of the church was padlocked.

Silently I stood looking at the house where I had been born. In my imagination nothing had changed and I expected Shep to come racing eager and barking to the gate. I looked for the hens and the red cattle in the far field but there were none. A huge steel hay barn had been erected behind the house and the three pine trees near the front path had been cut down. Cream coloured rambling roses no longer framed the hall door nor did white lace curtains float through an open window. I couldn't see the woods where Richard Meyer and I had looked for the white rabbit because the huge steel structure hid them – or maybe the woods had been cut down too? I didn't want to know.

But this place had once been my shelter and it overflowed with memories which concrete alterations could never erase, and although our bikes were not leaning against the wall anymore, I saw them there and in my imagination I saw the great heads of Sally and Nancy leaning over the fence. I tried to think about the progress of my life. How had I come from this place to a religious order and to a life of wandering from place to place in holy obedience? I remembered that day when Tom tried to hear Colin's confession and the wardrobe fell with them inside. I smiled as I recalled Tom's circus act when he planned to ride over me on the bike and crashed into Reverend O'Hara's car instead. And why, when I was sent to live with granny and I didn't get on with Sister Isobel – why had I ever thought of becoming a nun? Where had my vocation come from? I felt so attached again to my childhood home, memories of it had consoled me in a way that the house in Eskeriada never would. I had merged into the life of my family within the aura of this place, it was my heritage. I wondered how separate my brothers and I would become through all the years which lay ahead. Our binding memories lay here within these fields, these hedges, these woodlands and within the walls of a house now occupied by strangers. I knew that I would forever be a member of my family, nothing could change this. But I also knew that whatever burdens I might have to carry in the future could not be shared with them. I would miss them terribly when I got to America. At that moment in Lough Louchre, I felt an overwhelming sense of loss and desolation.

'Tom,' I asked, 'do you think we could go home on that road where Sam had the forge? You know the road which winds along by the mountains? Can we get back to Eskeriada that way?'

'That's a great idea,' he answered. 'I'll tell Joe, there's a bit of a mountain road but it comes out later onto the main road at Jameison's Cross. It's a lovely drive. Let's go.'

As I looked out at the fields and noticed the car climb higher and higher I felt totally at home. I was in a beautiful place and I was thankful to have a gift which recognised and was so aware of beauty. I wondered if everyone else saw things the way I did. I knew that my family were lovers of nature and I could tell that Bridget was also. But was what I saw the same as what they saw? Did we view the Irish landscape with the same passion and delight? I had no idea. I thought about the strange stability of these mountains and their eternal presence, grandeur and might. Within the convent I had, so far, been protected from ugliness and the sordid realities of crime and destruction. I had not read newspapers and there wasn't any television except what was watched privately by the chosen ones. I didn't hear radio programmes and I'd not had discussions with anybody about world events. There had been very little in my religious life to coarsen my mind. In the dusk of that evening as the light changed, the mountains remained calm and strong and I revered them. When the difficult times come, as I knew they would, I'll remember these mountains, I vowed silently. And like the poet, Wordsworth, I'll look to them in times of desperation hoping to hear within them, the "still sad music of humanity."

Mother Elizabeth welcomed me back to the convent in Galway. My family were with me. I would remain in Galway for five days and during this time the final arrangements would be made for the journey to America. Another Irish sister would be joining the group. She had recently come from England to have a holiday with her family in County Clare. I didn't know her because she had been professed some years before me but I learned that she was a teacher who had qualified in London. Mother Elizabeth treated my family to a lovely tea after which she sat and talked to us for some time. My mother was anxious to know when I would be back from America for holidays. She was told gently that Mother Angelus, who was travelling with us to America – to see us settled, would let her know about this. There were three sisters already in New York getting the convent furnished and sorting out educational matters. Altogether seven sisters would leave from Shannon Airport, including Mother General and her assistant, Mother Conchita. They would both return after two weeks. I absorbed all this information and wondered if Mother

Elizabeth was revealing the details for my benefit also. I would not see my family again before leaving Ireland and our goodbye's were emotional. Daddy sent his love to the girls and their families. I must phone them, he said, if I needed anything. I had their phone numbers hadn't I? Tom whispered that Joe was trying to get the photographs he'd taken developed quickly. If he managed to do this, he and Tom would hand them in at the convent before I left for the States.

'Don't forget,' Colin reminded me, 'that you'll have lots of visitors and make sure you don't develop that awful American twang.'

'I've had a wonderful holiday,' I was trying not to cry. 'I'll write and tell you everything about the journey and about West Cranberry. I will describe it all and Colin, we can compare notes about university life.'

I laughed, then adding that I just hoped I'd understand the lectures. My mother was blowing her nose as she got into the car.

'Ellie,' she called, 'you know how I wish you were not going so far away. I'm still very upset, you know. I will see Mother Angelus about your holidays she's not going to pull the wool over my eyes again. Don't worry, Ellie, we'll be meeting you at Shannon next summer, mark my words.'

'Don't worry about me,' I answered tearfully. 'I will write and I'll have lots to tell you all.'

When they had gone I discovered that easing back into convent life was simple. I was actually glad to have some respite from the constant chatter, tea drinking and business of home. Once again there was a sense of balance within the day. I had gladly left behind the hidden social undercurrents which flowed beneath town life. I was away from the outside world, safe within the predictable patterns of religious life.

Our flight from Shannon was scheduled for midnight. It was Saturday and we were to have some sleep beforehand. At three o'clock on that afternoon four sisters went to bed. Mother Angelus told us that we would be called at eight for a special supper with Mother

Angelus and Mother Conchita before our departure. The suitcases were lined up in the convent hallway - having been checked and rechecked. Mother Angelus had arrived the day before and had been greeted with all due ceremonial. Sister Jude, the other Irish sister would travel directly to Shannon Airport from her home. I hoped my mother would never hear about this.

'Sister Mary Jacob,' wake up.

It was the voice of Mother Elizabeth. Had I been asleep for so long, I couldn't believe it.

'Wake up, sister,' she called again. Opening my eyes I asked her if we were leaving now.

'No, dear,' she replied, looking at me very seriously. 'Mother Angelus wants you and all the other sisters in the refectory at once. Get dressed, sister and hurry downstairs. Don't keep Mother waiting.'

Feeling groggy and disorientated, I took my place at the long, wooden refectory table. Mother Angelus was seated at the top. Mother Conchita and Mother Elizabeth were seated on either side of her. I glimpsed Sister Davinia and the other nuns whom I expected had been awakened before the usual call for night duty. It seemed that all the sisters who were available had been rounded up and ordered to attend this gathering. What was going on? Mother Angelus was staring at me. Why? I lowered my eyes and shifted nervously.

'Sisters,' Mother Angelus began, 'a member of our congregation has behaved disgracefully. This is a sister in whom I had the utmost confidence. She is one of our pilgrims, one of our sisters who will be going to America. This would not be happening, I can assure you, had I known that she cannot be trusted. Unfortunately, with all the documentation in place and the flight booked I cannot change things now. But, Sister Mary Jacob, you are leaving here with a stain on your character. You are a great disappointment to the congregation. Do you not hear me speaking to you, sister? Kneel down at once.'

Chapter Thirteen
America

I felt faint. My thoughts were blurred. I couldn't think logically. I was aware of the angry voice of Mother Angelus. I was disgraced and all the sisters I knew in Galway were witnessing my fall. But what had I done? Mother Angelus addressed me, 'Sister Mary Jacob, look at this.'

I stared ahead and in her quivering hand I saw a photograph which Joe Scully had taken on the day we went to Lough Louchre. I stood tall and solemn, my hands enfolded in the sleeves of my habit beside Sergeant McEvoy. To the right of the picture a young Garda saluted. I couldn't believe my eyes. How had Mother Angelus come upon this photograph? And then I remembered. Joe, probably in Tom's company, had handed the photographs in to the convent. Of course, Mother Elizabeth had given the package to Mother Angelus who had opened it.

'Who are these policemen, answer me?' Mother Elizabeth demanded her voice rising sharply.

'Mother,' I whispered, 'that's Sergeant McEvoy, Judith's father. He is a good friend of our family.'

'A good friend of our family,' she mocked. 'This is your family now, sister and we don't know him, do we, sisters?'

'No, Mother,' a few voices answered.

'I am horrified by your lack of judgement, Sister Mary Jacob,' Mother Angelus continued. 'You are a sister who will have to be watched. You are a sister who cannot be trusted alone. Did you ask Mother Elizabeth if you could have your photograph taken?'

'No, Mother.'

'Mother Elizabeth, did you tell Sister Mary Jacob to telephone you if she wanted permission for anything or if she needed your advice?'

'Of course, Mother,' Mother Elizabeth answered sadly.

'And of course, you didn't do as you were told, sister. You had every opportunity to find out if being photographed was permissible. You didn't find out, did you, sister?'

'No Mother,' I replied.

'I am almost too horrified to look at some of these pictures, sisters.' Mother Angelus was unstoppable now. 'I don't think I should display them because they are quite scandalous. But I will show them because I want you all to know that Sister Mary Jacob has no strength of character. You couldn't say no, could you, sister? Your vanity has led you astray.'

Feeling as though I was in a trance of some sort, I had to remain kneeling while the rest of Joe's beautiful photographs were held up to gasps of horror. There I sat on the wall at the back of our garden. Luckily, the ladder which I had to climb to get there was not in the picture. But my feet were dangling and Colin sitting on the right side of me and Tom on my left held huge ice cream cones aloft. Naturally, I had an ice cream cone too but I was licking mine and obviously enjoying it. What would my lovely family think if they knew that a picture of them was being held up in the convent refectory as an example of my inordinate sin of pride? Another photograph showed me sitting on a garden bench in my father's flower garden between my parents. And behind me in the picture my brothers smiled gladly for the camera. How could this be wrong?

'And what is this?' Mother Angelus shouted. 'Surely sister, you were not visiting a horse riding stables? Were you,' she spluttered, 'horse riding?'

I couldn't believe how she thought of such a thing. The horse looking over the half door was obviously a farm horse. His grey muzzle and rheumy eyes a sure sign that he was retired. Hanging haphazardly from his mouth were a few strands of hay which made the horse look comical. I leaned against the old school door, my head just level with the horse's nose. I remembered Joe's complaints when he was taking this photograph.

'The old bugger won't smile,' he'd laughed

'No, Mother,' I mumbled. 'That is not a stable that is an old schoolhouse. It's where I once went to school. There's a new school…'

I heard a nervous titter and stopped. The disciplining of Sister Mary Jacob was becoming a charade. Mother held up more photographs and I had to explain the location, the characters and any possible reason as to why I should be featured in them. I was getting tired. I wanted to run from the refectory never to return. I was supposed to be going to America. This should have been a tremendous step forward on my religious journey. But I was castigated because I hadn't realised that there was a no photographs rule. This hadn't crossed my mind at all. I'd seen photographs of Mother General receiving important visitors. I'd seen photographs of other nuns too with people I'd assumed were family. Sometimes Mother General posed with a bishop and often a group of sisters were invited to join them for a group photo. I had been photographed by the bishop of Melbourne when he visited the convent farm. I could be photographed with pigs and cows and sheep but not with my own family. In the film which had inspired my vocation, the sisters were shown in the company of lay people and were seen singing and learning local dances. I couldn't reconcile this with the outcry over a few innocent photographs.

Often, during the years which followed this incident in the refectory, I considered what choices I had at that time. Why hadn't I done something? I hadn't because the hurt which I was experiencing then shattered my mind and heart. I was incapable of action. Often, I imagined myself running from the convent to the front desk in the hospital. Here, in my day dream, I asked Annie Doyle, the night receptionist, to let me use the phone. I phoned my parents begging them to come for me. Or sometimes I saw myself escaping to the small shop across the road where as student nurses we bought apples for an afternoon snack. I'd ask Mrs. Cody to hide me in her back kitchen until my parents who had been alerted came to fetch me. Often my escape route led me to the chaplain's quarters where I told him everything. He would be shocked, of course and he would insist on seeing Mother General so that he could give his opinion about this fiasco. And sometimes, I saw myself running into the streets of Galway, my habit flying in the wind – running and running until I reached the Atlantic Ocean where I jumped in to the crashing waves. Such memories were sore and sad. How I berated myself from time to time for not having had enough courage to go to the telephone in the convent and without any permission, calling my parents to come to my rescue. I could see them arriving and I even heard in my subconscious their bitter words. They would not have their daughter subjected to such abuse. How dare Mother General deceive everyone about the happy family spirit within her religious order. How glad they were that I had the good sense to phone them. They would tell everybody they knew to avoid these nuns at all costs. They would make sure that Colin wrote a true account of their practices in *The Shannon Valley Times,* these thoughts would drift on and on and on because there had been no courtesy or grace in the language used to deride me. I couldn't stand up to the injustice done to me because I didn't know how to. But was it an injustice? Or was this another trial from which I had to learn humility and graciousness?

When Mother Angelus had displayed all the offending photographs she was sated. I knew that the sisters who had been called to the refectory were not happy. I had ruined a visit from Mother General. I had caused her to become angry on the eve of beginning a new mission. I, who was one of the chosen ones, had failed them all. As Mother Conchita led Mother Angelus from the refectory she walked as if the whole weight of the world had collapsed around her. Her head was bowed her demeanour one of total and acute disappointment. Her lips moved in silent prayer for the salvation of my soul. I was ordered to the chapel where I was to remain until it was time to leave for the airport. A senior sister was appointed to stay there with me. I was not to move without permission. Mother Elizabeth came in silently. I heard her voice before I was aware of her presence.

'Sister,' she whispered. 'Don't worry about the photographs I will fix it all up with your mammy.' And she was gone.

Mother Angelus had ordered the destruction of all the photographs in Galway. My mother was to be contacted and asked to send on the negatives. She would think that they wanted copies made. Nobody asked me who had taken the pictures in the first place and I didn't say that these belonged to a young man named Joe Scully.

Later, as I sat in the back of a car, I watched while my companions received the kiss of peace and a holy embrace from their sisters. I was excluded and this exclusion hurt. Mother Angelus was assisted into the front seat of the car, her habit arranged discreetly around her ankles and a light rug placed over her knees. Mother Elizabeth would drive. On my left, Mother Conchita sat upright and attentive. On my right Sister Mary Agnes held three large brown leather bags one belonging to each superior. As the car slid away from the convent door I tried to look back but I couldn't because I was in the middle and wedged tightly. I knew that my fellow travellers were in a following car which also carried suit cases and bags. It was dark now and the night was dreary and uninteresting. There were no stars visible and as we left the city a mist rolling in from the sea enveloped us.

I felt so lonely, so filled with pain that I couldn't see anything to look forward to. I didn't want to think about the flight or what it would be like to soar into the sky and to be taken so far away from home. My imagination had deserted me. My sense of adventure had become stunted. I was carried along and I didn't care about my destination anymore. This journey should have been a highlight and an achievement but I travelled like a branded creature with all my weaknesses and shame exposed. Mother Angelus began reciting the rosary. When it was my turn to lead the prayers my voice sounded hard within the confines of the car. The words I uttered were cold and lifeless, without inner light and without feeling.

We reached the airport departure lounge. It was bright and airy. Waddling about we resembled prehistoric birds suddenly awakened after a long, long sleep. I looked at the four sisters who were travelling to America with me and I was taken aback. Each of us had been told to wear extra clothing because there were so many suitcases, so many bags and so many packages that weight had become a problem. Underneath my habit I was wearing a long flannelette nightdress. On top I had a wool cardigan which fastened at the neck. We each wore a long, brown, thick woollen cloak and our heavy winter shoes and long wool stockings. We were melting. We looked crumpled, untidy and dazed. Of course, Mother Angelus and Mother Conchita appeared perfect, they were not wearing any extra clothing, their habits were not creased, they moved gracefully.

Sister Jude arrived with her family. I watched them stream in behind her. She had, I realised, many siblings who were present, some with wife or husband. I had asked if my family could come to Shannon but I'd been told, 'no.' Our departure was to be quiet and dignified without any emotional farewells. Yet Sister Jude could have all these people with her. Why? I stood aside as directed and watched. I was a separate being belonging yet not included. Seeing me looking so forlorn and quiet, Sister Jude's father crossed the floor to where I stood.

'Sister, you look a little pale and nervous, are you afraid of flying?' He enquired.

I stared at him my thoughts poised between guilt and anxiety. I was afraid to speak.

'It's all right, sister,' he smiled. 'Actually, it's a great experience and you'll enjoy it. I've flown lots of times myself and I wish I was off to America now. Hey, come over and meet the wife, she'll give you some tips so that you won't be so worried. Come on.'

As I manoeuvred unsteadily towards the group Mother Elizabeth called my name.

'Sister Mary Jacob, you are to be checked in first. It's being done alphabetically. Your surname begins with D – Dardis. Come along, sister.'

'Dardis!' Sister Jude's father exclaimed. 'I have a good friend named Dan Dardis, would you happen to know him, sister?'

Looking desperately at Mother Elizabeth, I told him that Dan Dardis was my uncle. He was delighted and insisted on walking with me and Mother Elizabeth until we reached the check in desk.

'Her uncle is a sound man,' he told Mother Elizabeth. 'What a great business he's built up. I get all my horse boxes from him you know and he's never let me down. Someday we're going to Cheltenham together. I can't wait to tell him about this – what a coincidence – fancy meeting his niece here. And a fine lass you are too,' he added.

Mother Elizabeth smiled as she watched the scrutiny of my documents and the eventual handing over of my ticket to America.

'Next,' the check in girl announced, 'is Sister Jude Finnerty.'

Immediately, I knew who they were. The Finnerty's owned well established stables. They were horse breeders of distinction, their horses winning all over the country, in England and even abroad. They were wealthy and famous, their fame ensuring a right to bid their daughter farewell at the airport. Would my mother hear about this? I hoped not. But there was confusion at the desk where members of Sister Jude's family had gathered around her. She was searching frantically for something and rummaging over and over in whatever pockets she could reach. She too was overdressed for the occasion. It was her health certificate which couldn't be found. It was not with all her other documents and she couldn't enter America without it. Two sisters were sent with her to the Lady's Room. Their mission being, to sift through all of Sister Jude's attire until the document was located. Waddling back sometime later they admitted defeat. The other sisters were then dispatched with everyone hoping that the earlier party had missed something. Fervent prayers were being offered to St. Anthony while fellow passengers asked if all the sisters had suddenly taken ill. I wanted to laugh. I just wanted to hold my head back, to look up at the high ceiling and laugh and laugh as loudly as I could. There would be a wonderful echo. I wanted to do something spontaneously I wanted to really shock everybody. I didn't know how to handle the unreal situation in which I found myself. I was becoming frantic and panicky. I thought I was going mad. But when I tried, I couldn't hold my head back. The thick cardigan with the heavy cloak over it had reduced my neck space. My neck seemed to be resting on my shoulders. I had no neck. Then slowly and with great resignation the search party returned defeated. Sister Jude was crying. Mother Angelus' face was flushed and I was glad, glad that I was not the only one in trouble.

'What's wrong, Pet?' Mrs. Finnerty asked her daughter.

'Oh mammy,' she sobbed. 'I can't go to America, they won't let me in.'

'What are you talking about, why can't you go?' Her puzzled father asked.

'I can't find my health certificate, it's missing it's not with my other documents. It's not with my passport or in with the visa or anywhere else. We've searched and searched, it's missing.'

'Well, wait a minute sure I have an envelope here in my bag.' Announced Mrs. Finnerty. 'You gave it to me to mind for you, Pet. Don't you remember? Maybe that's what you're looking for?'

It was. Mother Angelus smiled and thanked the Lord.

Inside the aeroplane we struggled to get up the aisle. I sat beside a window with Mother Conchita beside me and Mother Angelus at the aisle seat. I was wedged into my place. When we were advised to fasten our seat belts I had great difficulty trying to locate it. I thought Mother Conchita had taken part of mine but I didn't dare say so. Eventually after much struggling and great efforts not to hit Mother Conchita in the ribs I was belted in. Across the aisle my companions sat in rows of two seats. I thought about Mother Elizabeth and the three sisters from the Galway convent who were probably half way home already. Why hadn't I insisted on returning with them? I tried to look out but the window was small and the early light outside was dull and grey. There was noise and shuddering. Smiling air hostesses walked around checking things within the cabin. We waited. Suddenly there was a great roar and I felt the plane move. It gathered speed gradually until we were racing down the runway. I felt excited for the first time in what appeared to have been hours and hours of tension. The plane banked, gathered momentum, sped along and nosed upwards. We soared into the sky. My stomach shot like a fiery liquid into my chest. I became light headed. As the noise and speed mingled my heart leaped. This was wonderful, it was truly amazing. Down below in the first light of an emerging dawn the River Shannon sparkled like scales twinkling on a great fish. Larger lights could be seen over Limerick and then we were gone.

We flew into the morning out over the Atlantic, upwards amongst the dimming stars and ever onwards towards New York. During the flight I drifted in and out of sleep. I dreamt about Lake Ailing. I saw the water hens with their tails up as they fished along the murky edges of the lake. The long reeds whistled in the wind and a low moaning sound crept from the surface of the water. I was trying to cross on the stepping stones which lay in an islet cut away by the flowing water. My arms were outstretched for balance and someone was holding my hand. It was Mother Conchita.

'Sister, stop that.' She ordered. 'You are disturbing our meditation, can you not sit quietly?'

'Mother, what is Sister Mary Jacob doing now?' Asked Mother Angelus. 'I hope she is not causing more trouble. Did I hear you cry out, sister?'

'I don't know.' I answered. 'I think I may have, Mother, when I was asleep.'

'Asleep! Sister, stay awake and praise God for this journey. Pray that you will be worthy to do His work. I still have grave doubts about you, Sister Mary Jacob. You will have to do penance for your disobedience. When we get to the convent in America you are to have your meals off the floor for one week. I will tell Reverend Mother Paula all about you, sister.'

The smiling hostess arrived with our meal. Perhaps I should ask about having it off the aeroplane floor. I imagined trying to stand up, trying to cross seats while carrying my tray and while swaddled in so much clothing. I could ask the hostess to clear a space for me and I'd have to explain my behaviour to all the passengers. Maybe Mother Angelus would provide a commentary. This was my first in flight dinner. At any other time I would have been intrigued. It looked so appetising, the blue green tray and the pretty cutlery setting off the covered dishes to perfection. But I wasn't hungry. I was filled with loathing. I observed Mother Conchita as she leaned to one side opening Mother Angelus' table napkin, setting out her knife and fork and taking the covers off her food. Why doesn't she eat it for her I thought sarcastically? I realised at that moment that I despised these women. I despised what I saw as a pseudo piety. I was filled with disdain for their superiority. Could they not let go? Why did

Mother Angelus have to go on and on about my wickedness. Why was everything taken to extremes within the Order? And where did holy poverty and simplicity fit in to the picture? These women were used to flying to various parts of the world, visiting convents, receiving accolades from church men and politicians, escaping the daily routine while arriving on red carpets to chasten the perceived guilty ones – the ones who were keeping the show on the road. They were written about in newspapers, they were interviewed, they were important. I sat there chewing but not tasting because I was consumed with bitterness.

☙❧

Father Benedict Ryan was very tall. And although he was not an old man his hair was snow white. He was dignified and welcoming. He wore a well pressed clerical black suit and a roman collar and his black shoes shone in the early morning heat. And it was hot. I couldn't believe it. I thought I would pass out. Here we were, the pilgrims coming to West Cranberry and dressed for the deep mid winter. The warm air felt suffocating, there wasn't a breeze anywhere and there wasn't any shelter where we waited for the cars. What did the parish priest think of his good sisters? What did he think when he saw us struggle through from immigration? Mother Angelus was leading the procession with Mother Conchita by her side. A grotesque company followed behind them. We looked half asleep, our clothes were creased our brows damp from perspiration and our hands were hot and clammy. Mother Angelus had been disgusted when she viewed us before we left the airport. But what could we do? We shuffled along keeping together as directed in an effort to conceal our dishevelled appearance. It was a total embarrassment. Two cars arrived to take us to our new convent. Each car looked like a miniature aeroplane. If only Tom and Joe could see them. These vehicles were so comfortable and roomy with welcoming fresh air coming in through special vents. Father Benedict asked us if we'd like to have breakfast. Mother Angelus answered abruptly. 'We've had an adequate breakfast on the plane.' She said.

'Sisters, anyone care for coffee? We could stop for some at a Rest Area later and have some pancakes – how about that?' He smiled.

'Gee, that's a super idea Father Ben,' the young curate laughed as he looked expectantly at us. 'I fancy some pancakes real bad.' And he winked.

We remained silent but some of us smiled until we saw that Mother Angelus was observing us. I knew then that there wouldn't be any pancakes. Mr. Cummins, a parishioner from West Cranberry, drove the car which took us onto the highway. Mother Angelus and Mother Conchita travelled ahead with the priests.

'You will be able to answer some of my questions as we travel.' Mother Angelus had said to Father Ryan. 'Of course there are many things which we will discuss later – of a private nature – but we have an opportunity now to cover some minor details.'

'Sure Mother, that's no problem,' he replied adding that he wondered if Father Palmer might travel with the young sisters. 'He will tell them all about the places through which we will be driving. He's quite an expert on New York State. And Mother,' he added, 'why not call me Father Ben and Father Palmer, Father John? All our parishioners do, you know.'

'Well, actually, I would like to have Father Palmer with us I would like to know about New York State myself, if you don't mind.' Mother Angelus replied while ignoring completely his suggestion of informality.

Soon we had left the city behind with its noise and heat and bustle, its yellow taxis and skyscrapers. I saw signs for Howard Johnson's ice cream and Dunkin Donuts. My mouth watered but there were no stops at any Rest Area along the route. However, New York State was so scenic it almost took my breath away. I never expected to see forests and lush farm lands with apple orchards and maple trees. Mr. Cummins pointed to the Hudson River which carried ferries and barges and larger vessels as it made its way to New York Harbour.

'It rises in the Adirondack Mountains,' he explained and, 'guess what, its tributary flows through West Cranberry, you will see it later?'

When we exited from the highway we drove through small neat towns and little villages. I was delighted. This was not the America I'd been thinking about. This was a peaceful place I realised as we drove through such a rural and picturesque environment. Here, houses were painted beautifully with wooden clap board sidings. There were neat lawns and children's bicycles propped against white fences. These scenes reminded me of the yearly calendar which Aunty Anna always sent. West Cranberry was a suburb of the city of Albany and following three hours of driving we were glad to be home. But the convent although newly built was a huge disappointment for me. We didn't reach it by driving up a shady avenue or find it nestling behind the old church. It stood directly off the main street, in full view of all the passing traffic. Behind the convent the priest's house was sheltered by a group of trees but we had nothing to shade us from the hot sun. There was a glare from the asphalt of a parking lot which edged close to the back of the convent. Indeed it appeared that our home had been built here on a number of parking spaces. There was no fencing, no lawn and very little space for one. And not a single tree or shrub to call our own. Inside, the building was modern, functional and split level in style. The chapel was pleasing with purple grapevine etchings on the long windows and beautiful carved wooden stalls. The kitchen, which was downstairs was white and bright and even had a dishwasher. But the recreation room and the refectory had not been approved by Mother Paula. In the basement, I spied armchairs and softly padded dining chairs which were being returned to the store from which they had come. Such luxuries would have no place in our life of austerity and penance. Upstairs, the bedrooms or cells, as we called them, were very attractive, painted in pastel shades with floral curtains as well as Venetian Blinds on the windows. I opened the wardrobe door and discovered a sink and a vanity unit as well as storage for our clothing. But there wouldn't be any vanity here – the mirror had already been painted over with white paint.

Mother Paula was the superior in West Cranberry. I was introduced to her by Mother Angelus almost as soon as we arrived.

'This,' she said, 'is Sister Mary Jacob.' Mother Paula smiled momentarily.

'She,' Mother Angelus continued, 'is a very disobedient sister. I'm having many regrets about her being here at all, Mother. She cannot be trusted and you will have to watch her closely. The bishop has put his faith in us to choose sisters who will do well in university and who will be a credit to the parish high school in the future. I greatly fear that Sister Mary Jacob will let us down. I am praying earnestly that this will not happen, Mother. She is to do penance, Mother, for the scandal she has given.'

'Yes, Mother. I will see to it that Sister Mary Jacob upholds the dignity and spirit of the Order here in America. Don't worry, Mother, I'm sure she will soon learn from the good example of the other members of the community here. They are all exemplary sisters, I'm sure of that. I am quite confident about them.'

I stood there forlorn and unhappy. What a shallow existence lay before me now. I'd be living here in this convent under constant and close observation. I became over anxious and very angry. I had no one to turn to, no one I could trust. I didn't know what choices I might have. The severity of Mother Angelus' reprimands and her publicly stated opinion of me had shattered any self confidence I might have possessed. She had made a public outrage out of what had been a private experience with my family. Even here, thousands of miles away from my birthplace, her tongue lashing fettered me. I couldn't distinguish between the outward humiliation and the potential for any spiritual growth emerging from this. I craved support and guidance. I needed to be able to enter my own heart and soul. But my heart was tightly closed and I was hollow inside. I'd hoped for peace and joy in religious life but this wasn't happening. I was vulnerable and I could think only of escape. My first meal in our American convent was taken kneeling on the lovely hard wood polished floor. But I was happy down there because I felt safe and out of sight, away from the self righteous. Speaking was permitted but I was excluded. After lunch Mother Angelus decided that there should be a tour of the new school. I joined the others until Mother Paula called me to one side.

'Sister, dear,' she said, 'you can see the school at some other time. You will not be teaching there for years anyway so it's not of immediate importance that you should see it now. Tonight we're having a typical English dinner in Mother's honour. We'll have roast beef with all the trimmings. I want you, sister, to prepare the vegetables. You'll find them left out in the larder. When you finish this task, sister, you may have a siesta. Be very quiet going upstairs, dear. Mother Angelus and Mother Conchita will be resting. Is that clear, dear?'

'No Mother,' I answered with contempt. 'It's not clear at all. I haven't a cat's notion of preparing any vegetables for Mother Angelus or anyone else.' I was glaring at her. 'You will have to ask someone else to do them, maybe one of your exemplary sisters will be happy to oblige. But I'm not staying here. I hate this place. And you can stop calling me, "dear," because I'm leaving.'

'Sister Mary Jacob,' she hissed. 'How dare you answer me in that fashion? Have you taken leave of your senses? You will do as you are told and thank God that you are here in America at all. From what I've heard you are not fit for the responsibility which you have been given.'

We were standing at the top of the stairs which led to the lower level of the convent. Mother Angelus and her retinue were about to ascend to where we were. Mother Paula suddenly grabbed my wrist and pulled me to one side in order to make room for them. I slipped over the edge of the step and tumbled to the bottom. Luckily, I didn't drag anyone along with me. Astounded, Mother Angelus peered at me while Mother Paula directed the others to the front door. How dare Mother Paula put a hand on me. I stood up.

'I can't believe this, Mother. Sister Mary Jacob is already showing her true colours. She has actually refused to prepare the vegetables for the evening meal. I can't believe her insolence.' Mother Paula was indignant.

'Is this true, sister?' Mother Angelus looked aghast.

'Yes,' I answered. 'It is true. I'm not here to be bullied all the time. Why do you have to go on and on about my faults. If I'm that bad just let me go. I don't want to be watched all the time and to be held up as an example of disobedience and whatever else you can think of. You say I'm untrustworthy. Well, all right then – I'm going home – now!'

Later, I was sitting in the office assigned for the use of Mother Angelus during her stay in St. Mary's. I had begun by automatically, if a little halfheartedly, kneeling to ask her pardon. But she was having none of that, not after my tears and my hysteria. I think I frightened the superiors and I frightened myself too because I couldn't stop shouting at them. I remembered my mother and her outbursts. Was I like her? Well, I'd show them not to treat me like a sinner.

'I can't do any more,' I'd screamed. 'I've tried and tried but nothing is good enough. You don't give credit for anything. You have your favourites who can do no wrong. Well, you can all get on with it now and leave me out of it because I'm going home.'

Mother Paula remained tight lipped when she was asked to have tea brought up to us.

'I think Sister Mary Jacob is overwrought,' Mother Angelus had said. 'All that travelling and the intense heat are affecting her. She and I will have a little chat, Mother.' She smiled.

My behaviour was out of character Mother Angelus believed. She knew that deep down I was a reliable and conscientious sister. Of course, I had a lot to learn but the potential for holiness was within me – hadn't she told me that herself when we first considered my vocation? Later, when we'd had our cup of tea and a little talk I must have a shower and a good sleep. We would start again with a clean sheet. But I had become cunning, I was playing games, I believed that at last I had the upper hand.

'It's no use Mother,' I sniffed. 'I know what you really think. I just want to go home. How can I live in this convent where I'm already singled out as a bad person? I've told you already how I've tried but it's not working. I'm not happy and I have to leave.'

'It was a mistake letting you go home for ten days,' Mother sighed. 'I should have sent a mature sister with you but I thought that you were reliable and that you had common sense. After all, you had spent many months with us in the School of Nursing. Yes, I made a mistake there, my dear. I expected too much.'

'Oh no, Mother, it wasn't a mistake at all,' I replied. 'I just know now that I should be at home for good. I want to telephone Aunty Anna. She lives in Long Island and I could go to her house first. She is a very good person and she will take care of me.'

'Sister, I am surprised at you. You must stop this talk at once. How can you possibly turn your back on your holy vocation just like that? Nothing very serious has happened. You made a mistake, face up to it, learn from it, dear. Wanting your Aunt to take care of you, indeed. Besides, how can you go back to Ireland? I know that your father is poor, do you want to be a burden to your family?'

'Poor,' I screamed. 'My father is not poor. Who do you think paid for me to go to secondary school and to nursing college? My father has a farm and my mother owns a high class drapery business. My brothers are at university. You know that I don't come from a poor family – you've seen the photographs, Mother!'

I was incensed as Mother Angelus ignored what I had to say and continued her warning by telling me that I would not be accepted anywhere if I left. I, she said, would not get a reference for a job. Who would give a recommendation to a girl who had left the convent? My parents, no matter what I might think, would be ashamed of me. Maybe I could work in the so called drapery shop but I wouldn't stay there for long because I was too impetuous. What would I do she asked. I was not qualified for anything and she would make sure that I could not complete my nursing in Galway. And she was absolutely sure, that given my history, I wouldn't be taken anyplace else either. Perhaps I could find work in a hotel or in an office but she doubted this.

'I'll go to Aunty Anna. I want to go this minute and you can't stop me. I can go to college over here I've already been accepted in what you say is a top American University. There won't be any problem about my future at all because my father wanted me to do this anyway. He didn't think I should be joining the convent. Or I could go straight home. My family said I must if I'm not happy.' I told her.

'Not happy, dear. How can you say that you are not happy? You, who have been chosen by the Lord to do His bidding. You have made your vows, what could bring greater happiness than this? You are being blinded by your own selfishness, the devil has you in his sights and you are sailing very close to the edge, Sister Mary Jacob. I'm thankful to the Almighty that all this has come about while I am here. I will help you through this terrible trail. Trust me, dear. The best sisters I know have come through similar and indeed even much darker nights. You are young and I think that this excuses some of your childishness. Grow up, sister and promise me that you will overcome these foolish thoughts.'

I felt very low. My self image had been severely dented. I tried to salvage some dignity some strength. But once again, the personality of Mother Angelus overwhelmed me. Her words had diminished me. How could I now think clearly enough to choose to stay on a path which I knew would be forever a difficult one? I needed desperately to belong but the emotional struggle and the longing for home was claiming all my inner resources. I needed a spark of light in this heart of darkness. I needed something to give me inner peace.

'As I've already said, you belong here in this religious family now just as much as you did when I first told you this,' Mother Angelus smiled. 'I'm disappointed because I thought you would have been strong enough to take your penance. But I do think you are strong, sister. I do think you have a long and wonderful spiritual journey ahead. Think about going to university and think about all the students you will have under your care later on. The world needs good religious working in the world now more than ever. Don't turn your back on St. Mary of the Wayside. Promise me that you will try very hard. I will ask Mother Paula to be particularly careful about your welfare while you get settled here in West Cranberry. We'll forget all these past transgressions, sister and begin again in the New World as it's called. What would the bishop think if he knew that one of our sisters, one specially chosen as a future teacher in his diocese wanted to take such an unworthy step? He would be shocked I'm sure and very disappointed. We will meet the bishop tomorrow,' she said. 'This will be a great honour for us all.'

Smiling serenely, Mother Angelus embraced me.

'Peace be with you, Sister Mary Jacob,' she smiled.

Chapter Fourteen
Kid Gloves

During the weeks which followed, Mother Paula and I danced around each other. Like boxers in the ring, we came forward and, without touching gloves, we retreated each time to our respective corners. In my subconscious mind, I was playing a game in which I was prepared to strike the first blow. If Mother Paula challenged me in any way, I would recreate a hysterical outburst just like the scene which, as I thought, had brought Mother Angelus to her senses. I reasoned that Mother Paula had been instructed to treat me with kid gloves. It wouldn't do at all for one of the sisters from Ireland to depart. At all costs the congregation must be protected from such a scandal. We had been to visit the bishop and he had been particularly interested in me not only because I was one of the sisters who would go to the university but because I had come all the way from Ireland.

I remembered this meeting very well. Mother Angelus led the procession into His Lordship's parlour where we were greeted by the bishop's secretary, Monsignor Nortz, who then presented us to the bishop. Mother Angelus was so proud that afternoon. I sensed her delight as well as her anxiety and her intense desire to let the bishop know that she was delivering her nuns into his protective care. We, her protégées, had been nurtured by her and had been trained within the holy cloisters of Mary's Way. She smiled and I supposed she had every right to do so. While we stood demurely in line Mother Angelus called us forward individually so that we could kneel to kiss the bishop's ring. At the same time Mother Paula explained to the bishop what work each of us would undertake. We were invited to sit, Mother Angelus at the bishop's right hand with Mother Conchita beside her. Mother Paula sat at his left. Since I was the junior I waited until last and I had to sit all alone on the edge of a massive sofa. Mother Angelus was charming. She told the bishop that she was very happy to have a community of sisters in the diocese of Albany. There was no doubt at all in her mind about our sincere willingness to face the challenges which lay ahead. Her sisters would be devoted to the education of the children entrusted to their care. The sisters who were going to university were conscientious students who would work hard and achieve the academic goals set for them. Her words amazed me. I knew little about university life in America and I wondered what Mother Angelus knew about it herself. Did she have any idea what she was talking about? If she now believed that I was conscientious and hard working she had certainly revised her opinion of me.

'Mother Angelus, you have helped me to fulfil a dream. I've uttered many devout prayers and made many sacrifices in order to have a Catholic High School built in East Cranberry.' The bishop spoke with deep emotion. 'I'm so glad that The Lord has seen fit to bless my work in this regard by bringing to fruition the sacrifices and hopes of the people of the parish.' And, he continued, 'may He bless you, Mother, and each of your good sisters.'

Mother Angelus thanked the bishop for his kind and encouraging words. She was preparing to say something else when turning to us all, the bishop asked, 'where is the little Irish sister who will be going to college?'

Blushing, I said in a small voice, 'I'm here, My Lord.'

Bishop Cullen rose from his chair. Immediately, following the example of Mother Angelus, we all stood up.

'Be seated, sisters,' the bishop smiled and crossing the room he sat beside me on the beautiful brocade sofa.

'Now sister,' he said as he leaned towards me, 'before we talk about Ireland don't say, "My Lord" just call me bishop.'

'Yes, My Lord,' I stuttered. 'I mean, yes, My Lord Bishop,' I continued.

Hearing a nervous titter I looked towards my fellow sisters. Some were smiling but Mother Angelus was twisting her mouth in an odd way and seeming to chew on the inside of her lower lip as she observed me. In this uncomfortable situation I felt awkward, I was being singled out and this was not acceptable. Such individual attention, especially from a bishop, was reserved for Mother Angelus and her chosen ones. I tried again.

'I'm sorry, my bishop. You see, in Ireland and in England we usually address a bishop as, "My Lord" but I'm sure we'll remember that here in The United States we should say bishop instead.'

'You are a fast learner,' he laughed. 'And I'm sure you'll do very well in college. Now tell me, where do you come from in Ireland?'

What was I to say? We were not permitted to tell anyone about our place of origin or about our family. This was terrible. Mother Paula came to the rescue.

'Excuse me, My Lord,' she simpered. 'Perhaps you do not recall that we have two sisters here from Ireland? Sister Jude, who is fully qualified, entered in Galway also although some years before Sister Mary Jacob.'

'Gee, of course I do know that we have two Irish sisters,' the bishop replied. 'How could I forget? I'm very pleased about this, you know and later I will speak to Sister Jude. But I just wanted a word with our little student here. Of course, you will all have to become students again for a time,' he added.

'Indeed, My Lord,' said Mother Angelus, seizing an opportunity to change the direction of the conversation. 'The sisters know very well that they will have much to learn. They are already adjusting to a different accent, different food and a difference in cultural background. But, you know, My Lord, when it comes to The Lord's work none of these things matter. The sisters will lead their students by example and by their prayerful devotion to their educational and spiritual needs.'

'Mother, do call me bishop, please. I realise that you have used the title, "My Lord," for a long time but you know something – this really throws me. Now I know how devoted the sisters will be to their work, Mother Angelus but I was not speaking about this. I just wanted to remind you that any sister who will be teaching in the High School in East Cranberry will have to do some further credits here in order to be registered as a High School teacher in New York State. Father Rob Moore is our liaison with the State Teacher Registration Board. He will see to all the paper work regarding additional credits and he will meet with you, Mother Paula, at the convent to go over everything in detail.'

A stunned silence followed. I don't think anyone expected this. Why would the qualifications of the sisters who had trained in England be unacceptable without further courses? It was outrageous and outrage was evident on the face of Mother Paula in particular. She, who would be the school principal, would have to do further courses in order to become registered. There must be some mistake surely but secretly, I was delighted. Looking at Mother Angelus, Mother Paula received a knowing look – she had permission to speak.

'My Lord, excuse me, I mean bishop. I think there may be some mistake. All the sisters here with the exception of our two students are highly qualified. Indeed, four of us already have many years classroom experience and I myself have been a school principal in Africa.'

The bishop winced.

'We were not told at any stage,' Mother Paula continued forcefully, 'that there would be any further academic requirements. You must realise, My Lor – I mean, bishop, that there will be a great deal of administration and class preparation to get through. How can the sisters be expected to study as well? Personally, I think such requirements are unnecessary. Perhaps when I speak to Father Moore I will be able to show him that any such perceived requirements must be waived.'

'I agree,' Mother Angelus spoke up sternly. 'I have taken my sisters out here on the understanding that their very superior skills would be more than welcome. They have all trained in Great Britain and it's very well accepted that teacher training there is the best in the world.'

Once more the bishop winced. A meeting which had begun so benignly was festering slightly. But the situation was saved by a knock on the parlour door and the ushering in, by Monsignor Nortz, of two smiling women who served us coffee.

During this introductory period to life in America, I admired the diligence and enthusiasm of my companions. If I needed good example, it was all around me. Yet, despite Mother Angelus' seeming concern for my welfare, I remained unsettled. I had sleepless nights and I was on guard mentally all the time. When the appointed Confessor, Father Leslie Vaughan, visited the convent for the first time, I decided to talk to him about my state of mind, my uncertainty and my hurt. Although I felt guilty and disloyal, I explained that I had been disobedient by having photographs taken of myself without permission. He actually laughed out loud.

'I don't get it,' he said. 'What was all the fuss about? A few photographs with your family, this is hardly a sin, sister and no fault at all if you didn't know the rule. Don't worry about this even if it did become a focus for your humiliation.' And he went on, to explain that these were just externals not the essence of religious life. 'You are not to worry about this, sister,' he advised again. 'And don't let them pick on you, because they will, if they see that you are weak. People who have power need a victim, someone they can hold up as an example to everyone else. It keeps the rest of the troops in order, believe me. Personally, as a young cleric I went through this sort of scenario too and it's not a lack of humility to oppose it. It taught me to be more respectful towards those I had some influence over in later years. You are a person in your own right, sister. You have given up much to get where you are now. Focus on the future and what the Good Lord wants from you here in America – you are on a learning curve, make the most of it.'

I was getting anxious because I'd already been in the confessional for quite a long time. Being the junior I had to go first. Meanwhile, Mother Angelus and Mother Conchita and the rest of the community awaited their turn in the chapel. Sometimes Father Leslie guffawed loudly and I was sure that he could be heard outside. But our new spiritual director was taking his duties seriously and apart from not understanding some of his Americanisms, I was confident that he was my kind of priest.

Mother Angelus knew that she was leaving a great legacy to posterity. Her sisters who were working all over the world would be an ever living proof of her existence. Nevertheless, she also wanted to leave something of her own individuality and personal talent as well. It became her custom to paint a mural in each new foundation. In the hospitals owned by the order she painted Guardian Angels in the Children's Ward or The Madonna and Child in the Labour Ward of the Maternity Wing. A school gave her new ideas and while in West Cranberry Mother Angelus announced that she was ready to begin a painting of the letters of the alphabet with accompanying pictures on the wall of the Kindergarten. Mother Paula was given a list of the paints and brushes which would be required and extra ones so that we could all assist Mother. I was appointed as Mother's aide at easel. It was a bit like being the theatre sister but instead of handing instruments I handed paints and brushes as required. Mother Angelus was an artist who could draw and paint effortlessly. She had a vision of what she wanted to produce in her imagination and she lost no time in getting on with the job. I would have liked to paint too but being Mother's assistant was considered an honour. I cleaned her brushes, washed her palette and brought a bowl of water and a towel when paint splattered her hands. We were reasonably relaxed and happy as we worked under mother's tutelage. There was a rich quietness in the air while each one created bright and cheerful symbols. But this calm was shattered when we heard women's voices in the corridor.

'Continue with your work, sisters,' Mother Angelus ordered as a bevy of young women burst into the room. There were high pitched exclamations, 'Oh my Gawd just look at that!'

'Gee!'

'Oh my gosh!'

'Wow!'

'Hey, Mother, you guys are such artists,' a blond woman shrilled. 'I can't believe it. These bare walls are alive, so bright, just wait until the kids see this.'

There was another din outside. Father John Palmer had arrived with other women, some were very large ladies too and they were all wearing shorts and sleeveless vests in every colour imaginable. I was shocked and I'm sure the other sisters were too. Fancy appearing in such attire in front of Mother General and in front of a priest. We averted our gaze and continued to paint as directed.

'Mother Angelus,' Father Palmer addressed her now. 'I've brought some of the mothers of the parish to meet you and the sisters,' he continued smiling happily. 'They will have their kids enrolled in our new school, some in High School and the little ones here in your special Kindergarten.'

'We do hope,' a lady spoke for the group, 'that you will be happy with our students who will come from the Junior School. I teach there,' she added, 'and The Sister's of Saint Cecilia who staff the school are delighted that you've come. They will arrange a brunch when they return from their holiday camp at Saranac so that we can all meet.'

What is she talking about I wondered? Nuns at holiday camp. And what is a brunch? And because I had no idea how the American Education system worked I hadn't realised that there were other nuns teaching in a Junior High and in an Elementary School in the next parish. Of course, had I thought about it, I would have wondered from where our High School students would originate? We were astounded a few mornings previously when Mother Paula announced that since there was a spare room in the school, the sisters would run a separate Kindergarten there for preschool children. This room was quite large and it was originally intended to be a lunch room for the nuns. It had toilet facilities and a small kitchen which would now be adapted for its new purpose. There was no way that we, Sisters of Saint Mary of the Wayside, would eat outside of the convent. We had The Divine Office to recite in the chapel before lunch too.

'We will get the children when they are at the beginning of their schooling and again when they are ready to finish.' Mother Paula explained. 'In the meantime we expect the parish here to build an Elementary School and a Junior High which we will staff but this will be in the future,' she smiled at Mother Angelus who nodded her approval.

There was no mention of any American nuns working nearby and nobody asked any questions. We accepted what we were told.

'Sister Mary Hyacinth will be in charge of the Kindergarten,' Mother Angelus declared as we sat around the table. It was during elevenses when we were supposedly allowed to relax. Sister Mary Hyacinth blushed furiously. I knew that she was not a teacher but had been sent to East Cranberry to be in charge of the household. She was a cook and I had overheard Mother Paula telling the bishop that she had qualifications in household management and horticulture. Mother Angelus was adamant, she had explained, that every sister should be properly trained for whatever duties she decided they would do as members of the Order.

'There is no garden space here for your vegetable planting and flowers, sister. This is a sacrifice, I know but you must accept it,' Mother Angelus said as she stared at her red faced subject.

I was sure that this was the first indication the poor nun had been given about her awesome role.

'You will be able to mind the Kindergarten class and still do the lunch and dinner for the sisters. After all, they only come to school for half the day, sister. 'You don't have to be a teacher to do this,' she added. 'After all, they're only babies.'

Mother Paula blanched but she said nothing and I wondered what the parents of these children would think if they'd overheard this pronouncement. I also wondered how Mother Paula would explain Sister Hyacinth's lack of credentials for this position to Father Rob Moore. Would Sister Hyacinth have to go to college too? Well, Mother had spoken and that was that.

Meanwhile some of the ladies had begun to chant like little children.

'A is for Apple, B is for Boat, C is for Rooster ... ?'

'Hey,' one young woman called out, 'you've made a mistake, sisters. You can't have C for Rooster.'

Mother Angelus turned around.

'No dear,' she smiled. 'Of course it's not C for Rooster. It is C for Cock.'

Indeed, it was a regal looking bird which she was painting, his feathers fluffed, his yellow beak open as he crowed in the morning light all red and gold with his fine head held high. Mother was working on his feet now and a bit annoyed to be so distracted. There was silence in the room. Father Palmer made an excuse to leave. I could tell that he was laughing. A couple of women followed him and they could be heard giggling in the corridor outside. There's something wrong I thought. The sisters near me looked puzzled as the visitors began to giggle too. They got into a huddle. I heard a mother say, 'they don't know it's so rude.' And then there was laughter, they laughed loudly holding each other, they shook and shook with laughter until they were red faced and had tears streaming down. We began to laugh too even though we had no idea what we were laughing at. Mother Angelus tried to look stern but even she couldn't prevent herself laughing as well.

Eventually, Mother Paula, recovering her composure, pleaded, 'Will someone please explain the joke for us because truly we have no idea what this merriment is all about?'

Again the women laughed hilariously. Nobody wanted to volunteer an explanation. Someone suggested asking Father Ben or Father John to explain things but this only encouraged more uproarious laughter.

'Please,' Mother Angelus snapped coldly, using her most forceful tone.

'I think we may have committed a faux pas. Is there something comical or perhaps inappropriate within our art work? I would like to know before we make any more errors. I sense that we are giving you all undue cause for hilarity.'

'Gee Mother, we are so sorry,' a young mother stepped forward. 'There is a problem all right. I will explain the situation to Mother Paula in private,' she offered. 'There is one symbol which is inappropriate but we understand that you sisters would not be aware of its significance.' There were nods of approval and a few giggles again.

'Of course they wouldn't, no way.' Someone else added.

The following day Mother's wonderful rooster was obliterated and in his place a pretty looking cow stared out from the wall. Mother Paula told us that we could not use a C for Cock, because the male bird was called a rooster in America. I think some of us realised that there was more to the meaning of cock than this.

We were allowed to write one letter home soon after our arrival in West Cranberry. In the meantime, my mother had written several letters to me. She asked all sorts of questions and made it clear that she wanted the answers. Had I heard from the aunts in Long Island or had I been in touch with them? Maybe they didn't know the name of our convent and its exact location? She was enclosing Aunty Anna's number so that I could phone her. Daddy was very anxious that I should get in touch with them. If I saw them again it would make my arrival in America more homely, he thought. I was petrified because I knew that I could not request a phone call to them or a visit from them either. Such premature petitions would certainly be frowned upon. I tried to put the whole matter out of my mind although I knew that Mother Paula had read my mother's correspondence carefully. I received a letter from Tom which surprised me because he was not keen on writing at all. Mother Paula perused it first and handed it to me with a questioning look. Tom's handwriting was not the most legible and I was amused to think that she was not able to decipher what he'd written. It was recreation time when I read:

Dear Ellie,

How are you? I am very well T.G. and so is Bridget. I like my job and the boss is very happy with what I'm doing. Bridget is now working for the summer in Murray's Medical Hall, in University Road. She likes it there and we can meet often because I'm in digs just outside the city. Colin is looking forward to university. I suppose you won't start until October either?

Mammy thinks you like America. I read the letter you sent and it sounds like a nice place with all those fields and trees and orchards which you saw on your journey to the convent. You are right I would really like to see those big cars. I told Joe about them. Hope you are getting used to the heat. I don't think

I'd like it that much.

I go to see Jerry almost every night now. His mother and father had him taken down to the hospital in Galway where your nuns are. I'm afraid the news is bad because he has cancer of the blood. His mother told mammy that they can't do anything. It's hard to believe but if you saw him you'd know that he's in a bad way. Maybe you can tell the nuns there that he is a friend and get them to take special care of him. I told him I'd ask you about this. He sends his love and says that you're lucky to be a nun now. I will let you know how he gets on with some new treatment the doctors are trying. He keeps hoping that there will be a cure.

The weather is not too bad for this time of year. Eugene and Irene send their regards. I went over to Capall Ban last Sunday and had a massive tea. The twins are great gas.

All the best for now and I hope you will write soon again because Mammy and Daddy are on the look out for a letter from America every day.

Bye for now,
Tom.

This letter from Tom shocked me and I was so sad. Poor Jerry, I had no idea that things were so bad for him. How could such a terrible illness take someone as fit and strong as he was? And he said that I was, "lucky to be a nun now." What did he mean? Was he glad that I could not see how sick he was or was he glad because I had not made any promise to be his girl forever? I didn't know what to think and in a way I suppose it was a relief to know for certain that I had no reason now to leave the convent. Soon, I'd have nobody waiting for me anymore because I knew enough to realise that Jerry would die. My thoughts were a mixture of selfishness, longing and fear. I longed to see Jerry once more so that I could tell him how much I had really loved him. I was afraid because I realised that if I ever wanted to go home in the future Jerry would not be there to comfort and support me. But I was being unrealistic, I had made my decision and Jerry's world had not stood still because of this. I had moved on but I expected everyone and everything else to remain as it was.

I felt hot tears sting the back of my eyes but I was not going to cry, not now while Mother Paula was looking at me. I put the letter into my sewing bag and continued to embroider a cushion cover. We were permitted to keep any correspondence for one day only – after this period my letter would be handed back to Mother Paula who would destroy it. I didn't own this letter but I knew that its contents would remain with me forever.

Following recreation Mother Paula asked me to follow her to her office. I felt nervous and I was still trying to keep my feelings under control.

'Sister,' she smiled. 'You and I have got off to a shaky start, I think. I know that you've been trying very hard to settle in here and I do want you to know that I'm here to help. Now am I right in thinking that you got bad news in your letter from Ireland? Do you want to tell me about it?'

I was amazed. This was the first real sign from Mother Paula that she was concerned about me. But I still wasn't going to cry.

'Yes, Mother,' I replied. 'There is bad news in Tom's letter, he's my brother and his best friend is dying. We all grew up together. Jerry was sick you see and he was in hospital in Donegal. His mother and father had him moved to Galway but it's no good.'

I had started talking now and I couldn't stop.

'They are trying some new treatment but Tom says that I wouldn't know Jerry if I saw him. He was a Civic Guard and he was stationed in Letterkenny, that's in Donegal. He loved it up there but he never got a chance to really do what he's trained for. I can't believe it.'

I had to bite my lip then to stop myself revealing anything about my past life and Jerry's part in it.

'Look sister, I understand what's happening to Jerry. It's very sad news indeed, dear but you are in the best place to help him. Pray that he will find comfort and have a happy death. The sisters will take good care of him. I will have him prayed for at Mass tomorrow and you may mention this in your next letter home. Later, sister, I will be talking to you and Sister Mary Zita about university. We have to go soon with Father Rob Moore to have you both registered for your courses. Now dear, if you want to talk to me about anything at any time you know that you can do so, don't you?'

Putting her arms around me she whispered, 'God Bless You.'

I was leaving her office when Mother Paula called, 'one minute, sister. I almost forgot. Your Aunt Anna telephoned. She asked to visit and I've told her to contact me at the beginning of August. She may come before we begin teaching here and before you go to university. You may also mention this in your next letter home.'

'Thank you, Mother, thank you very much,' I beamed delightedly.

Was there a new beginning for me, I wondered? I had the chance to become what I wanted to be, unlike Jerry. Was this a lesson telling me to get on with living in the present? And Mother Paula, well she wasn't so bad after all.

I wondered sometimes if the other sisters felt as I did and wished that Mother Conchita would pack the bags and that she and Mother Angelus would leave for their next destination. It was very difficult being in a small convent where three superiors vied for position. We, the junior sisters, seemed to be forever bowing and scraping to one or other of them. If a superior passed us in the tiny corridor we had to stand aside and bow without touching against even a sleeve of a Revered Mother's habit. When it was time for the Divine Office or Mass or other religious observance there was a scurry to the hall outside the convent chapel. Here we waited for Mother Angelus to arrive. Her choir veil would be held out to her by Mother Conchita and the pin to hold it in place offered head first into her right hand.

Mother Paula stood aside holding Mother Conchita's veil and pin while the Sister Vicaress, who was second in command in East Cranberry, did the same for Mother Paula. I, being the junior nun, had to wait to hand the choir veil to the Sister Vicaress. Meanwhile the rest of the community waited to process into the chapel ahead of the dignitaries whose missals, breviaries and hymn books were ready and waiting with the appropriate pages marked for them with a holy picture. Even though there was a hymn board in the chapel, Mother Paula wrote all the hymn numbers and the pages in perfect script on the best notepaper for Mother Angelus and Mother Conchita. The Sister Vicaress did the same for Mother Paula. We, the lesser mortals were constantly flustered while we tried to find the appropriate pages in our books using a holy picture – no thumbing with our fingers allowed. Morning Mass was celebrated in the convent by a curate from the neighbouring parish. He was Polish and he had been in America since boyhood. He was also a no frills person and it soon became obvious that he didn't like the English nuns and their desire to have a sung mass every morning. I overheard him telling Mother Paula that he did not have time to wait while, 'you good sisters warble along like little birds.' Mother Paula who had a very good singing voice didn't listen.

'It's the custom of our order to sing the mass whenever possible and since we are not involved in the school yet we will sing until September. We must raise our cheerful voices to the Lord whenever we can, Father.' She admonished.

Father Astrowski glared at her and got his revenge by drumming loudly on the altar with his fingers whenever we sang. He drummed out of time, refused to sing the parts assigned to the celebrant and cut us off in mid chant whenever he could. Mother Paula sang louder and encouraged us to do the same until Mother Angelus intervened, saying that she found such cacophonous singing an insult.

'Please desist from beating time on the altar,' she ordered the priest one morning after mass. She was sitting in the visitor's parlour with Mother Paula while I served the priest's breakfast.

'We have come here from England and we don't rush our worship of God especially during Holy Mass. I'm very surprised, Father that you have so little respect for your calling. I think it is very bad example for our young sisters to see you behave towards our singing of the Holy Mass in such a dismissive way.'

Father Astrowski stood and leaning over Mother Angelus bellowed, 'well, Mother, I do have other work to do today such as a visit to the prison and to the hobos lying at the railway station. There are a few other problems around the big city too like drug addiction, prostitution and the odd homicide – stabbings, shootings, things like that. But I don't suppose you or your little English choir would know or want to know about these things. No ma'am you stay safe in your little nest. If you want to sing *do, re, me* to the Lord that's fine but I'm out of here now – go trap yourself a singing priest from the monastery.'

I cleared the uneaten breakfast and the Polish priest never came to the convent again.

Obviously it was very awkward for Mother Paula with Mother General looking over her shoulder all the time. She, who was in charge of the community in East Cranberry could not be sure that her plans for each day and for each sister would go ahead without some changes. Often Mother Angelus decided that we should have a holiday. This meant a trip somewhere, usually to a church or shrine. One morning Mother Paula announced that the truck had arrived with all the new text books and supplies for the school. She had planned this day carefully and some parents and prospective students were coming in to help us at nine o'clock. Each sister had a class to arrange and those who were not teachers could help. Text books had to be taken to the rooms as well as chalk, paints, charts, maps and visual aids of all kinds. The school janitor and his assistant and fathers of students who had volunteered to help were ready for the second and third trucks which had transported the desks and chairs. It was very exciting and I was looking forward to a day away from the claustrophobic atmosphere of the convent. As Mother Paula gave instructions she was interrupted by Mother Angelus who declared that we would all go fishing. Mother Paula, becoming desperate pleaded with her.

'Mother, please,' she coaxed. 'It's not a good day for fishing because the stock has come for the school and I need each sister over there. Some parents have volunteered to help us to distribute the books and other materials and they have to be supervised. They don't know where things should go and I have to be there to give directions. I'm sorry, Mother. Perhaps we could go tomorrow or maybe you would like to look through some of the text books yourself, it would give you an idea of the education standard here in America? I'm really very sorry, Mother.'

'Nonsense,' Mother frowned. 'You can't need every sister in the school surely, Mother Paula? What are all those people doing outside? I see strong men and women all ready to work and those older boys and girls too. Two or three sisters will be enough to get on with things. Go and direct them, Mother and then get the car out.'

We set off on the fishing trip leaving Sister Cecily, Sister Lucinda and Sister Hyacinth at the school. Mother Paula looked distraught and pale as she drove us to what was known as Peter's Pond. Mr. Cummins had been assigned the task of finding a suitably secluded fishing ground for the sisters and this was it. To get to the pond Mother Paula had to drive along a rutted lane between two fields of sweet corn. The stalks of corn were so high and green that we became lost from view as soon as we entered the lane. The car bumped and rolled along as we tried to fend off the mosquitoes which quickly discovered the open car windows. Sister Ambrose, who was not looking well since morning, held her hand to her mouth and when the car got stuck in a particularly big clump of earth she made a hasty exit.

Peter's Pond was, as far as I could see – a mud puddle. There was a little jetty and a small boat tied up there but it was the height of summer and the deep water was some distance out. Sister Zita managed to loosen the rope and we helped her and Mother Angelus into the boat. They pushed off while the rest of us laid out the picnic, put worms on the hooks for Mother's use later and prayed for rain. When the boat returned with Mother Angelus and Sister Zita we saw an assortment of muddy, small and flat looking fish at their feet.

'Oh Mother,' we gushed, 'how wonderful, what a catch, did you enjoy being on the pond? Would you like a picnic now?'

They sat around on rugs placed on the rough grass and I brought the jug of homemade lemonade. There was a proper glass for each superior and a paper cup for the rest of us. There was one cup over and one nun missing – we had left Sister Ambrose behind in the corn field. This angered Mother Angelus.

'Where is sister?' She demanded. 'Who gave her permission to vacate the car? Go and find her at once, Sister Mary Jacob.'

I didn't have to walk very far before I saw Sister Ambrose stumbling along. Her face was red from the sun and streaked with tears. Her habit was covered in burs and dust, her shoes scuffed, her stockings torn.

'Mother Angelus is looking for you, sister,' I said. 'Here let me tidy you up and don't cry it will only make her mad. Just say that you got out of the car to help and that you didn't notice it move away. Don't say you felt sick because that will only make her mad too.'

We joined the group where Sister Ambrose had to kneel down to ask pardon for getting out of the car.

'For you penance, you will clean all these fish tonight and prepare them for breakfast,' Mother Angelus ordered.

I laughed, thinking we couldn't possibly eat such miserable specimens.

'And you, Sister Mary Jacob can take that smile off your face and help her,' she added.

We stayed up scaling and trying to fillet these awful fish until well after midnight. We said the rosary many times and hoped there would soon be an end to our trial. There was no flesh on the fish at all. What were we to do? And then to our horror we saw what had been happening. Our ferocious work had scattered fish scales all over the kitchen. They were on the window panes, the curtains, the floor, the fridge door, the cooker, the oven - everywhere we looked they gleamed at us in the light.

'Oh dear Jesus, we'll be murdered,' gasped Sister Ambrose.

I tried to remove some of these scales with a cloth but they were stuck fast. We tried a small brush but they just fell off and landed elsewhere. It was impossible. I took out the vacuum cleaner which woke Sister Hyacinth who slept in the room above the kitchen. She appeared in her night clothes and we screamed thinking it was Mother Angelus.

'What is going on here?' She whispered until seeing the fish scales everywhere she understood.

'You poor souls, what have you been doing at all? Dear God, fancy wanting to eat these miserable fish – the dirty little things. Now, keep quiet while I get some buckets of soapy water and we'll wash this place. You should both be in bed hours ago, such ridiculous carry on. Now say nothing in the morning.' She warned as we cleaned up and eventually went to bed.

I couldn't believe it. There in front of Mother Angelus was a lovely platter of succulent white fish for breakfast. She insisted that we each have a small taste from her catch. I glanced at Sister Hyacinth. She closed one eye.

'Jesus was a fisher of men,' Mother Angelus began. 'We must thank

Him for His gifts from the sea and the rivers and the lakes. We must think of those for whom we will fish on His behalf. Who would have thought that such a muddy pond would yield such an abundant catch? Mother Paula, you must arrange another expedition before I leave East Cranberry.'

Sister Hyacinth I thought, you'd better keep that freezer well stocked.

Chapter Fifteen
Speech from the Hard Shoulder

Mister Cummins sat outside in a long, black car which he had driven over from his own commercial garage. This vehicle had every modern comfort and he was so proud that he had thought of being chauffeur for Mother Angelus and Mother Conchita on their trip to the airport. Finally, they were leaving and we were all getting ready to accompany them in the smaller convent car which was now being loaded with baggage and picnic items. Mother Paula was busy checking that all Mother's needs were being attended to when the mail man arrived at the convent door.

'My goodness,' Mother Paula beamed, 'here is Sister Ambrose's driving test result.'

'Let me see,' Mother Angelus demanded as she took the letter from Mother Paula's hand and opened it in front of everybody.

'Sister, you have passed your driving test. Let us thank the Lord but it's no more than I would expect. This is, let's say, the first exam result for a Sister of St. Mary of the Wayside here in America. My dears, it will not be the last but I expect them all to be one hundred percent. We strive for perfection in all things and there's to be no second best.

Now, Sister Ambrose, you can prove your new found ability by driving the convent car to New York. There's no need at all, Mother Paula, for Mr. Cummins to accompany us - you can drive his car.'

Mother Paula looked quite shaken and even Mother Conchita shook her head in some disbelief.

'Mother, it's a long way to New York from East Cranberry and I don't think Sister Ambrose has enough experience to drive so many sisters in the car on the State Highway. It's quite daunting you know, even for those who have experience of it. You know that Mr. Cummins is a very skilled and safe driver. He is discreet too and he will ensure that we all reach our destination safely.'

Mr. Cummins was now standing with Father Ryan who had come out of the Parish House to say goodbye to Mother Angelus. Sensing that something unexpected was happening they came over to join us.

'Is everything prepared, Mother?' The priest enquired. 'I hope you have plenty of drinking water in each automobile because it's going to be a very hot day. Mr. Cummins will get you to the airport in good time so that you, Mother Angelus and Mother Conchita, will not have to rush at all. Now, is there anything else you good sisters need for the journey?'

'Actually, Father, we don't require the services of Mr. Cummins after all. It's so kind of him to offer to drive us but if I can drive his car Sister Ambrose, who has just passed her driving test, will take the convent car. This is the way Mother Angelus would prefer us to travel. We will be quite safe, Father.'

I don't think anyone who heard this exchange would have thought that Mother Paula really believed that this arrangement was in any way a safe one.

'No way,' Father Ryan spluttered. 'Pardon me, Mother, but you can't be serious about this. Sister Ambrose would not be safe on the State Highway. It's far too hazardous. Besides, she doesn't have her permanent licence yet, does she? If she's still on her temporary licence she will be in trouble should anything happen. No, Mother, it's out of the question.'

'Father Ryan,' Mother Angelus interrupted, 'I will say goodbye to you now. We must be on our way. Mr. Cummins has been most kind but we've made other arrangements. I'm quite sure he'll understand and Father, please assure him that we are most grateful for the use of such a fine car.'

'Hey, hang on there, Mother,' Mr. Cummins spoke up. 'I'm only delighted to bring the limo 'round for your use but it's another ball game to have an inexperienced driver take charge of the convent car with so many passengers. If you would prefer, Mother Angelus, I'll drive that car and Mother Paula can have the limo.'

But Mother Angelus was, quick as lightening, already sitting in the front of the limousine and beckoning to Mother Conchita and Mother Paula to join her. 'This is time wasting,' she said as she looked out the car window, 'and we must not waste the Good Lord's time, must we?'

Father Ryan strode to the passenger window and looming over her in total exasperation spoke sternly.

'Mother, I can't allow this. The bishop will be displeased and if anything happens along the route I'll have to answer to him and so will you, Mother.'

'Father,' replied Mother Angelus, using her sweetest smile. 'I do not have to answer to the bishop except in relation to the High School. We are a Pontifical Order and we answer only to His Holiness. Now, Father, don't worry, the Good Lord has us in the palm of His hand.'

Sister Ambrose gripped the steering wheel tightly looking more sickly than on the day when she got lost in the cornfield. Sister Hyacinth was beside her encouraging her and giving directions. We had been ordered by Mother Paula to keep within sight of Mr. Cummins's limousine at all times. I sat in the back of the convent car with Sister Jude. We were hemmed in by cases and assorted picnic baskets and bottles of water which we were supposed to keep immersed in small buckets of rapidly melting ice. Sister Ambrose was a small person who had large brown eyes in a rather square jawed face. I could see her in the rear view mirror and I didn't like what I saw. Her face was as red as a water melon's innards, her eyes were bulging and shining brightly and her jaw was set at an immovably rigid angle. We were speeding along, speeding faster and faster as the black car ahead of us disappeared into the distance.

'Sister, where is the exit from the turnpike?' Sister Ambrose shouted. 'Have we missed it? Where, in the name of God have they gone? Where is Mother Paula's car?

'You're alright, sister, I can see them now and we're near the exit. Don't forget to slow down because we've got to pay a toll.'

Luckily Sister Hyacinth had her wits about her. We caught up with Mother Paula and I could see Sister Zita looking at us from the rear window of the lead car. She had been chosen to travel with Mother in order to read aloud from a holy book. I had begun to think privately that Sister Zita was a favourite with Mother Angelus. She was a very handsome Sister, very charismatic, very bright and she knew how to play the system. Secretly I was not looking forward to being in college with her.

The highway was busy. Huge forty foot trucks swung past us leaving a great wake of air behind. We were like a ship being buffeted on the high seas. Caravans, trailing U Hauls from summer camps rolled alongside, large cars whizzed by and people stared at us while we tried to keep our veils from blowing away. Sister Ambrose held on tightly as we sped on in pursuit of Mother Paula. It was speed, speed, speed and still we couldn't keep up.

'Sister, you are driving too fast, you are way over the speed limit!' Sister Hyacinth screeched. 'Slow down, sister or we'll all be killed!'

She screamed again as we overtook all those trucks which had previously overtaken us. We jetted passed the cars giving the passengers a second chance to stare. We bounced from lane to lane as we avoided the Caravans and the U hauls. Sister Jude and I crashed against each other while the iced water trickled and splashed over us. I closed my eyes and remembered the roads around Lough Louchre which were never like this.

'Sister Ambrose, please slow down, we are not meant to go at such a speed we'll be arrested.' Sister Hyacinth was pleading with her now.

'But I have to keep up, I can't lose them, I don't know how to get off the exit for the airport, I've got to keep up, Mother Paula said that I must.'

'Look, sister,' this was Sister Jude speaking from the picnic area. 'Let them slow down for us. Surely Mother Paula must realise that we can't keep up this speed and that we can't see them. Slow down, sister, let them wait for us to catch up.'

'I can't, I can't,' came the desperate cry of the driver. 'Oh where are we at all?'

We were still on the highway and it was then as I looked back I realised that a car was following us also at great speed. It was Father Ryan with Mr. Cummins driving. Father Ryan had his arm out of the passenger window indicating that we should pull in, that we should try to stop.

'Look,' I cried, 'Father Ryan and Mr. Cummins are coming along behind us, slow down, Sister Ambrose until they reach us. Father Ryan is trying to tell us something, to move in or to stop, I think, Slow down, sister, it will be all right now.'

But Sister Ambrose was incapable of changing her driving technique. She wanted to know if Father Ryan was near us while she continued to go at breakneck speed. She kept calling out, her words lost in a haze of heat and melting tarmac.

'Mother Paula, where are you? Father Ryan, help us. O sweet Jesus, save us.'

Sister Hyacinth saw the toll booth and the signs indicating the exit which we needed. She also spotted the black limousine with Mother

Paula just ready to pay the toll.

'There they are,' she shouted. 'Quick, sister, catch them now before they move away. There's no one in front of us except them, Go on, now, now, now!'

Sister Ambrose, did and crashed slap bang into the back of the limo. I heard the sound of breaking glass and the thud of a back fender as it hit the ground. I closed my eyes for a split second and I tried to pray. Sister Ambrose was slumped over the steering wheel. She was shaking. Sister Hyacinth had her arms around her as Sister Jude reached forward with what had by now become hot water. I saw Sister Zita once again as she looked through the rear window this time in horror. She could see what we were about to hear – the State Troopers arriving.

We were all ordered to vacate our vehicles and the drivers were asked to produce documentation. But Mother Angelus remained in the car with Mother Conchita.

'Ladies,' said the officer very politely. 'I will have to ask you to oblige by vacating this vehicle. I know it's hot but you can stand over here in the shade.'

'Officer,' Mother Paula, spoke defiantly.

'You are speaking to our Mother Foundress. She has been here in the United States to open a new school. We are an English Order of nuns. We are taking Mother Angelus to the airport for her return flight to Great Britain. I can't explain how it's happened that our convent car has crashed into us. We were trying to keep together you see.'

'Ma'am, I reckon there's an airport in the sky somewhere too. I guess this is where you ladies were headin' and sure as hell gettin' closer to the departure gate. We've been trying to catch you guys from way back, now let's get on with the paper work.'

Mother Angelus was assisted from the limousine by Mother Conchita. Completely ignoring the police officers she grouped us all together on the hard shoulder.

'Sisters,' she began, 'I cannot believe that you would all behave so irresponsibly. Mother Paula, you told Sister Ambrose to keep up with us and did she? No. So here we are on the day when I'm leaving America standing with police officers while passers by are looking at us. How can I go away with this image in my mind? I feel that I must stay for longer because you, sisters, you are a big worry.'

Inwardly I groaned and I'm sure my companions did too. But at that very moment Father Ryan and Mr. Cummins arrived and pulled in beside the two cars which had been moved off the highway by the State Troopers. The priest shook hands with the officers and he and Mr. Cummins went into a huddle with them. There was much talk, gesticulating and even an odd smile.

'This is disgraceful,' Mother Angelus fumed. 'What were you thinking of, Sister Ambrose? Surely you are able to bring a car to a halt without causing such an unedifying scene? Gather over here, sisters and stop looking around, people are watching us and we must behave with due decorum. Now, we will have to alter our plans because as I've said already...'

'Mother Paula,' it was Father Ryan interrupting our roadside gathering. 'The State Troopers have to record this incident. Now Mr. Cummins and I have done our best to advise them that there were mitigating circumstances here – the imperative of getting you, Mother General, to the airport and the fact that you good sisters are new to the highway system here. What we must do now, is to see who is going to accept responsibility, firstly for speeding and secondly for the crash at the toll booth.'

Sister Ambrose was close to tears and Mother Paula looked very uncomfortable indeed. Mr. Cummins joined us to say that the cars had to be escorted by the police to a nearby garage. It was his personal opinion that there must be a faulty speedometer in the limo. How, in the name of all that's good and holy could Mother Paula drive at such a speed otherwise?

'It was indeed fortunate,' he said, 'that Father Ryan had decided to follow the two cars. He was, as it turned out, right to be worried about inexperienced drivers attempting the trip to New York.'

'Mr. Cummins, Mother Paula was not speeding, she is an experienced driver not a reckless one and that is why I wanted her to drive us to the airport in the first place,' Mother Angelus declared.

'Well, with all due respect, Mother General, if you'd allowed me to take charge of my vehicle at the beginning, I would have realised at once that there was a problem with the speedometer and I'd have substituted another vehicle. I didn't notice any problem as I drove to the convent because I was driving at a low speed. But on the highway, as the speed increased, it appears to me that the speedometer jammed and registered seventy continuously no matter what the driver did. An experienced American driver would have realised that something was wrong.'

'Mr. Cummins,' Mother Angelus began to preach once more but he was having none of it. We had to get to the garage now. We could take our places in the cars once more if we wished and the Troopers would go ahead of us or we could walk.

Mr. Cummins' theory was correct. The limousine was left at the garage so that a new speedometer could be fitted. Mr. Cummins would collect it on our return journey. Mother Angelus, Mother Conchita, Mother Paula and Sister Zita got into the convent car with Father Ryan driving. Mr. Cummins drove Father Ryan's car with Sister Hyacinth and three sisters on board. Sister Jude and I had no space because the picnic items for Mother and the cases and other baggage were more important. The State Troopers were still around and an officer was authorised to escort us to the airport – with Sister Jude and me as passengers in his car. Mother Angelus objected.

'Father Ryan,' she scolded, 'my sisters may not travel in a police car I will not permit this on any account. Is there a convent nearby where they can wait?'

'Mother,' he replied, I may not be His Holiness the Pope or even a bishop but this time you will follow my orders. Let's get the show on the road without any further problems.'

Sister Jude and I were already in the back of the State Trooper's wagon and with blue lights flashing we took the route to New York Airport. Here we watched anxiously until Mother General and Mother Conchita vanished from sight on their way to the departure gate.

On the way home to West Cranberry when we stopped at a Rest Area for coffee and doughnuts, the idea of a picnic having been abandoned, Father Ryan explained that Mother Paula was on record for breaking the speed limit but she would not have to appear in Court. Mr. Cummins would pay any fine. Mr. Cummins escaped a record because Father Ryan said he was his personal driver on a 'rescue mission, a sort of sick call' - trying to prevent an accident. Sister Ambrose was recorded for reckless driving but there wouldn't be any charges because she was not responsible for the fault in the speedometer. Mr. Cummins would see to the repair of the limousine too.

'Actually, the Troopers didn't write anything down that I could see,' Father Ryan explained with a sort of a nod and a wink. 'You probably won't hear anymore about this but please, please, please, don't ever go hot-rodding on the roads again, sisters.'

I was ecstatic, Mother Angelus and Mother Conchita had left, we were free at last and best of all I'd had the trip of my life in a State Trooper's car. What a story for Tom.

֎

It was mid August when the aunties came to visit. The days had become even more hot and sticky and we were in a state of continuous perspiration. It was so embarrassing. I could feel the sweat dripping down my back and behind my knees. Our head gear was soaking too and yellowing so much that the laundry became the busiest place in the convent. I knew already that the Americans were very conscious of body odour and I just hoped that I didn't smell. On the day of my aunt's visit I was thankfully permitted to change into a clean habit. To keep cool, I hid in the pantry which had a small window overlooking the parking lot and it was from here that I saw my relatives arrive. Two cars drew up – why two cars I wondered. I'd told Mother Paula that there would be just three ladies but here they were with an extended family in tow.

'Don't worry,' Sister Hyacinth advised as she joined me in the pantry. 'I'll take care of everything, there's plenty of fillings for sandwiches and lots of cake and I've got ice cream as well. Go upstairs now and meet them, sister.'

I was so happy that my visitors were modestly dressed. I'd been afraid that they'd arrive in shorts and skimpy tops. Mother Paula fussed over them all and I could see that she was impressed by the lovely dresses my aunts wore and by the good manners of Aunt Eileen's two daughters, Patti and Rose and by Aunt Helen's son, Michael, who looked very like my own brother Colin. A distant cousin named Barry Troy had come as well. He was famous – being a singer who had his own programme on New York City radio.

'I hope it's all right that so many of us have come. The girls were so keen, you know and when Barry offered to drive his car to East Cranberry, well it all just seemed so right. It's all right with you, is it, Ellie, hon?' Aunty Anna asked.

I could barely answer her because I was so overcome. Here they were, my father's sisters who had known him for more years than I, his daughter, had. They had lived with him in New York and now here they were fussing over me as if I was a long lost creature, a link which they had been searching for and had finally found.

'My God, doesn't she look so like Momma?'

'My Gosh, I think she looks like you, Anna, when you were in your twenties.'

'Patti, what do you think, isn't your cousin like an angel? The only one of these creatures in our family I'll bet,' Aunty Eileen laughed.

'Ellie, or should I call you Sister Mary Jacob, do you think Michael is like your dad in appearance?'

I sat there as close as I could to the cooling fan which had been left in the parlour by Mother Paula and I was speechless. Here were the aunties who had come to Ireland when I was still a school girl. They were warm and loving and loaded down with gifts for me but I was stiff and cold. I'd sat in granny Julia's house, beside the roaring fire, listening to them talk about their early life and about America. Now, here I was in America, sitting beside them and I was numb. But they carried on, Aunty Eileen telling me about her girl's education in a Catholic High School in New York. Their dad put their names down when they were born. And now, their children's names were filed away too even though they were just toddlers. In New York it's so important to get the kids into a good school she continued and the Catholic Schools are the best – the best discipline and morals too.

'Michael, tell your cousin about your plans for college,' Aunty Helen urged him.

'Well, I guess I'll be a Freshman in Villanova this Fall? You are going to college too aren't you, Ellie? It's going to be interesting. I don't suppose you are going on a Sport's Scholarship like me though. Do you play any sports in the convent?'

'No, I answered, we don't play any sports at all.'

They had only to look at me to know that this was true. I sat upright on the chair, I tried to loosen up but I couldn't. I wanted them to accept me as I was, a nun who had a book of rules by which I had to live. My life was beyond their understanding. I was afraid they would reject me because I couldn't cross that boundary which religion had somehow erected between us.

The topic changed as tea was being served by Sister Ruth.

'Your father has written to us lots of times,' Anna told me. 'Well, I'd have to say we've never heard so much from him in our lives, isn't that right, girls?'

They nodded and smiled. 'He's worried about you, Ellie,' she continued when Sister Ruth had left. 'He says they know very little about what's happening in your life out here. You know he was never that keen on the idea of you being in the convent.'

'Stop Anna,' Aunt Helen commanded. 'You'll upset Ellie.'

'Well, I think she ought to know so that she can write more news and reassure them that she is happy here. She's their only daughter for God's sake and Ireland is so far away.'

'Look,' I managed to intervene. 'There's not much to tell daddy now because we're trying to settle in. When I go to college I'll have lots more news to write I'm sure. Will you tell him that I'm doing fine and that I'm happy?'

I was upset because I'd written all about our exciting car journey to New York and the trip in the State Trooper's car. It was a great letter and I'd laughed out loud when I re-read it myself. They'll enjoy this I'd decided. But Mother Paula wouldn't allow the letter to be posted.

'What will your parents think?' She'd asked. 'Imagine them knowing that we were stopped by the police. You cannot send this sort of story home, sister. It's childish and unedifying and it's private convent business.'

I wasn't surprised that daddy was worried about me. The letters I'd written since had been bland and uninteresting but now I'd be able to tell him that his sisters had visited and he'd be happy. I was lucky to have such a father but I'd never told him this and now I probably never would. The realization hit me once again that I no longer belonged with my family. My father's nearest and dearest were trying to claim me, trying to tighten the bond which joined us all together, delighted that I, Sister Mary Jacob was a member of the clan and what was I doing? I was sitting here, prim and proper, smiling at the right time, congratulating politely, ignoring any painful memories, skirting around my feelings, lying, behaving in a manner which was so contrary to my inner nature. When inwardly I was crying out, wanting to say, 'your daughters are beautiful, they are competent and out going. Your son, Aunt Helen, does look like Colin and I do hope, Michael, that you will have a wonderful life. You, my aunties are really dear to me. You remind me of Capall Ban and of granny Julia and of the spring well and the cherry tree and the twins who will grow up and continue to keep the family heritage alive. I want you, Aunty Anna, to talk some sense to me, to say that you'll take me with you now. You told daddy years ago that I could go live with you – help me to do this because I want to be happy and carefree again, I'm so afraid of the future…'

But I didn't say these things and my thoughts were interrupted when Aunt Helen suggested that Barry should sing a song before they all left. Without hesitation he began:

If you ever go across the sea to Ireland,
It may be at the closing of your day
You will sit and watch the moonlight over Cladagh
And see the sun go down on Galway Bay.

His magnificent tenor voice lilted through the small convent, into the chapel to pleasantly disturb meditation, through the kitchen and upstairs to the very rafters. I glimpsed Sister Jude walking past with tears glistening in her eyes. I wept too as he continued.

'You're upset, Ellie,' Aunt Anna whispered, 'It's a very moving song and I'm gonna cry too. Don't worry sweetie, we'll all cry.' And we all did as Barry sang on,

And if there's going to be a life hereafter
And somehow I'm pretty sure there's going to be
I will ask the Lord to let me make my heaven
In that dear land across the Irish Sea.

When the song ended there was applause from the door of the parlour. Mother Paula had gathered the community to listen. She realised at once that here was a trained singer and her appreciation was obvious.

'You must all come again to visit Sister Mary Jacob,' she said as they were leaving. 'We do have rules about visits, as you know but perhaps Easter would be a nice time for you to return. Maybe you, Mr. Troy would be free to sing for the students and their parents at a future date. I'm sure there will be Fund Raising events for the High School and you would be such an addition to any programme. What do you think?'

Oh no, I should have known. Why couldn't Mother Paula keep her nose out of my family's business? I couldn't write home about our car chase but she could, with little introduction, try to use my cousin for her own ends. I was furious. But Barry was ready.

'Gee, Mother, you flatter me, you know. Now I'm really sorry but I'm contracted to the radio for months to come. During that time I don't, in fact, I can't, do private work. Call on me again sometime and we'll talk about it.'

When I walked with my family to their cars Aunty Anna had her arm linked in mine.

'That Rev. Mother of yours is some cookie,' she laughed. 'But don't worry about it, Ellie. Barry gets asked these favours all the time. Now if you ever need anything or you wanna talk, you must call me, right? Now tell me honestly is there anything you need?'

'I've got all I need here I told her, but do you think that you could send a present to Eugene and Irene's twins. I know this would make them very happy.'

'Absolutely,' Anna replied, 'I'd love to do this and I'll write to Irene because I'd like to be her friend and to hear all the latest news from Capall Bán. What a terrific idea. Ellie you're a real sweetie.'

'Oh Aunty Anna, thank you and thank you for coming, I know

it's a long way from where you live but it's been great.'

'Hon,' she beamed, 'It was no trouble, no trouble at all. We'd do anything for you and for your father. We all loved him so much and we cried buckets when he wrote to say he was not coming back to the States. God, he was so handsome and we were so proud of him. You know, one Sunday in each month he'd take us girls out for lunch – to The Commodore or The Waldorf Astoria no less. Wow, it was wonderful and you know what, Helen met her Mike in The Commodore?' He was the wine waiter. That's how come they have a wine importing business they're a smart couple and have done really well. Next time we'll bring some of the family you've not met so far and the babies as well.'

I wanted to ask her so much more but they had to leave. As they drove away, waving and blowing kisses I heard the bell for the Divine Office ring within the convent walls. That's where I had to be. But I couldn't concentrate. What if my mother had agreed to go to America when she and my father married? She wouldn't and she always said that the American crowd didn't like her because she stole their goose that laid the golden egg.

❧

We had become used to a structured daily life which resumed, following Mother Angelus' departure. So it was a shock when Mother Paula announced one morning that the Junior Sisters could not be in community with the finally professed nuns anymore. Mother Angelus had given some instruction before she left and she was very adamant about this, these changes were to happen as soon as possible. I could hardly believe it – there were just eight of us in America and we were to become an upstairs, downstairs society. Sister Zita, Sister Ruth and I were the Juniors and Sister Veronica, a finally professed nun, would be our Junior Mistress. A room downstairs, which was supposed to be the Library, was now our community room. The large room upstairs which was purpose built as a community room would be solely for the use of the Senior Sisters.

'You will report your faults to Sister Veronica,' Mother Paula explained. You will ask all permissions from her and she will conduct morning lesson with you and be responsible for your welfare. Our recreation will be separate although on special occasions we will be allowed to join together. However, I am answerable to Mother Angelus for your conduct outside the convent and you will report to me, on a weekly basis about your studies. If you encounter problems with your lectures, I will be able to sort these out. Your academic progress will be recorded and I will be sending a detailed report each month to Mother General.'

I felt that my dream about college and how I would escape through my studies was becoming a nightmare. Knowing that all my results would be scrutinised in the Motherhouse made me fearful and negative. What if I couldn't follow the lectures or if I failed some subject? My mind became fertile ground for a million negative ideas about myself. And what would we lose by not having daily interaction? Would we ever hear how the sisters were getting on in the school? Obviously there would not be any distribution of ideas which would help us when we had to teach. And we, being the students, would not be able to share our learning with the others. What were we going to talk about day after day at recreation, just four of us, always together. And I felt sorry for Sister Veronica who wasn't that much older than us. What did she know about the training and development of newly professed sisters? She would miss out on the discussions upstairs while trying to hold a pseudo mantle of wisdom over us. This divided authority just didn't make sense. And Sister Ruth who had just one year before final profession, I wondered how she felt about this segregation. Even though I was still young and inexperienced I realised that we were becoming too enclosed within our convent and within our Apostolate. Outside influences would not touch us if Mother Angelus had her way. To her, we were completely cared for spiritually and psychologically, within the Order she had founded. I didn't think so at all. But because I had made my agreement with God and with her, I accepted and I submitted.

It was the custom for a monthly bulletin to be dispatched from the Motherhouse to every St. Mary of the Wayside convent around the world. This gave news from each house. Usually, it was rather uninteresting telling of Retreats, Jumble Sales and of course, delightful visits from Mother Angelus. The bulletin for September 1962 provided a glowing account of the new mission in East Cranberry New York. Sister Zita and I were mentioned as being full time university students who were looking forward to bringing Christ into the lives of our fellow scholars. The Order would take a special interest in our progress and in the happenings in America. Another interesting piece of news for the sisters was the appointment of Sister Davinia and Sister Rosa to the Order's African mission in Kiwan in Zambia. I was sure that Sister Davinia would love this challenge. I wondered if my parents would hear this news at all. I would tell them when I wrote again and hope that my letter would not be censored. I would remind my father of the incident at my profession when he said he'd prefer me to be in America rather than in one of those African places.

Reverend Rob Moore and Mother Paula came with us when we went to register for our college courses. I couldn't believe my eyes. The university stretched for miles and miles. It had been designed for New Zealand the priest explained but they turned the design down. Nelson Rockefeller, the then Governor of New York thought it was ideal for Albany and it was. The Registrar who dealt with us was a delightful man. He was charmed, he said, to think that we had come all the way from England. I wanted to say Ireland but Mother Paula shot me a warning glance which said, I speak. Our courses were planned for us. Sister Zita would study Science and Education while I would pursue a programme in English and Education. The first year would be rather busy we were told because we had to include a language, mathematics, philosophy and either modern history or economic geography within our courses as well as speech training for debates and drama. Mother Paula was anxious to have us in as many classes together as possible.

'Will the text books will be expensive,' she queried, 'we don't want to duplicate if we can avoid this. We have a vow of Holy Poverty you see and the sisters must share.'

'This could be difficult,' Father Moore said as he looked at our schedules. 'The sisters may have a few overlapping lectures, Mother, but not that many because science includes lab work and tends to adhere to a different time table. We'll see what can be done but you realise of course, that Sister Mary Jacob will require many books for her English programme. I mean, apart from the general text books she will have required reading in English and American writings. I have the list here for her first semester, Mother, look.'

Mother Paula reddened to the roots of her eyebrows. It was a lengthy list but that was not the only problem.

'Father,' she cringed, 'surely the sisters are not expected to study some of the titles here. I mean what is there to study in such undesirable material as, *Sons and Lovers, The Catcher in the Rye* and those Virginia Wolfe titles? Really Father, I can't allow this Modern Novel module for Sister Mary Jacob.'

Father Moore looked confused and the registrar, looking amazed, spoke up.

'Mother,' he smiled, 'you want your sisters to study here? You want your sister to study English. Well, this is the modern world and these are the books she'll have to discuss with her students later on. She either does the course with all it entails or she doesn't.'

Father Moore, taking Mother Paula to one side, explained to her that there were other nuns studying at the university too. They had to do the required reading and they'd come to no harm as far as he was aware. But if she wanted to, he could introduce her to Sister Winifred. She was a nun from the Order of St. James the Confessor.

'This Order is highly regarded in the field of Education all along the Western Seaboard,' he told her.

Mother Paula could discuss her worries with this woman who was a renowned scholar. He would organise this if she wished. He could do it right now because the Order of St. James had a study house for their student nuns near the university campus and Sister Winifred lived there.

'Thank you, but there's no need, really. I'm sure I will be able to advise Sister Mary Jacob myself. I'm a college graduate too, you know and apart from my responsibility for the moral well being of my student sisters I can be very discerning when it comes to the written word whether it be in English or American, Father.'

The Fall arrived before the High school opened and before we were to begin college. We would have a special day together before our true work began, Mother Paula said, a holiday to celebrate the blessings which had been heaped upon us since our arrival in America. Father Leslie Vaughan was asked to celebrate a special mass of thanksgiving. Afterwards, with the car packed and ready we set off on what is known as a foliage drive. Mother Paula loved to drive and even though we, the juniors, were packed tightly into the back seats of the car, we were excited. Father Vaughan had suggested a route through the Adirondack Mountains. I couldn't believe the beauty which was all around us. The trees all golden yellows, bright scarlet and crimson reds, dark greens and purples rising over us with great protective canopies. The maple trees were old and noble looking, sometimes the outline of their distinctive leaves, were obvious as the sun shone through them. Leaves had begun to fall and along the wayside there were mounds of colour all waiting to become mulch as the season wore on. We drove through shaded areas too and left them behind to continue into what seemed like great fires of colour. Sometimes the route Mother Paula took became steep and, at other times, precarious, dark, and threatening, but we'd emerge again into the sunlight and gasp with delight to witness such beauty. For me, it was something mysterious. It was like how I'd felt during the drive with Tom and Bridget through the mountains above Lough Louchre. It made me long for peace, for peace within my soul and for certainty. But even though these trees had taken root for centuries, they were not masters of their own destiny and neither, I realised, was I.

Chapter Sixteen
On Campus

I couldn't believe that we'd come this far, it was a miracle I thought as I remembered the months which had passed since we began our studies. It had all been so difficult from that first late September morning when we caught the bus outside the church in East Cranberry and set off for the De Witt Clinton Railway Station in Albany. From here we took another bus directly to the college campus. The University was a New World. And because we had not been to any initiation days or to the week of orientation for Freshmen we were lost. Which bus stop was ours? Sister Zita, being the senior, was in charge of me and all matters to do with our college day. Suddenly spying Science Block she leaped from the bus leaving me sitting there in a panic. My sense of direction was terrible and having done so little thinking for myself in years I just stayed put. The bus toured the entire campus, round and round again and again with me sitting there incapable of stirring. I sensed the driver looking at me until eventually he spoke,

'Hey, sister, you lost or something. What building do you want?'
'I'm sort of lost, I think. Do you know where the Arts Block is?'

I asked.

'Gee sister, I know every block around here first hand and you're in luck. We're just outside the Lecture Hall now. It's called Emerson remember that for tomorrow, right?'

'Right,' I gasped as I thanked him and fled up the granite steps and into the building. The place was packed. Red faced and breathless I stood there clutching a canvas bag with a few text books, notebook and pen and a lunch wrapped in greaseproof paper inside. Heads turned, feet shuffled, someone in the back row moved over and I slunk into a seat trying desperately to get my bearings. The lecture hall was tiered and a tall, black haired and tweed suited lady stood beside a podium way below where I was. I looked at my schedule. Yes, this must be Imelda Goldstein, Professor of Nineteenth Century Literature.

Through her microphone she spoke to me, 'Sister Mary Jacob, right?' Would you like to come down nearer to the front, sister, there are some seats here. I have been telling the class that we could expect to have you with us all the way from England. We're very happy about this you know, because you will be able to contribute so much when we study the Nineteenth Century Novel.'

Nineteenth century Novel, I thought, what is that? In secondary school I remembered reading *Hard Times* by Dickens but I was not an expert on it or on any other novel. I stumbled down to the front while my fellow students stared and Imelda Goldstein smiled. When she resumed her lecture I saw how everyone wrote her words furiously in notebooks. I followed this example until it was time for discussion. I learned quickly that class participation was an imperative in the American University system. It counted for one third of the final marks at the end of a module. All around me hands were raised, students were on their feet, people called out for attention. It was so important to be noticed, to be identified to be assertive and opinionated. I wanted to hide, I had nothing to say, I didn't have an idea of my own I needed permission to speak. I sat there silent and mesmerised.

At lunch time I met Sister Zita as directed beside the statue of Benjamin Franklin close to the main gates of the university. Mother Paula had arranged with the Sisters of St. James for us to have lunch in their House of Studies. Sister Winifred couldn't understand why we could not have lunch with her community but I imagine she had, by now, accepted that we were different. A tiny room was reserved for us with a table and two chairs. Here, day after day, year after year we'd recite the midday office, say grace before and after meals and eat our sandwiches in total silence. If I needed a book for the afternoon classes I had to ask Sister Zita to lend it to me. Often there was a conflict in our schedule because she would need the book at the same time. This was terrible for me and caused endless anxiety. It was customary for students to write in the margins of their texts and to highlight passages. Sister Zita asked permission to do this but her highlighting and what I might have thought noteworthy didn't correspond. But my fellow students were very thoughtful and helpful too. One young man photocopied the most relevant sections from the text of *The Rise of the Novel* and gave it to me saying that he'd noticed that I didn't have this.

'Keep it hidden,' he'd said, 'because it's copyright and I shouldn't do this but I do it all the time. Let me know what other texts you need or individual pages. I'm happy to oblige.'

I only used his photocopies secretly when I had a free class and went to study upstairs in the Library. This was my first foray into subversive activity. In the library, I felt safe and comfortable. It was quiet and warm and often I'd fall asleep from sheer exhaustion. Sometimes, I surreptitiously looked through old files of *Time Magazine,* and I read countless articles about Jack and Jacqueline Kennedy. I was proud of him because he was the first Catholic President of the United States and because his ancestors were Irish. Even Mother Paula praised the Kennedys. It seemed to me that I was now living two lives – one a religious life and the other a frantic student existence. College was wonderful. It was buzzing with life and fervour and happiness and enthusiasm. The young people with whom I had to mix were outgoing and very questioning. They wanted to know all about us, why we had come to America, where we had come from, our former schooling, our ages and the make up of our families. It was difficult to avoid answering and nightly I was confessing to Sister Veronica, asking pardon for revealing some detail about myself. She became very cross each time and reminded me that I must keep custody of the eyes and the tongue.

Three Sisters of St. James the Confessor were doing the same course as me. They didn't seem to be filled with anxiety at all. They took everything in their stride and participated in class with fierce determination and smart ideas. I envied them because they were always so well prepared for class whereas I was still trying to get through some required reading as we travelled on the bus. One of them, Sister Vianney, told me that we had been invited to study with them in the evenings.

'We meet,' she explained, 'with our own tutor, Sister Catherine, who is an expert on English Literature and Education. She is also qualified in the other subjects which we have to study this year. We review the day's lectures with her and plan our assignments. Sister Winifred did ask your superior about you and Sister Zita joining us for an hour or two each evening. Father Rob Moore came up with the idea and Sister Winifred agreed. She thought it would be helpful since you are so new to the American system. We can't understand why your superior refused to allow this. We were looking forward to you coming over and to sharing our ideas. Don't you think it was a good idea?'

I was flabbergasted. It was a terrific idea and it would have helped us so much. For one thing, it would have prevented me from making a dreadful mistake with the first term paper which I had to submit. There was a manual which outlined the correct technique for submitting such papers but even though we had this we didn't know how to type and we didn't have the correct paper. When Sister Ruth asked Mother Paula for some paper for us, we were given off cuts from school craft paper. It was a creamy white and when I wrote on it in ink the words became all blotchy. What I handed in to Professor Goldstein was a disgrace and I blush even now when I think about it. I watched while the other students presented plastic folders with cover sheets where titles and names were beautifully typed. I tried to hide my assorted, grubby pages now held together with a paper clip beneath all the others. I was not surprised when a notice appeared on the board for Sister Mary Jacob to meet with Professor Goldstein two days later. She didn't know what to say. 'I don't understand this,' she'd frowned. Why had I not typed my paper and who told me to use such an assortment of sheets. Had I not done anything like this before, in High School, surely I must have typed papers there?'

I was mortified.

'I'm really sorry but you see I don't know how to type and we didn't do papers like this in school in Ireland. We had very large notebooks which we handed in each time.' I explained. 'I did ask for paper but this is all we've got and we have a vow of Poverty and we don't have a typewriter.'

Professor Goldstein adjusted her glasses and stared hard at me.

'I am Jewish and we have our customs too,' she said. 'But this takes the biscuit. I do think you will have to have what you need for your classes here and for the presentation of term papers and a thesis later on, poverty or no poverty. I don't know what to do about this now. I can't give you a grade because this does not conform to the standard at all. But, Sister, it's wonderful writing, so easy, so fluid, I'm enthralled. I know now that you are from Ireland and I can see the Gaelic lilt all over the place. You know something I feel like crying.'

'Don't cry,' I pleaded. 'I'm sorry I've upset you but I don't know what to do either.'

'I'm not upset, well yes, I suppose I am. It's sad to think that you are living such a hard life, a kid like you with so much talent. Well, you will be able to rewrite this paper, I'm sure. Here let me talk to someone and I'll get back to you later,' said the professor. 'We'll sort this out.'

Imagine my fear when she informed me later that she would be driving Sister Zita and me to East Cranberry after our lectures that day. The Professor had a meeting set up with Mother Paula. Oh what a favour this forthright woman did for us. From then onwards we wrote out our assignments in pen and afterwards Mother Paula had these typed up for us by the school secretary. Later, as the work became more intensive and other sisters, including Mother Paula had to present papers, the school secretary, her sister and her sister in law became our typing pool.

※

The posters were everywhere on the college campus. A group of men in Aran sweaters looked down on me. They were smiling and holding guitars and a banjo, they were Irish. A big concert was about to happen. The Clancy Brothers and Tommy Makem were touring the States. Students crowded round me.

'Did I know them, did I know Tommy Makem?'

'Would I like to go to the concert?'

'There are tickets for you sister and all your guys from the convent,' an entertainment committee representative told me.

'Wow, sister, you must be so excited.'

I would have been had I known who Makem and Clancy were. I had to pretend that I was excited and yes, I'd probably heard of them and no, we would not be permitted to attend the concert.

'You won't be there, sister,' someone gasped. 'And they've come all the way over from Ireland, they're famous.'

Well the concert was a hit. Everywhere I walked the following day there were groups of students singing Irish songs. My trusty photocopier friend, Steve, had this time managed to make a tape of each ballad. I was coaxed into a music room with some of my class so that I could hear snatches from them between lectures. The songs were wonderfully cheerful not at all like the sad Irish songs I'd been expecting to hear. We left together singing loudly,
> *All God's creatures have a place in the choir,*
> *Some sing low and some sing higher*
> *Some sing out loud on the telephone wire.*
> *And some just clap their wings or paws or anything they've got...*

That evening Sister Zita reported how she'd seen me on the stairs to a lecture hall, singing Irish songs while actually clapping my hands against the hands of another student, she wasn't sure if it was a girl or a boy. When Mother Paula asked me which it was I told her quite honestly that I didn't know.

At that time in America it was difficult to distinguish between the sexes. It was an era of long hair, of freedom, of flower power, of hallucinogenic drugs, of free love, of rock and roll and most disturbing of all for Mother Paula – it became the era of the Streaker. These bodies usually appeared at night, shooting from the college dorms chasing each other and racing for dear life like spectres all over the grounds. Mother Paula on reading about this activity in the college newsletter, called Sister Zita and me to her office.

'Sisters,' she began, 'do you know what streaking means?'

I looked at her blankly. Was she going to ask us to streak?

'Sister Zita, do you know what streaking means?'

'Yes Mother, it's running about in the nude.'

'Correct,' Mother Paula said colouring slightly. 'Now, sisters, such a despicable activity has become fashionable in many colleges including, I regret to say, on the Albany campus. Many misguided students believe that they will get concessions from the college authorities by behaving in this way. I believe it is a night time event but it can occur at dusk sometimes. What would you do, Sister Mary Jacob, if you encountered such a body on the campus?'

'Well,' I said, 'If it was alive I'd ignore it but if it appeared injured or dead I'd get help.'

'Sister, how dare you speak so flippantly about such disgraceful conduct? You will recite the Cross Prayers this evening because you are being very disrespectful. Sister Zita, please advise Sister Mary Jacob of the appropriate conduct under such circumstances.'

'Sister,' she whispered, 'we must avert our gaze, observe custody of the eyes and pray to Our Lady for pure and modest thoughts.'

Sometimes I despised Sister Zita. She was everything which I was not or so I convinced myself. She was really very attractive and the American people who met her were unhesitating in their praise of her beauty. How many times did I have to listen to them fawning over her and saying things like, 'Oh Sister Zita, you look like Ingrid Bergman, you are a real beauty.'

'How can such a stunning face and figure be hidden away in a nun's habit?'

'You should be in the movies.'

'Oh my Lord, how the poor men must pine away when they see you. It's just not fair, is it?'

No, I thought, it's not fair at all. Day after day I walked in her shadow during those early years in America, grieving because of my own seeming insignificance and my own inferior intelligence. She was the star beloved of lecturers. Students crowded round her to listen to her fine English accent, to bask in her smile, to admire her warmth and fun loving nature. She oozed sexuality. In the convent where she was a model nun she was placed on a pedestal. Here, she could do no wrong and even when she committed a misdemeanour, she was so penitential that it appeared in her favour. Her grades were superb while I just managed to scrape through in everything except English where I did really well. My resentment towards her and her success and charisma became so powerful that I began to feel physically sick when we had to meet for lunch or be together for a lecture. I had to confess my envy and jealousy to Father Leslie on more than one occasion.

'Why?' He asked, 'do you make yourself suffer on somebody else's account?'

'You are your own person and your quest for perfection is unique to you, sister. It is not a good thing to grieve because of another's success either spiritual or material. Don't measure your spiritual worth in this way. I believe, from talking to you, sister, that you are intelligent and honest in your endeavours. You want answers to many questions. In time, you must ask these questions with care and dignity. Right now, you are creating an image of perfection from a false premise. This won't work. Do you understand what I'm saying, sister?'

'I'm afraid I don't really get it,' I replied. 'You see, Father, I don't feel good enough to belong. I'm not able to fulfil the demands of college and religious life. The others seem to be able to do this but I'm always failing and I never measure up.'

Father Leslie Vaughan sighed. He told me that in his opinion I was a very dedicated sister, perhaps too dedicated for my own good.

'You are trying too hard as I've told you before,' he continued. 'And this sick feeling which you've talked about is a physical reaction to many things, not just a mild dose of envy. There are people who see it as their role and duty to chastise and to humiliate you. But,' he went on, 'it is how you treat yourself that matters. You must not put aside your own belief in true goodness and in your own ability to discover who you are. This is a little philosophical,' he laughed, 'but I hope you get the message. We'll talk along these lines some more later on.'

Indeed, it was very hard to keep the religious life uppermost as I progressed through college. We rose at four thirty in the morning so that we could meditate, chant the Divine Office, attend mass, have breakfast and listen to morning lesson before leaving for Albany. Sometimes I felt worn out before we even left the convent. I imagine I was not eating properly, resting properly or studying properly. There simply wasn't the time. When we got home on the bus there was tea and recreation followed by spiritual reading and then our chores to do. I worked in the laundry for a time where I'd try to study by placing a text book on the window sill above the ironing board. The sisters who were teaching stayed for an hour after school. They had to prepare lessons and do corrections. Sister Hyacinth organised the evening meal and if there was time between our chores being finished and this, we studied.

We had no idea that New York State could be so cold in winter. The season began slowly but by January, 1963, the earth was encased in snow which began as a blizzard during a Wednesday afternoon. I had never before experienced anything like this. While Sister Zita and I awaited the bus which was very late arriving on campus we stomped our feet up and down on the pavement trying to keep warm. Soon, the soles of our thin shoes were layered in ice. Students who travelled with us were wearing snow boots and parkas. We struggled in long skirts and light outer cloaks. With frozen fingers we held on to our book bags and battled against a fierce wind as we tried to clamber onto the vehicle. White figures moved along the pavements, clutching each other for safety and support, traffic looking like modern sculpture, crawled by. Some cars had stalled while others stopped for an occupant to emerge and make an effort to clear a snow covered windscreen. The cold was unbelievable it had become absolutely freezing I noticed that Sister Zita's lips were blue. When our second bus pulled out of Albany the driver got us as far as the bridge over the Hudson River and half way to East Cranberry before giving up and telling his passengers that, 'this was it,' he could go no farther.

We trudged towards home hoping and praying that we were going in the right direction. Everything was white and everyplace looked the same. As the wind howled and beat against us my eyes watered and tears froze on my face. Suddenly, out of nowhere a huge snow plough bore down upon us. We slithered away towards a tree lined fence, holding on to the icy wire as we went now knee deep in snow. Mr. Cummins and some other parishioners who were searching for us came upon us at some distance from the convent. We had passed it by and were on our way out of East Cranberry without knowing. Mother Paula and the community were very relieved when we were bundled into the convent by our rescuers.

'A warm bath, a hot whisky and a cosy bed should see them all right, Mother,' Mr Cummins told her. A hot whisky, what a thought, we might become alcoholics! Father Ryan, who had also been with the search party stayed behind to advise Mother Paula about personal and domestic safety during blizzards. All the High School students had been collected earlier in the day and the school, like all those around would be closed for three days. Before the end of the week we had each received a pair of black snow boots and a fur lined anorak which were a gift from the parish. And even though, as was the custom, we had to ask individually for permission to wear these I don't think Mother Paula asked permission from the Motherhouse for such additions to our wardrobe.

Springtime restored my spirits. It was a real awakening after the snow bound months and the weeks of slush which followed as the snow and ice melted. What a contrast to see the birds building nests in the branches of the trees which had weeks previously shone like crystal glass. Flowers blossomed in the fields and Mother Paula, who's love for a Sunday afternoon drive persisted, took us along very scenic country roads, through villages and past farms where red barns and huge silver silos dotted the landscape. Black and white cows grazed in lush green fields and mares with foals gazed upon us from their soft meadows. I loved this landscape with the bright blue sky overhead and white cumulus clouds moving slowly across. But I worried too because there was so much study still to do and because Mother Paula seemed oblivious to this need. Life was a constant catching up exercise and I hadn't learned to let go. I hadn't learned to accept reality to accept that there were some things I could do and others which were impossible.

❦

Our first summer became a time for surprises. We were to have a holiday. Mother Angelus had given permission for one week away at a lake where the Diocese had a holiday house. Bishop Cullen had personally visited the convent to offer the use of this facility. Each Order of nuns in the diocese availed of it, he told Mother Paula and the seminarians and priests went there as well. There was rota for its use so that nobody overlapped.

The house named St. Anthony's was amazing. It was set amongst pine trees, down a long drive, with the lake on three sides. Wild fowl and beaver lived along the lake shore and in the small tributaries of the Saranac River which flowed into it. The forest, we were told was home to the black bear, deer, racoons and wild cats. It was a complete escape and we had many happy hours of desegregation, swimming together in the cool deep water and relaxing at the small sandy, man made beach. Mother Paula had provided each sister with a very modest swimsuit. Mine was a dark navy with a red slash across the midriff. One afternoon we donned our costumes, took our towels and ran down the shaded path which led to the beach.

'Beat you to it,' Sister Ruth shouted as she careered along on sturdy athletic looking legs.

'Hang on, I'll race you,' shouted Sister Ambrose, her face reminding me of her look on that terrible day when she drove us madly along the highway.

Trotting behind them we watched as they climbed over some boulders where from the highest point, they dived disappearing with a mighty splash into ever widening rings of glistening water. When we reached the boulders we looked down only to gasp in disbelief. There were men swimming in the lake, there were men surrounding the sisters, there were shouts of, 'hi there, welcome to the water.'

'Gee, are you training for the Olympics?'

'Where have you girls come from?'

'Get back, sisters,' Mother Paula ordered from her perch, 'keep out of sight.'

We giggled, we couldn't help it, we were shocked and embarrassed and we didn't know how Mother Paula would attempt the rescue of her charges. Wrapping her large beach towel around her body, she stood atop the boulder, rather like a mountain goat surveying the horizon.

'Sisters,' she shouted, 'exit the water now.' Giggling followed from the audience.

'Sisters,' male voices echoed. 'We're swimming with nuns.'

'Well, what do you know, is this a first?' A male body joked.

'Sisters,' Mother Paula shouted again. 'Come out of the lake now.'

But Sister Ambrose and Sister Ruth remained threading water while submerging as much of themselves as possible. A priest, who had probably heard the shouting walked towards our group.

'Sisters, cover yourselves and stay back,' Mother Paula directed as she stood, towel wrapped to speak to him. 'Hi, I think there must be some mistake,' he smiled. 'I take it, you are nuns who have the use of St. Anthony's right now. I checked with the office and I was told that it would be all right to take the seminarians over for a swim today.'

'Well, I don't know who told you that, Father. I would just like your people to go away discreetly so that the sisters can come out of the water. Afterwards, your clerics may continue with their swim. I think we've had enough for one day.'

'By the way I'm Father Ronald Cox I teach in the seminary in Plattsburg.'

'Pleased to meet you,' Mother Paula replied without introducing herself or giving any further information. And unlike other Americans we'd met, Father Cox walked away without asking for any.

☙❧

We returned to college as work began on the construction of a new Catholic Elementary School for East Cranberry. It was at an angle to the High School and there was dust from the site blowing everywhere. I don't know how the sisters managed to conduct classes because there was so much noise. For once I was glad to be getting up early and to have so many hours away. College had become home to me, a place where I could let my thoughts roam and where I began to look on life in a different way. The rugged individualism which I noticed in the American psyche, their ability to question, their humility in the way they listened to other people's point of view impressed me. Within the convent, I didn't have the courage to challenge. The rules kept me safe and if I did have negative thoughts about our religious life I felt guilt and shame as a result. I was not so naive anymore that I thought that the world outside the convent was a safe place to be. There was violence and fear and the Vietnam war was claiming its victims every day. People were angry, students were resisting and draft dodging was spoken about. Aunty Eileen wrote asking me to pray for Michael – that he would not be called up and to pray for Pattie's husband, Roy, who was a commissioned officer now in Vietnam awaiting orders and expecting to be moved to the battle zone eventually. Reluctantly, Mother Paula gave me permission to reply saying that we would pray for them all. And we did pray for all the young men who were facing such an unknown future in America or away fighting. America became restless and even priests joined the demonstrations against the war and for racial justice. Some were arrested and even imprisoned. I read about all these happenings in *The New York Times* which was available in the college Library. I was very careful to do my outside reading there when I knew that Sister Zita was occupied in a lecture. When the crisis called The Bay of Pigs reached an impasse we were permitted to listen to President Kennedy's speech on television. Missiles were pointed at New York State from a base in Cuba. We were stunned we could all be blown up at any moment. It was surreal.

In 1963 President Kennedy went on a State Visit to Ireland. My mother wrote to tell me all about it. Tom and Bridget and Colin and his friends had gone to Dublin to see him. The cavalcade travelled across O'Connell Bridge and Colin, who had an assignment to write about it, was so near to the edge of the footpath that he could almost touch the President. Ireland was celebrating, she told me. He was so down to earth so friendly and handsome with a wonderful smile. The television showed him visiting his ancestral home in County Wexford and his speech at Shannon Airport when he was leaving had people in tears.

'I can't understand it,' she added, 'but for some reason your father keeps saying that he has no time for the Kennedy's.'

I knew all about the cavalcade in Dublin and I'd even seen marvellous photographs of his trip in *Time Magazine*. Tom wrote to me again during this time. Jerry Breen had lost his battle and he had died when Tom and the others were waiting to see President Kennedy pass by.

'Ellie,' he wrote, 'I'll never forgive myself for not being there with Jerry. I told him that I'd stay beside him and I didn't. Mammy says that he wouldn't have known anyway because he was in a coma. It's better for him, Ellie because there was no hope. I'll miss him. I know he was your best pal and he talked about you all the time…'

Although I was prepared to hear that Jerry had lost his battle, I was still terribly shaken by the news from Tom. Jerry, my best friend, was my first friend to die and I didn't know how to deal with such sadness. There wasn't anyone to talk to except Father Leslie and I didn't talk to him. I was unable to explain my thinking. I was fearful too that by now the confessor must surely see me as a real problem. I was forever troubled, anxious and questioning. Because we were insulated from most outside influences in our chosen way of life there were no new thoughts, no real discussion, nobody with a wealth of spiritual insights to pass on to us. I was very careful not to reveal what I'd been reading in college or to indicate that I had ideas of my own which didn't fit the norm. For such insubordination I knew that I could be taken out of college altogether, I would be punished. Somehow, we seemed to drag each other down keeping each other in a state of fear – fear of doing the wrong thing, of saying something out of place, of acting differently from everyone else. My inner feelings of falsehood and dishonesty continued. Was I still pretending to be what I was not?

Professor Goldstein remained my friend throughout college and there were others too who opened for me a world of new ideas and through whom I learned eventually to form an image of myself which was not so negative. Professor Ralph Craig was such a person. His field was American Literature and it was in his lecture and during a discussion of Thoreau's, *On Waldon Pond* that the intercom crackled and a voice spoke.

'Ladies and Gentlemen, there is some news coming in concerning the President of The United States. It appears that while he travelled though Dallas Texas in the Presidential Motorcade an incident occurred. Please remain seated wherever you are and we will relay the news as it comes in from Dallas.' We sat and waited. News came that the Governor of Texas had been wounded by a shotgun blast. The President had been taken to hospital for observation. It didn't sound too bad just rather frightening. Bobby Kennedy, the Attorney

General had been alerted. Streets in Dallas had been cordoned off, the National Guard had been called into action and buildings were being searched. A couple of President Kennedy's aides were seen walking around outside the hospital, there was no sign of Mrs. Kennedy. Then silence for a few seconds until the terrible words were spoken.

The President of America is dead.

There were screams and sobs from everywhere. Students stared in disbelief. The intercom continued to describe events, to spew out the words nobody wanted to hear. We were beyond listening, beyond hope, we were lost. College would be closed now, we heard and we should leave the main buildings. The chaplains and counsellors would be available to those who wished to talk. Announcements would appear in the newspapers and on T.V. to say when lectures would resume.

God Bless America.

I met Sister Zita at the bus stop and we didn't speak. Since it was too early for our usual bus she decided that we should walk to the De Witt Clinton stop to find a bus to East Cranberry. We moved slowly and in a daze while this awful news seeped deeper and deeper into our hearts. America the Beautiful had suddenly become blanketed in darkness. We saw its citizens in the streets of Albany standing in groups crying. Others, who were so totally distraught, literally banged their fists against the walls. I cried silently for Jacqueline Kennedy and for her children and for all the horror which must surely follow such an act of violence. Cars were driven slowly with radios blaring so that those who walked the streets could hear the latest news. At the traffic lights drivers sometimes forgot to move forward or were unable to do so because pedestrians crowded around to listen. They heard the same words over and over, yet waited there on the streets as if expecting to learn eventually that it had all been a mistake. But there was no mistake. President Kennedy was buried in Arlington Cemetery, on 25th November, 1963.

Life moved on, college resumed and we went back to our lectures fiercely determined to keep the torch alight which had been passed to a new generation of Americans. At the beginning, students clustered together to talk and to recall the days of Camelot. But the resilience of youth had its way too and soon there was laughter again and animated discussions during lectures. These exchanges focused very often on the themes of freedom, nationhood, liberty and justice. And beneath these ideals lurked an element of watchfulness. Somewhere out there evil lay in wait. It might stalk the corridors of the university or be embodied within some rebellious group. No individual wanted to be labelled a protester. But the group protests did continue and at the weekends students hired coaches to take them to the streets of Washington D.C. where unfurling banners they demanded a safe future for themselves and for their fellow man.

I don't know if in some way or another Mother Paula felt that we were exposed to some physical danger too. She became very anxious to have a wall or fencing erected around the convent. We needed privacy, she explained to Father Ryan and inside this fence if some tarmac was removed there would be room for a small lawn and a picnic table. He agreed and asked some of the parishioners to do this work voluntarily. Soon, the project became extended when it was decided by the men folk that a garage could be built as well. In this way, further shelter would be provided and the sisters could move about downstairs without being on view. It was quite amazing to see these men work together. Most of them were the father's of High School students while others looked forward to their younger children enrolling in the new Elementary School which was to be completed in a few months. A judge, a garbage collector, a builder, a bus driver, a farmer, a pharmacist indeed representatives from many walks of life came to work for us. I marvelled at this, how they cooperated, laughed and joked and got the job done. I was reminded of my father's admiration for this aspect of American life. It was the heritage he'd said from the days of the covered wagon when men went west and had to help each other on the way. I wondered about those of us inside the fence. We were bound together too but were we enabled to look out for each other?

'Sister,' Mother Paula addressed me one Saturday afternoon. 'You and I are going to the Builder's Provider. Sister Veronica has given her permission. The men who are doing the garage roof need some timber. We will get what they want and save them time.'

I could see that the carpenters were a little unsure about this but they deferred to Mother Paula. They explained exactly what they required and even drew diagrams of four by fours for her. Mother ordered the timber and we were both rather surprised when on going back to the car we discovered that the timber had been deposited beside it.

'Surely we are not expected to take this in the car, are we, sister? Go inside and get the manager for me.' Mother Paula seemed exasperated.

'Look,' he said, 'there's no problem about loading these few pieces into your wagon. Let down the back window and the back seats, ma'am and I'll lever them in. They can rest on the backs of the other seats.'

Swinging the four by fours around, he thrust them into the car. I was sure that every window would be broken. Mother Paula looked disbelievingly at what had by now become a very neat load. The planks were banded together one on top of the other with a striped red and white flag attached to the end. This fluttered in the breeze as we drove and indicated hazardous cargo to other road users. It was more dangerous than we'd imagined. Mother Paula was driving slowly when suddenly a car cut across in front of her at a busy intersection. As Mother Paula jammed on the brakes, trying to avoid a collision, our car veered towards the footpath and mounted the kerb with a massive jolt. The impact shifted the planks, I felt the full brunt of their weight against the back of my head. The car seat came adrift from its moorings, my legs buckled beneath me and I was trapped. As searing pain shot up my spine I tried to breathe – until the tranquillity of nothingness washed over me.

Chapter Seventeen
Wayside Rebels

Even now I find it difficult to recall the sequence of events which followed the car accident and which led to me being hospitalised in England. I was in the very hospital where I'd been cared for following the incident with the meat cleaver. I know that I spent Christmas in The Upstate Medical Centre in New York and that by mid January it was decided by the vascular specialist that I needed further surgery. Mother Paula informed me that it was Mother Angelus' wish that this should be done in England. I don't know why. Perhaps she didn't trust the American surgeons but it was more likely a matter of saving money. Sister Hyacinth travelled with me, she it appeared was most easily spared because a substitute teacher was available for the Kindergarten, who as Mother General had informed us months before, were only babies and didn't need a real teacher. The journey to London was long, tedious and painful. We went from New York to Boston. The snow lay deep outside and when the doors opened for further passengers to board we were frozen in our seats. A stewardess brought us blankets and I was given a hot drink when Sister Hyacinth explained that I'd been ill. I was very worried because I feared that once in England I might not get back to America. Mother General might come up with some new plan for me.

The hospital was very quiet, the Nursing Sisters going about their work with efficiency and speaking to me only if this was necessary.

'It's time for your physiotherapy sister.'

'Did you have any pain during the night, sister?'

'Mr. O'Keefe wants X-rays this morning, sister, come along now.'

'Have you got a spiritual book to read, dear?'

So you can imagine my surprise and delight when Sister Joanne appeared one morning. She had come over from the farm herself with the day's supply of eggs for the hospital kitchen.

'I heard that you were in here,' she smiled, 'and I was determined to come to see you. Sister Catherine won't say anything, so don't worry.'

We talked about America and about what had been going on in Mary's Way since I had left. Sister Joanne asked me if we were implementing Vatican II. Mother Angelus and her cronies were raising strong objections to any changes, she told me. As far as I could gather, I explained, we had just about accepted the mass in English in America and in community we sang the Divine Office in the vernacular too. Mother Paula only does what she is directed to do from here I told her.

'Well, you know, Sister Mary Jacob, I heard that the bishops in Ireland have told their Religious Orders to discontinue the practise of having Lay Sisters. These nuns must each have a place in the choir from now on. I knew an Order in the West of Ireland where the Lay Sisters were in pews away from the educated ones. They didn't recite the Divine Office, they even had different prayers.'

'I often wondered about the idea of Lay Sisters,' I told her. 'They did all the work it seems, while those who had schooling and a big dowry became teachers or nurses. I'm glad that it was never a custom in Our Congregation.'

'Oh don't be so sure about that,' she grimaced. 'Look at poor Sister

Cecily, always in the laundry, day after day, week after week, year after year. Sure she's never done anything else and Sister Matilda is the same. She's in the kitchen all the time – practically welded to the cooker by now. I think we have Lay Sisters all right, nuns who have not been educated even though the Order prides itself on giving everyone a status. I have discovered, she added, that many of the sisters who do the menial jobs have come from Orphanages. Don't repeat this, whatever you do,' she added, 'but just have a think about it.'

Looking at me quizzically, Sister Joanne asked if I'd heard what had happened in the hospital. Had I seen the special letter which was sent to each convent, asking us to pray for the sisters in St. Mary's Hospital I had not seen anything at all, what was it all about I wanted to know.

'Well, you must have noticed how quiet everyone is. Sister Rachel has been sent, as we say, to the Outer Hebrides and you know how the doctors admired her. She was the best matron they've ever had here and Sister Anne, she's somewhere in Africa now, whisked away in the night with Sister Madge who is in Ireland as far as I know although Sister Marguerite who has just returned from Galway told me that there's no sign of her there.'

'What was the nature of their crime?' I laughed. 'I know it's probably not funny but such drastic punishment, for what?'

'Actually, I think it's very funny,' she chuckled. 'Not the punishment, of course, but, following the directives of Vatican II the sisters looked for their rights. They wanted to alter the habits, to make them more suitable for nursing and for daily life too. There was a big meeting in the Motherhouse when they sent in a petition about this. Mother Angelus and the General Council said no. Mother Angelus, they were reminded, was our Foundress and it was she who had designed our habit which has all the meaning and symbolism associated with the Order of St. Mary of the Wayside. There would not be one iota of change.'

Sister Joanne continued in a low voice, telling me how the three disobedient sisters who needed our prayers, had, while on night duty, altered their habits. They arrived for morning mass wearing dresses which reached just below the knee. The large, brown, rosary beads was missing and they each wore a neat veil almost the same as the lay nurses and had their hair showing.

'Well, I wasn't there,' Sister Joanne, continued, 'but I wish I had been. I would have clapped them on the back. The lay nurses and doctors congratulated them thinking that they were authorised to try out a new style. Everyone thought it looked smart except the tell tales who had to rush off to Reverend Mother with the news. A show down followed when Mother Angelus arrived with her Council. We didn't even get a chance to say goodbye to the rebels. Some of the doctors, realising that Matron was being moved during the night, blockaded the convent car at the hospital gates until Sister Rachel persuaded them to let her through.'

Sister Joanne said that she did not want to tire me out, I was not to worry about what she had told me and when I was strong again, maybe I'd walk to the farm to see all my old friends and have another little chat. This would be a good goal to set myself.

'Lobelia is still around and she's as temperamental as ever. Now here are a few boiled sweets for you,' she whispered stuffing a paper bag under the pillow. 'Mr. Shiels brings them in all the time. Maybe I'll call in again next week. God bless you.'

'Give my best wishes to Mr. Shiels,' I called, as ever so softly she closed the door.

When Mr. O'Keefe told me that I was being discharged, conditionally and explained that I could now go to the Motherhouse for rest and recuperation, I had mixed feelings. Although the hospital had become boring and I wanted to get out of there, I was nervous about the future.

'I know that you will be well cared for in Mary's Way,' Mr. O'Keefe said as he smiled at Sister Catherine who stood beside him. 'However,

Sister Mary Jacob, I do want to see you next week and after that monthly depending on the speed of your return to full strength. I will write out these instructions and I want them followed to the letter.' As he said this he looked knowingly at Sister Catherine.

'Of course, Sir,' she replied. 'I will make sure that your orders are made known in the Motherhouse.'

'I almost forgot,' Mr. O'Keefe went on, 'to remind you that you must not over exert yourself, Sister Mary Jacob. So, no climbing stairs, carrying heavy books or bags and you must avoid crowds so there is to be no travel on public transport for the moment. We don't want you picking up infection now, do we?'

I had never before met the nun who came to collect me from the hospital. She may have been a little deaf because she didn't reply to anything I said and she only spoke once or twice. Once to say, 'damn' when a car passed her at speed and again to utter, 'shift your bloody arse' when a slow driver wouldn't get out of her way. Who is this woman, I wondered suspecting that while driving the car she was able to vent her frustrations in ways not possible within the cloister? Mother St. John the Baptist met me at the door of the Motherhouse and told me to go at once to the office of Mother Angelus.

'Mother is expecting you, dear,' she smiled, followed by the usual, 'and we must not keep Mother waiting must we.'

Mother was expecting others it seemed because when I reached her office there was a queue outside. I stood there on the polished wood floor as I had stood so many times before feeling anxious and bereft. I was alone again without the support system and directions which I'd had in the hospital. I was weak and nervous. I had been instructed by Mother St. John the Baptist to show Mr. O'Keefe's letter to Mother Angelus so that she would know how well I had recovered and what I would have to do in the future. When I was eventually kneeling painfully beside Mother and feeling upset that she didn't tell me to sit down I decided to be brave. This would, I assumed be a better tactic if I wanted to return to America. I wouldn't let her know how I was really feeling. I needn't have worried.

'What is this, sister,' she snapped when I handed her the instructions from the specialist in response to her matter of fact, 'how are you dear?'

'Oh I see. Well Sister Mary Jacob, we don't need this. It goes without question that you will be looked after here and as I see it since you are discharged from the hospital you are well enough to resume your religious life as before. You will be under the direction of Mother St. John the Baptist dear, and she will arrange for you to go to Ireland with Sister Hyacinth.'

While Mother Angelus spoke she slowly tore the instructions from Mr. O'Keefe into tiny pieces before handing them to me with a curt, 'for the waste basket, dear.'

'Ireland?' I gasped. 'Did you say I'm going to Ireland, Mother?'

I couldn't believe this, what was going on. Was I being sent after all to complete my nursing studies? My head was reeling.

'Well,' Mother Angelus frowned, 'I think it is best if you and Sister Hyacinth go to Ireland together before your return to America. Your accident has caused so much difficulty, dear, that the Order cannot afford to have you return again in two years when it would be time for your home visit. So you and Sister Hyacinth will be going to Galway and from there to your family home for two weeks. Afterwards, you will both leave for America from Shannon.'

I thought I would pass out. The best news was my impending return to America. But a home visit? Did my parents know about this? I knew that my mother would be furious to get such short notice. She would want to paint the house first and do all kinds of needless jobs before my return. And would Tom and Colin be free? And I felt awful and I knew that I didn't look good either. This was terrible. The voice of Mother Angelus droned on.

'You have missed a semester from college, sister. Now Mother

Paula tells me that you can make this up by covering the same courses in Summer School and she has arranged this for you already. The bishop had to be told about your accident. I expect he thought that it was very careless of you, dear, to sit in front with all those planks behind you in the car. I do worry about you sisters in New York State and I'm going out there in a few months to give you all some more advice and encouragement. And I have to explain the St. Mary of the Wayside interpretation of Vatican II. Some sisters are totally misguided about this, you know and it's my duty to keep the authentic spirit of the Order alive. I will be taking three other sisters to America,' she added, 'for the Elementary School and there will be other changes to make because you can't all live in that small convent. There will be hard work ahead for you, dear and I will expect you to give your all and not to count the cost.'

Well, I was right about my mother's reaction to my surprise visit. When she arrived with my father at the convent in Galway I could tell immediately how cross she was. Having looked me up and down and without a kiss or embrace she launched into an attack on Mother Elizabeth.

'What in the name of God is going on, Mother?' She demanded. 'Without very much notice we have our daughter on our doorstep looking like the dog's dinner. What has been happening to you, Ellie? We haven't even had a Christmas card not to mention a letter from you for at least two months and when I phoned you, Mother Elizabeth, you said that you didn't know anything. I had to telephone America to be told that my daughter had been in a car crash and was in hospital in England. And when I phoned The Motherhouse I was advised that I would hear from Mother Angelus "in due course". So this is how you treat the parents who have given a daughter into your care, is it? Supposing you had a brain tumour, Ellie and were in a coma, I bet we wouldn't even be told about this until after your death.'

'Come now, Eleanor,' my father coaxed as he put his arms around me. 'Ellie is coming home with us for a holiday and in a few days she will be right as rain again, won't you, chicken?'

'Of course,' I croaked. 'I've just got a sore throat. I probably picked it up while we were on the mail boat. It was crowded.'

'You travelled on the mail boat?' My mother shrieked. 'After a prolonged stay in hospital you travelled on the mail boat overnight and in this cold weather. Mother Elizabeth, I ask you. Why did my daughter not have a plane ticket to Ireland? I bet you and most certainly Mother Angelus would not travel on the mail boat. No wonder she's ill. If she doesn't recover enough to have a good holiday with her family I will hold Mother General entirely responsible and she will hear from me.'

Mother Elizabeth looked quite stricken during this tirade but she did what she could to ease the situation. My parents were persuaded to have a cup of tea before taking me to Eskeriada. And my mother didn't decline a glass of sherry when it was offered which mellowed her slightly. Yet the journey was tense and my homecoming from America was nothing like what I had imagined and indeed hoped for. I had dreamed of being at home in the summer time but this was March and the cold winds blew over the river while rain lashed the windscreen of the car. Our mood mirrored the weather and I longed for Tom to be with us to lighten the atmosphere. But he was working in Galway and couldn't get home until the weekend. Bridget would be with him said my mother tersely adding, 'more beds to be made and more work for me.' Colin was in London working on a college project. He could only manage a telephone call my mother explained and he was very upset because if he had known that I was in England he could have visited me there.

'I don't understand all the secrecy, Ellie.' She complained. 'It's not natural to keep us in the dark about your accident. What happened exactly, were you driving the car?'

'No, I wasn't, Reverend Mother Paula was and it wasn't her fault at all. A driver shot out in front of us without any warning and I was just unlucky.'

'Unlucky,' my mother smirked. 'Of course you were the unlucky one I bet Reverend Mother escaped without a scratch.'

I didn't answer because I knew that Mother Paula had indeed escaped without a scratch although she was naturally in deep shock. But she was back in charge of the school within a week while I was here on an unwanted and unscheduled holiday. That evening after supper, as we sat beside the roaring fire we tried to talk normally but I was scared because every word I spoke seemed to lead to a confrontation with my mother. I spoke about the auntie's visit and said I was looking forward to seeing them again. While this pleased my father greatly my mother used it as a means of attack.

'You actually said very little about them in your letters, Ellie.' She accused. 'Which I must say is no surprise. But I know that Irene heard from Anna and got presents for the twins. Anna told her that it was you who suggested this and all we get are dull and meaningless letters from you and never a gift from anyone in America. I mean you are attending university and studying English yet your letters home are useless. I wouldn't even show one to Aunty Pat. You know I have to pretend that we've heard all sorts of interesting news from you when people ask how you are getting on. It's very unfair, Ellie. What are you hiding?'

'I'm not hiding anything at all,' I said quietly. 'I just know that when you and daddy and the others come to America for holidays over the next few years I will be able to tell you so much and to show you everything that we're doing. This will be so much better than trying to write it all down. So you must come, like you promised.'

'You're a good one to talk about promises, Ellie. The Order you joined doesn't know what a promise means. And where do you think we will get the money to go flying off to America? Colin has to be supported still and business is not great now. You've had your head turned, Ellie, with all that high living the Americans go on with. But remember it's not the same here in Ireland, we have a long way to go.'

My father looked uncomfortable. Things were not all that bad he reasoned. We were better off than a lot of people and they would get to America he would see to it. That night I couldn't sleep. I could see my rag doll Judy staring down at me from the top of the wardrobe but I didn't tell her any secrets now. I just longed to return to America, to be back in college and to hide behind the safeguard of a convent routine. The following morning my father whispered to me, 'It's your mother's birthday today I thought I'd just remind you. Have you got anything to give to her, you know what she's like?'

I hadn't a thing. I had not been given anything to take home with me and this time Mother Elizabeth hadn't produced a tablecloth. What could I do?

'Don't fret, I'll send Kay from the shop across to the chemist and I'll get a bottle of perfume. You can give her that, Ellie,' he smiled.

But my mother was not fooled. She knew every item on every shelf in the chemist and she was not pleased that I had not brought her something from America. What would the neighbours say? What other mother would have a daughter come all the way from America with her "two hands hanging." People she barely knew brought her mementos from their holidays and Bridget never came without something nice for her and daddy. What kind of a girl was I? My cousin, who was a nun in an Irish Convent, was given money for her keep while at home. Was I given money, did I ask for money, no!

'Eleanor, please, that's enough. We don't need money from the convent in order to give Ellie a holiday at home. She's come here from the hospital anyway so how could she have presents for everyone. When we go over to America she will get you whatever you want, won't you, Ellie.'

'Oh yes,' my mother sneered, 'and you'll pay for it won't you, Owen just like you paid for this bottle of perfume. Well, thank you both very much.'

And to my horror, my mother ran out of the room and up the stairs. We heard the bedroom door slam as she settled into bed for the three awful days which followed. While my father and I tried to act normally, my mother turned her head to the wall whenever I entered my parent's bedroom. I'd ask her if there was anything she'd like and both daddy and I kept up a charade of her being ill and needing rest. So while we cooked the meals together and went for short drives, she read magazines, listened to the radio and had tasty snacks on a tray complete with embroidered cloth which I prepared and daddy delivered. When Kay needed advice in the shop my father had to climb the stairs to ask my mother's opinion. Sometimes she feigned sleep and at other times told him to ask Kay what she was being paid for.

'What is wrong with mammy?' I asked. 'Does she act in this way very often or is just because I'm here and didn't bring her anything? I wonder, daddy, if I should telephone Mother Elizabeth and have the nuns take me back to the convent in Galway. Maybe this would be the best thing to do?'

'Oh Ellie, don't even think of doing such a thing. It would only make matters worse. Can you imagine trying to come home again after leaving in such a way? No, your mother will appear one morning as if nothing has ever happened. I don't know why she gets into these states. I think she feels that she is losing control over you and the boys. And I have to agree with her that we should have been told about your accident. It really was a shock to find out about it when you were in England. I think your mother is afraid that she will gradually know nothing at all about you, Ellie. I wonder about this too. Is she right, Ellie? You can't blame her for worrying and for feeling left out. I think that in her heart she has not really given you to the convent at all. And the shop doesn't compensate for her loss. It just doesn't mean as much to her as it used to do either. She needs a new interest and

God knows there's not much going on here in Eskeriada to excite her or to give her an opening for her talents.'

'Whose talents are you talking about?' It was my mother, downstairs at last and looking a million dollars as they would say in the States. Aunty Pat had telephoned she announced and she was coming on the train for the weekend. And she'd invite Aunty Irene and the twins over for tea on Sunday afternoon. It would be great she beamed because we'd have a full house. I was delighted to see Aunty Pat but I sensed that she was suspicious and knew more about recent events in our house than she was letting on, she didn't try to discuss my mother with me at all and I didn't give her the opportunity to do so either. I was drawing away from everyone even Aunty Irene to whom I'd spoken before I went to America. I had not seen her since my arrival home because daddy decided that it would upset mammy if we went to Capall Ban without her. Uncle Eugene drove them over and when he came into our house for a few minutes he told me that he was glad to hear that I had seen his sisters in America. But he couldn't wait for tea because there were jobs to be done. Obviously he and my mother were still uncomfortable in each other's company. The twins had grown so much, they had started school and they brought some drawings for me. I admired the brightly crayoned pictures of a cow, a chicken, a pig and then an amazing looking black creature with a yellow face. 'She's our teacher, Sister Josepha. She's a nun, Ellie,' they chorused, 'but she doesn't look like you at all.' They talked and questioned incessantly.

'Ellie, where are your legs now?'

'Ellie, have you seen any cowboys and Indians?'

'Ellie, do you eat candy.'

When I told them that I moved on wheels and demonstrated this by gliding along the polished wooden floor, they chased me out of the parlour and up the stairs then down again and into the shop until my mother shouted.

'Stop, the three of you, you mustn't run about like that, Ellie. Remember you've had serious surgery. What would anyone think? Come here boys and don't mind Ellie – on wheels indeed. I'll oil your wheels for you miss, if you don't keep quiet.'

Everyone laughed as I collapsed on the sofa and the boys were taken away for a walk to the sweet shop with my mother and Aunty Pat. Tom and Bridget who had spent the weekend wrapped around each other had gone out too. While they were genuinely delighted to see me and asked so many questions about America and about University life I had the feeling that their visit was one of obligation and that they'd prefer be away someplace on their own.

My mother fussed over them and made a big display of the cake Bridget had brought.

'Look at this, Ellie,' she beamed, 'isn't Bridget gifted? She made and iced this cake herself. It's a work of art, Bridget.'

And it was. The cake was perfection itself but I couldn't wait for it to be cut, not for the taste alone but to see the end of that icing in shocking pink that shouted, 'welcome home, Ellie!' Is this what my mother misses I mused? Does she want to be seen to have a domestic role to play in my life also? Probably, but more than that she wants me to be submissive too and to make her feel important the way Bridget does. Maybe the realization as daddy had implied that my life is no longer under her control appals her. She is unable to come to terms with all the changes which are happening within the family. Perhaps her temper tantrums, her retreating to bed and her efforts to dominate are protest signals. But I knew only too well that I couldn't help her because she wouldn't listen to whatever I might try to say – and what could I say? What did I know about her life anymore? She reminded me of Mother Angelus because like her, the need to be centre stage seemed overwhelming.

Having helped Aunty Irene to clear away the tea things I retreated silently to the large brown velveteen covered easy chair in the sitting room. Colin's cat, Finnegan, made himself comfortable on my lap and we dozed as a huge fire roared and logs sizzled in the grate. There were voices disturbing my slumber. I heard them vaguely at first then more clearly as I awoke. What could I do? My father and Aunty Irene were standing outside the open parlour door not realising that I was nearby.

'You must do something, Owen. I mean Ellie looks very tired and frail. Did you see how she almost passed out when the boys were playing with her? I do realise how anxious you are. Speak to her. Is she happy out there in America at all?'

'God Almighty probably doesn't know the answer to that one, Irene,' he sighed. 'You know I'd do anything for Ellie. I'd even go to America myself and bring her home if I thought she was really unhappy. But it's so hard to know with her. When Anna wrote she said that she thought Ellie was doing well in the States.'

Dan and Bridget came here to see her last Thursday. And they were talking about Sister Jude. She's a Finnerty from Clare, the big racing stable people. She's in the convent in America with Ellie. Noel Finnerty was at Shannon when the nuns were setting off for America. He told Dan how he'd met Ellie and she was very nervous about the plane journey. He tried to reassure her. Can you imagine the ructions when Eleanor discovered that the Finnerty's were allowed to see their daughter off? You can't blame Eleanor I suppose because it looks as if who you are and what your family has, seems to matter in the convent just as much as it does in the parish. You can see that Ellie gives nothing away. She had never mentioned this Sister Jude to us. Eleanor got so cross with her about this. You know what I think Irene? I think that Ellie is just counting the days until she is off again. It's terrible.'

I sat rigid in the chair. Should I cough or get up to put some more logs on the fire? Should I do something to alert them to my presence? I did nothing.

'Owen, I know what you mean,' Irene said. 'Convent living is very different to what we imagine. In my experience the nuns live a life very unfamiliar to what we know. Remember it's all women together and women can be very powerful as a group. Those who get positions of authority are hell bent on keeping the system in place without any challenges. I know this from my nursing days, Owen. I think Ellie's identity and personality is slipping away from us all now. She is under the control of the Order.'

'That sounds awful,' my father gasped. 'You know I think she's lonely for home but, like you say, she can't admit this. She won't be disloyal to the nuns. What would you do, Irene?'

'I tell you Owen,' she replied. 'If I had had two girls instead of two boys I'd keep them well away from the clutches of any nuns. But look the Order she's with has a fine reputation so I think it's best to leave her alone this time. She's been through a lot and you don't want her going back to New York with bad memories of her visit. I think you should really encourage her to get a good degree and even further education if it's offered. Make sure Owen that if Ellie ever decides to ...'

The telephone rang resounding shrilly throughout the house. Aunty Irene knowing that it must be Colin and having said so to my father, ran downstairs to the front door, shouting back, 'Owen, I'll see where Eleanor is, she'll be furious if she misses Colin's call.'

I heard my father laughing as he spoke to my younger brother. I sidled out of the sitting room and hovered near him.

'The phone woke me,' I whispered. 'I was asleep. Keep talking to Colin while I splash some water on my face, I'm not awake yet.'

Colin's voice amazed me. He sounded so masculine, so much older than I'd remembered. There was sincerity in his tone and I did feel that he would have been glad to be in Eskeriada during my stay.

'How is God these days?' He chuckled. 'Tell Him I've a few questions for Him to answer. We must arrange an interview. You've the hot line, Ellie, can you arrange this?'

'No problem,' I laughed. 'I think it would be easier for you to interview God than you think.'

Tell me, Ellie, how are things States Side? What's college like? I need a long letter from you with all the details. You know when I finish in Galway next year I'm thinking of heading over there to do further studies. Would this be a good idea?'

My heart was suddenly filled with happiness.

'Oh Colin that's a terrific idea. You'd love America, I know you would. When you need information I'll help you all I can.'

Colin said he was upset to hear about my accident and very unhappy he didn't know I was in England. He could have come to see me when he'd arrived over there but now that he had his college project well under way he couldn't leave.

'And guess what, Ellie,' he enthused, 'I'm thrilled to be working in Fleet Street. This is where it all happens you know and if I get some contacts now it will be ideal for the future. I'm so sorry, but I haven't a hope in hell of seeing Ireland for another month. Hey, are you going back to America from London, Ellie?'

I didn't get time to answer because my mother came charging up the stairs and snatched the receiver from my hand. As I walked away I could hear her, 'Oh, Colin! I nearly missed your call. We took the twins out for sweets. Yes, of course Ellie's fine. Now I must tell you ...'

I left her there chattering away. Tom and Bridget were getting ready to leave and I had to say goodbye to them.

'I've hardly managed to have a chat with you at all,' I said to Tom. 'I hope you and Bridget are enjoying your jobs. Do you like your work?'

'Look, Ellie,' he replied. 'I know that this has been a rather rushed weekend for us and we really did think we'd manage to take you out somewhere for a drive and a good old talk about everything. But you know how it is. If I suggested this mammy would want to come as well and,' he laughed, 'you know the way she takes over.' But don't worry, Ellie, we are saving hard and we'll make it to America. Maybe for our honeymoon,' he whispered.

'That would be wonderful, Tom. And I really do understand.'

Bridget hugged me while also warning me to take care of myself.

'I know what college is like but you mustn't overdo things when you go back,' she admonished, 'You are not back to full health at all since your accident. Tell the Reverend Mother in America that you must have more rest and a good tonic. I could always recommend one.'

'Thank you,' I smiled. 'I could do with a good caring pharmacist like you, Bridget. Tom has made a wise choice. He always knew how to look after himself.'

Laughing, they went outside to the car, just as Uncle Eugene drew up to the curb. We were all together on the street including mammy. The twins kissed me before Irene had time to wipe the residue of sticky sweets from their mouths. Aunty Pat clattering about on her high heels wished everyone well and hugged whoever was within reach including my father who got in her way.

'Why am I saying goodbye to you?' She laughed.

'He'd do anything to hug a well endowed lady,' Uncle Eugene quipped, knowing I'm sure, that my mother, who was not so well endowed, stood within earshot. She called out sharply, 'come here, Owen, can you find the iron doorstop before this hall door closes over in the wind?'

I had not been into my mother's drapery shop since I'd arrived. It was rather old fashioned looking I thought and I could understand now why the American aunties had thought so too. The colours and styles were not as cheerful as those worn in the States but I did notice that my mother had the place well stocked and the garments attractively displayed. I wasn't sure if she had done the displays herself or if it was the work of Kay who was employed by her. I'd not seen many of the neighbours until St. Patrick's Day when my mother invited close family friends to the house. She was so disappointed though that Fr. Cyril was away.

'It's such a shame,' she explained to her friends, 'because you know he is very fond of Ellie.'

He was, I discovered, in England, in Stratford on Avon with a group of young clerical students. They had gone over to see some Shakespearian plays my mother explained admiringly.

'I wonder if you nuns will attend worthwhile plays, Ellie, in America. Have your rules about not going to places of public entertainment changed at all? Of course, I don't believe the Americans could compete with The Royal Shakespeare Company.'

Where had all this come from? I knew soon enough. Father Knickers had visited Eskeriada before his cultural journey. Had he known about my hospital stay he would, she knew, have come to see me by hook or by crook. But since she, my mother, didn't know about this for such a long time, what could she do? It was too late then to contact the dear man.

'Oh I laughed,' dismissing any reference to Fr. Knickers. 'Not only do we attend dramas, we study them in depth too.'

Joe and Judith who had married the year before were at the party. Judith was expecting their first child and we laughed over our innocence when as children we believed that her mother had a supply of babies for the town. I was sad to meet Jerry Breen's parents. They tried to be brave about their loss but I could tell that it was not easy for them.

'We always thought that you and Jerry would get married, Ellie. Well, not after you'd decided to enter I mean. It was a hopeless dream for Jerry but it kept him going. He talked about you a lot. That was a ferocious accident you had Ellie. Your mother told me about it. When I think of it, we could have lost you as well as Jerry. We do look on you as one of our own. It's strange I know and I hope you don't mind.'

'Not at all,' I told her. 'Jerry was my very best friend. I pray for him every day.'

May Kenny and her husband Martin began to tell me about their son who would begin university the following October. They were very proud of Kieran. I didn't know him very well because he was younger than us. Kieran was adopted which was the reason why the Kenny's kept him, according to my mother, 'wrapped in cotton wool.'

'He's a great young fellow,' Martin Kenny enthused. 'He's going to be a doctor. Now can you beat that, our boy a doctor, it's a long hard course of study but he's well able for it, isn't he May?'

'He is indeed,' she agreed. 'He has a fine brain don't know where he got it from. My father was a well educated man you know but the brains were lost on me I'm afraid. And on you too, Martin, you weren't that good at the school books were you?'

Ignoring his wife Martin Kenny asked me what the students were like in American Universities.

'I believe most young yanks have cars and drive to college. I've heard though that the standard is not as good as it is here in Ireland. Is this true? What do you think of the education over there, Ellie?'

I told him that it was first class.

'There are so many degree choices for the student,' I explained. 'It's an education system that looks to the future and prepares the students for professions or for employment, which will be there for them in the years ahead. There are many types of universities in the states,' I added, 'and I'm fortunate to attend what is known as an Ivy League College.'

I'm not sure if this impressed Martin Kenny or not but my mother looked at me and smiled a well done, Ellie, smile. And such a smile of approval made me very happy. The following morning was quiet until Aunty Pat came clattering downstairs with her bags. Daddy was taking her down the road to the train station.

'Ellie, come here, you little love,' she called out. 'You will be glad to have some peace and quiet at last. This weekend's been a real break for me. I just hope that you're not worn out, Eleanor. Now the two of you deserve a nice treat and I've left some lovely biscuits and a bottle of sherry on the table so get to it, girls.'

Chapter Eighteen
Recovery

I couldn't believe my eyes. Tom and Bridget were standing outside the convent door in Galway. It was afternoon and Sister Hyacinth and I were packed and ready to leave for Shannon.

'Have you come to say goodbye again?' I asked them.

'Are you surprised, Ellie?' Tom beamed. 'Well, you are going to be even more surprised because we're driving you and Sister Hyacinth all the way to Shannon.'

'What!' I cried. 'I don't believe this! Does Mother Elizabeth know?'

'Of course I know,' Mother Elizabeth spoke from behind me. 'Your brother is very persuasive, Sister Mary Jacob, he wondered why I should take two nuns away from their duties to go all the way to the airport and drive back from there at night. He had a point of course so off you go now and God bless you all.'

As Mother Elizabeth gave me the kiss of peace she whispered.

'This drive by your brother is my decision. I did not hear from the Motherhouse that any particular sister should drive you. Do you understand, dear?'

I understood.

What a wonderful journey we had. Sister Hyacinth I could tell was as happy as I was. She came from County Clare she told Bridget and her family had a small guest house in Ballyvaughan. There wasn't much going on there at this time of the year although some of the rare wild flowers unique to the place were beginning to appear. She enjoyed walking on the strange rocky land of the Burren and helping her brother in law to find lost sheep. Her parents were dead and she had just one sister. Within the convent walls I would never have heard such family details. I told her about my mother's shop and about the neighbours and Tom spoke about the farm where he, Colin, and I had been born.

'No wonder Sister Mary Jacob was such a good little farm hand in Mary's Way,' she laughed. 'Sister Joanne, who is still in charge there, depended on her a lot, I know that. She's from County Clare too, sister. We went to the same national school.'

'Oh, the Banner County,' laughed Tom. 'I do love those banner spuds from Clare with loads of butter and salt.'

We were soon at Shannon Airport and I was relaxed and content. There was no search for lost documents this time or threats of further punishment for misdeeds. Tom and Bridget would see us in America, they promised. And did I know, Tom asked, that Aunty Pat was planning a surprise trip over with my mother? I suspected this I said, adding, 'I hope they come, Tom. It would be so good for mammy to know where I am and to see it all for herself. She would love it, I'm sure. But, Tom,' I warned him, 'please don't surprise me! I will have to have permission to see them when they come.'

'Don't worry, I know all about your odd rules and regulations,' he laughed. 'We'll make sure mammy understands too. Anyway, she will be going with Pat. No better woman to keep her under control,' he winked. 'And by the way, she doesn't know that we are here. Say nothing, Ellie. If daddy still drove at night they could both be seeing you off but he doesn't. So what mammy doesn't know won't trouble her.'

'What a lovely pair,' Sister Hyacinth was saying as we settled into our seats on the plane. She asked me how I was feeling and if I'd be able for college again.

'I don't know what's going on?' She muttered. 'We are moving to a new convent, did you know this, sister? And Mother Angelus will be out in America again in a couple of months. Then God help us all!'

I knew from Mother Angelus about her plans to come to America soon with possibly three or even four additional sisters for the school, I replied, but I'd heard nothing about a new convent.

'Who knows what they're up to, sister. I don't know who gets all these bright ideas. I mean the school is being run like a hospital ward and from the Motherhouse too. Mother Paula doesn't seem to be able to write on the blackboard without getting permission from Mother General.'

I agreed with Sister Hyacinth and I told her that I was glad I'd be in college during the summer. At least I might avoid some of the drama which I inherently associated with a visit from Mother Angelus. Arriving at New York Airport we took a connecting flight to Syracuse N.Y. on an aptly named Pilgrim aeroplane. This was a tiny, eight seat commuter. Syracuse N.Y. is a city to the north of Albany. We would be collected there. But on approaching Syracuse the pilot announced that weather conditions had altered very suddenly and he now had to, with a blizzard impending, divert to Rome. I gasped in disbelief and horror. Rome!

'It's Rome N.Y.' Sister Hyacinth laughed, 'have you forgotten your American geography already?'

Of course, I did remember but I was worried. Suppose we were stranded in Rome? Then what would happen to the sisters who were to collect us? They would be on the highway to Syracuse already. Sister Hyacinth was worried too and on landing in Rome she ran to a telephone to advise Mother Paula about our predicament. The sisters had indeed left the convent. She would have them paged in Syracuse and they would continue driving from there to Rome.

'I explained to Mother Paula about the weather conditions up here and I did suggest that we might get in touch with a local convent because I'm sure there's a couple we could phone. Then we, including Sister Ruth and Sister Jude who are coming to collect us could stay until the roads are safe. Would you believe, sister, she wouldn't hear of such a thing. We are to stay here, have patience and trust in the Lord. I'm so worried about the sisters who are driving. I mean its dark out there and the roads will be treacherous. What reckless carry on in the name of obedience?'

I agreed. The hours passed slowly. The night grew darker outside and snowflakes were whipped into the shed like terminal whenever an outside door opened. It was eerie. There was nobody to be seen later on except a man who was cleaning the floor while wrapped in a yellow parka and wearing thick, red gloves. He brought us coffee from a vending machine.

'Ladies, you must try to keep warm,' he advised. 'The heating system is out of action so when you've had this coffee, get up, walk around and shake it all about. You get my meaning?'

We got his meaning. I was so cold. The iciness was piercing through me like spears rammed in from the soles of my feet to the top of my head. As we shivered Sister Hyacinth hugged the styrofoam cup in an effort to warm her hands. Before dawn broke an official appeared who, on seeing us surrounded by our baggage and half asleep, invited us into his office where he left us alone with an electric fire giving minimal heat and comfort. To us it was heaven and as we thawed, out Sister Hyacinth spoke.

'This reminds me,' she said, 'of the days when we had to sleep in Nissan Huts behind St. Mary's Hospital. That's when Sister Joanne and I were Novices. We were working on the wards, cleaning and dusting and being general dog's bodies,' she laughed. 'But you know, sister, it wasn't funny because several of the young sisters including Sister Joanne got tuberculosis there. We were so cold at night and in the morning the water which had been put into the wash basins was frozen over. I'll never forget it. Eventually, the Health Authorities wondered why so many girls from St. Mary's were tuberculosis patients. There was an unexpected inspection and a screening of everyone. The huts were demolished immediately and our diet improved too. I always thought this was such a terrible disgrace for a Nursing Order but they brazened it out and it's never been referred to again. I'm sure you've never heard about this, sister?'

'No, never,' I replied. 'What else went on years ago, I wanted to know?'

'Well, I shouldn't tell you this but a small number of the sisters became quite unbalanced. Some of them had suffered during the war years, you know. I knew of one or two who actually drove ambulances at that time. Maybe they saw the convent as a refuge after such hardships, I don't know. I do recall one lunch time when the sister who was reader suddenly flung the spiritual book into the air. She began to shout and even though the Junior Mistress ran to stop her it was impossible to do so. The poor nun was distraught but she was young. I imagine she had a psychiatric problem although some of the things she ranted and raved about were very close to the bone.'

'What happened to her?'

'Well, I do know that she was taken off to hospital, a public psychiatric place near London. And would you believe it, sister? When a nun from Mary's Way was taken there she would have a special grey habit to wear in the vain hope that nobody would know where she'd come from.'

'This is unbelievable,' I gasped. 'You must know so much, sister about the history of the Order. Please tell me more.'

'No, Sister Mary Jacob,' I know I have been speaking too much about the bad days when I should have been silent. I hope I have not scandalised or frightened you. If you are very scrupulous and feel you will have to report our conversation to Sister Veronica I'll understand. But we've been so relaxed travelling together outside the convent walls. I do hope with all my heart that I've done you no harm.'

'Not at all,' I assured her. 'I'm a guilty party too so don't worry. I hope there will be changes in the future. Did you hear about all the trouble in St. Mary's Hospital when ... ?'

We stopped speaking when we saw Sister Ambrose and Sister Jude approaching. They looked really tired and shaken. What a terrible journey they'd had too. It was fortunate that they made it safely to the airport. The traffic police told them to wait for at least two hours before trying to drive back to Albany. It would take that time at least for the snow ploughs to clear the highway. This was awful after our long flight and an all night delay. But it was good to see the engineers arrive to sort out the heating because we had to leave the official's office when the day staff arrived. We had more coffee and sat together huddled in silence until Sister Ambrose was assured that the roads had been sanded and we could travel. Three hours later Mother Paula welcomed us home and following a hot meal we were sent to bed. I couldn't believe the state of my room. It was piled high with boxes. In the wardrobe all my clothes were randomly folded or stuffed onto a shelf to make room for piles of curtains, blankets and towels. What was happening? I didn't know and I was far too tired to think about this. Falling into bed I slept and I didn't move until I heard Sister Zita walk along the corridor, ringing the rising bell and calling out, 'praise to Mary, Our Lady of the Wayside.'

'Thanks Be to God,' I muttered. Then, added silently, 'thanks for nothing.'

Nothing had changed in East Cranberry. I was back again with my companions. Nobody spoke and except for those in charge nobody welcomed us back or asked if I was better. Sister Veronica did explain that my room had been used to store some items which were being assembled for our move to the new convent. I could help with all this packing later but for now Mother Paula wanted to talk to me and she would explain what my immediate duties would be. Sister Hyacinth passing me on the stairs, smiled ruefully. I had a friend now within the convent. We had spoken. Together we had broken the silence. I had at the beginning of my religious life agreed to be silent and to respect the silence of others. Would Mother Paula suspect my betrayal? Had Sister Hyacinth confessed her fault? Even though I felt guilty and disloyal to my word I was determined to say nothing at all. I was responsible for my own thoughts and for my own values which could not, I reasoned, be imprisoned by anyone. Mother Paula did say that she was very sorry for the suffering I'd had to endure following our accident but this was all part of God's plan for me. If I accepted this cross as a gift from God, which she was sure I did, then I would become a better and a stronger religious.

'Offer up all the inconvenience, dear, this is another step on your journey to perfection. Think about the sufferings of Our Lord,' she admonished as I continued to kneel while my injured leg became painfully cramped beneath me. I already knew that I would have to attend Summer School which didn't start until June. Meanwhile, Mother Paula had spoken to Sister Veronica and together they had agreed that I could do Sister Hyacinth's work in the convent and help out also with the preparation of the house which would become our new convent. I was not a great cook even though I had experience in the kitchen at Mary's Grove. Sister Hyacinth quietly advised me to make life as easy for myself as possible. She had her menu for each day in a notebook which she gave to me as well as foolproof methods for cooking dishes to serve eight people exactly. I was very happy to be left alone in the convent for most of the day. I worked out a plan which gave me at least an hour of free time which I devoted to reading, resting or attempting to meditate. As I tried to pray in the chapel the hum of traffic from the highway was the only sound to break the silence within. I really didn't know what starting point my companions used as a means towards meditation. In the Novitiate we were given ideas from the great mystics but I never could follow any particular steps towards this. Now I sat alone going over and over the good and the bad in my life so far. My thoughts became more and more inward looking. I was fragile in mind and body, I had been physically injured, I was frightened in case I would not be able to resume my studies. Again I was pretending. I was concealing my outer wounds in the same way that I concealed so many inner ones.

I was dusting and polishing in our downstairs community room for Junior Sisters when I had an idea. Sister Zita did not have a philosophy lecture on Tuesday and she didn't have child psychology on Wednesday. Did she leave her text books and notes in her locker? I looked and there they were. What an opportunity for me to get ahead before summer school. I would take time from my stolen chapel visits to study. But if I asked permission to do this what would happen? I was sure I would be refused. I didn't ask permission to use our books and to read through Sister Zita's superb notes. While sometimes actually copying her work I held a pen in one hand and a duster in the other in case I might be disturbed. Was this stealing? I decided not to think about it in this way. After all, we did hold all things in common. Didn't we?

※

The doorbell rang one afternoon about a week after my return to West Cranberry. I opened the door and Father Leslie Vaughan stood there. It was Friday, the day for confessions and I'd forgotten.

'Oh my God! Sister Mary Jacob, you've come back to us,' he laughed and, much to my surprise, putting his arms around me he kissed me.

I was delighted and confused. Here was a person who was really happy to see me.

'I was afraid that you'd never come back again to East Cranberry,' he smiled. 'Nobody here seemed to know where you were or what was happening to you. Are you alright? You do look very thin.'

'Sister is perfectly well now, Father.' Sister Veronica who had come upstairs informed him. I blushed and scurried inside totally embarrassed to know that I, being the junior would have to go to confession first. I needn't have worried. Father Leslie was so encouraging. I was angry I said. I was angry with Mother Paula, with Mother General and even with my own mother. These assertive women upset me. I felt diminished in their presence. Destructive and uncharitable thoughts about them filled my mind.

'You have suffered,' Father Leslie explained, 'and this suffering has challenged you. I know that it is very hard to accept illness graciously. Your whole routine has been upset, sister. You are naturally anxious about the future and feel that you have no support not even from your own mother and your religious superiors. Is this how you feel?'

'Yes,' I replied.

'You must try not to think in this way.' He spoke softly. 'I'm sure everyone wishes you to be strong again. I know I do, Sister Mary Jacob. Use your convalescence to move forward into a new understanding of your life. Learn to forgive – yourself first of all and then all those who without realising this, may have hurt you. They have their own burdens and their own pain. I know that you don't have friendships within the convent which allow you to express a kinship with each other. This is a pity I think, but sister, it doesn't mean that your fellow religious are without concern for you.'

'Father,' I said, 'I think I've been stealing?'

'What? Stealing what, sister?'

I thought he was laughing but I continued by explaining how I'd discovered another sister's college work and I'd used it without her knowing and without permission. I wanted a head start for college I explained. I was so worried about my studies and the reports which were periodically sent to Mother General.

'Oh, sister, don't worry about this. If there's an opportunity to do a little extra study on your own, take it. I suppose, strictly speaking, you should ask permission but gee, I don't know, sister, are you harming anyone? Maybe you are harming yourself and if you think so then you alone know what you must do about it.'

His words encouraged me even though I did feel that while Father Leslie did not judge me he would not accept any more excuses or whinging. I had been confused and unable to move forward. I was now determined to put my trust in God and to ask Him for courage – courage to confront my anger and misdeeds and to change them into a force for good.

On the first weekend following my return to America I saw the building which was to become our new convent. Each sister had been assigned a duty there in an effort to have everything ready before Mother Angelus' arrival at the end of May. This house, a very large grey clapboard building with white trim had been constructed in the old semi-colonial style. It was beautiful, it's wooden veranda surrounded by decorative railings, its long sash windows reflecting the early spring sunlight. Long ago, the house had belonged to a newspaper magnate and his large family. It had been left in a bequest to the diocese complete with furnishings and contents, and, although it needed lots of tender loving care, it still retained a comfortable and stable ambience. I could tell that there had been much activity within its walls already. Floors had been sanded, interior walls painted white, window frames repaired, internal doors mended and new very plain light fittings installed. It smelled of wood, paint, resin and beeswax. Sister Veronica showed me the large room which would become the chapel and the upstairs rooms we would occupy for sleeping. What a wonderful house I thought as I peeped into the new sewing room and the library.

'Unfortunately,' Sister Veronica explained, 'there are only two bathrooms but Mother Paula has asked that another be installed downstairs in that small room beside the main hall door. Now, Sister Mary Jacob, she continued as we inspected the kitchen, it will be your task to sort through all the cupboards in the house especially here in the kitchen and next door in the original dining room. There are all sorts of glasses, cutlery, platters, bowls and dishes in these cupboards which we intend to distribute to anyone who is interested in having these. Father Ryan has suggested that trestle tables be placed in the Parish Hall. The school janitor will do this and then you can arrange the items nicely on these, sister. The parishioners will be able to view the displays and choose to take whatever they fancy. Father Ryan will suggest that each one who takes something away should leave a donation.

'You won't have to do this all by yourself Sister Mary Jacob,' she smiled. 'We will all help when we have some free time.'

How I wished I could have shipped all the beautiful china, glass and silver I handled during the next two weeks back to Ireland. My mother and Aunty Irene and Aunty Pat would have such a wonderful time choosing pieces for their homes. My mother loved antique furniture and all old things. What a surprise it would have been for her to get her hands on items which were being offered to the parishioners. Should I try to contact the aunties, I wondered? Would they like any of these treasures? I'd never been to visit them in their houses so I didn't know. In any case they didn't belong to this parish and would tell daddy about my suggestion. This would cause mammy to become envious. No it was better just to do what I had been told to do and to enjoy my own association with the past furnishings of our soon to be convent. I would not be sorry at all to leave our original dwelling. It was so very clinical and without character. From now on it would be the home for two curates as well as supplying office space and meeting rooms for the parish. Our new convent was in a sheltered place and while it would be a longer walk to the school, it was much more private. And best of all, there was a wonderful garden behind the house. A huge wrought iron gate beneath a stone arch led into this hideaway. Tall trees surrounded the lawn area while shrubs and arbours hid secret niches where one could sit and pray. The walk around this sanctuary was cloister like, paved with grey/green slabs and sheltered by box hedging. It could have been made for us I thought. But we had to concentrate on the house now because it had to be ready for occupancy before Mother Angelus arrived in America.

When Mother Angelus came with a companion named Sister Fidelma they immediately inspected every nook and cranny of our new residence. Mother Paula scurried after them and announced happily, 'Mother likes it, she really likes it.' There was only one place deemed to be totally unsuitable for Sisters of St. Mary of the Wayside. It was the new bathroom. This was far too extravagantly furnished and too near to the front hall and the chapel. I had thought so myself but the bathroom had been gifted to the convent by a group of parishioners. They had installed all the fittings and chosen the décor which was indeed out of keeping with our basic lifestyle. Marble effect tiles lined the walls and gleamed in the reflected light from a red and blue toned stained glass window. The bath was an old roll top Victorian style tub which was gracefully adorned by elegant gold taps. A mahogany vanity unit with gilt edged mirror hung above the washbasin. The toilet was a perfect throne having a wide mahogany seat and a golden chain hanging invitingly from a mighty cistern. The end of this chain was complemented by a fat, brass angel whose legs one had to pull in order to flush the toilet. Such outright rejection of the new bathroom posed a dilemma for Mother Paula. She would speak to Father Ryan, she said. Perhaps it was possible to change the fittings without offending those who had presented the bathroom to us in the first place. Alternatively, this bathroom could be kept for the use of visitors only.

'See to this quickly,' Mother Angelus ordered.

I was shrewd enough to suspect, that while Mother Angelus began her visitation to the convent in good humour, telling us the latest news from the Order's houses around the world, recounting funny incidents which she, naturally had played on the unsuspecting and telling mild mannered jokes at which we laughed heartily without knowing what the punch line was supposed to be – I suspected all the while that within a few days her mood would change and we'd be called to account for our actions, our misdeeds and our failures. And very soon indeed we were in crisis.

Sister Brendan and Sister Therese were Primary School teachers who had been assigned to the new school. My friend from those parlour days, Sister Gabriel had come to teach drama. And Sister Julianna, who was Irish, joined the staff in the High School, I returned home from summer school one afternoon with Sister Jude during Mother's first week in America, to discover that the convent was empty and a note had been pinned on the notice board for us. We were to collect Sister Brendan and Sister Therese from the course which they had been registered for following their arrival in America. We were to make sandwiches and take a large fruit cake from the larder then drive to Crystal Lake in the Catskill Mountains. Where on earth was Crystal Lake? And where on earth was the summer dwelling of Mr. Knox, the local Bank Manager who had offered the use of his house along with it's fishing facilities to Mother General?

'We will have to phone Father Ryan for directions,' Sister Jude decided. 'He will surely know where the place is because I expect he's been up there.'

Father Ryan was not at home but Father Palmer knew where it was. We could follow him and he'd bring his new fellow curate Father McIntyre along for the ride.

We were not happy. Mother General would not like to have the two curates hanging around. Maybe we would be able to give them a gentle warning without upsetting them. After all, we surmised, there must be lovely places farther up in the mountains to which they could drive and where they could dine out if they wished. Spying the lake shimmering in the distance, Sister Jude hooted the horn and signalled for the priests to stop. She explained our situation to them as delicately as possible and they took her advice. 'But,' said Father Palmer, 'I do think we should just say hi to Mother General before we drive on. It would be rude not to, don't you think?'

This was agreed. We arrived alongside the lake shore to find Mother's fishing stool outside and a plaid rug spread out on the grass. There was nobody around. Maybe they saw the curates coming and scurried inside. Perhaps they were in swimsuits. We looked at each other blankly. Yes, this was indeed the house named Crystal Cloud. But before we could think, Father Palmer had opened the front door and walked inside. Following with Father McIntyre what a sight awaited us. Mother Angelus was seated in an old rocking chair her eyes blazing with suppressed anger. Sister Zita stood tall in front of the electric cooker while other sisters were in groups pale and nervous looking while they listened to Mother. But the strangest sight of all was Sister Julianna. She was sitting on a wooden kitchen chair in the middle of the room wrapped in a white sheet from head to toe. Overhead, her habit and undergarments were swaying on a temporary clothes line above an electric heater. Was this a sinister ritual which I'd known nothing about?

'Oh my Gawd what the hells happened, sisters?' Father Palmer said in a stunned voice. 'Did someone fall into the water? Is everyone safe here?'

Mother Paula stepped forward.

'Please, Father,' she pleaded. 'Please leave. We're all fine. There was just a slight mishap and a sister fell into the lake. There's no problem at all, believe me. Thank you so much for helping the sisters to find Crystal Lake,' she added, pushing him and Father McIntyre outside. Mother Angelus remained silent until she heard their car drive away.

We were then treated to a vivid description of how two foolish sisters had taken a boat out onto the lake.

'Sister Ambrose, you knew nothing about rowing a boat nothing at all, did you? Why did you volunteer to take Sister Julianna out there?'

'Mother, you did . . '

Mother Paula tried to intervene. I realised that Mother Paula was trying to save the situation. It was very obvious from her look of exasperation that Mother Angelus had ordered Sister Ambrose to row the boat in the first place. Soon we had the whole picture. The two nuns on returning to the mooring attempted to tie up the boat. As Sister Ambrose manoeuvred the craft close to the edge, Sister Julianna, thinking that she was home and dry, stepped out of it and went straight down, feet first, into the water. But worse was to follow. Sister Ambrose realising what had happened and being unable to manage the boat now or to see Sister Julianna anywhere actually screamed and screamed until perfect strangers came running to her aid.

'So undignified, sister,' accused Mother Angelus, 'after all you've learned about religious decorum. And to know that two male doctors who had a holiday house at some distance away actually heard you. Well, they had to dive into the lake to rescue you because, Sister Julianna, you did nothing at all to help yourself.'

'Mother, please, Sister Julianna does not know how to ...'

But Mother General becoming even more furious continued.

'And if this was not enough indignity to be heaped upon us. Could you credit it, sisters, these men had to administer the kiss of life to Sister Julianna? Why can I not come to America without having so much anxiety about your conduct? Imagine a Senior Sister, dripping wet and covered in mud having to have the kiss of life on a lake shore. What will the parishioners think? And all of you were sisters chosen to lead the way in America, fine examples you are indeed.'

'I am so sorry, Mother,' Sister Julianna bleated as she tried to kneel down to beg pardon. But being so tightly and modestly mummified within the folds of the sheet she fell over and was unable to get up again. Sister Hyacinth and Sister Jude ran to assist the poor mortified lady. What a way to be treated after such a terrifying ordeal. Sister Julianna was certainly in shock and what a scary welcome for the new sisters. From my own experience I knew only too well how they must be feeling. Mother Paula looked very upset. We'd all had enough of this drama and longed for the cup of tea and a sandwich which she now suggested.

'Yes, we will have tea,' Mother Angelus agreed. 'Sister Zita, boil the kettle at once.' Sister Zita turned around and without realising that one electric ring had not been turned off from earlier put her hand down directly on top of it. She yelled in pain and rushing to the sink plunged her hand into cold water.

'I'll fetch the doctors again,' Sister Ruth offered.

'No you will not!' Mother Angelus barked. 'We will pack up everything and go back to East Cranberry at once because I am very worried about the Divine Office. And it's time for Vespers.'

How could one woman hold us in her power like this? What gave her so much authority? Why didn't someone stand up to her and question the reason for such behaviour? She didn't own us yet she could generate irrational fear. Was our fear and trembling bringing us closer to God or closer to becoming unbalanced? As we drove back to East Cranberry, these thoughts circulated in my mind. Did anyone else think as I did? The cult of silence prevented me from finding out.

※

Once a month, a priest from the nearby monastery of Friars Minor, came to give a talk to the nuns. I waited in great expectation each time wondering which priest would show up. One or two of them were old school and boring but the younger ones presented exciting ideas and I sensed were mischievous enough to try to shake up the old system of blind obedience which we espoused so ardently. During Mother Angelus' stay a friar came who was an intellectual, a well known theologian and spiritual director. He spoke for about half an hour and during his talk I could see Mother Angelus beginning to look both furious and uncomfortable.

'We have been living our life,' he said, 'following the teachings of the Church which until now we accepted as absolutes. But dear sisters, there are exciting moves afoot. There's freshness in the air and a quest for meaningful change. We must be grateful to Pope John XXIII and to theologians such as Cardinal Ratzinger and Hans Kung for their enlightened views. The Church is moving into a new age and we must be willing to embrace and to discuss unsettling ideas and practices with an openness which has not existed before. I do know that you, Mother General, if I may be bold enough to address you personally, have founded a modern Order. You are leading women who will be, in the future, at the cutting edge of this renewal. No longer should any of us have to look over our shoulder. No longer should we feel restrained and unable to express our views. No longer should we have to put our commitment to an institution before our commitment to self. We must each realise our full potential in order to serve as Religious in a new way. Youth must have it's say at parish, school and community level. The Holy Father has opened the windows, sisters. Can you feel the breath of the Holy Spirit enlightening your mind?'

When I took tea to Father Sebastian in the new parlour, he and Mother Angelus were in deep discussion. Sister Fidelma sat beside her while Mother Paula, looking anxious hovered beside the tea pot. I knew that there was an argument here just waiting to happen, and it wouldn't do for Mother General to be the winner once again unless she had an audience. As I walked slowly away Mother General launched her attack. I waited out of sight.

'Father,' she began, 'I am really surprised that you would express such free and undisciplined thoughts in front of our young sisters. I do know that Vatican II was called by Our Holy Father in order to discuss theological and other issues pertaining to tradition and ritual. But to suggest, Father, that the sisters should think as individuals and not adhere to the Rules and Constitution of the Order, is, to my mind, dangerous.'

'Mother,' he admonished, 'you are jumping to conclusions here. I never advised the sisters to abandon the Rules and Constitution of the Order. How could I do this? This is the Rule by which they live. But I do believe Mother, and I won't hesitate to say it, that there comes a time when even these rules and customs must be studied carefully. Many religious observe outdated rules at the present time which I'm sure hinder rather than help the spiritual growth of the individual.'

Mother Angelus did not agree with him. The customs and traditions of the past were tried and trusted, she countered. Many of the saints who adorned the church were religious whose lives of humility and obedience were an example to everyone. To lose all this would be an affront to The Lord. No, she couldn't agree with Father Sebastian at all. He told her again that she had misunderstood. He was not suggesting a free for all. But he did think that within all religious orders there was room for growth and discovery.

'We religious live in a controlled environment,' he concluded, as he finished his tea and stood up. 'We must not resist change which is for the better,' he said on parting. 'If the hopes of many within the Church are not realised Mother Angelus, there will be disappointment, disillusion and defections. And you know what Mother, it's those at the top who will be responsible for this.'

'Good Bye, Father,' Mother Angelus spoke pointedly. It was certain that Mother Paula would be told never to invite Father Sebastian to speak to us again.

Living in our new convent and with many new companions I felt happier than I'd been for a long time. Soon Mother Angelus would leave and life would return to normal. Summer School was my escape.

Sister Jude travelled with me now but she had lectures in a completely different building. I think that being on my own in class helped me to feel less inhibited. But it was so hot from eleven o'clock onwards. Sometimes the varnish melted on the wooden seats in the grounds and one had to be careful not to sit in the direct sunlight. Mother Paula who was very conscientious about hygiene had a rota of bath times arranged for each sister. Our list was pinned to the board in the Junior Sister's Community Room. Sister Gabriel, whom I was so delighted to see in America and who had waved to me when nobody was looking, disregarded such childish ideas. Having worked hard in the garden until perspiration dripped all over her she abandoned her tools and made a beeline for the visitor's bathroom. I watched as she entered the sanctum, towel over her arm and toilet bag in readiness. She was going to sample the hedonistic delights of this condemned bathroom before its status changed. What relief for her bones as she sank into inches of warm water in that fine tub. What was she dreaming about as she splashed and soaked using the best bath oil which was for decoration only? She sang and Mother Angelus who was meditating in the chapel heard her. Well, I think every sister in the convent heard the happy, dream like melody.

I dreamt that I dwelt in marble halls,
With vassals and serfs at my side,

Mother General, Mother Paula and Sister Fidelma were not amused.

'Sister Mary Jacob, what is that?' Inquired Mother Angelus as she stood in the hallway?

I shook my head. I wasn't going to say anything. Mother Paula came rushing from her office.

'Mother, is something the matter?' She asked.

'Who is in there?' Mother Angelus demanded while banging loudly on the bathroom door. The singing continued.

But I also dreamt, which pleased me most,

That you lov'd me still the same.
'Sister, please do stop your singing in there,' Mother Paula ordered.
That you lov'd me. You lov'd me still the same.
Sister Gabriel warbled on regardless.

Nuns appeared on the main staircase and listened some in horror and others with amusement as the drama unfolded below them.

'Sister, in the name of holy obedience you must refrain from singing.' Mother Angelus shouted.

I knew that Sister Gabriel was slightly deaf and totally so when the occasion demanded. Did she think that Mother General wanted to hear the refrain again? Whether she did or not Sister Gabriel carried on singing.

That you lov'd me, you lov'd me still the same.

'This is disgraceful,' Mother Angelus fumed. 'Did you give sister your permission to use the visitor's bathroom, Mother Paula? Do you permit the sisters to sing while bathing?'

'No, no, no, Mother,' she cried anxiously. 'I don't know why sister thought she could use this particular bathroom. She is new here of course and...'

I dreamt that suitors sought my hand,
floated from inside accompanied by great splashing sounds,
And with vows no maiden heart could withstand
They pledg'd their faith to me ...

'Sister, do you hear me, come out this minute. Do you hear me?' There was laughter on the stairs when the response drifted into the hall,

But I also dreamt, which pleased me most,
That you lov'd me still the same...

'Sister, in the name of Saint Mary of the Wayside identify yourself,' challenged an exasperated Mother Angelus. 'Who is in the bath?'

'Just little ole me,' came the response.

'Come out at once, it's Sister Gabriel isn't it? Come out here, Sister, now!'

There was a great slurping sound as water drained from the bath and gushed wildly through the outside drainpipe. When the bathroom door opened the assailants were enveloped in a heady mist of perfumed steam and moisture. Sister Gabriel peering out from behind the door with shining nose and mischievous eyes, smiled her sweetest smile.

'So sorry, Mother,' she said. 'Were you looking for me?'

Chapter Nineteen
The Singer not the Song

Perhaps Sister Gabriel's singing ignited something within Mother Angelus because she decided that we all needed to practice the Divine Office daily in reparation for such disrespect from the bathroom beside the chapel. She was director of the choir. Each sister had to assume in turn, the role of chantress or leader, the one who would intone a psalm. Mother Angelus was not a wonderful singer, her voice was loud and raucous but she chanted with vigour and determination. When she called on me to take my place as chantress I froze. No sound would come. I was not a great singer either my voice being soft and light.

'I can't hear you, sister!' She bellowed. 'Sing out loudly for the glory of God.'

Not a sound would come, not a murmur, not a squeak. There was something wrong with my throat or was it my ears? I felt choked. Or was it plain fright?

'Sister Therese, stand beside Sister Mary Jacob and sing the introduction so that she can hear it.' Mother Angelus directed.

Sister Therese was a new sister who had come to take over the

Kindergarten from Sister Hyacinth. She was young and fair and very pretty and she could sing. The indignity of subjecting me to a demonstration from the most Junior Sister was, I knew, a deliberate choice by Mother Angelus.

'Sing a new song to The Lord,' she intoned.

'Sing that now, Sister Mary Jacob,' Mother Angelus roared.

I tried while Sister Therese singing along ever so discreetly assisted me.

'Louder, louder, louder,' the order came until I was finally screaming at the top of my lungs.

What a scene Father Palmer encountered when he came for morning mass. Mother Angelus was standing in the sanctuary, psalm book in hand ordering someone to sing.

'Sister Jude, line one!'

'Sister Zita, line two!'

'Sister Hyacinth line three!'

'Sister Mary Jacob line four! Again sister, again sister, again, again, again!'

I was mortified, close to tears, a wreck. I wanted to run from the chapel. The priest sidled towards the sacristy looking askance at the red faces and the drooping heads and he jumped sky high when Mother Angelus shouted, 'Next!' We'd been subjected to choir practice for two hours at least. Did he doubt our sanity? He'd already got a picture of the episode at Crystal Lake and now this. I was really upset because I knew that when Mother Angelus set her sights on a particular sister there was no letting go. I could feel the tears coming. I covered my face with my hands. Suddenly I felt a firm grip upon my wrist. I was hauled from my place in the choir, in the middle of mass, by Mother Angelus. Visions of Sister Isobel and a Corpus Christi procession assailed me. Dazed, I looked at her.

'Sister, you have defamed the house of God, you are not fit to be in His presence. How dare you shed tears in front of a priest! You will go down to the refectory now and sing psalm twenty two without stopping until mass is over. And close the door, I don't want to hear you in the chapel.'

I went downstairs alright but not to the refectory and certainly not to sing. I looked for the keys to the convent car. I would drive away from this place. I would go all the way to Long Island to my Aunt Anna. As I searched Mother Paula appeared looking worried.

'Sister, what are you doing?' She wanted to know. 'Look, do not get so upset about what Mother Angelus has done. It's for your own good. She is here to help us all. Do whatever she asks, dear, for the sake of your fellow sisters. This is difficult for everyone.'

'She is going to pick on me, I know it,' I replied. 'I have seen all this before and it's not my fault if others are upset. I didn't start it, she did. Now I want the car keys because I'm going to my aunties'.

'But, dear,' she cajoled, 'you can't drive, you haven't even taken your driving test yet.'

'If you don't give me the keys I'll go upstairs and ask Father Palmer to drive me. He has seen so much carry on now that I'm sure he'd be glad to help me escape.'

'Escape? Who is talking about escape?' It was Mother Angelus.

I didn't answer her because I despised her. Our home had been filled with music. My mother sang and Colin could play several instruments. I had begun to learn the recorder until that pursuit was ruined for me by a disreputable priest. Now Mother Angelus was accusing me of making a mockery of liturgical music, this perfect music which enriched the soul taking it into the presence of the Divine. I heard music everywhere in my life. I heard it in Lough Louchre through the reeds which sang in the wind. I heard it on our farm under the woodland trees and in the cooing of the pigeons and the cries of the birds. I'd heard the music of nature and I'd been nourished by its eternal blessing. No one would take this away from me, certainly not a power hungry woman who failed to distinguish the singer from the song.

Breakfast was tense. Mother Angelus took her place and was served her usual fresh orange juice and toast. Sister Zita whose burnt hand had become septic and was now bandaged, rushed to her side with a finger bowl and small towel as Mother topped her boiled egg, scooped out the contents and discarded the shell. There was silence. We had almost finished and I suppose everyone wondered what next when the doorbell rang to the tune of *Ave Maria*.

'Sister Jude, please see who is calling.' Mother Paula whispered.

It was Father Ryan. He would like to take Mother Angelus to Auriesville, to the Shrine of the Jesuit Martyrs. Would this be agreeable to Mother or had she other plans? He could take three other sisters along as well. What a relief when I was not included in the party. Who had sent Father Ryan to save us I wondered?

Because it was Saturday I had to spend some time helping Sister Hyacinth in the kitchen. She had the car keys now. I had seen Mother Paula give them to her with whispered admonitions. In the pantry I just stood blaming myself for being a coward, feeling ashamed and guilty because I'd made life difficult for others. I was useless. Sister Hyacinth came in. She spoke softly.

'Sister, don't mind her. It doesn't matter what others think. Now don't go blaming yourself, she would have picked on somebody else if it wasn't you. Don't take all her chastisements personally. It says more about Mother Angelus than it does about you. I have learned to let this sort of thing pass over me like water off a duck.'

'Really,' I replied, rather too sharply because I did know in my heart that Sister Hyacinth was trying to help me.

'Oh indeed, we've all had a tongue lashing from Mother General at one time or another believe me. But she wasn't always so ferocious. She was a woman of great vision and courage. Think of all the convents we have throughout the world. This didn't happen without her strength of character and her ability to deal with bishops and

Governments. And she is very spiritual and wants the best for us all.'

'Do you really think so? Mother General doesn't have the vision to see that Vatican II will be good for us, does she? From what I've heard she's resisting change at every opportunity. You should have heard her in the parlour after Father Sebastian's talk. She practically told him that he was leading us all astray.'

'Well, she doesn't want what she has built up to slip away and perhaps she can see into the future better than we can, Sister Mary Jacob. My advice to you now is to do whatever she says even if it means biting your tongue. My own opinion is that she's not a well woman.'

There was a sound outside the pantry door. Sister Hyacinth put her finger to her lips.

'Yes, rice is a very good idea,' she enthused. 'If Mother Angelus and the others are not here in time for supper it will be quite easy to do some fresh rice for them. The mince and vegetables will only improve with keeping anyway. Suddenly she opened the door. Sister Zita stood there.

'Do you want something, dear?' Sister Hyacinth asked.

'No thank you, sister. I was just looking for my Biology text.'

'I'm sure you know that there are only cookery books in here,' was Sister Hyacinth's pointed reply.

Before leaving East Cranberry for an onward journey to New Zealand, Mother Angelus gave a farewell talk to the community.

'Jesus has wept here in East Cranberry,' she began. 'I am leaving now with a heavy heart because I am so worried about you all. There are influences abroad which are not in keeping with our spirit. I charge you, Mother Paula to be vigilant so that no sister will be led astray. Last Saturday, Father Ryan took us to that wonderful Shrine where two Jesuit priests lost their lives. They befriended the Indians, worked and prayed with them and thought that they had gained their trust. But they were mistaken. The Indians deceived them and murdered them. They are martyrs. In Africa, even as I speak, priests and nuns are suffering in the name of Christ. In some places they have been killed and even eaten. What a glorious sacrifice they've made. I hope that in the future, we will have martyrs too.'

Some of my companions were looking rather sickly. I had no intention of being killed or eaten and doubted if anyone else in the room had either. But since one never really knew what the other was thinking I had no way of finding out. There was very little to look forward to in my life at this time. I was angry and my anger became anxiety. I felt that all my faults had been exposed again by Mother Angelus. There was no encouragement from any source. I carried a burden that I couldn't describe to anyone, a burden which I couldn't describe even to myself. My thoughts were negative. My inner self seemed to be lost in a well of suffering. I had tried very hard to forgive Mother Angelus, to take to heart what Sister Hyacinth had told me about her courage and insights, but she had done nothing to repair the hurt she had caused within me. I knew our philosophy dictated suffering as a means towards perfection but was doing damage to any individual necessary for the spiritual progress of the entire institution? Daily my very soul was being conditioned until I began to think that I had no choices.

※

There was one month left of Summer School. I used this as a means of flight from my thoughts and miseries. Professor Ralph Craig had been very pleased to see me on campus again. He made a point of referring to Irish poets and writers as often as possible. He'd ask my opinion and often catch up with me later to discuss some writing. Gradually, he became the focus of my day. I looked forward to class because I felt a connection with his ideas. I belonged in his world of poetry. I became more spontaneous in his presence until gradually, without being totally aware of this I actively sought his company. I was vulnerable and he knew this. He was concerned. He realised that I was in pain but when he asked me what was causing it, I fled. I fled back to the convent. I was not ready to enter my own heart to find what was lurking there. In the convent I had refuge within an identity which had been forged for me. My self image was impoverished but nobody not even Ralph Craig, I vowed, would ever know my inner thoughts and feelings.

That summer of 1965 ended with a holiday for two weeks. We were given a house deep in the woods near a lake. It was within a Nature Reserve with only one other dwelling on the farther shore. There were Canadian style canoes at our disposal, trails through the forest and a safe bathing area. The house itself had been built in three sections. The original owner had taken his bride there in the 1930's. They had occupied the centre block. Later, as the family grew, sleeping quarters and a larger kitchen were built. It was a wonderful place, a real escape where one could be alone. In the early morning loons cried from the water, an osprey could be seen in flight above the pines while chipmunks came to eat beech nuts from my hand. The sisters sometimes formed like minded groups for walks to collect leaves and wild grasses for arrangements, others sketched, chatted or listened to records and relaxed. It was not acceptable for two sisters to be alone but this was happening. I wondered if anyone else noticed the comradeship which had so rapidly developed between Mother Paula and Sister Therese. They spent time together talking and laughing. And while they were always within sight of others it was somehow understood that they were not to be disturbed. But we were all disturbed one afternoon when the Park Rangers came to warn us about a black bear that had made his way down from the Adirondacks.

'It's a dangerous animal, sisters,' they warned, 'so don't get any ideas about having him as a pet! Stay close to your house and don't go off alone into the forest until we've got him caged.'

This was interesting and there were countless false sighting's of the bear when we'd run into the house almost hysterical with laughter generated from fear. Then we heard it – a loud rifle blast. Had they shot the bear? Everything was quiet until we saw it, a red and white scarf being waved from the house across the lake. Did somebody need help? There were no telephones here. Mother Paula decided that we should walk in a body for safety, to the far side of the lake. Something was happening there. We came upon an elderly lady standing at the front door of the house, a rifle aimed at the gable.

'It's my fault,' she explained, 'my husband is an invalid and I thought it would be nice for him to see the bear through the front window. I left food for him – what a beautiful creature – the bear I mean not my husband although he was beautiful once.' She laughed nervously. 'The bear came every night and we watched him until the Rangers explained how dangerous he could be. I was frightened,' she explained, 'but I didn't tell the men what I'd been doing. I stopped leaving the food though and the bear became angry. He climbed onto the conservatory roof, you see and we were terrified. My husband was in bed looking up at the glass roof and this mighty bear was up there looking down at him. There was nothing I could do except fire a shot to scare him off. I was afraid the glass roof would collapse.'

'What a terrifying ordeal for you both,' Mother Paula said sympathetically. She asked if we could do anything to help. Would she like us to stay with them for a while? But the Rangers had heard the shot too. Setting up a bear trap outside the house they captured the animal that night and quickly took him home to the mountains.

☙❧

My return to full time study was a little like the bear going back to his mountain. I was in my preferred environment again and I felt free. No longer did Sister Zita look over my shoulder. We were in our final year and occupied because we were specialising in our degree subjects. We didn't meet during the day except for lunch, and this suited me very well. I became friendly with many students who had been with me since the beginning and I still enjoyed a little clandestine reading in the library but, most of all, I looked forward to my English lectures, especially one presented by Professor Ralph Craig. I could have chosen some other course but since his subject for the semester was a comparative study of selected Irish and American writings I felt drawn to the topic. In my heart I realised that I was taking a risk. In my heart I knew that my interest was not only in the literature. I wanted to be near Ralph Craig again. I wanted to listen to his voice to see his gestures to be aware of the light in his eyes. What was wrong with me? After all the warnings I'd received in the convent about custody of the eyes and control of the emotions, I pulsed with a deep longing. I wanted to belong to a place, to an academic discipline, to a meaningful life but most of all I wanted to whisper my longing for completeness to another human being. Did Ralph Craig hear my silent whisperings? Did he know that my most hidden thoughts were of him? Did he see in my downcast eyes the real conflict within as I tried to define what was happening to me? This was a terrifying situation. Within the convent a simple caress was taboo, sex was not up for discussion. The physical self was sterile, a sterility gladly embraced so that our love could be pure and preserved for God alone. I now viewed this commitment with fear. Did I want to be like this? I had given my word that I accepted the vow of chastity and that I willingly presented it to God as an eternal gift. Did I really know what I had forfeited? Did anybody explain to me that what I was missing was an intrinsic and vital element of my very being? Nobody did which made me more determined to find out for myself.

'Sister, I am so glad to see you back this semester. How are you now? Have you recovered fully from your accident?'

Ralph Craig had discovered me in the library, but, to my horror, on the table in front of me and impossible to miss was a volume entitled *That Undiscovered Country - Called Sex*. Swiftly my face reached boiling point. I tried to hide the title of the book but he took it into his hand and studied it.

'I've heard of this,' he smiled, 'but I haven't read it, have you?'

I wanted to say that it was here on the table when I arrived but I knew he'd realise this was not the truth.

'No, I haven't read it. I probably won't. It's not the book I asked for at the desk. I think it's been left here in error.'

'Have you time for a coffee, Sister Mary Jacob? I know I could do with one and I'd like to talk to you about Ireland.'

I gathered my things while he pulled out my library chair and waited.

'Thank you very much,' I gasped. 'I must go now, enjoy your coffee.'

What had I done? Where could I go? This was terrible. I'd made a complete fool of myself. All the freedom I'd imagined I had was just an illusion. I despised myself. Could I survive the personal consequences of the damage I'd done? I had turned my back on the teachings of Mother Angelus. I'd deceived the bishop who had singled me out for special attention. What could I do now? I couldn't tell Father Leslie Vaughan about my thoughts, could I? And how on earth could I face Ralph Craig again? He would have no time for me in the future, how could he? And with this thought I felt a light go out in my soul. Of course Professor Craig had not taken offence. He waited beside a notice board next day to say that he was sorry. He thought it was alright to ask me for coffee. He'd seen Sisters of St. James in the Cafeteria so why not me? I didn't answer. I was flustered and agitated.

'Sister, you seem scared. Here, let's go for a coffee today. I'll ask a couple of the students to join us for a little discussion. You'll see that the Cafeteria is a great place. There are lots of ideas floating about in there.' He laughed. 'It would be interesting for you. What do you say?'

'I'll go,' I told him.

And he was right. The Cafeteria which was an assortment of long tables, tables for two or four and intimate alcoves, was the noisiest place I'd come across on campus. The coffee smell seeped into every crevice of the building where dunkin donuts which had been piled high on the hot counter looked like miniature pyramids. I loved it and seeing three St. James's there gave me courage. Two students joined us. I stopped worrying. Even if Sister Zita saw me here, what could she do? Our college life had been more restricted than I'd ever imagined. There was a whole area of academic living of which we knew nothing. Outside the lecture halls, discussions raged, ideas surfaced, debates were conceived and learning through this sharing of knowledge grew stronger. We had no such debates in the convent. There we listened and although a question could be asked it was usually a discreet, meaningless one. I knew that I was changing. I was becoming more daring by going to the cafeteria every day. I didn't have personal money to buy a coffee but when I sat down a lady would come from behind the counter with a cup for me and a donut too. I knew that Ralph Craig had organised this. I never thanked him directly instead I'd say, 'such wonderful coffee today and the donut, well, what can I say?' He'd look at me and smile. I longed for closeness but I couldn't reveal my longing. I'd been practising for years, learning how to keep my feelings under control. Now that these feelings threatened to erupt I knew that whenever this happened their force would be more than I could contain. My constant thoughts of Ralph made me jittery. I let things fall in the convent, forgot to switch on the cooker, burned a hole in Mother Paula's habit when I was ironing it and had to perform cross prayers almost every day. But I didn't care. I was happy. My college work improved, I found study enjoyable because I wanted to impress him. His encouragement meant everything to me. His praise meant more to me than Gods. I signed up for his lectures after Christmas. He knew that I would do this because it was a continuation of his Irish American topic. Did he know that I had deeper reasons? He did.

'Mary Jacob,' he addressed me one morning as we walked to the cafeteria. There was snow on the ground and icicles hanging from the large maple trees. I was cold even though I'd got my snow boots now and a warm cardigan inside my cloak. Yet, I felt that I could stay outdoors forever because I loved the scenes of winter in Upstate New York. Our new convent became a dream place at this time of the year. The garden was covered in layers of whiteness as ice glistened around the unused stone fountain. The grey clapboard which wrapped itself around the convent looked like cotton wool in places where small pockets of frozen snow glimmered. Light shone hazily through the long windows in the early dawn and at evening time the scene was like a Christmas Card.

'Do you ever long to be able to do just what you want? Do you ever long to escape from your life as a nun? I mean do you think about the kind of individual you want to be, really? I'm not putting this very well but I'm asking because I care about you and I want to know who is hiding behind those robes?'

Again I wanted to run, to hide from these questions which I had tried not to ask of myself. I yearned for protection for shelter and if it didn't lie within the convent anymore where would I find it?

We were sitting inside now, thawing out gradually and I answered.

'Yes, Ralph. Naturally I long for freedom. But I don't know what freedom really is. In the convent we vow to obey. It's explained to us that this vow gives us the greatest freedom of all. We don't have to worry anymore about choices. We do what we are told knowing that this directive has come straight from God Himself. I don't know if this is true freedom or not. To me it's sometimes feels as if I'm in a cage but it's a cage I've chosen.'

'Wow! Who claims to have this wisdom to know what God wishes from another individual? This idea is bizarre. You must have very powerful leaders. Do you ever doubt what they say? I mean do you have discussions about this? Don't tell me that you've handed over your own way of thinking to others.'

'That would be impossible,' I replied. 'I can think for myself but...'

'But what?' He persisted.

'Please,' I begged him, 'I don't want to talk about this anymore. We don't discuss matters relating to the convent or our Rule and Constitution with outsiders.'

'Am I an outsider? Mary Jacob. Tell me, am I an outsider?'

'No Ralph, you are not an outsider.' I answered.

His question disturbed me. I didn't know who I was or what defined me as an individual. I was now as Mother Angelus would say, on the slippery slope. I was like a person wearing a disguise, saying what was expected from me while thinking something else. I loved somebody, a flesh and blood being, another person, a man. Was this enough to free me so that I could reveal to him my inner thoughts and feelings? Whether it was or not I didn't discover immediately. But happiness enfolded me as I danced through life recklessly longing for the fleshpots of Egypt.

'W.B. Yeats, the Irish poet and Henry David Thoreau the American Essayist had many ideas in common.' Professor Ralph told us. 'Yeats had been introduced to Thoreau's writing by his own father. And years later when he read Thoreau's *On Walden Pond* he had been very impressed. Thoreau's experiment to live close to nature and to have nature provide for his every need inspired Yeats.'

'Indeed,' as Ralph Craig, who was an authority on Thoreau, pointed out, 'Yates had planned at one time to live in imitation of Thoreau. Life on an island would be an escape for the poet when the monotony of the everyday became too burdensome. Here he would dream his own dream.'

Yeats had written a poem about his chosen island which existed close to his boyhood home. This was the island of Innisfree, in Lough

Gill, County Sligo, Ireland.

'It's a poem of wonderful intensity,' Ralph Craig told his class. The atmosphere is indescribably beautiful because Yeats' use of alliteration and repetition is remarkable. I have here,' he continued, 'a recording of Yeats reading, *The Lake Isle of Innisfree*. I think we should listen to the poet now and you can think about the work for discussion tomorrow.'

There were gasps of delight from the students until the voice of Yeats, sonorous and slow filed the hall:

I will arise and go now, and go to Innisfree,
 And a small cabin build there, of straw and wattles made;
Nine bean rows will I have there, a hive for the honey bee,

We listened enthralled as he continued,

I will arise and go now, for always night and day
 I hear lake water lapping with low sounds on the shore;
While I stand on the roadway or on the pavements grey,
 I hear it in the deep heart's core.

What I heard in my deep heart's core as I listened were the cries of water hens on Lough Ailing, the weaving of sweet grasses in Monabeag and the continuous lapping of the river beneath the bridge in Eskeriada. I had packed away so many memories from where I had first belonged. Unpacking these memories became too much for me. I lowered my head as the tears fell. When I knew that the lecture hall had emptied I looked up again. Ralph Craig was standing very still at the podium. We stared at each other. I gathered my notes as swiftly as possible and left my seat. But he was faster. Taking three steps at a time he came through the steeped isle between the rows of seats and faced me. 'Mary Jacob,' he whispered, 'I'm so sorry, I had no idea how much that poem would mean to you. I love you, Mary Jacob, I really do.' As he enfolded me in his arms I knew that whatever else might happen in my life this moment of tenderness would stay with me always.

The convent was strangely quiet when we arrived home from college that day but Sister Veronica was waiting inside the door,

'Sisters, hurry now and remove those cloaks and change your footwear. Mother Paula is waiting for you in the refectory with the community.' Oh no, I thought. I'd been discovered. Someone had seen me day after day with Ralph Craig. This was the end of everything. Mother Angelus would surely arrive on the next plane. I began to shake.

'If you are cold, dear, you may leave your cardigan on,' Sister Veronica said, 'but hurry sister we are all waiting.'

The community were seated and Mother Paula looking grave acknowledged our arrival.

'Sisters, there has been a communication from Mary's Way which concerns us all. An extraordinary General Chapter will be held there at Easter. Mother Angelus has been advised to rest indefinitely. She will not be able to carry on her usual duties although naturally she will be involved in decision making and she will be kept up to date about everything within the Order. What we have to do, sisters, is to select a delegate who will represent us at this Chapter where a sister will be appointed to become acting Mother General. The delegate must be a finally professed sister but each member of the community is entitled to vote. I have drawn up a list of potential delegates. Please tick the box in front of the sister you want to send to Mary's Way. Then fold the paper in four and place it in the box which Sister Therese will bring round. I don't need to say, I'm sure that your paper should be kept covered with the blue sheet which accompanies it and your vote kept confidential. I suggest that we should each say a silent prayer before voting.

Mother Paula was selected as the delegate from West Cranberry. And while it would create difficulties having her absent from the school she looked pleased and immediately made plans for her departure to England.

What a relief to discover that the meeting in the refectory was not about me. But the very possibility made me consider carefully the risks I had been taking. Someday gossip would spread about us. Indeed, Sister Winifred had come to the cafeteria just the other day. She was looking for one of her student sisters amongst the crowd. I had noticed the Sisters of St. James were never without a companion nun when they went for coffee with class mates. Sister Winifred glanced at me. Did she notice that I was alone with the Professor? Would she say anything? These were situations I had to think about. What would I say if I was ever confronted about this over familiar friendship? I was making life very complicated for myself. And now that Mother Paula had gone I didn't want to make difficulties for Sister Hyacinth who had become acting superior in the interim. It was noticeable how Sister Therese appeared to go into mourning when Mother Paula had departed for the Chapter. She picked at her food, sat staring ahead in the chapel and had to ask if Sister Hyacinth could help her with Kindergarten. Sister Veronica scolded her and wouldn't allow her to come to recreation for two evenings in a row because of her sad demeanour.

'What is the matter with you, sister?' I heard her ask. 'If you are ill tell me what is wrong. You can't go around with a long face, dear. When you decide to be happy in the Lord you may join us again.'

Then out of the blue I got a letter from Tom to say that Aunty Pat had arranged everything and that she and my mother would be in New York for Easter. Sister Hyacinth, who glanced at the letter smiled as she handed it to me. Knowing that she would give them a warm welcome I was happier than I'd ever expected to be about my mother's arrival. They came to the convent on Good Friday when we were attending the solemn Stations of the Cross in the Parish Church. We processed behind Father Ryan, the curates and the altar boys, stopping at each station for prayers. At the tenth station I overheard.

'Eleanor, there she is.' It was Aunty Pat wrapped in a long fur coat and beside her was my mother also in furs. She was pretending to be prayerful while looking at me out of the corner of her eye. I was so glad that Sister Hyacinth was in charge now. I didn't think that Mother Paula would make any concessions for my visitors, but Sister Hyacinth, knowing something about my family and having met Tom and Bridget, made a big fuss of them. She knew, of course not to refer to our journey to Shannon Airport with them. Sister Veronica tried to assert her authority by restricting the number of days on which my mother and Aunty Pat could visit the convent. She was overruled.

'Look, sister, these women have come all the way from Ireland. It's a wonderful time for them and we mustn't spoil it. We can include them in some outings which I have planned for the community during the Easter holidays and we must allow Sister Mary Jacob to have time alone with them too. The Good Lord will smile on our generosity, don't you think?'

For a week, my mother and Aunty Pat enjoyed the hospitality of the convent. Although they had to stay in a small hotel locally, they always had afternoon tea and their evening meal in our parlour. Sister Hyacinth asked me what food they might like and she went out of her way to tempt them with all kinds of delicacies. Mammy was a different person, appreciative of everything that was done for herself and my aunt. When we toured the local area she was enthralled by the red barns and the huge fields of corn and the tall pines and maple trees.

'We had a farm once,' she said. 'It was wonderful too. I miss it although I had to work hard there during the bad years. I miss the woods and the wild flowers and lilac which we picked, do you remember that Ellie?'

I remembered and I was shocked. I'd been so selfish for such a long time I'd never imagined my mother missing her life in the country. I thought that the woods and the flowers and the secret hiding places around the farm were mine, that they belonged to me. But my mother had her magic places too and her memories which we'd never spoken about before. Although Easter was late that year the days were still crisp while here and there dark piles of hard packed snow reminded us of winter. I felt closer to my mother now than ever before. She remarked one day that I certainly looked better than I did when I'd been home after my stay in England. But she couldn't resist adding, 'How I wish that Reverend Mother of yours was here now. I would give her a piece of my mind. She kept us in the dark about your accident, Ellie. Just who do these people think they are?'

'Eleanor,' Aunty Pat coaxed. 'You promised not to go on about this. You can see how content Ellie is now and we're having the holiday of a lifetime because of her being here in America.'

I was content at this time because Ralph Craig inspired, encouraged and loved me as an individual. He did not diminish me and through him I learned not to think quite so destructively of others. I learned about my own worth because he lavished praise on my writing and my ideas. He was my light in the dead place of self denial. He brought peace to my soul and in return I worshipped him.

I was given permission to show my visitors some photographs of East Cranberry after a blizzard and others taken during the Fall when the colours of the leaves and grasses were so spectacular.

'You must come here again, Eleanor,' Aunty Pat exclaimed! 'When the trees look like this. And you must have Owen with you next time. You know how the girls especially Helen went on about him not travelling. I think they would have preferred to see him rather than me.'

'That's silly, Pat. Helen has comments about everything and everyone. They know very well that Owen wanted you to be with me. He will come next time when he has his new hip replacement.'

'New hip? I didn't know that daddy has to get a new hip,' I said. 'When will this happen? Will he go to our hospital in Galway?'

It would happen in a couple of months, my mother told me. 'He's been trying to put it off pretending that he's not in pain'.

But at last, he had admitted that a hip replacement would be best. And then my mother revealing her other self turned to me accusingly, 'I don't know how much sympathy you have for people in pain, Ellie. It seems to me that you nuns look out for yourselves and total strangers too but don't care about your family at all. I couldn't believe it when Eileen wrote to your father about Roy. He's been so badly injured in Vietnam and you didn't even have the manners to get in touch with them. I wouldn't mind but they went out of their way so often to drive up here to see you.'

Sister Hyacinth came into the parlour just then and hearing my mother's sharp remarks she asked her what had happened to Roy. My mother didn't have all the details but when she returned to New York for her homeward journey she would see him in the military hospital.

'It's so embarrassing, Sister Hyacinth,' she said. 'I wondered why Eileen was so cool with me when we met in Long Island. The poor woman is distraught. I mean one expects terrible things to happen in a war zone but not to your own son-in-law. Ellie couldn't even send a card. It's outrageous.'

'But I knew nothing about this,' I stammered. 'Nobody wrote or telephoned. When did it happen?'

'I can't believe you didn't know, Ellie,' mammy said with disgust in her voice. 'Eileen phoned and she told me a nun named Mother Agnellus spoke to her. She was told that you would receive the news as soon as you came in from the university.'

'Oh it must have been...' Seeing Sister Hyacinth making frantic eye signals I stopped dead.

'I wonder,' she said, 'if Eileen phoned a wrong number and by coincidence reached some other convent. It certainly was not a message we received here. All incoming messages are written down and I would have known. Besides, we have nobody in the convent called Mother Agnellus.'

'I don't know what to think,' my mother answered. 'It's been the only bad aspect to our wonderful holiday here, isn't that right, Pat.'

'I am really sorry about this mix up, Sister Hyacinth told her. Now if you Mrs. Dardis would like to telephone Sister Mary Jacob's aunt from here perhaps we can sort this out. There has been some terrible mistake and tomorrow I will ask Father Palmer to offer mass for the recovery of this brave man. If you would both like to come to the convent chapel you can participate. I hope this will be of some help to the family.'

My mother was very pleased and Aunty Eileen was most gracious in accepting our apologies. The idea of a special mass being offered for Roy delighted her. I could have hugged Sister Hyacinth who had a way of dealing with problems which amazed me. But Mother Agnellus – well we both knew who that was.

Chapter Twenty
The Curate's Trouser's

My cousin Michael came to collect my visitors for their trip back to Long island. Michael, having already completed two years at Villanova University, was keen to talk to me about our studies. Sister Hyacinth told him that Father McIntyre, our new curate, had graduated from Villanova. If Michael called to the former convent they could have a quick meeting. She would telephone to arrange this. I said goodbye to my mother and Aunty Pat who promised to telephone from New York before leaving for Dublin in a few days.

'It's been such a wonderful holiday, Ellie.' My mother smiled. 'I never expected to enjoy myself so much. I've kept a diary of each day,' she went on, 'and when you come home next year we will be able to go through it and remember everything we've done together. Your father won't miss an iota of my trip because I've got it all in writing for him.'

'That was a terrific idea, mammy. And I'm so glad that you've had such a good time and that you saw the University where I study and so many other places too. Now you'll know what I'm talking about when I write.'

'She will indeed,' Aunty Pat laughed. 'We'll be talking about

America from now until kingdom come. But Ellie, it's been marvellous. I can see why you like being here so much. You're a great little trooper, isn't she, Eleanor?'

'Well, she is.' My mother smiled as she tried to hold back the tears. Michael drove away as my mother and Aunty Pat waved frantic good byes. They drove to our former convent where he met Father McIntyre. When my mother phoned from New York she couldn't stop laughing.

'You won't believe this, Ellie,' she giggled. 'You just won't believe it. Michael reversed that big ranch wagon of his into the clothes line which the curates had Strung between two trees. The back window on the wagon was down, it's electric you know. Well, he raised the window and somehow caught the legs of a pair of priest's trousers in it. We drove along the highway with the trousers waving in the wind.' She laughed so much now that Aunty Pat had to take over.

'Oh, Ellie,' she tittered, 'I'll never forget it. People were hooting at us and waving. And we waved back. "Such friendly people" your mother said. "They must know we're from Ireland?"'

Michael was mortified. The trousers were in the post. Would I tell Father McIntyre because he might think that they've been taken as a prank? This was a good story at recreation. Even Sister Veronica had to laugh when led by Sister Ambrose we chorused, 'Oh Father where's your trousers?'

My mother and Mother Paula must have past each other in the skies because one had hardly time to depart before the other returned. Father Ryan, Sister Ruth and Sister Jude went to New York to meet her. We were surprised when they arrived home with Sister Olivia as well. She was a very senior nun and I didn't know if she was a teacher and I hadn't expected our community to increase to twelve so quickly. We heard nothing about the Chapter until the next morning when we assembled all together in the Senior's Community Room. From now on any small communities, meaning those with twelve sisters or less, would not have separate Junior/Senior lessons, community rooms or bathrooms. This was Mother Bernadine's wish.

'Mother Paula!' Sister Hyacinth gasped. 'What is this about Mother Bernadine's wish, Mother?'

'She is our Mother General now,' Mother Paula said, 'and she will come to America as soon as she possibly can. She is very interested in seeing the school. Mother says that she would like to have a better insight into our work as teachers because most of her dealings so far have been in the area of nursing.'

Sister Hyacinth's face was bright red as she spluttered, 'You mean that the delegates voted for Mother Bernadine to replace our Foundress?'

'Why, of course, sister. Don't sound so surprised. Mother Bernadine has been Mother's administrator for years. She of all people knows Mother's wishes and she will see to it that nothing of her teaching will be lost.'

The room was very quiet. Mother Paula continued with more news from the Motherhouse. It was evident that some didn't hear a word she said. I knew Mother Bernadine by sight only. She was tall and she looked physically robust. Whenever Mother General was on her travels Mother Bernadine took charge of the business of the congregation. Sister Olivia who had a habit of rolling her eyes to heaven and looking bored fascinated me. I could see that she and Sister Hyacinth were of like mind about the elevation of Mother Bernadine when this rolling of eyes became more rapid, lips tightened into a thin line and sets of teeth were very obviously clenched. Sister Hyacinth's colour which had heightened even more was a sure indication that the news from Mary's Way was not good.

❧

Sister Zita and I graduated that summer and by September we had a class and a room of our own in the High School. What a change for me. I was thrown in at the deep end with very few classroom management skills to fall back on. During our rather skimpy education lectures we had done plenty of theory but classroom teaching practice didn't exist for potential High School teachers. We had been allowed to watch Sister Jude and Sister Veronica in action once or twice but there just wasn't time to see enough within the school which might have assisted us later. How I admired my fellow teachers. They loved their students and were unstinting in their imparting of knowledge to them. How they managed to keep one step ahead preparing classes and correcting homework as well as giving time to an individual in difficulty amazed me. They were loved in return, something I had not been aware of because our teaching selves and our religious life were so separate. Sister Zita took to the classroom like a duck to water. The students adored her. She always had a band of followers wherever she went. They laughed and were happy in her presence they would do anything for her. Students longed to be in her class, they all wanted to be scientists. I didn't have this sort of charm or charisma. I did enjoy teaching English but I worried in case I didn't gain the confidence of my students. What if the parents who were very involved in the children's progress were to become critical of me? I missed college so much and those coffee breaks with Ralph Craig. When Mother Paula called me to her office one Saturday morning I could only think the worst. There had been a complaint from a student or perhaps a parent.

'Sister,' she smiled, 'you will be doing an MA. It's Mother Bernadine's wish that our education should be on a par with other religious here in the States. I've been speaking to Sister Winifred who as you know is in charge of the students from the Order of St. James. She tells me that all their nuns pursue further studies. Now you will have to proceed with a post graduate degree in English. You will need a professor to guide you. Is there anyone whom you think we could approach to be your Director?

'Thank you, mother,' I spoke so politely trying not to reveal my utter delight. 'I could approach Professor Craig. I have taken his American Literature courses and I think I would be able to manage a thesis in this area. This could be very useful for my teaching too, Mother,' I suggested hopefully.

'Well, dear, we will apply for both you and Sister Zita and I think three other sister to pursue further studies. You do know, sister,' she added, 'that these studies will have to be done at night class and in Summer School. Do you think you will be able to organise your school work here and do this study as well?'

I had no doubts. Such prospects lightened my step and I knew that I became more animated in class from that morning onwards. I had something to look forward to. I hoped that Ralph Craig would be happy to be my director. It would mean consultations in his rooms and other meetings which would appear legitimate. Suddenly it became easy to do my best because I was happy. Our long day of prayer, school, convent duties and recreation didn't deplete my energy anymore. I felt that I was being rewarded for my dedication. I was beginning to put a value on myself to see that I was of some worth in this world and that I could now express my dream. But what was my dream? Did I live in the real world at all or was I in a fantasy land. I had changed. I had not been enjoying my life until the possibility of meeting Ralph Craig again became so real. And what would he think? I had scuttled away following our graduation ceremony without saying goodbye. I knew that I could do nothing for myself if I was not loved. Ralph Craig loved me. Would this be enough?

'Yes,' he told Mother Paula, 'I will be happy to oversee Sister Mary Jacob's post graduate work. I already have many areas which she might like to look at for a possible thesis. She is a very keen scholar. I will be delighted to assist her. You can begin your research at any time, sister,' he smiled, 'although officially your degree studies will begin this coming May if you are taking Summer School into account.'

'Thank you,' Mother Paula smiled. 'Our sisters will do night classes and summer school. They are all in full time teaching now, you understand.'

'I'm aware of that, it's the situation with many religious who study here but I'm sure that Sister Mary Jacob will cope admirably.'

He was always so positive about my ability so much so that my ideas about myself became positive too when I was with him. I was not doing anything wrong, I told myself. His caring for me inspired me to lead a better and more productive religious life. Surely this was a good thing?

~~~

Father Benedict Ryan had a massive heart attack the day after the official blessing and opening of the new Elementary School. It had never occurred to us that one day he would no longer be our Parish Priest. He had welcomed us to America and given us a home in East Cranberry. There must have been occasions when our Britishness irritated him but he never said so. His warmth and encouragement and his loyalty although never taken for granted had become accepted. He was gone now. When Mother Paula, Sister Hyacinth and Sister Jude visited him in the hospital he told them that he would have to retire.

'I will live with my widowed sister,' he'd said. 'It's time I handed over the reins anyway. But,' and he laughed, 'I've had the best years of my life since you good sisters came to the parish.'

Mother Paula was visibly upset. Father Ryan would visit us when he was better, she remarked. We all knew how much he had helped her as she steered the new venture forward. He would have been such a support now when the elementary school was ready to open. It was not to be. Father Ryan recovered but he never came back to East Cranberry. Instead, we went to see him from time to time.

His replacement, Father Coyle, arrived in East Cranberry like a whirlwind. He charged around the school corridors pouncing into classrooms at will. He shouted to the students and called Mother Paula, 'Your Royal Religiousness.'

'Father,' she admonished, 'Not in front of the students.'

The two of them clashed. Talk about a red rag to a bull. And he was bullish. This was his parish, these were his schools and we were his nuns! But there was another side to Father Coyle and if Mother Paula had played her cards right he would have been putty in our hands. He was a potential sugar daddy.

I was not the originator of these theories, Ralph was. I had gone to his office to decide on my field of research. I told him what was happening in the parish because I had a great need to talk to someone. He enjoyed listening to my accounts and suggested that a thesis on the goings on in East Cranberry would be very interesting. But his tone changed as he continued, 'I don't know how you can stand it. I mean a girl of your intelligence. How can you live such a routine life, so ordered, so constricted, It makes me mad just to think about you living a life based on fear rather than love.'

'I'm not afraid,' I countered. 'Tell me what am I afraid of?'

'Yes, you are afraid. Think about it, Mary Jacob, think about the people who scare you.'

While Mother Paula registered her displeasure with Father Coyle's behaviour at every opportunity, her concern for Sister Therese increased. This sister had taken charge of the Kindergarten where from time to time she was assisted by Sister Hyacinth or by Sister Olivia who was in charge of the school library. Why did she need these senior nuns to help? I didn't know and neither did Sister Gabriel who raised an eyebrow as we passed by the classroom door one morning.

'What a strange carry on,' Sister Gabriel commented. 'Surely Olivia has better things to do than watching over kids at a sand table. Do you know what she told me? Sister Therese gets everything she wants for those little kiddies. I know for a fact that Sister Zita needed some science equipment – did she get it, no. Mother Paula purchased another reading plan for Kindergarten instead. Sister Therese has a different reading programme for every four children in there. And you know something, it's the parents who are doing the Fund Raising and the money is not just for Kindergarten.'

It did occur to me that we should not be talking like this but a trend had begun where certain sisters had little chats with one another from time to time. It was a development which hadn't really registered with me because I was so busy now. There was so much class preparation to do and essays to look at. I was feeling swamped. There was still no support system and nobody I could run to for help, yet expectations remained high and unrealistic. I knew that soon there would be more to do than I could cope with, and I unlike Sister Therese wouldn't be able to send for Sister Hyacinth. When Sister Therese began to have nightmares it was disturbing. A terrible screaming would awaken us in the middle of the night. When I looked out of my bedroom door I could see the other nuns peeping out too. Invariably Mother Paula would scurry past on her way to console the sufferer. Later I'd hear clattering about and whispering from the kitchen as Mother Paula prepared hot milk for sister. Then one by one the lights would go out as we tried to go back to sleep. What was going on I wondered. I wanted to talk to Sister Hyacinth or to Sister Gabriel but there never seemed to be an opportunity to do this. The night time horrors which were being visited upon Sister Therese became worse until she began to walk in her sleep and to visit and cry out plaintively to other nuns. Something had to be done and Mother Paula did it. She took Sister Therese into her own room. I don't know when this move happened, it was done secretly. The screaming stopped. Sister Therese became happier in herself and Mother Paula bustled about looking as if she was ready to burst into song at any moment. I'm sure that some of the senior nuns asked questions and were satisfied with the answers they received. But maybe they didn't ask and were, like me, glad to get a good night's sleep. Father Coyle continued his intrusions on our life. He wanted to take us all to dinner in a High Class Restaurant. We'd have T bone steaks, salads and a dessert trolley which was beyond our imaginations. Mother Paula resisted.

'Look Your Royal Religiousness,' he bellowed, 'there won't be any other clients around. The place is owned by my brother in law. He will do a special lunch for us. I want him to meet you all. I've been telling him about you ladies from England and Ireland. Come along now, it won't matter if you get tomato sauce on your wimple – what the hell, Royal Religiousness, nobody will care.'

Sister Hyacinth told me that Mother Paula had asked her opinion.

'I told Mother go along with him this time. It would be so rude to refuse and he is such a difficult character, you wouldn't know how he'd react,' she said wincing visibly. Father Coyle was delighted. He was so generous but totally without any understanding of our rules. As he had promised, we were the only people there apart from Father Palmer and Father McIntyre and the meal was wonderful. When the waiter asked what wine we would like Mother Paula explained that we didn't take wine. Orange juice would be very acceptable, she smiled. It was very good orange juice.

'I like this very much, Father, it's quite exceptional,' Sister Gabriel told him as he refilled her glass and they cast a knowing look at each other. Father Coyle insisted on refilling every one's glass. I had never seen such a demand for orange juice in the convent or such indulgence either. Mother Paula smiled at us all, Sister Olivia fell asleep. Sister Jude offered to demonstrate an Irish jig which luckily Sister Hyacinth was sober enough to prevent. I felt drowsy. I thought I saw Ralph Craig at the end of the table.

'Hi,' I said, 'having a good time. Do I know you? You were here last night, right? You are my very, very own Professor of mud ponds are you not?'

'Oh no, I'm your very, very own Professor of crystal lakes,' the new curate guffawed.

All night long we were sick. Mother Paula almost needed another rota for the bathrooms. The brass angel had the indignity of having his legs pulled time after time as sisters ran hither and thither looking for a place to vomit. Sister Gabriel was the only sober soul in the house. She knew that we were drinking Buck's Fizz but she'd said nothing. It was good for us, we needed lightening up. And she knew enough about drink from her former life, she said, to drink plenty of water in between.

'But sister,' I moaned, 'my head is killing me. How will we all face school.'

School was becoming unpredictable. Sometimes Mother Paula disappeared because she had to see to Sister Therese who was supposedly sick. Sister Jude who was the assistant principal was always on hand to sort out classes when this happened. Often we'd have to double up or ask Sister Olivia to sit with a group. This was not a desirable situation. It wouldn't be long, Sister Gabriel believed until some student went home with a story. Sister Zita was a pillar of strength during these flights by Mother Paula and Sister Therese but doubling up in the lab was hazardous. One afternoon when she'd volunteered to take two classes for science some white rats escaped. Sister Zita was doing research on these for her thesis. The students would love to hear all about this, she reasoned. It would be a topic which would keep her now large group enthralled. The caged animals were on the laboratory bench. Sister Zita had microscopes arranged and her overhead projector organised. Now she would take a rat, she opened the cage door and a girl screamed. Sister Zita lost concentration and four rats in all departed for freedom.

'Keep the lab doors closed,' she shouted but it was too late. Girls were atop the lab benches, boys were crawling on the floor hunting and shouting, the doors were open, the noise could be heard along the corridor. Father Coyle, who was charging up the stairs, encountered head on four rats intent on escape. He was furious. What was going on here? Where was the Janitor? This building was not clean, it would have to be fumigated, our students must be sent home, some body telephone pest control. It took all Sister Jude's expertise to calm him down. But he was angry. This was no place to keep rats. If Sister Zita wanted to experiment on these vermin she could do it in the convent. If her Royal Religiousness wanted the nuns to chase rodents around there that was fine but in his school, no way. And where was Mother Paula? He was looking for her. The bishop was on his way and Father Coyle would be taking him around the two schools. We were to organise the students. Have them ready to greet the bishop.

'Alright Father,' Sister Jude smiled. 'This will be a lovely surprise for the students. I will organise everything. You do know of course that we have just one hour before the school buses come.'

'Yes, yes, I know. But where is Her Royal Religiousness. I want the bishop to have tea in the new convent.'

'Of course, Father. Don't worry at all. Bring the bishop to the school whenever you are ready. And we'll be happy to serve tea later in the convent.'

Father Coyle sat on the stairs and mopped his brow while Sister Jude made frantic gestures to me while mouthing, 'go to the convent and get them over here at once.' I scurried away holding up my skirts while trying to avoid the muddy areas along the path. Mrs. Beale, the school secretary was sitting with my class who wanted to know all about the rats.

'Don't tell them,' I warned her. 'It will be all over the parish soon enough.'

The excitement, the dampness outside and the anxiety about leaving my class with the secretary affected me so much that I had to run to the nearest toilet as soon as I reached the convent. The marble hall was most convenient. I dashed in and there in the big bath were Mother Paula and Sister Therese. I shut my eyes tightly. I opened them. They were still there in front of me naked, in the bath together. What were they doing?

'I'm sorry, sister,' Mother Paula said in shock. 'I forgot to lock the door. It's alright I was just helping Sister Therese you see she needed...'

I couldn't think straight.

'Quick,' I ordered. 'Get out of there both of you and come to the school and Kindergarten. The bishop wants his tea. Father Coyle is chasing rats. Come at once.'

The two bathers began to emerge from the water, 'No, no, wait, wait,' I spluttered as I, throwing them a towel, ran from the front door and back to my classroom like a bat out of hell.

I didn't expect Mother Paula to call me to her office to offer an explanation for that rendezvous in the bath. She behaved as if nothing had happened until I began to wonder if I'd imagined it. But I hadn't. Her dangerous liaison with Sister Therese continued. Mother Bernadine's arrival was imminent. What would she do now, I wondered and would any sister have the courage to speak out?

⇜⇝

Mother Bernadine was so sweet. She smiled benignly, her beautiful grey eyes full of love and appreciation. And we were nearly all fooled. If I'd considered Mother Angelus a hard task-master she was mild by comparison. Our new Mother General was determined to keep all the old customs alive. She now had a privileged position and was determined to get every benefit which adhered to it. Luckily, she was not a keen fisher woman but she loved to play cards and she had to win every time. It was so stupid. Here we were, grown women, professional people catering to her whims. And she could be cruel too. Father Coyle arranged a special mass of thanksgiving. We would thank God together, he explained to Mother Bernadine.

It was marvellous to have two catholic schools catering for the educational needs of the parish. And to have her nuns here, well, he was overwhelmed with gratitude.

'What a cagey old boy,' Sister Gabriel muttered.

The church was packed that morning. Sister Brendan was delegated to go back to the convent at a certain point. She had to put the bacon and sausages into the oven for our special celebratory breakfast and then return for the remainder of the mass. But Father Coyle wasn't thinking about bacon and sausage. He was thinking about a feast written about in the gospel. A delighted father had prepared a lavish welcome for his prodigal son. This sermon would make an impression on Mother Bernadine. He'd show the English what drama was all about. I could read the signs clearly. Father Coyle while waving his arms and turning from side to side preached to the congregation.

'Oh yes, the older son was upset. Why wouldn't he be? This guy had stayed at home. He had worked for his dad. And guess what? Did he get any reward? No. Well, his old man did say that he'd have it all one day. What good was that? One day could be a long time coming. He made his case. "Father," he said, "my brother has spent his inheritance. He's been reckless, he's been living the good life and for him what do you do? You tell me father, what do you do?" The father didn't answer right away. "Well, I'll tell you, Father, loud and clear. For that waster you killed, yes killed - *the catted falf*." There was silence. Father Coyle looked puzzled because there was a loud laugh somewhere in the body of the church. This was taken up elsewhere until soon the entire congregation roared and applauded. Father Coyle didn't seem to realise his mistake. Thinking that his sermon had his intended effect he smiled broadly, held his arms out wide to his flock, bowed and went back to the altar to continue the solemn part of the mass. I laughed too and Sister Gabriel who was sitting beside me whispered. 'There's nothing like a good laugh.' I couldn't see my companions in the bench beside me. I couldn't see Mother

Bernadine either but I wondered if she managed a smile.

Returning to the convent the smell of burning drifted towards us. The bacon was cremated and the sausages too. Mother Bernadine raged. Sister Brendan was on her knees inside the front door. Sister Olivia was ordered to take the burnt offerings from the oven. Sister Brendan had to shovel the remains onto a metal tray.

'You will eat this for breakfast each day until it's all gone.' Mother Bernadine shouted. 'We have a vow of holy poverty we have a vow of obedience. We have trained you to be a teacher and what happens? You cannot even cook bacon and sausage. Can you not do anything right?'

I was sickened at the thought of anyone suggesting that this debris should be eaten. Surely Mother Paula would intervene. She didn't and Sister Brendan, sandwiching some burnt bacon between two slices of bread, began her penance that morning.

'Mother,' Sister Gabriel spoke, 'perhaps we could all help Sister Brendan to eat the bacon and sausage. It will go mouldy and she'll be sick.'

'How dare you,' Mother gasped. 'How dare you, Sister Gabriel, are you challenging my authority? By all means, you can assist, yes go ahead.'

Sister Gabriel retrieving a stringy, blackened sausage took it ever so delicately between her fingers and ate as if she was dining on caviar.

'She's a dreadful woman, always was, she gave the sisters a terrible time in St. Mary's Hospital years ago. How anyone could vote to have her as Mother General is beyond me. Not a thing will change while she's in control. Hopefully someone will be brave enough to burn her bacon one of these days,' Sister Hyacinth fumed. I was in the kitchen with her when, taking Sister Brendan's penitential tray, she flung the entire contents into the bin.

We walked timorously around the convent sorry that school holidays had arrived and there wasn't that escape anymore. Sister Zita now shared a room with Sister Therese as far away from Mother Bernadine's quarters as possible. I could tell that Mother Paula was nervous but she had a strategy to keep Mother and her companion Sister Cecilia occupied. Each day she planned a trip or a visit which would enhance Mother's reputation as the leader of our Order. Meanwhile we were directed to organise a concert for mother. She was expecting some very special entertainment from the teachers. Sister Gabriel, being an art and drama teacher took charge and for days while Mother was being entertained elsewhere, we rehearsed, made masks and sorted music. Sister Brendan knew a play which her practice class in England had performed. She and Sister Gabriel adapted this for our show. It was called *Little Blue Riding Hood*.

The VIPs assembled in the dress circle in our large Community Room. Here on a makeshift stage chairs from the refectory had been scattered about – these were trees. We had painted huge leaves and hung them on the chair backs in case there would be any doubt. There were just five actors and one of these, Sister Therese, was in charge of the gramophone. Beside her, the recordings to be used throughout the performance were stacked and numbered in order of need.

Behind a screen Sister Gabriel was the narrator. Later she would become a woodcutter and following this role she'd recline on a camp bed as the grandmother. Each of us had double roles and joined forces sometimes as elves or song birds.

The performance began when Sister Zita playing a fox rather than a wolf appeared wearing a large painted foxy face. Striding between the chairs – now – trees, she sang along with a recording of *A Wandering Minstrel I*. I don't think she could see very well because instead of going off left, she stood in front of Mother Bernadine pointing her long, black, pointed nose into the box of chocolates which Sister Cecilia held open for Mother.

'Be off with yourself!' Mother Bernadine scolded. Everybody laughed. This was a good beginning.

The story unfolded. The forest dwellers were poor. The fox was taking everything. We elves got together and jumping up and down sadly sang,

> *We ain't got the money for the mortgage on the cow,*
> *the cow, the cow. Moo, moo.*
> *No we ain't got the money for the mortgage on the cow,*
> *the cow, the cow. Moo, moo.*

Even Sister Zita's wonderful mooing sounds left the audience unmoved and impassive. Our woodcutter appeared to save us. When Sister Gabriel who had arranged her cloak to resemble a pair of trousers, raised her leg and put her foot on a chair seat, the audience gasped in horror. Meanwhile the record player was blasting out,

> *Give me land lots of land,*
> *Under starry skies above,*
> *Don't fence me in.*

It's a little worrying for a cast when the audience who are expected to be laughing heartily become quiet. But in the best traditions of the show must go on we persevered. Ballet style I tip toed onto the stage wearing a blue painted face mask. Well I was Blue Riding Hood after all. I cried as plaintively as I could, 'I'm lost, granny where are you? I'm lost.' *Amazing Grace* boomed around the walls. This was the wrong record I was sure of that as I tried to join in, "I once was lost but now I'm found ..." The recording stopped suddenly but someone in the audience kept singing, "was blind but now I see."

Locating granny behind the screen of leaves I revealed her to the audience. Lying on her bed she grinned widely through goofy teeth. Clutched in her left hand was a half empty bottle of altar wine. Sister Therese, our musical director, played from a Bob Dylan song and when it reached the words *Kiss me and smile for me* the audience walked out. What terrible humiliation for the cast. The reviews came sharp and fast. Imagine teachers presenting such a juvenile form of entertainment. Mother General was worried about the standards which we are setting for our students. When she was a young nurse they did brilliant concerts for Mother Angelus. Our nursing sisters would put us to shame. There wasn't even an acknowledgement of the artistry which went into the crafting of our wonderful masks. There was no credit given for our ingenuity, our creativity and the way we moved about in such a confined space.

'And from where may I ask did that modern jet plane record come?' Mother Bernadine enquired. 'It's not at all suitable for a convent collection. Sister Cecilia I want you to check all the music here in this convent. You have my authority to dispose of whatever you may find unsuitable.'

'Bob Dylan's *I'm Leaving on a Jet Plane* is a very good modern piece of music, Mother.' Sister Zita had the nerve to say. 'I borrowed it, Mother, from one of our students.'

'I forbid you to borrow anything,' Mother Bernadine said turning to face her. 'You will not bring aspects of the outside world in here either in music or books or pictures or ideas. No modern trends – do you hear me?'

It had been a shattering experience. Mother Bernadine stood up and as she turned we saw it, a big cut out leaf painted bright green, was stuck to her bottom. Who had left this on her chair? Mother Bernadine was so keen to chastise us that she'd not noticed it. Mother Paula whipped it away as she ushered Mother from the refectory.

Like Mother Angelus before her, our new Mother General met us individually for a private talk. She told me as Mother Angelus had done before that I belonged to the Order and she knew how much God loved me but she was anxious in case I'd be unduly influenced by the outside world. I must be careful in the university where she knew that ideas contrary to our beliefs abounded. The devil was lying in wait. I must be on guard always. I must pray to our Lady for protection. Did I have any questions to ask? I wanted to ask why she was such a hypocrite. How could she come to America and within a week have a wonderful hard working and dedicated sister on her knees eating burnt bacon and sausage. Where was Our Lady in all of this? I wasn't naïve anymore about the strength of a communal system. I knew only too well the compulsion under which we laboured to see good in the meanest of companions. But I saw nothing positive or good in the appointment of Mother Bernadine to the top position in our Order. Mother Paula was a good, intelligent woman, but how on earth could she go to England and with others reward a crazy person by giving her a position of authority? And I did think that Mother Bernadine was unbalanced. I found it hard to believe that the misery women like her could inflict on her subordinates was a good thing, a godly thing or a means towards the saving of one's soul. But I was clever now and I gave nothing away. I was a hypocrite too when it suited. 'Mother,' I smiled at her knowing full well the risk I was taking. 'Mother, I just wondered if you might have made a decision about my holiday in Ireland. Do you think it might be next year?'

There was a sharp intake of breath. Oh no, I'd said the wrong thing. Mother Bernadine smiled at me.

'Don't worry, dear. This will all happen. I will have a little talk with Mother Paula about the sisters' home visits before I leave.'

Maybe she's not so bad after all I thought happily. I might even get home for Tom and Bridget's wedding.

Sister Hyacinth wanted to know if I got on well during my session with Mother.

'It's hard to say. She's so sweet sometimes and at other times she frightens me. I can't make her out, can you? You know it's possible I'll get home next year. Tom and Bridget are getting married. Wouldn't it be great? I know I wouldn't be able to go to the reception but ...'

'Sister Mary Jacob, I hope all your dreams come true,' Sister Hyacinth spoke kindly, 'but I've been in this Order now for almost thirty years and it's sad to have to say it but I don't believe anything those in power say anymore and I trust them even less.'

These words shocked me but they shouldn't have. I had been in the convent long enough myself to realise that praise and encouragement had a very minor role to play in the lives of all of us except for a favoured few. Mother Bernadine and many of her contemporaries had joined the convent when they were young. They had been given positions of authority at an early stage in their religious life and they clung to their status grimly. I understood their background but I still couldn't excuse or forgive the abuse of our spiritual selves. These women put our psychological and physical well being at risk. I couldn't excuse this because they were, like I was, professional people. I prayed that I would always treat my students with care and understanding. I didn't want to be like Mother Bernadine who would have to carry the burden of having, done unto others what may have been done unto her.

Chapter Twenty One
Compromise

Leaving us depleted in mind and body, Mother Bernadine, trailing clouds of glory departed for her next destination. We had attempted to raise with her some ideas from Vatican II but without much success. We knew that the Sister's of Saint James were already implementing changes. They had discussions and an open minded approach to renewal. Sister Vianney, who continued to be my friend, explained with great enthusiasm how they were, as a community, trying to adapt the ideas of their Founder to suit the modern world. This was one of the tenets from the Council. But we were a modern Order already, Mother Bernadine had explained. We had no need to change in the way that other religious had to. Our Foundress was still with us and for this blessing we must be eternally grateful. Her inspiration to found the Order of Saint Mary of the Wayside was a living guide in the midst of so called change. How she pitied other nuns who would have to move with the times. 'We have always had discussions,' she beamed, 'and our sisters are free to speak their mind.'

'Don't you agree Mother Paula?'

When she feebly replied, 'yes Mother,' a gasp of disbelief

reverberated around the table.

'I think your community does not entirely agree with you, Mother Paula. Who uttered that sound of disapproval?' Mother Bernadine enquired.

Nobody spoke, heads were lowered. Mother Bernadine decided to ask us individually if we felt free to speak. I was a coward in the ranks of "yes, Mother," "of course, Mother," "absolutely, Mother". 'And what about you, Sister Gabriel?' Mother beamed. 'You are a sensible and experienced sister, what do you think?'

'I think, Mother,' she replied, 'that we are living in cloud cuckoo land. We can't speak freely at all. We don't speak – full stop. And what do we listen to? The same old seven wonders of our institution. There is no deep, meaningful discussion here, Mother. We are wedded to the Order. I don't think we can distinguish between it and our individual vocation anymore.'

'What a wonderful performance, sister.' Mother Bernadine scowled. 'You are a drama teacher. Indeed I believe you were an actress in a former existence. But, dear, you are not on stage in this convent. You are first and foremost a religious wedded as you say to the Rules and Constitution of the Order. You have every help to persevere in your vocation, sister. But I will not and I repeat will not have you scandalise your fellow religious. Get down on your knees now and ask pardon for such an outburst.'

This was a mistake. From my limited teaching experience I knew it was a mistake. Mother Bernadine should have removed the offending party and herself to a private place or arrange to discuss the matter later. But she had been challenged in public and she had to conquer in public too. Sister Gabriel knelt down and while asking pardon from her sisters said, 'I'm an elder, dear sisters and I do have insights which come with age. I will not have my spirit crushed at this point in my life. I think we do need change. We can still do this while preserving our spirit and traditions. I'm just sorry that it's not going to happen while... .'

'You have said quite enough, thank you, sister,' Mother Bernadine interrupted. 'Mother Paula I want you to have a serious talk with Sister Gabriel and sister, you are to read our Rule and Constitution today from cover to cover and every single day for the next week.'

⁓⁕⁓

Unrest continued in America throughout the sixties. When I scurried to Ralph's office to discuss my thesis we talked about the Founding Father's dream for independence. I was trying to formulate a study based on the idea of freedom and individualism as seen in early American literature. Would this focus on religious, political or social freedom or be a combination of all three? Whatever we decided I was determined to make my study cover as many months as possible so that I could be with Ralph. He told me that the students in The Sorbonne in France had rioted. Even the Trade Unions and civilians had joined in. It's all anti war, he explained. Did I know that some Vietnam Veterans had gone to Washington D.C and thrown back their medals outside The White House? They had revealed to newspaper journalists how North Vietnam prisoners were tortured by American troops. "We have blood on our hands," they had chanted. Did I know that Robert Kennedy promised to end the Vietnam War? He also pledged to work even harder for Civil Rights following the shooting dead of a number of black students by police in Kent State University. There was arson and destruction everywhere because young people were fed up being told how and what to think. This was their only way of speaking out, of diverting their energy, of questioning authority, of seeking moral and sexual freedom. They are rejecting all those ideals which until now Americans considered most important Ralph explained. Did I know about all this? Did I understand the reasoning behind all this agitation? I knew nothing and I understood even less.

Around this time Sister Vianney asked me if I was making progress with my research.

'Don't get too attached to your professor,' she advised. 'He's a bit fresh, a bit fond of the gals. I don't think any of us would be allowed to have him for a director.'

'I'm getting along fine. He respects the fact that I'm a nun, I'm confident about that,' I told her. 'Otherwise Mother Paula would not have agreed to us working together.'

'Fine,' she smiled, adding, 'he's a real smart guy.'

We faced another long snowy winter trudging along the narrow road from the convent to the school. Our students loved to meet us on the way so that they could help to carry books and bags. Our days were difficult. Teaching was demanding. In East Cranberry the parents were professional or business people who wanted good results for their children. They had all contributed towards the cost of the school buildings and were very proud of that success. And Father Coyle was relentless in his tormenting of Mother Paula. When he discovered that students in the tenth grade were using maths books which she'd had sent over from England he exploded. We could hear him all over the building when he'd located her.

'Your Royal Religiousness, what is this all about? Are American text books not good enough for you? Don't you know that the education department stipulates the books students in this State of New York are to use?'

When she tried to explain that the English maths books were just an additional tool and were only used now and again for testing he wouldn't listen. They were to be disposed of. He never wanted to see them again. Mother Paula had learned that it was best to agree with Father Coyle which didn't mean at all that she followed his orders. The school enrolment had increased and Mother Paula was not a teaching principal anymore. Sister Jude became principal of the Elementary School and Sister Therese continued to control Kindergarten which was almost an independent entity. We all came down with flu during the winter of '67. One by one we took to our beds while the stronger nuns tried to keep classes going with the help of supply teachers. Snow fell thick and fast. Curled beneath the blankets I consoled myself by thinking about Ralph. It occurred to me that I knew very little about him personally, and, being honest, I had to admit that Sister Vianney's words had shaken me a little. But Ralph was totally wrapped up in his field of study. His reputation was phenomenal and he was frequently called away as a guest speaker. He and I were so well suited. I believed, that if ever I should leave the convent, which he encouraged me to do, he would be there for me. I knew this, but did I really know him or what I wanted? He was years older than I but my father was older than my mother too and that didn't matter. I felt no guilt as I dreamed about us being together. In these dreams I carved an identity for myself, but I was to learn all too soon that I should have listened to Sister Vianney.

I struggled back to college still feeling weak but anxious to get some more research out of the way. A seminar was taking place in the English Department also which would probably give me some useful references for my own thesis. Sister Zita, Sister Julianna and Sister Ruth were participating too. But beforehand I just had to see Ralph. 'I must let him know that I've recovered and I'm ready for study,' I said to the others, 'and I need some journals from his office too.' I was excited because I knew that he would welcome me with open arms. My pace quickened and I smiled to myself as I neared his door. It was closed, he never closed his door. It was his policy to be accessible to students at all times. I knocked, I turned the knob and the door flew open. Facing me was a beautiful looking woman. She was tall with dark bobbed hair. Her clothes were perfect.

'Wow Ralph, a little nun is it? Are you for real sister?' She asked, 'or are you going to a fancy dress? Oh Ralphie isn't she the cutest little thing. Is she studying under you too? I'm emphasising "under" honey,' she smiled, 'but you wouldn't understand that would you, sister. By the way, what is your name?'

Hearing warning bells I said nothing. What was this all about? Who is she? My head was reeling, I began to cough. She patted me on the back, I pushed her away.

'Oh, oh, don't like to be touched do we, sister. I'm so sorry. For a while I really didn't think you were for real. I mean Ralph here, well, he can be a little kinky sometimes can't you, darling?'

Oh my God, what had I been thinking about? What could I do? Ralph Craig just stood there in silence.

'Don't you think you should explain our relationship to your eh whatever? She's a little embarrassed, or would you like me to do that for you?'

'I don't want your explanation,' I gasped.

'Oh but I think you do because I suspect you may have a little thing going for one another. I know all the signs. He may now be your caring professor, sister but he sure has designs on you, I can tell. It happens all the time. His modus operandi is so refined. But, gee! Ralph a little nun! How could you? He's my ex husband. I'm Amanda Morton Craig. And you are?'

I didn't answer.

'A young nun of loose habits, perhaps,' she quipped.

'That remark is uncalled for Amanda, would you please go to the cafeteria and I'll be along in a few minutes. Once again, dear, you are jumping to conclusions. Your active imagination will never cease to amaze me. Your paranoia is breathtaking. I have to give some guidelines to my student. I'm sorry that you have been so embarrassed, sister.'

'Guidelines, guidelines don't let me interrupt,' she smirked as, taking her fur trimmed coat and shiny leather briefcase she waltzed out the door.

'Mary Jacob, I'm so sorry about this. I had no idea that Amanda was coming for this seminar. You must have heard of her. Surely you knew that I'd been married? She is a professor and author, very well known for her Medieval Studies.'

'Well, there's nothing medieval about her,' I cried. 'You have been leading me up the garden path. You never spoke about a wife, ex or otherwise. I didn't know you are divorced. In Ireland divorce is a sin.'

'Ssh, ssh!' He whispered. 'Come here to me you beautiful innocent girl. I love you dearly. Now what are we going to do about this. Are you prepared to leave that awful convent, Mary Jacob? Are you prepared to cast in your lot with me? We could go away to some other part of America. I'll get a position no problem.'

I felt a terrible sense of loss then, a terrible sense of betrayal and a grief which crushed me. What remained to be lived for now? I could crawl back to the convent as a marked soul, a disloyal follower of Christ, a reject. Or I could take up his meaningless offer. He would never leave the university and go elsewhere with me. I had been stupid. I had read a great deal more into Ralph Craig's admiration than he had ever intended. I looked at him with loathing. More than ten years before when I was eighteen I'd been deceived by Aidan Flood. I was still eighteen physiologically and what was worse I was also an emotional cripple. I couldn't stand up for myself. The anger which I felt about my personal deficiencies was now directed at him. Grabbing his carved book ends of Huckelberry Finn I threw them at him. I swiped papers from his desk. I charged after him as he ran from me. I became my mother. Standing behind a wing backed chair he ducked as missiles were hurled at his head. He made a run for the door. I gathered *The Complete Works of Nathaniel Hawthorne* six volumes in all and flung them one by one after him. There was a thud and another and another followed by a loud crash and a sob. Sister Zita stumbled through the door dazed and shocked. Blood was streaming from her face as she held a hand over her left eye.

To say that all hell broke loose would not describe the aftermath of this incident. Sister Zita's eye was closed and black the following morning. The bruising had travelled down her magnificent face and across her nose. Her right eye was bloodshot and she couldn't appear in the classroom. Mother Paula was closeted away all morning in the convent office with Sister Hyacinth and Sister Olivia. When Father Coyle stormed the convent looking for an explanation as to why there were so many supply teachers in the classrooms Her Royal Religiousness told Sister Ambrose to advise him to, 'mind his own business.' Which she did.

'What the... It is my business!' He roared. 'Where is Her Royal Religiousness? Tell her to come here at once. I want to know what is going on.'

'Why don't you just take a hike, Father and leave us alone for once. You are a right God dam nuisance.'

Little Sister Ambrose could be tough.

'Well, what do you know?' Father Coyle was laughing as he walked away.

I was ordered to go to Mother Paula's office. She had already interviewed the nuns who were with me the evening before. Sister Zita could only say that she was on her way to collect me for the seminar. I had taken so long with Professor Craig that she thought I'd be late and we wouldn't get seats together. She remembered nothing else except hearing a raised voice which she knew was mine. The other nuns knew nothing. They discovered us in the corridor where Sister Zita was nursing a bloodied eye. Professor Craig was standing by saying something about a bookcase toppling over and books scattering around.

'This does not make any sense at all,' Mother Paula said as she looked at me severely. 'Books don't just fly through the air willy nilly.

Sister Zita is tall; how could a book hit her in the eye unless it had been aimed at her face? Sister Mary Jacob, did you deliberately throw a book at Sister Zita?'

'Oh no, Mother, it was an accident. It happened the way Professor Craig said it did.'

'Indeed?' She answered while pursing her lips. 'And tell me, dear, what has been going on between you and Professor Craig?'

I looked desperately at Sister Hyacinth who raised her eyes in total disbelief.

'Nothing has been going on, Mother. What do you mean anyway by going on? He is my professor, he oversees my research, he outlines a plan for my thesis, that's all.'

'Sister, don't make me cross, I'm not talking about academic pursuits and you know this very well. Sister Winifred, from The Sister's of Saint James mentioned to me some time ago that you were in the coffee shop with Professor Craig. She did say that there were other students at the table too. I said nothing at the time and now I know this was an oversight. Did you get permission to go to the coffee shop, sister?'

'No, Mother, I didn't but we were having discussions there every day and I thought it was alright to go.'

'So you went more than once then?' Mother Paula was really shocked now. 'And you didn't ask a senior sister's permission to do this when you were on campus during summer school?'

Mother Paula turned to Sister Hyacinth and Sister Olivia.

'It's typical isn't it? That by small disobediences we are led to greater deceptions. The Rules of the Congregation are in place to protect us. If we ignore these rules, we risk so much.'

'What have you risked, Sister Mary Jacob? Have you risked your vocation? Have you broken your vow of chastity as well as your vow of obedience? Have you discussed your life as a religious with an outsider? Have you forfeited your vocation for a man? I want to know what you have done – Now!'

'I will tell you nothing, Mother,' I whispered.

'Sister, swear to me in front of your sisters here who care about the Order and its reputation. Swear to me that you were not intimate with this man.'

I knew from all my readings what intimate with a man meant but I was daring. Just who did she think she was? How could she ask me such things in front of the others? Shock and disappointment and most bitter medicine of all – being found out made me reckless.

'Intimate, Mother? What exactly do you mean?' I asked as I stared boldly at her.

'Well,' she said, her colour rising. 'Let's begin at the beginning, did he ever kiss you?'

I looked at her. I had reduced her to asking such a question. I knew she hated this and the trouble I had brought upon the convent. She would have to report my terrible conduct to Mother Bernadine who might very well land on the next plane from England. Mother Paula would be held accountable for not watching over me. I had come to America as a flawed sister and I'd not changed. The air hung cold between us. The snow flurries thickened against the window. Sister Hyacinth coughed and I smiled.

'Mother that's for me to know,' I answered, 'and for you to find out.'

Overnight my personal dream had become a threatening nightmare. The atmosphere within the convent, like a solid entity, hung between me and my sisters in religion. I was guilty of recklessness, disloyalty and deceit I would be judged again and punished again.

'Sister Mary Jacob, what have you been doing?' It was Sister Hyacinth who cornered me. 'I know for a fact,' she said, 'that Mother Paula will not risk bringing Mother Bernadine back here, not with Sister Therese behaving as she is. Are you sure that you have nothing to tell me? I want to help you.'

'There's nothing to tell you. I was just stupid, that's all.'

'Then go to Mother Paula and ask forgiveness for you thoughtless conduct. Do this for everyone's sake.'

Each morning during the week which followed I had to kneel in the refectory in front of Sister Zita and the community. There I kissed her feet and asked her pardon for accidentally hitting her with a book. Mother Paula was adamant that I should use the word accidentally.

'You may not be aware of this, sister, but to hit a fellow religious with intent to do physical harm is contrary to canon law. I'm assuming that you didn't intend to hurt Sister Zita. I hope I'm right.'

'Of course I didn't intend to injure her,' I answered without emotion.

'Look, dear,' Mother Paula cajoled, 'You must talk to Father Leslie about all of this. I am not your confessor and there are things which are within your heart and soul which I have no right to delve into. But you are hurting, sister. I know that you must be, or at least I hope, you are feeling guilt and blame and shame but you alone have acted without decorum and without any sense of respect for yourself or your fellow religious. You have been very foolish and you have put yourself in the way of temptation. You have brought a feeling of unrest into the community. Please, for everyone's sake, confess your sins and be happy again. And,' she added, 'I have asked Sister Winifred to organise a different academic director for you. This will be done discreetly. You will have no further contact with Professor Craig.'

When my mother wrote, telling me that she was so excited because Tom and Bridget were now engaged I felt little emotion. They would get married next May. I must be there,

'We're giving you plenty of notice, there will be no excuses. Tell me if you think I should write to the Mother General about this just to make sure. We've met Bridget's parents, they're lovely people. They have heard all about you and they are looking forward to meeting you. Colin was home for the engagement party. He's in great form but no sign of a girlfriend yet. He says he's too busy.'

All that terrible week the snow fell and the school was closed. We ploughed our way to the classrooms to get some work done but the days became monotonous for me and I had too much time to think. I wanted to walk away from everything. I had nothing to look forward to and very little to look back upon. I knew permission would not be given for me to go to my brother's wedding. Did I have the will to suggest a holiday in Ireland at that time without mentioning this? I was tired of subterfuge. Sometimes at night I felt so lonely, so out of touch with reality. I didn't belong anywhere I was in limbo, suspended between the dream and the reality. I hated myself and felt I could never be accepted by the community after all the trouble I'd caused. I was consumed by negative thoughts. My mind had been conditioned to be a fertile ground for such self rejection. Must I continue this life of always looking over my shoulder, always watching what I'd think and say? My hopes had not been realised, change was outlawed. I had based my belief and my faith on people in authority and I knew now that by doing so I would never achieve my full potential. I could not clearly express a personal dream because I was living the dream of other people. I did not love my life anymore it had become a heavy meaningless load. Should I return home, go back to Eskeriada and to my family? They said that they would welcome me with open arms but I wasn't so sure about this anymore. I would be looked upon as a social disgrace. I imagined Tom's wedding and guests nudging each other. I heard their whispered comments.

'That's Tom's sister, Ellie, she was a nun, you know. She left just a few months ago. Can you believe it? The father seems delighted but the mother's furious I heard. Well, you can't blame her. She even went off to America to visit Ellie and didn't shut up about that holiday for months afterwards. "My daughter, Sister Mary Jacob this and my daughter Sister Mary Jacob that." What is she going to do with the girl now?'

Night after night I lay awake staring into this bottomless pit. Only

I knew what this burden was. I wanted to shake it off, to be free of it forever. There was nothing vital left in my soul and I had brought all of this on myself. I was responsible. Carrying my heavy weight of pain I climbed to the flat roof of the Kindergarten. It was past midnight and a large, bright, yellow moon glimmered and reflected upon the snow. Stars shone in a clear sky. Tall trees stood on guard like witnesses. I looked up into the heavens. It was magnificent. I thought about granny Ethel and granny Julia and Michelangelo. I wanted them. I belonged wherever they were. Far below cushions of snow awaited my descent. I knew that I would fall through the icy sheet which lay on top of this. I would go through the snow like an arrow with all the weight of my troublesome body to ensure a quick freeze demise.

'Sister Mary Jacob, Mary Jacob, Mary Jacob, Mary Jac...'
Strong arms enfolded me. It was Sister Hyacinth.
'Come with me, what are you thinking of out here at this time of night. How did you manage to get onto the roof? Sister Olivia is here too. She saw you leaving the convent. She was in the bathroom and thanks be to God she saw you from the window. You've been sleepwalking, I think. Are you awake now? Wake up, sister.'

Trembling I let them take me back to the convent. Mother Paula was at the front door looking pale and anxious. I was taken into a warm kitchen and given, like Sister Therese, warm milk with whiskey in it. When Sister Olivia had placed a hot water bottle in my bed I climbed in and slept fitfully. Whenever I awoke I was aware that Sister Hyacinth was sitting there beside me - always.

It was very difficult for me to confess my sins to Father Leslie but I didn't have a choice. I couldn't carry on without talking to someone. I needn't have worried. He was so understanding, so full of sympathy and so helpful.

'If I was in your shoes I wouldn't have done any better,' he told me 'We must all go through these times of confusion and uncertainty. If we didn't how could we ever grow or understand other people, you with your students for example. Failure can be a good thing if you use it as a teacher. You must have more trust in yourself' he went on, 'and in the Order too. I know its run now by a few fuddy duddies but it won't be like this forever. Younger nuns won't accept the old ways for much longer. You have a lot going for you sister and you should be out there leading them instead of feeling so sorry for yourself.'

'But I loved someone, I loved a man so much that I would have given up my vocation for him.' I whispered.

'No, you wouldn't have. Think about it. What would you do when it came down to the wire? Run out the convent door and leap into his car and away? I don't think so. We all have another self, sister, a longing for what we can't have or have vowed to renounce. Its part of our human condition and from time to time it will deceive us and lead us astray. But our longing must be for God. And remember, sister, it's not so wonderful out there. The world can be a hard task master. Think of all the people in violent marriages who keep hoping that their partner will wake up one day a changed person.'

'Well, that's what I think about the convent,' I told him. 'I keep going because for some reason I expect change. I always hope that tomorrow may be different. I also expect to wake up to find that people are more open, more loving, I suppose.'

He told me to grow up. Perhaps I needed to be more open and more understanding too. This rebuke made me furious.

'There's a system of favouritism here,' I said. 'Some sisters can do whatever they like. I mean I saw one the other day – a sister who oozes sexuality and she was on the back of the curate's skidoo. Mother Paula was laughing and even encouraging her to stay on the machine for another round of the playground. And you won't believe this but I think there's a particular friendship going on within the convent too. Nobody speaks about this but when I am accused of being overly familiar with a professor I have to kiss feet and beg for forgiveness. Do you know that I went onto the school roof? I was ready to kill myself.'

'Hey, Hey, slow down there's no need to become so upset. Look, why are you so worried about what the others do?'

'Because they seem to be very worried about what I do, right?'

'O.K.' He conceded, 'let's start again. So everything is not rosy in the convent. I know this. But sister, it's not so serious that you have to die because of it. Are you jealous of the others? If you are, don't be. They each have choices too and like us all, they will have to answer for their decisions. It's an unnatural situation having all women or all men living together. It's not wrong for a person to love another person. You don't know the nature of this love. Don't be hard on your fellow religious, don't judge them, they are all doing their best.'

There was much more I wanted to say. I wanted to tell him about the bathing episode in the marble hall that would put a flea in his ear but I couldn't bring myself to do this. I had already given Father Leslie much to think about. Perhaps by reading between the lines he would put two and two together. But if he did, it didn't alter the happenings during the coming nights. Sister Therese became hysterical again and all Mother Paula's ministrations were useless. We were kept awake for hours week after week. Sister Ruth developed stomach ulcers. Sister Gabriel taking herself off to the chapel played, *Lead kindly light amidst the encircling gloom*, on the organ over and over. I never want to hear that hymn again. Sister Hyacinth and Sister Olivia hovered around Mother's room or went to prepare the hot drinks which we now all accepted as part of the nightly ritual. One night I spied Sister Ambrose sitting in bed knitting furiously while Sister Zita, glasses perched on her bruised nose which had turned a dirty yellow, read from her spiritual book. For how much longer could we endure these sleepless nights I wondered and what if Father Coyle became aware of the situation? One night he almost did.

Two patrol cars drew up outside the hall door. Blue lights flashed and swirled across the convent windows. The doorbell rang and rang shrilly throughout the house. Mother Paula called for anyone who was dry and dressed and looking respectable to go downstairs and let the officers in. I ran through the hall and switched on lights in the parlour. To my astonishment Father Coyle was with the police. I became suspicious. I'd have to be very careful now. I mustn't say anything.

'This is not the Reverend Mother,' Father Coyle announced. 'Where is she, sister?'

'Good night Father, good night officers,' Mother Paula appeared with Sister Olivia. 'It's three o'clock in the morning,' she said looking questioningly at the men. 'Why are you here? This is a convent and your visit is highly irregular.'

'Well, whatever has been going on is highly...'

'Pardon me, Father,' an officer spoke, 'I will handle this.'

'Reverend Mother, did you hear any screaming in the convent garden within the last hour? We had a report from a house nearby saying that there seemed to be some sort of commotion out there. Indeed, from what we have noted there was a lot of shrieking and crying as if a person was being attacked. Have you been aware of this? Were any of your sisters awakened by cries do you know? Are all your nuns accounted for?'

Sister Olivia volunteered to go upstairs. She would check on each sister. They were all in bed and asleep earlier, she said, but of course having two patrol cars with flashing lights outside would have every sister awake.

'We sleep very well, a clear conscience is a great help you know.' She spoke with a smile while looking pointedly at Father Coyle.

Upstairs sisters were frantically trying to hide their wet clothes and boots. Sister Ruth had produced clean nightdresses from the hot press. Cold hands and feet were soaked in hot water. As few lights as possible had been switched on. Sister Hyacinth directed operations in a whisper. Sister Zita sat with Sister Therese who was wrapped in a blanket and crying softly. Sister Olivia put her finger to her lips. She pretended to open each door, call out a name and close the door. Then indicating that we should get to bed fast she returned to the parlour.

'All present and correct,' she beamed.

'We would like to inspect you garden, Reverend Mother,' the senior officer said.

'What now?' Mother Paula raised her eyebrows.

'Yes, he said now,' Father Coyle, shouted. 'Let's see what's out there.'

We knew only too well what was out there. As we stood to one side, the high beams of the officer's torches revealed deep fissures in the snow which had drifts of almost five feet in places. Here and there crushed white mounds of it glistened and boot prints gaped from their surface. There was slush in places where the snow had melted as feet floundered and bodies fell.

'What the...' Father Coyle spluttered. 'Were you nuns having a snow ball fight?'

'What a ridiculous notion Father,' Mother Paula scoffed.

'There's no snow balls out here said the second officer. But there's been a chase of some kind. There's no blood though. It's not animals either because there are some boot prints. Animals don't wear snow boots as far as I know'. We laughed. 'I suspect some kids have been horsing around. I'm just surprised you were not woken up by this, sisters.'

'Oh but you have a clear conscience isn't that right your Royal Religiousness?' Father Coyle quipped. 'All the same, I wonder if you were having a snow ball fight.'

We were left shaken after this experience. There had indeed been a chase. Sister Therese had gone out to the garden in the snow and in her nightdress. Realising that she was missing Mother Paula wakened us, we would have to find her. Nobody believed that she would go outside in the cold except me. I had done it. It was a while before I saw her standing knee deep in the snow. I called to her and she ran. I called to the others. We tried to head her off as she struggled forward towards the small gate leading into the lane. Hither and thither we tried to move with our arms flaying about as we attempted to balance. Frequently our feet became wedged between layers of snow and ice. Trying to rescue one another we'd fallen down in a tangled heap of habits. Mother Paula had thanked us all for our cooperation. Sister Therese was not well but with our sisterly love and compassion Mother was confident that she would recover very soon.

I crept back to college, but there was always a nun at my shoulder now watching where I was going and what I was doing. Professor Stephen Langtry welcomed me saying that he was, 'happy to be of assistance.' There was no mention of Ralph Craig even though I had to review all the work I'd done with him with my new director. He was an older member of the faculty, a professor emeritus who took me on when he heard that I was from Ireland.

'I don't lecture much these times unless I'm invited,' he explained. 'I'm a sort of honorary citizen around the place now. From time to time I need a refreshing discussion I'm glad you've come along, sister. And you're from Ireland too. I've been to Ireland, you know.'

Professor Langtry had spent a year in University College Dublin at the then Earlsforth Terrace Campus.

'I remember it so well,' he smiled. 'You know, sister I spent as much time as I could in the theatre. I've been to The Abbey, The Gaiety and The Gate. I had the privilege of meeting Michael MacLiammoir. What a magnificent actor, what a wonderful voice and presence. I was introduced to Hilton Edwards too, another fine man.'

'I went to a play in Dublin once,' I told him. 'We were studying *Hamlet* for our Leaving Certificate. I can't remember which theatre we went to. I think it must have been The Gate. Cyril Cusack was Hamlet.'

'And what did you think of him?'

'I didn't like his Hamlet at all. I thought he was too small for that role. And he sounded so peevish. "To be eeh, or not to be eeh," you know that sort of constant whinging.'

The professor laughed.

'Peevish is a good word. And I agree with you that he probably was not the schoolgirl's ideal Hamlet. But Cyril Cusack is a very fine actor all the same even if he does overdo the eeh, eeh's'

We laughed and I knew then that we would get along fine. I began to feel more content. I began to claw back elements of my life which I had lost. I rededicated myself to my vocation and I tried very hard to obey and support Mother Paula. I learned to walk away from confrontation, I kept my head down as I tried to prevent anyone having cause to judge or punish me. I tried to let go of all the negative things which had ruled my life in the past. I looked forward instead of back. I worked hard at trying to reclaim my place in the community. I wanted so much to belong. But we can never really be divorced from the past and when the Newsletter came from Mary's Way telling of Sister Cecily's deathbed scene I was appalled. It described how the sisters in the Motherhouse at that time were assembled around her bed. Each held a lighted candle. I pictured Mother Angelus and Mother Bernadine leaning over Sister Cecily asking her to beg pardon from her sisters for all her faults before the Lord took her. I imagined the room, the dying sister writhing in pain and Mother Angelus, whose habits this woman had laundered for years and years, asking her to beg pardon. Pardon for what? This nun had never uttered a wrong word or done a bad deed during all of her religious life. She had not been a sophisticated person, she was simple and kind and helpful. She died, we were told, defiantly without begging pardon and because of this we must pray that Our Lady would obtain forgiveness for her in the next world. Sister Gabriel slunk into my classroom a few days later while our students were having a Physical Education class in the gym.

'Wasn't that sickening about dear old Sister Cecily?' She said. 'What are these people thinking about? Sister had a right to her dignity at the end and they couldn't even give her that. It would make me afraid to die.' She half smiled.

'Well, she's free now, she has escaped their clutches,' I answered. 'And they have only diminished themselves by trying to diminish Sister Cecily. I was thinking about her,' I added. 'She was gentle, loyal, funny and holy and she did many good turns for us when we were novices. I can remember her washing and drying our farm gear on the quiet so that we wouldn't be all smells and mud after a wet day down there. There are many nuns like her and they never get the reverence and care which some of the others seem to enjoy.'

'I know what you mean Mary Jacob and I sometimes wonder for how long the young ones will put up with the sort of spiritual abuse which Sister Cecily embraced. I believe that the older nuns and I'm an older person, have been giving away our lives to a religious system that is unworthy of us.

Chapter Twenty Two
What Happens Now?

Mother Paula didn't like having to leave Sister Therese in anyone else's care but the bishop was holding a conference for all the religious in the diocese which we were expected to attend. Ecumenism was a topic which would be discussed in small groups first with the leader of each group reporting its findings at the end of the session. Mother Paula was to lead a group. This was an honour for the English nuns. It was January. Sister Gabriel had a very bad chest cold and I'd hurt my leg again when I slipped on the front steps. We had to stay at home in the convent. We were charged with minding Sister Therese. We were to take her a cup of tea at eleven, ensure that she got up and dressed for lunch and observe her when she went to the chapel making sure that she sat up all the time, there was to be no kneeling.

'Keep the outer doors locked,' Mother Paula instructed me. 'Sister won't want to go out I'm sure but we don't want any more accidents, do we?'

'No mother,' I smiled. 'Don't worry, mother, everything will be fine.'

We checked on Sister Therese. She was tucked up in bed fast asleep. Her bed had been moved close to Mother Paula's. In fact they were side by side.

'Very friendly,' Sister Gabriel chuckled.

'Very friendly indeed,' I laughed.

When our chores for the morning were done Sister Gabriel and I had our elevenses. We sat at the kitchen table with mugs of steaming coffee in front of us. Sister Gabriel had insisted on making this with hot milk.

'Well, her ladyship upstairs gets this all the time,' she said as she delicately slid a piece of apple tart, which Sister Hyacinth had left for us, onto her plate.

'What do you think is the matter with Sister Therese anyway?' I asked. 'Is she really ill? I mean is she a mental wreck or what?'

'I have no idea,' Sister Gabriel frowned. 'She is a genius and you know what they say about genius.'

'My brother Colin is a genius,' I told her, 'but he doesn't carry on the way she does.'

'It is awful because Sister Therese is very affable and so sweet natured by times. You'd never guess that she causes so much trouble, would you? I don't know if she's aware of her carry on half of the time. She must be, she's not stupid, she's just so intense I don't know what to think. But I know, Mary Jacob this can't continue because we are all suffering now.'

'I don't know why Mother Paula protects her like this,' I said crossly. 'I mean she'd throw me to the wolf without a second thought. You know what I mean?'

Sister Gabriel knew what I meant. But she was very happy this morning, she explained. She hated meetings and these talking shops. The Church wasn't going to change very much and she hoped it wouldn't because she liked the traditions which had come to us over centuries.

'I mean, I can take a certain amount of moving with the times but only a certain amount. It should be meaningful change not just a cosmetic exercise. There was a conference of religious when you were in hospital in England, Mary Jacob. Mother Paula made a right exhibition of us then. Did you hear about it?'

I hadn't heard anything at all. Nuns from every order in up State New York were attending talks in the Diocesan Conference Centre Sister Gabriel explained. Lunch was provided which was self service. Bishop Cullen stood in the queue chatting to some nuns. Mother Paula was shocked. The bishop of the diocese was carrying his own tray while nuns stood by. Such disrespect was uncalled for. We'd show the American nuns a thing or two about good manners. Sister Ruth was commissioned to be the bishop's assistant. On the instructions of Mother Paula she approached the bishop from the side and slid her hands underneath his lunch tray.

'Hey, hey,' the bishop chuckled. 'You want my lunch do you, sister? Well, it's a mighty fine lunch and I've not finished choosing my menu yet.'

The nuns who were beside him wondered what was going on. Gradually the extremely noisy scene became quiet. Sister Ruth was heard to say, 'Bishop, I would like to carry your tray for you. Where is your table? I will take your meal over to it and come back for whatever else you want.'

'Don't get excited, sister,' he cautioned. 'I like to choose my own lunch. I like this idea of queuing because it gives me a chance to meet the sisters. It's a day out for me and I love it.'

The bishop's tray was loaded. He had a tumbler of water and a glass of orange juice and a large plate of delicious food – and he wasn't going to part with it. Sister Ruth, acting under holy obedience tried to wrench the tray away. The bishop hung on, the nuns cheered. Mother Paula looked for Monsignor Nortz, who in her opinion, should have been at the bishop's side. He too was serving himself and he was laughing heartily while shouting, 'hang on in there, bishop!'

Sister Ruth apologised. She had been made to look a fool.

'Mother Paula,' the bishop called down the line of diners, 'try some sweet potatoes, they are very good.'

'There was more laughter and I do believe,' Sister Gabriel concluded 'that in some quarters we are now known as, "The Sweet Potatoes."'

I couldn't stop laughing as I pictured the scene. Sister Gabriel laughed too.

'We really are the...'

There was an almighty crash overhead. Taking the stairs two at a time we had trouble opening the door to Mother Paula's room. Sister Gabriel was breathless and coughing badly. I wasn't strong enough to push the door in against some obstacle which was jammed behind it. We put our shoulders against the door and slowly, ever so slowly made enough space to enter the room. A large wardrobe lay face down on the floor. Where was Sister Therese? There was perfect silence, not a moan or a groan to indicate a human presence. She was in the wardrobe!

'Oh My God, what are we going to do? She's in the wardrobe. Maybe she's injured, maybe she's dead. Gabriel, what are we going to do?'

Sister Gabriel was white as a sheet. She was wheezing now.

'We'll have to get Father Coyle and the curates. We can't lift that heavy piece of furniture by ourselves. This is terrible. What on earth was she thinking of?'

I couldn't agree to us running for Father Coyle or the curates. This was the last thing we needed. I knew that he had suspicions still about our romp in the snow filled garden. I imagined the repercussions if he was to discover a nun in a wardrobe. We were in enough trouble already. Mother Paula would blame us for not watching sister more carefully.

'No, no, we can't involve the priests,' I cried. 'We've got to get her out of there somehow by ourselves. Think, Gabriel, think.'

Sister Gabriel was now banging on the upturned back of the

wardrobe. Still not a sound emanated from within. I recalled my brothers when they used our parent's wardrobe as a confessional and it fell. Daddy was there then, there was help but what were we two frail nuns to do. Suddenly Sister Gabriel shouted, 'I've got an idea. Don't leave the room, Mary Jacob stay here!'

Very quickly she returned from the basement brandishing a saw, a screwdriver, a pair of pliers, a chisel and other assorted weapons. Setting to work she tried to prise the back of the wardrobe away along the edge. But the furniture was so old and so tightly held together that she couldn't even put a knife in there.

'Keep your head down Sister Therese and close your eyes,' she cried as brandishing the heavy hammer above her head she brought it down with full force onto the chisel which I held at an angle against the back of the wardrobe. A jagged gash appeared and Sister Gabriel reaching for the small pointed saw cut a larger peep hole but on peering in could see nothing at all.

'She's not in here, where on earth is she?'

'Let me have a look,' I was feeling panicky now. 'Here, let me look.'

Placing my hand on the opening I tried to look inside. I leaned forward until some of the now weakened wood gave way. A large piece was rent downwards and it splintered. Sister Therese was in there alright. She was curled into a tight ball but she was alive and breathing.

We heard the convent car arriving. We heard Mother Paula's voice and then we heard her rapid footsteps along the upstairs corridor. We waited. Sister Therese was awake sitting on the bed but saying nothing. The disfigured wardrobe was facing Mother Paula as she came in. She didn't see it, she didn't see us. She ran to Sister Therese who began to sob. They embraced. Sister Gabriel looked heavenwards. I looked at the badly scratched floor. I saw determination in the set of Sister Gabriel's jaw. She was the first to speak.

'Mother Paula,' she said firmly. 'The day and night time dramas which have become a part of our religious life here cannot go on. I want to know what help you are getting for Sister Therese. Unless she's a very skilled actress and I think I'd know one when I'd see one, she needs psychiatric support. Surely you agree that this is the case now?'

'Sister, don't speak like that in front of Sister Therese. She does not need psychiatric help. She is not ill, she is just tired. I trusted you to look after her and what has happened? What did you say to upset her and why is the wardrobe damaged like that?'

'We didn't say a thing, Mother,' I interjected. 'Sister Therese got into the wardrobe herself. One minute we looked in and she's asleep, the next minute she's bringing furniture down around the place. Is she possessed, Mother? I heard one time about a woman who was possessed by the devil and she used to ...'

Sister Therese began to wail loudly. Mother Paula glared at me as she tried to comfort our very disturbed sister.

'Sister, leave the room this very minute. You are terrifying Sister Therese. How can you even think such terrible things?'

'Well, Mother, if I may say so, she terrifies us often enough and I just want to know what you intend to do about it. I will not leave this room until you promise to do something.'

Mother Paula agreed to take Sister Therese to a psychiatrist. She would make an appointment immediately.

'I have suggested this to her already,' she told us, 'but sister is afraid that she will be brought back to Mary's Way. You know that I am obliged to tell Mother General when any sister is seriously ill? I am afraid to. Sister would probably be sent to a Psychiatric Hospital in England. This would probably mean an end to her teaching and an end to her mission here in East Cranberry.'

'I know about that place. When any sister of ours is admitted there she must wear grey. No one must know that she belongs to the Order of Saint Mary of the Wayside. Isn't that right Mother?'

I was ignored.

'Well, she doesn't do much teaching anyway, does she, Mother?' Sister Gabriel spoke scornfully. 'But we're not going to say anything, are we Sister Mary Jacob?'

'We're not,' I agreed and brazingly added, 'this is a scandal you know. Mother, you are putting her welfare before the needs of the rest of the community. If Mother Bernadine knew about this situation she would be here tomorrow.'

'Sister, I won't have you speak like that. Just who do you think you are? You are being educated above your station. You have already well and truly disgraced yourself. I didn't report your flighty dalliance to Mother Bernadine. Don't push me too hard sister, don't threaten me because I could still do it.'

'Touché,' I replied softly.

I left the room. I could hear Sister Gabriel saying, 'Mother, look I'm probably older than you are. I have had many hard knocks out in the world before I joined the convent. There are things which don't bother me because I've learned how to let them pass me by. However, there are young sisters here and they are baffled. You've got to think about everyone, Mother.'

I felt an overwhelming sadness. What were we doing to each other? We were a little band of religious tucked away in a beautiful part of New York State and we were shouting at one another, blaming each other, challenging each other. I felt pity for Mother Paula. I wondered what frustrations had led to her fixation with Sister Therese. We all longed to be needed, to be loved, to go with our best instincts, to have an outlet for our feminine nature. Where did the disappointments lie in the life of Mother Paula? What rejection had she suffered which now propelled her heedlessly into the arms of a deeply troubled companion. We were not permitted to display even the most normal signs of affection. Such denial of our basic selves could not be a good thing. I understood Mother Paula's reluctance to report this crisis. This in itself showed the lack of trust between the

Motherhouse and us, the workers in the field. We were so insulated as an Order, so controlled, so fearful of rebuke, of letting the side down of being made a scapegoat that we said nothing. This inordinate fear was like a sore which festered from the inside. What did the other nuns really think? Surely Sister Hyacinth and Sister Olivia had discussed the situation with Mother Paula. It won't be long I thought nervously until someone lets slip an unguarded word or reports this to the Motherhouse. And then Mother Bernadine, like the great dinosaur she is, and with sadistic fury, will grind us into the earth.

※

I knew that I was sitting on the fence. The priest who came to give the monthly talk and to hear confessions told me so. I didn't know him and I felt free to speak. I explained that religious life had once again become a huge burden for me. It was not at all what I had longed for. It was a travesty. I wore a mask, I was a pretend nun.

'You're not,' he countered, 'not at all. You are an intelligent person who cannot take all the petty nonsense which has attached itself to religious life. We are all discussing ways to move forward but I gather your bosses are not too keen. They don't want to lose their positions or to have their own cosy, self serving lives exposed. You can tackle this sister, head-on, or just let it pass you by but you can't sit on the fence forever. If you straddle the fence you will sooner or later fall on one side or the other. And you know what the bad thing is here – if you wait for something to happen this will not have been of your own free choice. This is something you might regret later.'

He was right of course, but life went on, and I didn't think about anything much except my classroom work and completing my MA. Father Coyle decided to have a concert in the church. He invited the local Protestant Church Choir, the Mennonite Men's Choir, the Public High School and anyone else within singing distance of East

Cranberry to participate. The tickets went on sale and the funds raised would be distributed to local charities of all denominations. This would be the parish effort to promote ecumenism. Mother Paula objected. The schools would not be involved she told him. It was sacrilegious to hold a concert in a consecrated building. She could not have Sister Brendan, who trained the school choirs, having hand, act, or part, in this mockery within the church.

'Aha, but I have already approached Sister Brendan,' said the priest, 'and guess what, Mother, she thinks it's fantastic, she's all for it.'

Mother Paula and Sister Brendan argued.

'You will not conduct the school children for a concert in the church, sister,' Mother Paula told her. 'You have no right to agree to this without consulting me in the first place. I will have to talk to Mother Bernadine. I will phone her if you insist on disobeying me, sister.'

'But, mother,' Sister Brendan spoke coolly, 'You are not the manager of the Elementary School or of the High School, Father Coyle is, we just work for him. I have discussed the elementary choirs participation with Sister Jude, she is very happy for the children to be a part of this. And I expect Father Palmer will tell you, mother that he will have the High School choir there too.'

Mother Paula, banging her dessert spoon on the table after lunch, told us to remain for a few minutes because she had something to say. She had telephoned to Mary's Way, she had spoken to Mother Bernadine. Naturally Mother was horrified that we would consider participation in a concert which was being held in the parish church. Any involvement by the sisters was forbidden. Mutiny followed. Sister Brendan declared openly that the Motherhouse had no business interfering and most of us agreed. Sister Brendan would do what the parish priest wanted regarding the school choir. The parents will want this too,' Sister Jude insisted.

'Since when has it become a sin to sing in Church, Mother?' She asked.

'It would be a much more profitable thing for us all, Mother,' Sister Brendan said fiercely, 'if you reported some matters which are more disturbing within this community than children from the parish singing a few songs in church.'

The wound had been lanced. We walked away silently. Sister Hyacinth and Sister Olivia followed Mother Paula upstairs. Sister Therese went to bed.

When the evening came for the concert, the car parks around the church and the schools were packed. Parents were dressed to the nines. Father Coyle strutted around welcoming his parishioners and those who were visiting. There would be a little party in the church hall afterwards he told them. There was such an air of excitement everywhere except in the convent. Mother Paula knelt in the chapel with her head bowed as we left. Sister Therese was there too sitting up and staring straight ahead. I went to the parish church with Sister Gabriel we were to help keep order back stage. The choirs would sing from the sanctuary standing on the steps in front of the altar. Beautiful floral arrangement adorned the pillars and the pews were decorated with ribbons. The children had designed the programme covers.

'Buy your programmes quickly,' Father McIntyre warned, 'they will be collector's items one day.' The audience clapped.

Sister Gabriel spotted Sister Zita peeping out from the side chapel.

'Look,' she whispered, 'there's a spy in the camp.'

There was no sign of Sister Ruth or Sister Veronica. Sister Jude was busy helping to organise the elementary school students. Sister Hyacinth took care of the tiny ones who had been abandoned so often by Sister Therese. Father Palmer whose High School Choir would be the first to perform was helped by Sister Ambrose who I noticed had her sleeves rolled up.

It was a wonderful night. As the choirs sang, sometimes joined by the audience, I forgot about the troubled life we were now leading.

The sisters were smiling, their countenance as should be, radiating inner peace and happiness. At the end there were tears and cheers and a standing ovation as everyone joined in the final chorus from the battle hymn of the republic.

When the conductors of each choir had each been presented with a bouquet of flowers Father Coyle thanked everyone. He thanked Sister Jude and Sister Brendan and of course, Mother Paula for – then very pointedly he asked, 'Where are you, mother? Don't be shy just come forward so that we can show our appreciation.' She wasn't there to come forward and he knew it.

'Bastard,' whispered Sister Gabriel. 'He's a right bastard. You didn't hear that did you, sister? A mere slip of the tongue. Sorry.'

I was in the kitchen when Sister Brendan came in with her bouquet of flowers. Mother Paula, her face tight, white, and twisted was boiling milk for Sister Therese. She didn't ask if the concert had been successful. She just didn't look at us or speak.

'Mother, please, I have some flowers here. They were given to me by the choir. May I put them in the chapel? They are really beautiful don't you think?'

'Since when have you been worried about what I think, sister?' Mother Paula replied with biting sarcasm. 'Those things are the fruit of disloyalty and disobedience. You may go now, sister and put them in the outside trash can they will not adorn the house of God in this convent.'

Sister Brendan turning on her heel walked silently from the kitchen carrying the bouquet with her.

'Mother,' I said, 'If Sister Therese had conducted the choir, if Sister Therese had been presented with a bouquet would you tell her to trash it? I don't think so, do you?'

Mother Paula was very angry as she swung around. She held onto the handle of the saucepan. The contents quivered. She was shaking so much that milk spilled over the cooker, some of it splashed onto

Mother Paula while the rest splattered the floor. I didn't even offer to help her to clean up - but the smell of burning milk followed me upstairs.

Sister Hyacinth was the person to tell me that Sister Brendan was leaving the convent in America.

'She might just leave the Order altogether,' she whispered, 'and if she does I can't blame her.'

'How do you know all this?' I asked as once again we had a little word in the pantry. I could tell that Sister Hyacinth was upset. She knew about it because Mother Paula had received a missive from Mary's Way to say that Mother Bernadine would be in America the following week.

'It's terrible, I can't endure that woman and its school term too, what is she thinking of? I told Mother Paula that she should make a suggestion immediately. Have Mother General postpone her trip until the summer. There's snow around now and it's so cold. My God, she'll be under our feet all the time.'

'I don't believe this,' I stammered. 'Why now? Has she been told about Therese too?'

'No, it's like I said, it's really because of Brendan. She wrote to the General Council saying that she will leave. She wants to go now. She didn't tell Mother Paula anything. She just wrote her letter and got Mrs. Beale to mail it with the school post. Mother Bernadine is coming over to try to sweet talk her out of this I suppose. But God only knows what else will come out in the wash now.'

'Sister Brendan,' she said, 'didn't want to be in America when Mother Bernadine arrived. She was not going to bow down anymore, kiss feet or eat burnt bacon. I heard her say this to Mother Paula, they were having a right old ding dong, but I think she has to wait here. I don't believe that Mother Bernadine's false charms will work on Brendan though because she's had enough.'

I was not surprised to hear this and I supposed that the incident with the bouquet of flowers was the final straw for Sister Brendan. From her own experiences she had to draw her own conclusions and make a decision. Had she seen deep within herself what choice she would have to make? I wished I could be sure of the future so that I could see through life's mysteries more clearly. Had I the commitment to continue in the direction I had chosen? Would I find from so many bitter losses something worth living for? I was far from knowing at that time that for me the bitterest loss of all was about to happen.

The convent was empty. It was a cold windy February day. Snowdrops tried to push their way through the frozen earth. Here and there beneath the hedge some bright crocus had appeared only to wither away in an icy blast. Mother Paula and some senior nuns had gone on a massive shopping trip in preparation for Mother General's stay. Every room in the convent had been cleaned and polished. Sister Brendan went about her chores tight lipped. Sister Therese had made a miraculous recovery. She took her place in community once more until I began to wonder why I had ever imagined her to be deranged. Mother Paula moved into Sister Zita's room and Sister Zita now shared with Sister Therese. The visitors would have their own suite in another part of the convent. I was polishing the chapel floor when the phone in the hall rang.

'Good morning,' I said, 'St. Mary's can I help you?'

'Help me!' My mother screamed down the line. 'Help me, what are you doing over there?'

'I'm in the convent, why are you phoning me, are you in New York?'

'Ellie, I thought you were on your way home. What are you doing, why are you not on your way to Shannon?'

Is my mother deranged too, I wondered. What is she on about? Why is she expecting me to be at Shannon?

'Mammy, what is wrong with you? Why are you expecting me to be at Shannon Airport?'

'My God!' She gasped, 'Ellie, do you not know about your father?

The day before yesterday he had a stroke, here in the house. The doctor gave him forty eight hours to live. Daddy is waiting for you and you are still in America. Oh Ellie.'

I had to tell her I knew nothing about this. I was becoming hysterical. My mother was the one who was now trying to calm me by telephone.

'Listen to me, Ellie,' she coaxed. 'I will telephone the Motherhouse again. Yesterday morning Mother Bernadine, that's her name isn't it? told me that she would personally see to it that you would be on the very next plane to Shannon. Tom and Colin are here waiting for word to collect you. Daddy is upstairs and Dan and Eugene are with him. Aunty Pat and Uncle William are on their way!

'But mammy, why is daddy not in hospital? The nuns in Galway would look after him. Maybe he will be alright. People don't always die following a stroke, you know.'

'I know,' she replied, 'but daddy, Oh Ellie he is not one of the fortunate ones. He was not taken to hospital because the doctor said that the journey alone would kill him.'

Mammy and the boys had agreed that he should die at home with his family around him. The aunties were awaiting news. If I was going to New York they wanted to see me off from there.

'Don't worry,' I told her. 'I will be on the next plane out of here. I will go to Father Coyle. I know that he will arrange everything. I will phone you back in half an hour. I ran to the hall door and opened it. Standing there all smiles was Mother Bernadine. Mother Paula was there too with Sister Olivia and Mother General's companion, a nun I didn't know.

'Let me pass!' I yelled at them. 'I am going to the priest's house. Father Coyle and the curates will show more compassion than any of you. How could you, how could you not tell me that my father is dying? He may even be dead by now!'

Mother Paula stood in front of me.

'You are distraught, dear,' she said. 'The news is not that serious and I do have your tickets here. You will be going to Ireland tonight. Mother Bernadine wants to have a little chat with you first.'

'She doesn't need to have any chat with me,' I cried. 'She's already had a chat with my mother. She knows how critically ill daddy is.'

Mother Paula ushered me inside. The community on hearing voices came along to welcome Mother Bernadine.

'Listen,' I shouted at them, 'my father is dying. He has been given a short time to live. This happened the day before yesterday. And who told me the news? My mother had to – in a phone call from home just a few minutes ago.'

'Sisters,' Mother Bernadine addressed them. 'Her father is not dying at all. Sister is frightened. I have spoken to the sisters in Galway and they say that there is no need to worry. Just leave me alone with Sister Mary Jacob. I'll talk to her quietly.'

Mother Paula and Mother's companion fussed over her. She had just travelled such a long journey surely she'd like a cup of tea. Perhaps she needed to freshen up first. But no Mother was so concerned about me. We would have our little chat and then we'd all have supper before I'd leave for New York.

'Do telephone sisters Aunties, Mother Bernadine directed Mother Paula. They can meet Sister Mary Jacob and see her through at the airport. You would like that wouldn't you, sister?' She smiled.

'How can you?' I sobbed. 'How can you stand there and talk about the sisters in Galway knowing what is wrong with daddy. He's not even in their hospital. He's at home. And it was my mother who told you that my aunts would collect me in New York. You are lying to me and I despise you.'

I was not sorry for what I'd said even though Mother Paula speaking on my behalf said that I was. Mother Bernadine brushed it all aside as if it was of no consequence at all. When my father recovered perhaps my mother would like to come to America again for a holiday. My father could come also and the Order would pay for this. Mother Paula must pack some gifts with my things. I must not go to Ireland empty handed. And she must give me money too whatever I wanted I could have.

'I want nothing I told her, nothing at all. I just want to go home to my father. I want to see him before he dies. If I'm late, I will never forgive you.'

Aunty Anna and Aunty Helen met me when the small plane in which I had travelled from Albany landed. It was nine o'clock at night and New York was a maze of lights. The American cousins were waiting for me in Aunty Eileen's house in Long island. Phone calls were made to those who couldn't be there and I had to speak to them all. They hoped that the news about daddy would be good. They all loved him so much. When we were settled and having coffee after dinner Aunty Eileen suggested that I go into the study and phone Ireland for news. They will be happy to know that you are with us, she said and tell them about your flight. I believe you will arrive in Shannon at about seven thirty in the morning Irish time. Joe Scully answered the phone in Eskeriada and I knew at once that I was too late.

'Ellie, I'm so sorry but they've just taken you father to the church. Now I'll meet you at the airport, just give me the time you expect to arrive. Judith will come with me. Now look, Ellie, there's nothing you could have done, your father had a very peaceful end. We will see to it that you get here in time for his funeral. I'll tell your mother and the boys that you're on your way. They will be very happy to see you. Promise me that you won't worry, Ellie.'

'I could have been in time but they wouldn't let me,' I cried.

Aunty Anna was beside me.

'Oh no, he's gone, dear Owen, how we'll miss you. Oh Ellie, you poor child come out into the heat. Owen has passed away,' she told the others who began to weep for him.

The aunties held me close as I cried and cried.

'I could have been in time but they wouldn't let me,' I sobbed.

―❦―

Coming into Shannon Airport on that dull February morning I couldn't see the green fields or the bright homesteads. I was shattered in mind and body. I couldn't imagine being at home without daddy's calm presence. He had taught me so many things. I learned the art of gentleness and serenity from him. He had such respect for himself and for other people. He loved the land and all of nature and he'd passed this love onto me. And above all else he taught me that nothing is ever too late no matter how desolate the scene or situation.

Joe and Judith ran to me. Under the lights in the airport their faces looked green. I wondered if my face looked green too. How tired they must be. How many hours had they already spent with Tom and Colin? How many cups of tea had Judith made for people who were calling to the house? And they had their two small children to worry about too although I knew that Judith's mother would be caring for them. Joe and Judith were true friends who would never leave us in times of pain and loss, and they didn't judge me or ask why I was not home earlier. They wanted to protect me, to comfort me, to be there when they were needed. Joe decided we should have something to eat before setting off. 'The roads are very icy,' he said. 'I wouldn't be at all surprised if we have snow on the way although it seems almost too cold for it.'

'There are huge banks of snow around East Cranberry,' I told him. 'We've had very bad blizzards this winter but we are prepared for these. I think it's different in Ireland. Do you have snow tires or chains?' I asked.

'Not at all, Ellie,' Joe laughed. 'We just hope that an old tractor will turn up to pull us out when we're in trouble.'

My suitcase was being loaded into the boot of the car. I was about to sit into the front seat at Judith's insistence when two nuns appeared beside us. I thought I was dreaming was this what they called jet lag?

'Sister,' it was Mother Elizabeth speaking. 'You are to come to Galway with us. It's Mother Bernadine's wish. She telephoned from America, we are to look after you now. We will take you to see your family this afternoon.'

'Hey, now!' Joe was shocked. 'Hang on a minute, sister. You are not taking Ellie anywhere. She's coming with us. We are taking her home.'

I got out of the car and almost slipped on the icy road. Sister Alphonse whom I now recognised tried to take my arm. She almost slipped as well. Joe came to our rescue and Judith who was hanging onto the rear door handle trying to keep upright pushed me back into the front seat.

'We are going for some breakfast and you are welcome to join us, sisters. We have to go now because we must get to Eskeriada before eleven o'clock. If you are not staying then drive back carefully to Galway, the roads are treacherous.'

'But Sister Mary Jacob has to come with us. Mother says so. Please let her come,' Sister Alphonse pleaded.

'No, definitely not and I, Joe Scully say so,' Joe answered.

'What on earth are they up to?' Judith wanted to know as we drove away from Shannon Airport.

'I mean don't they even think about the loss you've suffered, Ellie. Anyone would imagine that you were on your way to a party not your father's funeral.'

I started to cry. I told them everything that had happened since my mother telephoned America where I just by chance answered the phone. They were shocked. They didn't know that this sort of thing went on in convents. Judith didn't think that the nuns in Eskeriada behaved in this way. I didn't either. You should have joined them, Ellie it might have been a safer bet she laughed. The hotel was warm and there was a delicious smell of frying bacon and sausage wafting from the kitchen. Joe was starving, he informed us. He would have a full breakfast, the whole works. I opted for bacon and sausage and Judith did as well. 'I've gone off scrambled eggs,' she told me, 'because the children want them all the time.'

'Holy Christ!' Joe exclaimed. 'We've got company. Don't look back, Ellie but the eyes of God are upon you.'

'Joe, stop that, what a thing to say.' Judith glared at him.

'Hey, just look, Judith, they're here.'

'Who's here?' She asked as she looked around the dining room.

There they were, Mother Elizabeth and Sister Alphonse sitting at a table. Joe went over to them. He was very polite. Would they like to have breakfast?

'No, thank you very much we are waiting for Sister Mary Jacob,' was the reply.

'Well you can wait until the cows come home, sisters,' Joe advised them. 'I've told you she's coming with us and that's final.'

There was another struggle outside the hotel as the nuns pulled me by the left arm and Joe and Judith pulled me by the right. I was slipping and sliding all over the place.

'Stop it!' I yelled as loudly as I could. People stared. 'Sisters, let go of my arm at once,' I ordered. 'I will not go to Galway. You can telephone Mother Bernadine from here, from this hotel. Tell her I said no!'

They walked away. I called after them.

'You do know that my father is dead. Don't pretend that you don't? What about some words of sympathy?' They didn't turn around or pretend to hear me.

When we reached Eskeriada cars lined each side of the street outside our house. We had missed the funeral because of the terrible road conditions. Joe had insisted that I get into the back of the car with Judith just in case we'd have any bad skid. We huddled together with a plaid rug wrapped around our knees.

'Joe,' I said, 'don't try anything foolish. You have two small children at home and I want you and Judith to be safe for them. Nobody expects you to do the impossible so just take it nice and easy.'

I saw the black ribbon tied to our front door. I saw the curtains drawn in the house. I saw the blinds all closed in the shop. I saw Tom when he opened the door to see if there was any sign of us. He came to Joe's car and he helped me out.

'Ellie,' he said, 'it's great that you are here at last. I was worried because everyone is talking about the state of the roads. There have been a few bad accidents around here. But I knew that Joe would do it.' He put his arm around me.

'Mammy is bearing up very well,' he told me. 'It hasn't registered with her yet that daddy is dead. Now don't mind if she gets upset when she sees you. She has been waiting for you for such a long time.'

She looked older and pale and drawn and for a moment she didn't seem to realise that it was I who knelt there beside her.

'Mammy are you alright? I came just as soon as I could. Everything seemed to go wrong, the plane was delayed the roads were terrible. I'm sorry I missed the funeral mass. Joe did everything he could ... .'

'Oh, Joe,' she looked around for him. 'Joe and Judith what would we do without them and all the neighbours too? But Ellie, you should have been here, he wanted you at the end before he stopped speaking altogether. Those nuns of yours have a lot to answer for. I'll never forget what they've put us through and I'll never forgive them.'

'I could have been in time but they wouldn't let me,' I sobbed.

Aunty Pat came over and hugged me.

'You're frozen,' she said, 'come in closer to the fire and get warm. We have soup and sandwiches all ready for you whenever you feel you can eat something.'

Tom said that he was going to the graveyard. He wanted to check on daddy's grave before it got too dark. Maybe I would like to come. I didn't have to but maybe . .

I wanted to go, I wanted to get away from all the sympathy being offered me. I couldn't believe my father would not walk in the door at any minute to ask what sort of flight I'd had. It was impossible to believe he had gone and that he would not be coming back, that he would never again arrive home from Capall Ban for his tea. Dusk was falling. The frost, like crisp white linen covered some of the mounds farther uphill in the cemetery. A few stars were already appearing in the sky. The crows were flying home to their nests. My father's grave was obvious. It was a new knoll of earth in the shadow of a tall tree near to the huge iron gates. It was covered with floral wreaths and bouquets of flowers. 'I must take the cards off the rest of these,' said Tom as he wandered around the grave looking at the wreaths and tidying them. He settled the bouquets like a colourful eiderdown over our father almost as though he was tucking him in for the night. Underneath all of this my father lay. But I saw him in my mind as he was that long ago day in Capall Ban. I was skipping while granny spoke earnestly to him. She was rubbing his arm reassuringly. I hoped that they were together now and that once again she would lay her comforting hand on his.

'He got a great send off, Ellie, there's no doubt about that. But you know, Ellie, I should have seen it coming. They didn't want to do his hip. They were worried about blood pressure or something. I'd forgotten how old he was becoming. He never seemed to change until recently. I should have thought about it. I mean he was so much older than mammy. Colin said something when he came back from London the last time but I didn't take it in, I suppose.'

We were walking back to the car. I told Tom that I felt awful for not having being there.

'It was not my fault,' I explained, 'I could have been in time but they wouldn't let me go until Mother Bernadine arrived in America. It was terrible. And when the two of them from Galway arrived at Shannon, well you should have heard Joe, he was great. I think Mother

Bernadine is afraid I won't go back, Tom. There has been a lot of odd things happening out there in the convent in America. I'm a bit fed up with it all.'

'They seem to be a bit of a funny crowd alright,' Tom laughed. 'I mean they're not like the nuns in the convent here at all. Do you think, Ellie, that you might have backed the wrong horse?'

The house was still filled with people as though they were reluctant to leave, reluctant to have us face the reality that our family was now changed forever. Dan and his wife Bridie were chatting to Eugene and Irene. The twins Peter and Paul who were now almost eleven were very helpful. They were serving tea and sandwiches continuously. Colin offered drinks to those who wanted them. My mother was drinking brandy.

'It's good for her,' said Aunty Pat. 'It will warm her up and a drop wouldn't do you any harm either Ellie, you are like a ghost. 'I'll tell you what,' she said, 'why don't you run upstairs and have a hot bath and change your clothes? You've been travelling for hours, you poor thing. Oh, your suitcase is in our room,' she added. 'I don't know who put it there but William will move it later. Use my room now it's nice and warm in there.'

I lay in the large bath tub. It was so wonderful to be at home and to be surrounded by familiar things. My father's shaving brush was on the shelf above the washbasin. A painting which Colin had done when he was a child hung on the wall. It was a ship whose sails were now discoloured and whose funnel didn't smoke anymore. My mother's glass perfume bottle stood on a wire tray with the stopper beside it and her pink hairbrush, discarded it seemed in haste, sported a tuft of silver hairs. Wrapping a bath towel around me I scurried to Aunty Pat's room. I opened the suitcase and took out the clothes I needed. Half way through dressing myself I stopped. Some of Aunty Pat's things lay on the bed. I tried on her beautiful black coat. It reached to mid calf. I arranged the fur collar around my neck, it felt so comfortable. Her smart ankle boots were the correct size but I did find the heels rather high. I took her hat into my hands. It was a little pill box with black netting. It was perfect. I fixed the veil over my eyes. I looked through it at my reflection in the mirror. It smiled shyly at me.

'What happens now?' I asked.

There was no reply. I walked out of the room I teetered on the high heels. I held onto the banisters as voices rose and fell while I descended. When I reached the second floor landing I stood there listening.

'Better than a long illness do you remember old Jimmy Moran ...?'

'Ah, she'll be alright, Eleanor is stronger than you'd think.'

'A great age, sure you'd never have believed it.'

'...boys are done for but what about Ellie, she looks bad, miserable, poor creature ... a long journey right enough.'

'Oh yes, I'm staying for a few days. William will go back tomorrow.'

'No they won't get married until next year. Bridget is a good ...'

I moved towards the door and I stood there. The buttons on Aunty Pat's coat reflected lights from the fire. Glasses clinked, someone coughed. There was a smell of cigarette smoke and gradually there was silence. Colin couldn't take his eyes off me. Someone gasped in disbelief, the twins whispered, 'Ellie.'

I saw the faces, the eyes blinking, the cups and glasses held aloft, a sandwich half way to a mouth. There was an explosion as a log burst asunder in the fireplace, sparks flew up the chimney. My mother put her hands to her face. She took them away again.

'Good God in heaven Ellie,' she laughed. 'I don't believe it, you're the image of your granny Julia.'

Lightning Source UK Ltd.
Milton Keynes UK
175172UK00001B/17/P